RODERICK HUDSON

was born in New York, April 15th, 1843.
He lived most of his life in England, and
was eventually naturalised in 1915. He
died in Chelsea on February 28th, 1916.

FIRST PUBLISHED IN GREAT BRITAIN © 1879
THIS EDITION FIRST PUBLISHED IN 1947 BY
JOHN LEHMANN LTD

RODERICK
HUDSON

BY

HENRY JAMES

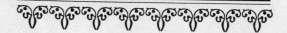

JOHN LEHMANN

MCMXLVII

FIRST PUBLISHED IN GREAT BRITAIN IN 1879.
THIS EDITION FIRST PUBLISHED IN 1947 BY
JOHN LEHMANN LTD.
MADE AND PRINTED IN GREAT BRITAIN BY
MESSRS. PURNELL AND SONS, LTD.,
(PAULTON) AND LONDON.

NOTE TO THE PRESENT EDITION

HENRY JAMES was thirty-one when, in 1874, he wrote *Roderick Hudson*, and though he had not yet reached the dignity of an expatriate he was something more than the American doing Europe; he was beginning to realise that Europe was the part of the " mere, mad phantasmagoria and dime museum" of the world which was for him. It was not until the end of the year, after he had finished the "absorbing task" of his novel that he more or less made up his mind to remain in Europe and to "study England," about which he knew at this time very little. Thus 1874 was one of the most important years of his life, the year of his great decision and of the novel which marks the end of his literary apprenticeship.

Roderick Hudson had been commissioned for serialisation in the *Atlantic Monthly* by James' friend, W. D. Howells, and he began working seriously on it in his rooms in the great, dusty Piazza Sta. Maria Novella, in Florence,[1] to which he and his brother had moved from Rome after William had contracted malaria—one wonders if it were not the presence of his brother and the knowledge of his inevitable disapproval of a decision to stay, as much as absorption in the novel, that made him delay his planning.

The novel appeared in the *Atlantic Monthly* during the whole of 1875, was published in book form in Boston the following year, but only appeared in England, somewhat revised, three years later.

James, himself, had a natural affection for this, the first work of his maturity. In a letter to his beloved Robert Louis Stevenson (who had just written in admiration of the book) in 1887, he modestly writes: "I am really delighted you can find something at this late day in that work in which my diminutive muse first tried to elongate her little legs. It is a book of considerable good faith, but I think of limited skill. Besides, directly my productions are finished, or at least thrust out to earn their living, they seem to *me* dead." His revision of it for the New York edition of 1909, which is followed in the present edition, was an act only of careful refurbishing—in a letter he writes: ". . . to attempt to touch the *substance* of the thing would be as foolish as it would be (in a *done* and impenetrable structure) impracticable. What I have tried for is mere revision of surface and expression, as the thing

[1] The book was finished in East 25th Street, New York.

v

is positively in many places quite *vilely* written." There is a detailed study of this revision by Miss Helene Harvitt[1] in which she claims that polishing has spoilt the crisp outlines of the style, a view which is challenged by Professor F. O. Mathiessen,[2] who is a great defender of the revisions.

In 1913, three years before his death, Henry James was asked by a "delightful young man from Texas" to give him a list of five of his novels which he should read. *Roderick Hudson* heads the first of the two lists offered—the "not so advanced" group—along with *A Portrait of a Lady, Princess Cassamassima, The Wings of a Dove,* and *The Golden Bowl,* so we can be sure that he was faithful in his affection until the last.

MICHAEL SWAN

[1] 'How Henry James Revised *Roderick Hudson*; a study in style.' P.M.L.A. (March 1924), pp. 203–27.
[2] 'Henry James: The Major Phase.' O.U.P., 1946.

PREFACE

RODERICK HUDSON was begun in Florence in the spring of 1874, designed from the first for serial publication in the *Atlantic Monthly*, where it opened in January 1875 and persisted through the year. I yield to the pleasure of placing these circumstances on record, as I shall place others, and as I have yielded to the need of renewing acquaintance with the book after a quarter of a century. This revival of an all but extinct relation with an early work may often produce for an artist, I think, more kinds of interest and emotion than he shall find it easy to express, and yet will light not a little, to his eyes, that veiled face of his Muse which he is condemned for ever and all anxiously to study. The art of representation bristles with questions the very terms of which are difficult to apply and to appreciate; but whatever makes it arduous makes it, for our refreshment, infinite, causes the practice of it, with experience, to spread round us in a widening, not in a narrowing circle. Therefore it is that experience has to organise, for convenience and cheer, some system of observation—for fear, in the admirable immensity, of losing its way. We see it as pausing from time to time to consult its notes, to measure, for guidance, as many aspects and distances as possible, as many steps taken and obstacles mastered and fruits gathered and beauties enjoyed. Everything counts, nothing is superfluous in such a survey; the explorer's note-book strikes me here as endlessly receptive. This accordingly is what I mean by the contributive value—or put it simply as, to one's own sense, the beguiling charm—of the *accessory* facts in a given artistic case. This is why, as one looks back, the private history of any sincere work, however modest its pretensions, looms with its own completeness in the rich, ambiguous æsthetic air, and seems at once to borrow a dignity and to mark, so to say, a station. This is why, reading over, for revision, correction and republication, the volumes here in hand, I find myself, all attentively, in presence of some such recording scroll or engraved commemorative table—from which the "private" character, moreover, quite insists on dropping out. These notes represent, over a considerable course, the continuity of an artist's endeavour, the growth of his whole operative consciousness and, best of all, perhaps, their own tendency to multiply, with the implication, thereby, of a memory much enriched. Addicted to "stories" and inclined to retrospect, he fondly takes, under this backward view, his whole unfolding, his process of production, for a thrilling tale, almost for a wondrous adventure, only asking himself at what stage of remembrance the mark of the relevant will begin to fail. He frankly proposes to take this mark everywhere for granted.

Roderick Hudson was my first attempt at a novel, a long fiction with a "complicated" subject, and I recall again the quite uplifted sense with which my idea, such as it was, permitted me at last to put quite out to sea. I had but hugged the shore on sundry previous small occasions; bumping about, to acquire skill, in the shallow waters and sandy coves of the "short story" and master as yet of no vessel constructed to carry a sail. The subject of *Roderick* figured to me vividly this employment of canvas, and I have not forgotten, even after long years, how the blue southern sea seemed to spread immediately before me and the breath of the spice-islands to be already in the breeze. Yet it must even then have begun for me too, the ache of fear, that was to become so familiar, of being unduly tempted and led on by "developments"; which is but the desperate discipline of the question involved in them. They are of the very essence of the novelist's process, and it is by their aid, fundamentally, that his idea takes form and lives; but they impose on him, through the principle of continuity that rides them, a proportionate anxiety. They are the very condition of interest, which languishes and drops without them; the painter's subject consisting ever, obviously, of the related state, to each other, of certain figures and things. To exhibit these relations, once they have all been recognised, is to "treat" his idea, which involves neglecting none of those that directly minister to interest; the degree of that directness remaining meanwhile a matter of highly difficult appreciation, and one on which felicity of form and composition, as a part of the total effect, mercilessly rests. Up to what point is such and such a development *indispensable* to the interest ? What is the point beyond which it ceases to be rigorously so ? Where, for the complete expression of one's subject, does a particular relation stop—giving way to some other not concerned in that expression ?

Really, universally, relations stop nowhere, and the exquisite problem of the artist is eternally but to draw, by a geometry of his own, the circle within which they shall happily *appear* to do so. He is in the perpetual predicament that the continuity of things is the whole matter, for him, of comedy and tragedy; that this continuity is never, by the space of an instant or an inch, broken, and that, to do anything at all, he has at once intensely to consult and intensely to ignore it. All of which will perhaps pass but for a supersubtle way of pointing the plain moral that a young embroiderer of the canvas of life soon began to work in terror, fairly, of the vast expanse of that surface, of the boundless number of its distinct perforations for the needle, and of the tendency inherent in his many-coloured flowers and figures to cover and consume as many as possible of the little holes. The development of the flower, of the figure, involved thus an immense counting of holes and a careful selection among them. That would have been, it seemed to him, a brave enough process, were it not the very nature of the holes so to invite, to solicit, to persuade, to practise positively a thousand lures and deceits. The prime effect of so sustained a system, so prepared a surface, is to lead on and on; while the fascination of following resides, by the same token, in the presumability *somewhere* of a convenient, of a visibly-appointed stopping-place. Art would be easy indeed if, by a fond power disposed to "patronise" it, such conveniences, such simplifications, had been provided. We have, as the case stands, to invent and establish them, to arrive at them by a difficult, dire process of selection and comparison, of surrender and sacrifice. The very meaning of expertness is acquired courage to brace one's self for the cruel crisis from the moment one sees it grimly loom.

Roderick Hudson was further, was earnestly pursued during a summer partly spent in the Black Forest and (as I had returned to America early in September) during three months passed near Boston. It is one of the silver threads of the recoverable texture of that embarrassed phase, however, that the book was not finished when it had to begin appearing in monthly fragments: a fact in the light of which I find myself live over again, and quite with wonderment and tenderness, so intimate an experience of difficulty and delay. To have "liked" so much writing it, to have worked out with such conviction the pale embroidery, and yet not, at the end of so many months, to have come through, was clearly still to have fallen short of any facility and any confidence: though the long-drawn process now most appeals to memory, I confess, by this very quality of shy and groping duration. One fact about it indeed outlives all others; the fact that, as the loved Italy was the scene of my fiction—so much more loved than one has ever been able, even after fifty efforts, to say !—and as having had to leave it persisted as an inward ache, so there was soreness in still contriving, after a fashion, to hang about it and in prolonging, from month to month, the illusion of the golden air. Little enough of that medium may the novel, read over to-day, seem to supply; yet half the actual interest lurks for me in the earnest, baffled intention of making it felt. A whole side of the old consciousness, under this mild pressure, flushes up and prevails again; a reminder, ever so penetrating, of the quantity of "evocation" involved in my plan, and of the quantity I must even have supposed myself to achieve. I take the lingering perception of all this, I may add—that is of the various admonitions of the whole reminiscence—for a signal instance of the way a work of art, however small, if but sufficiently sincere, may vivify and even dignify the accidents and incidents of its growth.

I must that winter (which I again like to put on record that I spent in New York) have brought up my last instalments in due time, for I recall no haunting anxiety: what I do recall perfectly is the felt pleasure, during those months—and in East Twenty-fifth Street !—of trying, on the other side of the world, still to surround with the appropriate local glow the characters that had combined, to my vision, the previous year in Florence. A benediction, a great advantage, as seemed to me, had so from the first rested on them, and to nurse them along was really to sit again in the high, charming, shabby old room which had originally overarched them and which, in the hot May and June, had looked out, through the slits of cooling shutters, at the rather dusty but ever-romantic glare of Piazza Santa Maria Novella. The house formed the corner (I delight to specify) of Via della Scala, and I fear that what the early chapters of the book most "render" to me to-day is not the umbrageous air of their New England town, but the view of the small cab-stand sleepily disposed—long before the days of strident electric cars—round the rococo obelisk of the Piazza, which is supported on its pedestal, if I remember rightly, by four delightful little elephants. (That, at any rate, is how the object in question, deprecating verification, comes back to me with the clatter of the horse-pails, the discussions, in the intervals of repose under well-drawn hoods, of the unbuttoned *cocchieri*, sons of the most garrulous of races, and the occasional stillness as of the noonday desert.)

Pathetic, as we say, on the other hand, no doubt, to reperusal, the manner in which the evocation, so far as attempted, of the small New England town of my first two chapters, fails of intensity—if intensity, in such a connexion, had been indeed to be looked for. *Could* I verily, by the terms of my little plan, have "gone in" for it at the best, and even though one of these terms was the projection, for my fable, at the outset, of some more or less vivid antithesis to a state of civilisation providing for "art"? What I wanted, in essence, was the image of some perfectly humane community which was yet all incapable of providing for it, and I had to take what my scant experience furnished me. I remember feeling meanwhile no drawback in this scantness, but a complete, an exquisite little adequacy, so that the presentation arrived at would quite have served its purpose, I think, had I not misled myself into naming my place. To name a place, in fiction, is to pretend in some degree to represent it—and I speak here of course but of the use of existing names, the only ones that carry weight. I wanted one that carried weight—so at least I supposed; but obviously I was wrong, since my effect lay, so superficially, and could only lie, in the local *type*, as to which I had my handful of impressions. The particular local case was another matter, and I was to see again, after long years, the case into which, all recklessly, the opening passages of *Roderick Hudson* put their foot. I was to have nothing then, on the spot, to sustain me but the rather feeble plea that I had not *pretended* so very much to "do" Northampton Mass. The plea was charmingly allowed, but nothing could have been more to the point than the way in which, in such a situation, the whole question of the novelist's "doing," with its eternal wealth, or in other words its eternal torment of interest, once more came up. He embarks, rash adventurer, under the star of "representation," and is pledged thereby to remember that the art of interesting us in things—once these things are the right ones for his case—can *only* be the art of representing them. This relation to them, for invoked interest, involves his accordingly "doing"; and it is for him to settle with his intelligence what that variable process shall commit him to.

Its fortune rests primarily, beyond doubt, on somebody's having, under suggestion, a *sense* for it—even the reader will do, on occasion, when the writer, as so often happens, completely falls out. The way in which this sense has been, or has not been, applied constitutes, at all events, in respect to any fiction, the very ground of critical appreciation. Such appreciation takes account, primarily, of the thing, in the case, to have *been* done, and I now see what, for the first and second chapters of *Roderick*, that was. It was a peaceful, rural New England community *quelconque*—it was not, it was under no necessity of being, Northampton Mass. But one nestled, technically, in those days, and with yearning, in the great shadow of Balzac; his august example, little as the secret might ever be guessed, towered for me over the scene; so that what was clearer than anything else was how, if it was a question of Saumur, of Limoges, of Guérande, he "did" Saumur, did Limoges, did Guérande. I remember how, in my feebler fashion, I yearned over the preliminary presentation of my small square patch of the American scene, and yet was not sufficiently on my guard to see how easily his high practice might be delusive for my case. Balzac talked of Nemours and Provins: therefore why shouldn't one, with fond fatuity, talk of almost the only small American *ville de province* of which one had happened to lay up, long before, a pleased vision ? The reason was plain: one was not in the least, in one's prudence, emulating his systematic closeness. It didn't confuse the question either that he would verily, after all, addressed as he was to a due density in his material, have found little enough in Northampton Mass to tackle. He tackled no group of appearances, no presented face of the social organism (conspicuity thus attending it), *but* to make something of it. To name it simply and not in some degree tackle it would have seemed to him an act reflecting on his general course the deepest dishonour. Therefore it was that, as the moral of these many remarks, I "named," under his contagion, when I was really most conscious of not being held to it; and therefore it was, above all, that for all the effect of representation I was to achieve, I might have let the occasion pass. A "fancy" indication would have served my turn—except that I should so have failed perhaps of a pretext for my present insistence.

Since I do insist, at all events, I find this ghostly interest perhaps even more reasserted for me by the questions begotten within the very covers of the book, those that wander and idle there as in some sweet old overtangled walled garden, a safe paradise of self-criticism. Here it is that if there be air for it to breathe at all, the critical question swarms, and here it is, in particular, that one of the happy hours of the painter's long day may strike. I speak of the painter in general and of his relation to the old picture, the work of his hand, that has been lost to sight and that, when found again, is put back on the easel for measure of what time and the weather may, in the interval, have done to it. Has it too fatally faded, has it blackened or "sunk," or otherwise abdicated, or has it only, blest thought, strengthened, for its allotted duration, and taken up, in its degree, poor dear brave thing, some shade of the all appreciable, yet all indescribable grace that we know as pictorial "tone" ? The anxious artist has to wipe it over, in the first place, to see; he has to "clean it up," say, or to varnish it anew, or at the least to place it in a light, for any right judgement of its aspect or its worth. But the very uncertainties themselves yield a thrill, and if subject and treatment, working together, have had their felicity, the artist, the prime creator, may find a strange charm in this stage of the connexion. It helps him to live back into a forgotten state, into convictions, credulities too early spent perhaps, it breathes upon the dead reasons of things, buried as they are in the texture of the work, and makes them revive, so that the actual appearances and the old motives fall together once more, and a lesson and a moral and a consecrating final light are somehow disengaged.

All this, I mean of course, if the case will wonderfully take any such pressure, if the work doesn't break down under even such mild over-hauling. The author knows well enough how easily that may happen—which he in fact frequently enough sees it do. The old reasons then are too dead to revive; they were not, it is plain, good enough reasons to live. The only possible relation of the present mind to the thing is to dismiss it altogether. On the other hand, when it is not dismissed—as the only detachment is the detachment of aversion—the creative intimacy is reaffirmed, and appreciation, critical apprehension, insists on becoming as active as it can. Who shall say, granted this, where it shall not begin and where it shall consent to end ? The painter who passes over his old sunk canvas the wet sponge that shows him what may still come out again makes his criticism essentially active. When having seen, while his momentary glaze remains, that the canvas *has* kept a few buried secrets, he proceeds to repeat the process with due care and with a bottle of varnish and a brush, he is "living back," as I say, to the top of his bent, is taking up the old relation, so workable apparently, yet, and there is nothing logically to stay him from follow-ing it all the way. I have felt myself then, on looking over past produc-tions, the painter making use again and again of the tentative wet sponge. The sunk surface has here and there, beyond doubt, refused to respond: the buried secrets, the intentions, are buried too deep to rise again, and were indeed, it would appear, not much worth the burying. Not so, however, when the moistened canvas does obscurely flush and when resort to the varnish-bottle is thereby immediately indicated. The simplest figure for my revision of this present array of earlier, later, larger, smaller, canvases, is to say that I have achieved it by the very aid of the varnish-bottle. It is true of them throughout that, in words I have had occasion to use in another connexion (where too I had revised with a view to "possible amendment of form and enhancement of meaning"), I have "nowhere scrupled to re-write a sentence or a passage on judging it susceptible of a better turn."

To re-read *Roderick Hudson* was to find one remark so promptly and so urgently prescribed that I could at once only take it as pointing almost too stern a moral. It stared me in the face that the time-scheme of the story is quite inadequate, and positively to that degree that the fault but just fails to wreck it. The thing escapes, I conceive, with its life: the effect sought is fortunately more achieved than missed, since the interest of the subject bears down, auspiciously dissimulates, this particular flaw in the treatment. Everything occurs, none the less, too punctually and moves too fast: Roderick's disintegration, a gradual process, and of which the exhibitional interest is exactly that it *is* gradual and occasional, and thereby traceable and watchable, swallows two years in a mouthful, proceeds quite *not* by years, but by weeks and months, and thus renders the whole view the disservice of appearing to present him as a morbidly special case. The very claim of the fable is naturally that he *is* special, that his great gift makes and keeps him highly exceptional; but that is not for a moment supposed to preclude his appearing typical (of the general type) as well; for the fictive hero successfully appeals to us only as an eminent instance, as eminent as we like, of our own conscious kind. My mistake on Roderick's behalf—and not in the least of conception, but of composition and expression—is that, at the rate at which he falls to pieces, he seems to place himself beyond our understanding and our sympathy. These are not our rates, we say; we ourselves certainly, under like pressure,—for what is it after all?—would make more of a fight. We conceive going to pieces—nothing is easier, since we see people do it, one way or another, all round us; but this young man must either have had less of the principle of development to have had so much of the principle of collapse, or less of the principle of collapse to have had so much of the principle of development. "On the basis of so great a weakness," one hears the reader say, "where was your idea of the interest? On the basis of so great an interest, where is the provision for so much weakness?" One feels indeed, in the light of this challenge, on how much too scantly projected and suggested a field poor Roderick and his large capacity for ruin are made to turn round. It has all begun too soon, as I say, and too simply, and the determinant function attributed to Christina Light, the character of well-nigh sole agent of his catastrophe that this unfortunate young woman has forced upon her, fails to commend itself to our sense of truth and proportion.

It was not, however, that I was at ease on this score even in the first fond good faith of composition; I felt too, all the while, how many more ups and downs, how many more adventures and complications my young man would have had to know, how much more experience it would have taken, in short, either to make him go under or to make him triumph. The greater complexity, the superior truth, was all more or less present to me; only the question was, too dreadfully, how make it present to the reader? How boil down so many facts in the alembic, so that the distilled result, the produced appearance, should have intensity, lucidity, brevity, beauty, all the merits required for my effect? How, when it was already so difficult, as I found, to proceed even as I *was* proceeding? It didn't help, alas, it only maddened, to remember that Balzac would have known how, and would have yet asked no additional credit for it. All the difficulty I could dodge still struck me, at any rate, as leaving more than enough; and yet I was already consciously in presence, here, of the most interesting question the artist has to consider. To give the image and the sense of certain things while still keeping them subordinate to his plan, keeping them in relation to matters more immediate and apparent, to give all the sense, in a word, without all the substance or all the surface, and so to summarise and foreshorten, so to make values both rich and sharp, that the mere procession of items and profiles is not only, for the occasion, super-seded, but is, for essential quality, almost "compromised"—such a case of delicacy proposes itself at every turn to the painter of life who wishes both to treat his chosen subject and to confine his necessary picture. It is only by doing such things that art becomes exquisite, and it is only by positively becoming exquisite that it keeps clear of becoming vulgar, repudiates the coarse industries that masquerade in its name. This eternal time-question is accordingly, for the novelist, always there and always formidable; always insisting on the *effect* of the great lapse and passage, of the "dark backward and abysm," by the terms of truth, and on the effect of compression, of composition and form, by the terms of literary arrangement. It is really a business to terrify all but stout hearts into abject omission and mutilation, though the terror would indeed be more general were the general consciousness of the difficulty greater. It is not by consciousness of difficulty, in truth, that the story-teller is mostly ridden; so prodigious a number of stories would otherwise scarce get themselves (shall it be called?) "told." None was ever very well told, I think, under the law of mere elimination —inordinately as that device appears in many quarters to be depended on. I remember doing my best not to be reduced to it for *Roderick*, at the same time that I did so helplessly and consciously beg a thousand questions. What I clung to as my principle of simplification was the precious truth that I was dealing, after all, essentially with an Action, and that no action, further, was ever made historically vivid without a certain factitious compactness; though this logic indeed opened up horizons and abysses of its own. But into these we must plunge on some other occasion.

It was at any rate under an admonition or two fished out of their depths that I must have tightened my hold of the remedy afforded, such as it was, for the absence of those more adequate illustrations of Roderick's character and history. Since one was dealing with an Action one might borrow a scrap of the Dramatist's all-in-all, his intensity—which the novelist so often ruefully envies him as a fortune in itself. The amount of illustration I could allow to the grounds of my young man's disaster was unquestionably meagre, but I might perhaps make it lively; I might produce illusion if I should be able to achieve intensity. It was for that I must have tried, I now see, with such art as I could command; but I make out in another quarter above all what really saved me. My subject, all blissfully, in face of difficulties, had defined itself—and this in spite of the title of the book—as not directly, in the least, my young sculptor's adventure. This it had been but indirectly, being all the while in essence and in final effect another man's, his friend's and patron's, view and experience of him. One's luck was to have felt one's subject right—whether instinct or calculation, in those dim days, most served; and the circumstance even amounts perhaps to a little lesson that when this has happily occurred faults may show, faults may disfigure, and yet not upset the work. It remains in equilibrium by having found its centre, the point of command of all the rest. From this centre the subject has been treated, from this centre the interest has spread, and so, whatever else it may do or may not do, the thing has acknowledged a principle of composition and contrives at least to hang together. We see in such a case why it should so hang; we escape that dreariest displeasure it is open to experiments in this general order to inflict, the sense of any hanging-together precluded as by the very terms of the case.

The centre of interest throughout *Roderick* is in Rowland Mallet's consciousness, and the drama is the very drama of that consciousness—which I had of course to make sufficiently acute in order to enable it, like a set and lighted scene, to hold the play. By making it acute, meanwhile, one made its own movement—or rather, strictly, its movement in the particular connexion—interesting; this movement really being quite the stuff of one's thesis. It had, naturally, Rowland's consciousness, not to be *too* acute—which would have disconnected it and made it superhuman: the beautiful little problem was to keep it connected, connected intimately, with the general human exposure, and thereby bedimmed and befooled and bewildered, anxious, restless, fallible, and yet to endow it with such intelligence that the appearances reflected in it, and constituting together there the situation and the "story," should become by that fact intelligible. Discernible from the first the joy of such a "job" as this making of his relation to everything involved a sufficiently limited, a sufficiently pathetic, tragic, comic, ironic, personal state to be thoroughly natural, and yet at the same time a sufficiently clear medium to represent a whole. This whole was to be the sum of what "happened" to him, or in other words his total adventure; but as what happened to him was above all to feel certain things happening to others, to Roderick, to Christina, to Mary Garland, to Mrs. Hudson, to the Cavaliere, to the Prince, so the beauty of the constructional game was to preserve in everything its especial value for *him*. The ironic effect of his having fallen in love with the girl who is herself in love with Roderick, though he is unwitting, at the time, of that secret—the conception of this last irony, I must add, has remained happier than my execution of it; which should logically have involved the reader's being put into position to take more closely home the impression made by Mary Garland. The ground has not been laid for it, and when that is the case one builds all vainly in the air: one patches up one's superstructure, one paints it in the prettiest colours, one hangs fine old tapestry and rare brocade over its window-sills, one flies emblazoned banners from its roof—the building none the less totters and refuses to stand square.

It is not really *worked-in* that Roderick himself could have pledged his faith in such a quarter, much more at such a crisis, before leaving America: and that weakness, clearly, produces a limp in the whole march of the fable. Just so, though there was no reason on earth (unless I except one, presently to be mentioned) why Rowland should *not*, at Northampton, have conceived a passion, or as near an approach to one as he was capable of, for a remarkable young woman there suddenly dawning on his sight, a particular fundamental care was required for the vivification of that possibility. The care, unfortunately, has not been skilfully enough taken, in spite of the later patching-up of the girl's figure. We fail to accept it, on the actual showing, as that of a young person irresistible at any moment, and above all irresistible at a moment of the liveliest *other* preoccupation, as that of the weaver of (even the highly conditioned) spell that the narrative imputes to her. The spell of attraction is cast upon young men by young women in all sorts of ways, and the novel has no more constant office than to remind us of that. But Mary Garland's way doesn't, indubitably, convince us; any more than we are truly convinced, I think, that Rowland's destiny, or say his nature, would have made him accessible at the same hour to two quite distinct commotions, each a very deep one, of his whole personal economy. Rigidly viewed, each of these upheavals of his sensibility must have been exclusive of other upheavals, yet the reader is asked to accept them as working together. They are different vibrations, but the whole sense of the situation depicted is that they should each have been of the strongest, too strong to walk hand in hand. Therefore it is that when, on the ship, under the stars, Roderick suddenly takes his friend into the confidence of his engagement, we instinctively disallow the friend's title to discomfiture. The whole picture presents him as for the time on the mounting wave, exposed highly enough, no doubt, to a hundred discomfitures, but least exposed to that one. The damage to verisimilitude is deep.

The difficulty had been from the first that I required my antithesis —my antithesis to Christina Light, one of the main terms of the subject. One is ridden by the law that antithesis, to be efficient, shall be both direct and complete. Directness seemed to fail unless Mary should be, so to speak, "plain", Christina being essentially so "coloured"; and completeness seemed to fail unless she too should have her potency. She could moreover, by which I mean the antithetic young woman could, perfectly have had it; only success would have been then in the narrator's art to attest it. Christina's own presence and action are, on the other hand, I think, all firm ground; the truth probably being that the ideal antithesis rarely does "come off," and that it has to content itself for the most part with a strong term and a weak term, and even then to feel itself lucky. If one of the terms *is* strong, that perhaps may pass, in the most difficult of the arts, for a triumph. I remember at all events feeling, toward the end of *Roderick*, that the Princess Casamassima had been launched, that, wound-up with the right silver key, she would go on a certain time by the motion communicated; thanks to which I knew the pity, the real pang of losing sight of her. I desired as in no other such case I can recall to preserve, to recover the vision; and I have seemed to myself in re-reading the book quite to understand why. The multiplication of touches had produced even more life than the subject required, and that life, in other conditions, in some other prime relation, would still have somehow to be spent. Thus one would watch for her and waylay her at some turn of the road to come—all that was to be needed was to give her time. This I did in fact, meeting her again and taking her up later on.

HENRY JAMES

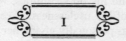

I

ROWLAND MALLET had made his arrangements to sail for Europe on the 5th of September, and having in the interval a fortnight to spare, he determined to spend it with his cousin Cecilia, the widow of a nephew of his father. He was urged by the reflexion that an affectionate farewell might help to exonerate him from the charge of neglect frequently preferred by this lady. It was not that the young man disliked her; he regarded her, on the contrary, with a tender admiration and had not forgotten how when his cousin brought her home on her marriage he seemed to feel the upward sweep of the empty bough from which the golden fruit had been plucked. He then and there, for himself, accepted the prospect of bachelorhood. The truth was that, as it will be part of the entertainment of this narrative to exhibit, Rowland Mallet had an uncomfortably sensitive conscience, and that, in spite of the seeming paradox, his visits to Cecilia were rare because she and her misfortunes were often uppermost in it. Her misfortunes were three in number: first, she had lost her husband; second, she had lost her money, or the greater part of it; and third, she lived at Northampton, Massachusetts. Mallet's compassion was really wasted, because Cecilia was a very clever woman and a skilful counter-plotter to adversity. She had made herself a charming home, her economies were not obtrusive, and there was always a cheerful flutter in the folds of her crape. It was the consciousness of all this that puzzled Mallet whenever he felt tempted to put in his oar. He had money and he had time, but he never could decide just how to place these gifts gracefully at Cecilia's service. He was no longer at all in the humour to marry her; that fancy had in these eight years died a very natural death. And yet her extreme cleverness seemed somehow to make charity difficult and patronage impossible. He would rather have chopped off his hand than offer her a cheque, a piece of useful furniture or a black silk dress; and yet there was pity for him in seeing such a bright proud woman live in such a small dull way. Cecilia had moreover a turn for sarcasm, and her smile, which was her pretty feature, was never so pretty as when her sprightly phrase had a lurking scratch in it. Rowland remembered

21

that for him she was all smiles, and suspected awkwardly that he ministered not a little to her sense of the irony of things. And in truth, with
his means, his leisure and his opportunities, what had he done? He
had a lively suspicion of his uselessness. Cecilia meanwhile cut out
her own dresses, and was personally giving her little girl the education
of a princess.

This time, however, he presented himself bravely enough; for in the
way of activity it was something definite at least to be going to Europe
and to be meaning to spend the winter in Rome. Cecilia met him in
the early dusk at the gate of her little garden, amid a studied combination of horticultural odours. A rosy widow of twenty-eight, half-cousin,
half-hostess, doing the honours of a fragrant cottage on a midsummer
evening, was a phenomenon to which all the young man's senses were
able to rise. Cecilia was always gracious, but this evening she was
positively in spirits. She was in a happy mood, and Mallet imagined
there was a private reason for it—a reason quite distinct from her
pleasure in receiving her honoured kinsman. The next day he flattered
himself he was on the way to discover it.

For the present, after tea, as they sat on the rose-framed porch,
while Rowland held his younger cousin between his knees, and she,
enjoying her situation, listened timorously for the stroke of bedtime,
Cecilia insisted on talking more about her visitor than about herself.
"What is it you mean to do in Europe?" she asked lightly, giving a
turn to the frill of her sleeve—just such a turn as seemed to Mallet to
bring out all the latent difficulties of the question.

"Why, very much what I do here," he answered. "No great harm!"

"Is it true," Cecilia asked, "that here you do no great harm? Isn't
a man like you doing a certain harm when he isn't doing some positive
good?"

"Isn't that compliment rather ambiguous?" he inquired in return.

"No," she answered, "you know what I think of you. You have a
turn for doing nice things and behaving yourself properly. You have
it, in the first place, in your character. You mean, if you will pardon
my putting it so, thoroughly well. Ask Bessie if you don't hold her
more gently and comfortably than any of her other admirers."

"He holds me more comfortably than Mr. Hudson," Bessie declared
roundly.

Rowland, not knowing Mr. Hudson, could but half appreciate the
eulogy, and Cecilia went on to develop her idea. "Your circumstances,
in the second place, suggest the idea of some sort of social usefulness.

You're intelligent and are well informed, and your benevolence, if one may call it benevolence, would be discriminating. You're rich and unoccupied, so that it might be abundant. Therefore I say you're a man to do something on a large scale. Bestir yourself, dear Rowland, or we may be taught to think that Virtue herself is setting a bad example."

"Heaven forbid," cried Rowland, "that I should set the examples of virtue ! I'm quite willing to follow them, however, and if I don't do something on the grand scale it is that my genius is altogether imitative and that I've not recently encountered any very striking models of grandeur. Pray, what shall I do ? Found an orphan asylum or build a dormitory for Harvard College ? I'm not rich enough to do either in an ideally handsome way, and I confess that yet a while I feel too young to strike my *grand coup*. I'm holding myself ready for inspiration. I'm waiting till something takes my fancy irresistibly. If inspiration comes at forty it will be a hundred pities to have tied up my money-bag at thirty."

"Well, of course I give you decent time," said Cecilia. "It's only a word to the wise—a notification that you're expected not to run your course without having done something handsome for your fellow-men."

Nine o'clock sounded, and Bessie with each stroke courted a closer embrace. But a single winged word from her mother overleaped her successive intrenchments. She turned and kissed her cousin, depositing an irrepressible tear on his moustache. Then she went and said her prayers to her mother; it was evident she was being admirably brought up. Rowland, with the permission of his hostess, lighted a cigar and puffed it a while in silence. Cecilia's interest in his career seemed very agreeable. That Mallet was without vanity I by no means intend to affirm; but there had been times when, seeing him accept with scarce less deference advice even more peremptory than this lady's, you might have asked yourself what had become of his proper pride. Now, in the sweet-smelling starlight, he felt gently wooed to egotism. There was a project connected with his going abroad which it was on his tongue's end to communicate. It had no relation to hospitals or dormitories, and yet it would have sounded very generous. But it was not because it would have sounded generous that poor Mallet at last puffed it away in the fumes of his cigar. Useful though it might be, it expressed too imperfectly the young man's own personal conception of usefulness. He was extremely fond of all the arts and had an almost passionate enjoyment of pictures. He had seen a great many and judged them sagaciously. It had occurred to him some time before that it would be the work of a good citizen to go abroad and with all expedition and secrecy purchase certain valuable specimens of the Dutch and Italian schools, as to which he had received private proposals, and then present his treasures out of hand to an American city, not unknown to æsthetic fame, in which at that time there prevailed a good deal of fruitless aspiration toward an art-museum. He had seen himself in imagination, more than once, in the mouldy old saloon of a Florentine palace, turning toward the deep embrasure of the window some scarcely-faded Ghirlandaio or Botticelli while a host in reduced circumstances pointed out the lovely drawing of a hand. But he imparted none of these visions to Cecilia, and he suddenly swept them away with the declaration that he was of course an idle useless creature and that he should probably be even more so in Europe than at home. "The only thing is," he said, "that there I shall *seem* to be doing something. I shall be better beguiled, and shall be therefore, I suppose, in a better humour with life. You may say that that's just the humour a useless man should keep out of. He should cultivate humility and depression. I did a good many things when I was in Europe before, but I spent no winter in Rome. Every one assures me that this is a peculiar refinement of bliss; you must have noticed the almost priggish ecstasy with which those who have enjoyed it talk about it. It's evidently a sort of glorified loafing: a passive life there, thanks to the number and the quality of one's impressions, takes on a respectable likeness to an active pursuit. It's always lotus-eating, only you sit down at table and the lotuses are served up on rococo china. It's all very well, but I have a distinct prevision of this—that if Roman life doesn't do something substantial to make you happier it must contribute rather to unhinge or upset you. It seems to me a rash thing for a sensitive soul deliberately to cultivate its sensibilities by rambling too often among the ruins of the Palatine or riding too often in the shadow of the crumbling aqueducts. In such recreations the chords of feeling grow tense, and after-life, to spare your æsthetic nerves, must play upon them with a touch as dainty as the tread of Mignon when she danced her egg-dance."

"I should have said, my dear Rowland, with all recognition of your eloquence," Cecilia said with a laugh, "that your nerves were tough—that your eggs were hard !"

"That being stupid, you mean, I might be happy ? Upon my word, I'm not so happy as that ! I'm clever enough to want more than I've got. I'm tired of myself, my own thoughts, my own affairs, my own eternal company. True happiness, we are told, consists in getting out of one's self; but the point is not only to get out—you must stay out; and to stay out you must have some absorbing errand. Unfortunately I have no errand, and nobody will trust me with one. I want to care for something or for somebody. And I want to care, don't you see? with a certain intensity; even, if you can believe it, with a certain passion. I can't just now be intense and passionate about a hospital or a dormitory. Do you know I sometimes think that I'm a man of genius half-finished? The genius has been left out, the faculty of expression is wanting; but the need for expression remains, and I spend my days groping for the latch of a closed door."

"What an immense number of words," said Cecilia after a pause, "to say you want to fall in love! I've no doubt you've as good a genius for that as any one if you would only trust it a little more."

"Of course I've thought of that, and I assure you I hold myself ready. But evidently I'm not inflammable. Is there in Northampton by chance some perfect epitome of the graces?"

"Of the graces?" said Cecilia, raising her eyebrows and suppressing too distinct a consciousness of being herself a finished embodiment of several. "The household virtues, in all their rigour, are better represented. There are some excellent young women, and there are two or three very pretty girls. I'll have them all here to tea, one by one, if you like."

"I should particularly like it; especially as I should give you a chance to see by the profundity of my attention that if I'm not happy it's not for want of taking pains."

Cecilia was silent a little; and then, "On the whole," she resumed, "I don't think there are any worth putting you in possible suspense about. You've seen as good samples as we can show you."

"Are you very, very sure?" asked the young man, rising and throwing away his cigar-end.

"Upon my word," cried Cecilia, "one would suppose I wished to keep you for myself! Of course I'm very, very sure. But, as the penalty of your insinuations, I shall invite the plainest and prosiest damsel who can be found—of *them* we have our assortment!—and leave you alone with her."

Rowland smiled. "Even against her," he said, "I should be sorry to conclude until I had given her my respectful attention."

This little profession of ideal chivalry (which closed the conversation) was not quite so fanciful on his lips as it would have been on those of many another man; as a rapid glance at his antecedents may help to make the reader perceive. His life had held side by side many hard things and many soft. He had sprung from a stiff Puritan stock and had been brought up to think much more intently of the duties of our earthly pilgrimage than of its privileges and pleasures. His progenitors had submitted in the matter of dogmatic theology to the relaxing influences of recent years; but if Rowland's youthful consciousness was not chilled by the menace of long punishment for brief transgression, he had at least been made to feel that there ran through all things a strain of right and of wrong as different, after all, in their complexion, as the texture, to the spiritual sense, of Sundays and week-days. His father, a chip of the primal Puritan block, had been a man of an icy smile and a stony frown. He had always bestowed on his son, on principle, more frowns than smiles, and if the lad had not been turned to stone himself it was because nature had blessed him inwardly with a well of vivifying waters. Mrs. Mallet had been a Miss Rowland, the daughter of a retired sea-captain once famous on the ships that sailed from Salem and Newburyport. He had brought to port many a cargo which crowned the edifice of fortunes already almost colossal, but he had also done a little sagacious trading on his own account, and he was able to retire, prematurely for so seaworthy a maritime organism, upon a pension of his own providing. He was to be seen for a year on the Salem wharves, smoking the best tobacco and contemplating the seaward horizon with an inveteracy which superficial minds interpreted as a sign of repentance. At last, one evening, he disappeared beneath it, as he had often done before; this time, however, not as a commissioned navigator, but simply as an amateur of a critical turn likely to prove oppressive to the officer in command of the vessel. Five months later his place at home knew him again, and made the acquaintance also of a handsome, light-coloured young woman, of redundant contour, speaking a foreign tongue. The foreign tongue proved after much conflicting research to be the idiom of Amsterdam, and the young woman, which was stranger still, to be Captain Rowland's wife. Why he had gone forth so suddenly across the seas to marry her, what had happened between them before, and whether—though it was of questionable propriety for a good citizen to espouse a young person of mysterious origin who did her hair in fantastically elaborate plaits and in whose appearance "figure"

26

enjoyed such striking predominance—he would not have had a heavy weight on his conscience if he had remained an irresponsible bachelor: these questions, and many others bearing with varying degrees of immediacy on the subject, were much propounded but scantily answered, and this history need not be charged with resolving them. Mrs. Rowland, for so handsome a woman, proved a tranquil neighbour and an excellent housewife. Her extremely fresh complexion, however, was always suffused with an air of apathetic homesickness, and she played her part in American society chiefly by having the little squares of brick pavement in front of her dwelling scoured and polished as nearly as possible into the likeness of Dutch tiles. Rowland Mallet remembered having seen her as a child—an immensely stout white-faced lady, wearing a high cap of very stiff tulle, speaking English with a formidable accent and suffering from dropsy. Captain Rowland was a little bronzed and wizened man, with eccentric opinions. He advocated the creation of a public promenade along the sea, with arbours and little green tables for the consumption of beer, and a platform, surrounded by Chinese lanterns, for dancing. He especially desired the town library to be opened on Sundays; though, as he never entered it on week-days, it was easy to turn the proposition into ridicule. Therefore if Mrs. Mallet was a woman of an exquisite moral tone it was not that she had inherited her temper from forefathers with a turn for casuistry. Jonas Mallet at the time of his marriage was conducting with silent shrewdness a small unpromising business. Both his shrewdness and his silence increased with his years, and at the close of his life he was an extremely well-dressed, well-brushed gentleman with a frigid grey eye, who said little to anybody, but of whom everybody said that he had a very handsome fortune. He was not a sentimental father, and the introduction into Rowland's life of that grim ghost of the wholesome by which I spoke of it just now as haunted dated from early boyhood. Mr. Mallet, whenever he looked at his son, felt extreme compunction at having made a fortune. He remembered that the fruit had not dropped ripe from the tree into his own mouth, and he determined it should be no fault of his if the boy were corrupted by luxury. Rowland therefore, except for a good deal of expensive instruction in foreign tongues and abstruse sciences, received the education of a poor man's son. His fare was plain, his temper familiar with the discipline of patched trousers and his habits marked by an exaggerated simplicity which was kept up really at great expense. He was banished to the country for months together, in the midst of servants who had strict injunctions to see that he suffered no serious harm, but were as strictly forbidden to wait upon him. As no school could be found conducted on principles sufficiently rigorous, he was attended at home by an instructor who had set a high price—high for Jonas Mallet—on the understanding that he was to illustrate the beauty of abstinence not only by precept but by example. Rowland passed for a child of ordinary parts, and certainly, during his younger years, was an excellent imitation of the boy—most usual of boys—who has inherited nothing whatever that is to make his presence on earth shine from afar. He was passive, pliable, frank, extremely slow at his books and inordinately fond of trout-fishing. His hair, a memento of his Dutch ancestry, was of the fairest shade of yellow, his complexion absurdly rosy and the measurement of his middle, when he was about ten years old, quite alarmingly large. This, however, was but an episode in his growth; he became afterwards a fresh-coloured, yellow-bearded man, but was never accused of anything more material than a manly stoutness. He emerged from childhood a simple, wholesome, round-eyed lad, with no suspicion that a less circuitous course might have been taken to make him happy, but with a vague sense that his young experience was not a fair sample of human freedom, and that he was to make a great many discoveries. When he was about fifteen he achieved a momentous one. He ascertained that his mother was a saint. She had always been a very vivid presence in his life, but of an intensity so mild, so diffused and so regulated that his sense was fully opened to it only by the danger of losing her. She had an illness which for many months was liable at any moment to carry her off, and during her long-arrested convalescence she removed the mask that she had worn for years by her husband's order. Rowland spent his days at her side, and felt before long as if he had made a new friend. All his impressions of this period were to be commented upon and interpreted during the comparative ease of the future, and it was only at the later time that he understood how his mother had been for fifteen long years a woman heavily depressed, and her marriage an irredeemable error which she had spent her life in trying to look in the face. She had found nothing to oppose to her husband's rigid and consistent will but the appearance of absolute compliance; her courage had sunk, and she had lived for a while in a sort of spiritual torpor. But at last, as her child emerged from babyhood, she had begun to find a certain charm in patience, to discover the uses of ingenuity, and to learn that somehow or other one can always arrange one's life. She had cultivated from this time forward a little plot of independent feeling, and it was of this private precinct that before her death she had given her son the key. Rowland's allowance at college was barely sufficient to maintain him decently, and, his degree nevertheless achieved, he was taken into his father's counting-house to do small drudgery on a proportionate stipend. For three years he earned his living as regularly as the obscure functionary in fustian who swept out the place. Mr. Mallet was consistent, but the perfection of his consistency was known only on his death. He left but a third of his property to his son, devoting the remainder to various public institutions and local charities. Rowland's third was a very easy competence, and he never felt a moment's jealousy of his fellow-pensioners; but when one of the establishments which had figured most advantageously in his father's will bethought itself to affirm the existence of a later instrument in which it had been still more handsomely treated, the young man felt a sudden passionate need to repel the claim by process of law. There was a sharp contest, but he gained his case; immediately after which he made in another quarter a donation of the disputed sum. He cared nothing for the money, but he had felt a just desire to protest against a star which seemed determined only not to pamper him. It struck him that he could put up with a little pampering. And yet he treated himself to a very modest quantity and submitted without reserve to the great national discipline which began in 1861. When the Civil War broke out he immediately obtained a commission, doing his duty afterwards, for the three first long years, by the aid of much grinding of the teeth. His duty happened to remain, for the most part, obscure, but he never lost a certain private satisfaction in remembering that on two or three occasions it had been performed, if not with glory, at least with a noted propriety. He had disentangled himself from business, and after the war he felt a deep disinclination to take up again the harsh and broken threads. He had no desire to make money, he had money enough; and although he knew, and was frequently reminded, that a young man is the better for a fixed occupation, he could perceive no advantage to his soul in his driving a lucrative trade. Yet few young men of means and leisure ever made less of a parade of idleness, and indeed idleness in any degree could hardly be laid at the door of a personage who took life in the conscious, serious, anxious fashion of our friend. It often seemed to Mallet that he wholly lacked the prime requisite of an expert *flâneur*—the simple, sensuous, confident relish of pleasure. He had frequent fits of melancholy in which he declared that he was neither fish nor flesh nor good red herring. His was neither an irresponsibly contemplative nature nor a sturdily practical one, and he was for ever looking in vain for the uses of the things that please and the charm of the things that sustain. He was an awkward mixture of moral and æsthetic curiosity, and yet he would have made an ineffective reformer and an indifferent artist. It seemed to him that the glow of happiness must be found either in action of some thoroughly keen kind on behalf of an idea, or in producing a masterpiece in one of the arts. Oftenest, perhaps, he wished he had been a vigorous young man of genius without a penny. As it was, he could only buy pictures and not paint them; and in the way of action he had to content himself with making a rule to render scrupulous justice to fine strokes of it in others. On the whole he had an incorruptible modesty. With his blooming complexion and his quiet grey eyes he felt the friction of existence more than was suspected; but he asked no allowance on grounds of temper, he assumed that fate had treated him inordinately well and that he had no excuse for taking an ill-natured view of life, and he engaged to believe that all women were fair, all men were brave and the world a delightful place of sojourn, until the contrary should be distinctly proved.

Cecilia's blooming garden and shady porch had seemed so friendly to repose and a cigar that she reproached him the next morning with indifference to her ordered little parlour, not less in its way a monument to her ingenious taste. "And by the way," she added as he followed her in, "if I refused last night to show you a pretty girl, I can at least show you a remarkably pretty boy."

She threw open a window and pointed to a statuette which occupied a place of honour among the ornaments of the room. Rowland looked at it a moment and then turned to her with an exclamation of surprise. She gave him a rapid glance, perceived that her statuette was of striking interest, and then smiled knowingly, as if this were a familiar idea. "Who in the world did it, and how did you ever come by it?" Rowland had visibly received a sharp impression.

"Oh," said Cecilia, adjusting the light, "it's a little thing of poor Mr. Hudson's."

"And who the deuce is poor Mr. Hudson?" asked Rowland. But he was absorbed; he lost her immediate reply. The statuette, in bronze, something more than two feet high, represented a naked youth drinking from a gourd. The attitude was perfectly simple. The lad was squarely planted on his feet, with his legs a little apart; his back was slightly hollowed, his head thrown back; his hands were raised to support the rustic cup. There was a loosened fillet of wild flowers about his head, and his eyes, under their dropped lids, looked straight into the cup. On the base was scratched the Greek word Δίψα, Thirst. The figure might have been some beautiful youth of ancient fable—Hylas or Narcissus, Paris or Endymion. Its beauty was the beauty of natural movement; nothing had been sought to be represented but the perfection of an attitude. This had been attentively studied—it was rendered with charming truth. Rowland demanded more light, dropped his head on this side and that, uttered vague exclamations. He said to himself, as he had said more than once in the Louvre and the Vatican, "We ugly mortals, what beautiful creatures we are!" Nothing for a long time had given him so much pleasure. "Hudson—Hudson," he asked again; "who may Hudson be?"

"A young man of this very place," said Cecilia.

"A young man? How young?"

"I suppose he's three or four and twenty."

"Of this very place, you say—of Northampton, Massachusetts?"

"He lives here, but his people belong to Virginia."

"Is he a sculptor then by profession?"

"Oh, no—he's studying Law."

Rowland burst out laughing. "He has found something in Blackstone that I never did. He makes statues like this then simply for his pleasure?"

Cecilia, with a smile, gave a little toss of her head. "He makes them perhaps sometimes for mine!"

"I congratulate you," said Rowland, "on having so generous a provider. I wonder if he could be induced to do anything for a mere man?"

"For you? Oh, this was a matter of friendship. I saw the figure when he had modelled it in clay, and of course I greatly admired it. He said nothing at the time, but a week ago, on my birthday, he arrived in a buggy, with his treasure done up in a morsel of old blanket. He had had it cast at the foundry at Chicopee; I believe it's a beautiful piece of bronze. begged He me, in the most natural way in the world, to accept."

"He has, upon my word, a grand conception of the natural!" With which Rowland fell to admiring the statue again.

"Really then," said Cecilia, "it's a very remarkable thing?"

"Why, my dear cousin," Rowland answered, "Mr. Hudson of Virginia is an extraordinary——" Then suddenly stopping, "Is he a great friend of yours?" he asked.

"A great friend?" Cecilia hesitated. "I regard him practically as a child."

"Well," said Rowland, "he's a very precocious child! Tell me something about him. I should like to see him."

Cecilia was obliged to go to her daughter's music-lesson, but she assured Rowland that she would arrange for him a meeting with the young sculptor. He was a frequent visitor, and as he had not called for some days it was quite possible he would come that evening. Rowland, left alone, examined the statuette at his leisure, and returned more than once during the day to take another look at it. He discovered its weak points, but its charm was of finest essence. It had taken form under the breath of genius. Rowland envied the happy youth who, in a New England village, without aid or encouragement, without models or examples, had found it so easy to produce a lovely work.

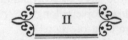

II

In the evening, as he was smoking his cigar on the verandah, a light quick step pressed the gravel of the garden-path, and in a moment a young man, rising before them, had made his bow to Cecilia. It indicated either that he was an extreme intimate or was scantly versed in the common social forms. Cecilia, who was sitting near the steps, pointed to a neighbouring chair, but her visitor abruptly sought a place on a step at her feet and began to fan himself vigorously with his hat, breaking out into loud dispraise of the high temperature. "I'm simply dripping wet!" he observed without ceremony.

"You walk too fast," said Cecilia. "You do everything too fast."

"I know it, I know it!" he cried, passing his hand through his abundant dark hair and making it stand out in a picturesque shock. "I can't dawdle over things if I try. If I do anything at all I must do it *so*. There's something inside of me that drives me. A demon of unrest!"

Cecilia gave a light laugh, and Rowland leaned forward in his hammock. He had placed himself in it at Bessie's request and was playing that he was her baby and that she was rocking him to sleep. She sat beside him swinging the hammock to and fro and chanting a lullaby. When he raised himself she pushed him back and said that the baby must finish its nap. "But I want to see the gentleman with the driving demon," said Rowland.

"Do demons know how to drive?" Bessie demanded. "It's only old Mr. Hudson."

"Very well, I want to see old Mr. Hudson."

"Oh, never mind *him!*" said Bessie, with the brevity of contempt.

"You speak as if you didn't like him."

"I don't!" Bessie affirmed, putting Rowland to bed again.

The hammock was swung at the end of the verandah, in the thickest shade of the climbing plants, and this fragment of dialogue had passed unnoticed. Rowland submitted a while longer to be cradled and contented himself with listening to Mr. Hudson's voice. It was a soft and not altogether masculine organ, and pitched on this occasion in a somewhat plaintive and pettish key. The young man's mood seemed fretful; he complained of the gnats, of the dust, of a shoe that hurt him, of having gone on an errand a mile to the other side of the town and found that the person he was in search of had left Northampton an hour before.

"Won't you have a cup of tea?" Cecilia asked. "Perhaps that will restore your equanimity."

"Ay, by keeping me awake all night!" said Mr. Hudson. "At the best, to go down to the office is like getting into a bath with the water frozen. With my nerves set on edge by a sleepless night I should sit and shiver at home. That's always charming for my mother."

"Your mother's well, I hope?"

"Oh, mother's as usual."

"And Miss Garland?"

"Miss Garland's as usual, too. Every one, every thing's as usual. Nothing ever happens in this benighted town."

"I beg your pardon; things do happen sometimes," said Cecilia. "Here's a dear cousin of mine arrived on purpose to sing to you the praises of your little bronze." And she called to Rowland to come and be introduced to Mr. Hudson. The young man sprang up with alacrity, and Rowland, coming forward to shake hands, had a good look at him in the light projected from the parlour window. Something seemed to shine out of Hudson's face as a warning against random compliments.

"Your statuette seems to me very interesting," Rowland gravely said. "It has given me immense pleasure."

"And my cousin really knows what things are worth," Cecilia went on. "My cousin's a judge and a critic."

Hudson smiled and stared. "A judge—a critic?" he echoed, laughing. "He's the first then I've ever seen! Let me see what they look like"; and he drew Rowland nearer to the light. "Have they all such good heads as that? I should like to model yours."

"Oh do it!" said Cecilia. "It will keep him with us a while. He's running off otherwise to Europe."

"Ah, off to Europe!" Hudson exclaimed with a melancholy cadence as they sat down. "Happy, happy man!"

But the note seemed to Rowland struck rather at random, for he failed to catch it again in the boyish candour of the visitor's talk. Hudson was a tall slim youth, with a singularly mobile and intelligent face. Rowland was struck at first only with its responsive vivacity, but it had presently affected him as full of a beauty of its own. The features were admirably chiselled and finished, and a frank smile played over them as gracefully as a breeze among flowers. The fault of the young man's whole structure was an excessive want of breadth. The forehead, though high and brave, was narrow; the jaw and the shoulders were narrow, and the result was an air of insufficient physical substance. But Mallet afterwards learned that this fair and slender stripling could draw upon a fund of nervous force outlasting and outwearying the endurance of sturdier temperaments. And certainly there was life enough in his eye to furnish an immortality. It was a generous dark grey eye, subject to an intermittent kindling glow which would have made a ruder visage striking, and which gave at times to Hudson's harmonious face an altogether extraordinary beauty. There was to Rowland's sympathetic sense a slightly pitiful disparity between the young sculptor's distinguished mask and the shabby gentility of his costume. Arrayed for a rural visit, a visit to a pretty woman, he was clad from head to foot in a white linen suit which had never been remarkable for the felicity of its cut and which had now quite lost its vivifying and redeeming crispness. He wore a bright red cravat, passed through a ring altogether too splendid to be valuable; he pulled and twisted, as he sat, a pair of yellow kid gloves; he emphasised his conversation with great dashes and flourishes of a silver-tipped walking-stick, and he kept constantly taking off and putting on one of those slouched sombreros which are the traditional property of the Virginian or Carolinian of romance. When his hat was on he was almost romantic, in spite of his mock elegance; and when it was off and he sat nursing it and turning it about and not knowing what to do with it, he could hardly be said to be awkward. He evidently had a native relish for rich accessories, and he appropriated what came to his hand. This was visible in his talk, which abounded in the superlative and the sweeping. His plastic sense took in conversation altogether the turn of colour.

Rowland, who was a temperate talker, sat by in silence, while Cecilia, who had told him that she desired his opinion upon her friend, used a good deal of characteristic art in leading the young man on to put himself before them. She perfectly succeeded, and Hudson rattled away for an hour with a volubility in which the innocence of youth and the assurance of felt and unwonted success were singularly blended. He gave his opinion on twenty topics, he opened up the crystal flood of local gossip, he described his repulsive routine at the office of Messrs. Striker and Spooner, counsellors-at-law, and he gave with a hundred happy touches an account of the annual boat-race between Harvard and Yale, which he had lately admired at Worcester. He had looked at the straining oarsmen and the swaying crowd and the whole great shining summer scene with the eye of the artist and of the lover of displayed life. For Rowland meanwhile the time passed well; Cecilia's visitor held his attention fast. Whenever Hudson surpassed himself in confidence or in magniloquence his hostess broke into a long, light, ambiguous laugh.

"Do you find me more of a fool than usual?" the young man then demanded. "Have I said anything so ridiculous?"

"Go on, go on," Cecilia replied. "You're but too much your wondrous self. Show Mr. Mallet how Mr. Striker read the Declaration of Independence on the 4th of July."

Hudson, like many men with a turn for the plastic arts, was an excellent mimic, and he represented with equal truth and drollery the accent and attitude of a pompous country lawyer sustaining the burden of this heavy honour of our national festival. The sonorous twang, the see-saw gestures, the patriotic pronunciation were vividly reproduced. But Cecilia's manner and the young man's quick response ruffled a little poor Rowland's responsive mind. He wondered if his cousin were not sacrificing the faculty of reverence in her bright beneficiary to her need for amusement. Hudson made no serious rejoinder to Rowland's compliment on his statuette until he rose to go. Rowland judged he would have forgotten it, and supposed the oversight to be a sign of the indifference of conscious power. But

Hudson stood a moment before he said good-night, twirled his sombrero and hesitated for the first time. He gave Rowland a clear, penetrating glance, and then with a wonderfully frank, appealing smile, "You absolutely meant," he asked, "what you said a while ago about that thing of mine? It's good—essentially good?"

"I really meant it," said Rowland, laying a kindly hand on his shoulder. "It's very good indeed. It's as you say, essentially good. That's just the beauty and the interest of it."

Hudson's eyes glowed and expanded; he looked for some time in silence at this strange utterer of sweet sounds. "I have a notion you really know," he said at last. "But if you don't, you see, it doesn't much matter."

"My cousin asked me to-day," said Cecilia, "if I supposed you knew yourself how good it is."

Hudson stared, flushing a little. "Perhaps not, then!"

"That may very well be," said Rowland. "I read in a book the other day that great talent in action—in fact the book said genius—is a kind of safe somnambulism. The artist performs great feats in a lucky dream. We mustn't wake him up lest he should lose his balance."

"Oh, when he's back in bed again!" Hudson answered with a laugh. "Yes, call it a lucky dream. It was a very happy one."

"Tell me this," said Rowland. "Did you mean anything very particular by your young Water-drinker? Does he represent an idea? Is he a pointed symbol?"

Hudson raised his eyebrows and gently stroked his hair. "Why, he's youth, you know; he's innocence, he's health, he's strength, he's curiosity. Yes, he's a lot of grand things."

"And is the cup also a symbol?"

"The cup is knowledge, pleasure, experience. Anything of that kind."

"Then he's drinking very deep," said Rowland.

Hudson gave an approving nod. "Well, poor wretch, you wouldn't have him die of thirst, would you?" But without awaiting a reply he called good-night from the garden-path and lost himself in the darkness.

"Well, what do you make of him?" asked Cecilia, returning a short time afterwards from a visit of investigation in respect to the number of Bessie's blankets.

Rowland replied after a little by a question of his own. "Isn't he a case of what's called the artistic temperament? That's interesting to see, for the ' likes ' of *us*."

"Speak for your own temperament! But he's a very odd creature," Cecilia conceded.

"Who are his people? what has been his education?" Rowland asked.

"He has had no education beyond what he has picked up with little trouble for himself. His mother is a widow, of a Massachusetts country family, a little timid, tremulous woman, always troubled, always on pins and needles about her son. She had some property herself and married a Virginia gentleman—an owner of lands and slaves. He turned out, I believe, quite a dreadful sort of person and made great havoc with the resources, whatever they were, that she always speaks of as their fortune. Everything, or almost everything, melted away, including Mr. Hudson himself. This is literally true, for he drank himself to death. Ten years ago his wife was left a widow, with scanty means and a couple of growing boys. She paid her husband's debts as best she could and came to establish herself here, where, by the death of a charitable relative, she had inherited an old-fashioned ruinous house. Roderick, our friend, was her pride and joy; but Stephen, the elder, was her comfort and support. I remember him later; he was a plain-faced, sturdy, practical lad, very different from his brother and in his way, I imagine, the making of a useful man. When the war broke out he found the New England blood running thicker in his veins than the Virginian, and immediately obtained a commission. He fell in some small hole-and-corner engagement, leaving his mother inconsolable. Roderick, however, has given her plenty to think about, and she has induced him by some mysterious art to take up a profession that he abhors and for which he is about as fit as I am to drive a locomotive. He grew up *à la grâce de Dieu*; he had no guidance—he could bear no control; he could only be horribly spoiled. Three or four years ago he broke off his connexion with a small college in this part of the state, where, I'm afraid, he had given a good deal more attention to novels and billiards than to mathematics and Greek. Since then he has been reading law at the rate of a page a day. If he's ever admitted to practice I'm afraid all my friendship will scarce avail to make me give him my business. Good, bad or indifferent, the boy's, as you say, an artist—an artist to his fingers' ends."

"Why, then," asked Rowland, "doesn't he go right in for what he can do?"

"For several reasons. In the first place I don't think he more than

37

half suspects his ability. The flame smoulders, but it's never fanned by the breath of criticism. He sees nothing, hears nothing, to help him to self-knowledge. He's hopelessly discontented, but he doesn't know where to look for help. Then his mother, as she one day confessed to me, has a holy horror of a profession which consists exclusively, as she supposes, in making figures of people divested of all clothing. Sculpture, to her mind, is an insidious form of immorality, and for a young man of possibly loose leanings she considers the law a much safer training. Her father was, by her account, an eminent judge, she has two brothers at the bar, and her elder son had made a very promising beginning in the same line. She wishes the tradition to be kept up. I'm pretty sure the law won't make Roderick's fortune, and I'm afraid it will spoil his temper."

"What sort of a temper do you call it?"

"Oh, one to be trusted on the whole. It's subject, like our New England summer, to sudden changes—which yet don't prevent our *having* a summer, and a magnificent one. I have known it to breathe flame and fury at ten o'clock in the evening, and soft, sweet music early on the morrow. It's a very entertaining temper to observe. Fortunately I can observe it dispassionately, for I'm the only person in the place he has not quarrelled with."

"Has he then no companionship? Who's the Miss Garland you asked about?"

"A young woman staying with his mother, a sort of far-away cousin; a good, plain, honest girl, but not a person to represent sport for the artistic temperament or to minister to the joy of life. Roderick has a good share of the old Southern arrogance; he has the aristocratic temperament. He'll have nothing to do with the small towns-people; he says they're 'ignoble.' He can't endure his mother's friends —the old ladies and the ministers and the tea-party people; they bore him to death. So he comes and lounges here and rails at every thing and every one."

This youthful scoffer reappeared a couple of evenings later and confirmed the friendly feeling he had excited on Rowland's part. He was in an easier mood than before, he chattered less extravagantly and asked Rowland a number of rather primitive questions about the condition of the fine arts in New York and Boston. Cecilia, when he had gone, said that this had been the grateful effect of Rowland's eulogy of his work. Roderick was acutely sensitive, and Rowland's intelligent praise had steadied him: he had heard absolutely for the first time in his life the voice of taste and of authority. Rowland recognised afresh, recognised them as irresistible things, his personal charm and his presumable gift. He had an indefinable attraction— the something tender and divine of unspotted, exuberant, confident youth. The next day was Sunday, and Rowland proposed that they should take a long walk and that Roderick should show him the country. The young man assented gleefully, and in the morning, as Rowland, at the garden gate, was giving his hostess God-speed on her way to church, he came striding along the grassy margin of the road and out-whistling the music of the church-bells. It was one of those lovely days of the last of August when summer seems to balance in the scale with autumn. "Remember the day and take care you rob no orchards," said Cecilia as they separated.

The young men walked away at a steady pace, over hill and dale, through woods and fields, and at last found themselves on a grassy elevation studded with mossy rocks and red cedars. Just beneath them, in a great shining curve, flowed the generous Connecticut. They flung themselves on the grass and tossed stones into the river; they talked, they fell into intimacy, like old friends. Rowland lit a cigar and Roderick refused one with a grimace of extravagant disgust. He thought them vile things; he didn't see how decent people could tolerate them. Rowland was amused—he wondered what it was that made this ill-mannered speech seem perfectly inoffensive on his companion's lips. He belonged to the race of mortals, to be pitied or envied according as we view the matter, who are not held to a strict account for their aggressions. Looking at him as he lay stretched in the shade, Rowland vaguely likened him to some beautiful, supple, restless, bright-eyed animal, whose motions should have no deeper warrant than the tremulous delicacy of its structure and seem graceful to many persons even when they should be least convenient. Rowland watched the shadows on Mount Holyoke, listened to the gurgle of the river and sniffed the balsam of the pines. A gentle breeze had begun to tickle their summits and brought the smell of the mown grass across from the elm-dotted river-meadows. He sat up beside his companion and looked away at the far-spreading view, which affected him as melting for them both into such vast continuities and possibilities of possession. It touched him to the heart; suddenly a strange feeling of prospective regret took possession of him. Something seemed to tell him that later, in a foreign land, he should be haunted by it, should remember it all with longing and regret.

"It's a wretched business," he said, "this virtual quarrel of ours with our own country, this everlasting impatience that so many of us feel to get out of it. Can there be no battle then, and is one's only safety in flight? This is an American day, an American landscape, an American atmosphere. It certainly has its merits, and some day when I'm shivering with ague in classic Italy I shall accuse myself of having slighted them."

Roderick rose on still lighter wings to this genial flight, declaring that America was quite good enough for *him*, and that he had always thought it the duty of an honest citizen to stand by his own country and help it on. He had evidently thought nothing whatever about it —he was launching his doctrine on the inspiration of the moment. The doctrine expanded with the occasion, and he declared that he was above all an advocate for American art. He didn't see why we shouldn't produce the greatest works in the world. We were the biggest people, and we ought to have the biggest conceptions. The biggest conceptions, of course, would bring forth in time the biggest performances. We had only to be true to ourselves, to pitch in and not be afraid, to fling Imitation overboard and fix our eyes upon our National Individuality. "I declare," he cried, "there's a career for a man, and I have twenty minds to embrace it on the spot—to be the typical, original, *ab*original American artist! It's inspiring!"

Rowland burst out laughing and told him that he liked his practice better than his theory and that a saner impulse than this had inspired his little Water-drinker. Roderick took no offence and three minutes afterwards was talking volubly of some humbler theme—only half heeded by his friend, who had returned to cogitation. At last Rowland delivered himself of the upshot of his thought. "How should you like," he suddenly demanded, "to go to Rome?"

Hudson stared, and with an emphasis which speedily consigned our National Individuality to perdition, responded that he should like it first-rate. "And I should like, by the same token," he added, "to go to Athens, to Constantinople, to Damascus, to the holy city of Benares, where there's a golden statue of Brahma twenty feet tall."

"No," said Rowland with a certain literalness, "if you were to go to Rome you would have to settle down and work. Athens might help you, but for the present I shouldn't recommend Benares."

"It will be time to arrange details when I begin to pack my trunk," Hudson remarked.

"If you mean to turn sculptor the sooner you pack your trunk the better."

"Oh, but I'm a practical man! What's the smallest sum per annum on which one can keep alive the sacred fire?"

"What's the largest sum at your disposal?" Rowland returned.

Roderick stroked his light moustache, gave it a twist, and then announced, as with due importance, "Three hundred dollars."

"The money question could be arranged," said Rowland. "There are ways, you know, of raising money."

" 'Know?' How should I know? I never yet discovered one."

"One of them consists," said Rowland, "in having a friend with a good deal more than he wants and in not being too proud to accept a part of it."

Roderick stared a moment and his face flushed. "Do you mean —do you mean——?" He stammered, he panted; he was greatly excited.

Rowland got up, blushing a little, and Roderick sprang to his feet. "In three words, if it's in you really to go in for sculpture, you ought to get to Rome and study the antique. To get to Rome you need money. I'm fond of fine statues and busts, but unfortunately I can't make them myself. I have to order them from those who know how. I order a dozen from you, to be executed at your convenience. To help you I pay you in advance."

Roderick pushed off his hat and pressed his forehead, still gazing at his companion. "Upon my soul, you *believe* in me!" he cried at last.

"Allow me to explain," said Rowland. "I believe in you if you're prepared to work and to wait and to struggle and to exercise a great many virtues. And then I'm afraid to say it, to force it upon you, lest I should disturb you more than I should help you. You must decide for yourself. I simply offer you an opportunity."

Hudson, with his face intensely lighted, stood for some time profoundly meditative. "You've not seen my other things," he said suddenly. "Come and look at them."

"Now?"

"Yes, now. We'll walk home. We'll settle the question."

He passed his hand through Rowland's arm and they retraced their steps. They reached the town and made their way along a broad country street, dusky with the shade of magnificent elms. Rowland felt his companion's arm tremble in his own. They stopped at a large white house flanked with melancholy hemlocks, and passed through a little front garden paved with moss-coated bricks and ornamented with parterres enclosed in ragged box edges. The mansion had an air of antiquated dignity, but it had seen its best days and evidently sheltered a shrunken household. Mrs. Hudson, Rowland was sure, might be seen in the garden of a morning, in a white apron and a pair of old gloves, engaged in frugal horticulture. Roderick's studio was behind, in the basement; a large empty room with the paper peeling off the walls. This represented, in the fashion of fifty years ago, a series of small fantastic landscapes of a hideous pattern, and the young sculptor had presumably torn it away in great scraps at moments of æsthetic exasperation. On a board in a corner was a heap of clay, and on the floor, against the wall, stood some dozen medallions, busts and figures in various stages of completion. To exhibit them Roderick had to place them one by one on the end of a long packing-box which served as a pedestal. He did so silently, making no explanations and looking at them himself with a strange air of refreshed credulity. Most of the things were portraits, and the three at which he looked longest were finished busts. One was a colossal head of a negro, tossed back, defiant, with distended nostrils; one was the portrait of a young man whom Rowland immediately perceived by the resemblance to be his lost brother; the last represented a gentleman with a pointed nose, a long close-shaven upper lip and a tuft on the end of his chin. This was a face peculiarly unadapted to sculpture; but as a piece of modelling it was the best, and it was admirable. It reminded Rowland, in its homely veracity, its quaint closeness, of the works of the early Italian Renaissance. On the pedestal was cut the name—Barnaby Striker, Esq. Rowland recognised in these characters the legal luminary from whom his companion had undertaken to borrow the vital heat, and though the irony of portraiture was not gross it betrayed comically to one who could relish the secret that the features of the original had often been at the mercy of an exasperated eye. Beside these appeared several rough studies of the nude and two or three figures of a fanciful kind. The most noticeable (and it had singular beauty) was a small modelled design for a sepulchral monument, that evidently of Stephen Hudson. The young soldier lay sleeping eternally with his hand on his sword, the image of one of the crusaders Roderick had dreamed of in one of the cathedrals he had never seen.

Rowland made no haste to pronounce; too much depended on his judgement. "Upon my word," cried his friend at last, "they seem to *me*, you know, very decent, not too helpless!"

And in truth as Rowland looked he saw they were strong. They were youthful, awkward, ignorant; the effort often was more apparent than the success. But the effort was signally powerful and intelligent; it seemed to Rowland that with its aim clearer it might easily hit the highest mark. Here and there indeed the mark had already been hit with a masterly ring. Rowland turned to Hudson, who stood with his hands in his pockets and his hair very much crumpled, looking at him askance. The light of admiration was in Rowland's eyes, and it caused the young man's handsome watching face to shine out in response. Rowland said at last simply: "You've only to work hard."

"I think I know what that means," Roderick answered. He turned away, threw himself on a rickety chair, and sat for some moments with his elbows on his knees and his head in his hands. "Work— work?" he said at last, looking up. "Ah, if I could only begin!" He glanced round the room a moment, and his eye encountered on the mantel-shelf the inimitable presence of Mr. Barnaby Striker. His smile vanished—he stared at it with an air of concentrated enmity. "I want to begin," he cried, "and I can't make a better beginning than this! Good-bye, Mr. Barnaby Striker!" He strode across the room, seized a hammer that lay at hand, and before Rowland could interfere, in the interest of art if not of morals, dealt a merciless blow upon Mr. Striker's skull. The bust cracked into a dozen pieces, which toppled with a great crash upon the floor. Rowland relished neither the destruction of the image nor his companion's expression in working it, but as he was about to express his displeasure the door opened and gave passage to a fresh-looking girl. She came in with a rapid step and startled face, as if she had been alarmed by the noise. Meeting the heap of shattered clay and the hammer in Roderick's hand, she gave a cry of horror. Her voice died away as she saw Rowland was a stranger, but she had sounded her reproach. "Why, Roderick, what on earth have you done?"

Roderick gave a joyous kick to the shapeless fragments. "I've driven the money-changers out of the temple!"

The traces retained shape enough to be recognised, and she gave a little moan of pity. She seemed not to understand the young man's allegory, but none the less to feel that it pointed to some great purpose, which must yet be an evil one from its being expressed in such a lawless fashion, and to perceive that Rowland was in some way accountable for it. She looked at him with prompt disapproval and turned away through the open door. Rowland looked after her with immediate interest.

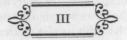

III

EARLY ON the morrow he received a visit from his new friend. Roderick was in a state of extreme exhilaration, tempered, however, by a certain amount of righteous wrath. He had had a row at home, as he called it, but had remained master of the situation. He had shaken the dust of Mr. Striker's office from his feet.

"I had it out last night with my mother," he said. "I dreaded the scene, for she takes things terribly hard. She doesn't scold nor storm, and she doesn't argue nor insist. She sits with her eyes full of tears that never fall, and looks at me, when I vex her, as if I were a monster of depravity. And the trouble is that I was born to vex her. She doesn't trust me; she never has, and she never will. I don't know what I've done to set her against me, but ever since I can remember I've been looked at with tears. The trouble is," he went on, giving a twist to his moustache, "I've been too great a mollycoddle. I've been sprawling all my days by the maternal fireside, and my dear mother has grown used to bullying me. I've made myself cheap! If I'm not in my bed by eleven o'clock the cook's sent out to explore for me with a lantern. When I think of it I'm quite sick of my meekness. It's rather a hard fate, to live like a tame cat and to pass for a desperado. I should like for six months to lead Mrs. Hudson the life some fellows lead their mothers!"

"Allow me to believe," said Rowland, "that you'd like nothing of the sort. If you've acted as a gentleman don't spoil it by pretending you'd have preferred to be a brute. You've been very happy in spite of your virtues, and there are worse fates in the world than being loved too well. I've not had the pleasure of seeing your mother, but I'll lay you a wager that this is where the shoe pinches. She's passionately fond of you, and her hopes, like all intense hopes, are next neighbours to alarms and despairs." Rowland, as he spoke, had an instinctive vision of the sentiments infallibly entertained for this beautiful and amusing youth by the women of his house.

Roderick frowned, and with an impatient gesture, "I do her justice," he cried; "may she never do me less!" Then after a moment's hesitation, "I'll tell you the perfect truth," he went on; "I have to fill a double place. I have to be my brother as well as myself. It's a good deal to ask of a man, especially when he has so little talent as I for being what he's not. When we were both young together I was the curled darling. I had the silver mug and the biggest piece of pudding, and I stayed indoors to be kissed by the ladies while he made mud-pies in the garden. In fact, you know, he was much more the right thing. When he was brought home that horrible night with a piece of shell in his skull, my poor mother began to think she hadn't loved him enough. I remember, as she hung round my neck sobbing, before his coffin, she told me that I must be to her everything that he would have been. I made no end of vows, but I haven't kept them all. I've been very different from Stephen. I've been idle, restless, egotistical, discontented. I've done no vulgar harm, I believe, but I've done no vulgar good. My brother, if he had lived, would have made fifty thousand dollars and had the parlour done up. My mother, brooding night and day on her bereavement, has come to fix her ideal in little attentions of that sort. Judged by that standard I'm nowhere."

Rowland was at a loss what to believe of this account of his friend's domestic circumstances; it had an honourable candour, but would be probably open to control. "You must lose no time in producing some important thing," he answered; "then with the proceeds you can do up the whole house."

"So I've told her; but she only half believes in 'art', anyway. She can see no good in my modelling from the life; it seems to her a snare of the enemy. She would fain see me all my days tethered to the law like a browsing goat to a stake. In that way I'm kept before her. 'It's a more natural occupation!'—that's all I can get out of her. A more natural damnation! Is it a fact that artists in general are such bold, bad men? I've never had the pleasure of knowing one, so I can't refute her with an example. She has the advantage of me, because she formerly knew a portrait-painter at Richmond, who did her miniature in black lace mittens (you may see it on the parlour table) and who used to drink raw brandy and beat his wife. I promised her last night that whatever I might do to my wife, I would never beat my mother, and that as for brandy, raw or diluted, I detested it. She sat silently crying for an hour, during which I expended treasures of eloquence. It's a good thing to have to take stock of one's intentions, and I assure you that pleading my cause, I became agreeably impressed with the elevated character of my own. I kissed her solemnly at last and told her that I had said everything and that she must make the best of it.

This morning she had dried her eyes, but I warrant you it isn't a racket-ing house. I long to be out of it!"

"I'm extremely sorry to have brought things to such a crisis," said Rowland. "I owe your mother some amends; will it be possible for me to see her?"

"If you'll see her it will smooth matters vastly; though, to tell the truth, she'll need all her courage to face you, for she considers you an agent of the foul fiend. She doesn't see why you should have come here and set me by the ears: you're made to poison ingenuous minds and desolate doting mothers. I leave it to you personally to answer these charges. You see, what she can't forgive—what she'll not really ever forgive—is your taking me off to Rome. Rome's an evil word in my mother's vocabulary, to be said below the breath, as you'd repeat some profanity or tell a 'low' story. Northampton Mass is in just the centre of Christendom, and Rome far off in the mere margin, benighted heathendom too at that, into which it can do no proper moral man any good to penetrate. And there was I but yesterday a regular attendant at that repository of every virtue, Mr. Striker's office!"

"And does Mr. Striker know of your decision?" Rowland asked.

"Why, sure! Mr. Striker, you must know, is not simply a good-natured attorney who lets me dog's-ear his law-books. He's a parti-cular friend and general adviser. He looks after my mother's property and kindly consents to regard me as part of it. Our opinions have always been as opposite as the poles, but I freely forgive him his zealous attempts to unscrew my headpiece and set it on another way. He never understood me, and it was useless to try to make him. We speak a different language—we're made of a different clay. I had a fit of rage yesterday, when I smashed his bust, at the thought of all the bad blood he had stirred up in me: it did me good and it's all over now. I don't hate him any more; I'm rather sorry for him. See how you've improved me! I must have seemed to him wilfully, wickedly stupid, and I'm sure he only tolerated me on account of his great regard for my mother. This morning I took the bull by the horns. I picked up an armful of law-books that have been gathering the dust in my room for the last year and a half, and presented myself at the office. 'Allow me to put these back in their places,' I said. 'I shall never have need for them more—never more, never more, never more!' 'So you've learned everything they contain?' says the great Striker, leering over his spectacles: 'better late than never!' 'I've learned nothing that you can teach me,' I cried. 'But I shall tax your patience no longer. I'm going to be a sculptor. I'm going to Rome to work at *that*. So now there! I won't bid you good-bye just yet; I shall see you again. But I bid good-bye here with enthusiasm to these four detested walls —to this living tomb! I didn't know till now how I hated the place! My compliments to Mr. Spooner, and my thanks for all you've not made of me!"

"I'm glad to know you're to see Mr. Striker again," Rowland answered, correcting a primary inclination to show himself as taking this report for an amusing burlesque of the facts. "You certainly owe him a respectful farewell, even if he has not understood you. I confess you rather strike *me* at moments as a little of a hard sum. There's another person," he presently added, "whose opinion as to your new career I should like to hear. What does your friend Miss Garland think?"

Hudson looked at him keenly, with a slight change of colour. Then with a conscious smile, "What makes you suppose she thinks anything?" he asked.

"Because, though I saw her but for a moment yesterday, she struck me, just in that moment, as a decidedly positive quantity, and I'm sure she has opinions."

The smile on Roderick's mobile face turned dim. "Oh, she thinks what I think!" he answered.

Before the two young men separated Rowland attempted to give as harmonious a shape as possible to his companion's future. "I've launched you, as I may say," he said, "and I feel as if I ought to see you into port. I'm older than you and know the world better, and it seems well that we should voyage a while together. It's on my conscience that I ought to take you to Rome, walk you through the Vatican, and then lock you up with a heap of clay. I sail on the 5th of September; can you make your preparations to start with me?"

Roderick assented to all this with an air of luxurious surrender to his friend's wisdom that expressed more than any formal pledge. "I've no preparations to make," he said with a smile, raising his arms and letting them fall as if to indicate his unencumbered condition. "What I'm to take with me I carry here!" And he tapped his forehead.

"Happy man!" murmured Rowland with a sigh, thinking of the light stowage in his own organism, in the region indicated by Roderick, and of the heavy one of bags and boxes in deposit at his banker's.

When his companion had left him he went in search of Cecilia. She was sitting at work at a shady window, and welcomed him to a low chintz-covered chair. He sat sometime thoughtfully snipping wool with her scissors; he expected criticism and he was bracing himself. At last he told her of Roderick's decision and of his own part in the matter. Cecilia, besides an extreme surprise, exhibited a certain fine displeasure at his not having asked her advice.

"What would you have said then if I had?" he demanded.

"I should have said in the first place, 'Oh, for pity's sake, don't carry off the person in all Northampton who most amuses me!' I should have said in the second place 'Nonsense! the boy's doing very well. Let well alone!'"

"That in the first five minutes. What would you have said later?"

"That for a man who's generally averse to meddling, you were suddenly rather officious." Rowland's countenance fell; he frowned in silence. Cecilia looked at him askance; gradually the spark of irritation faded from her eye. "Pardon my sharpness," she resumed at last. "But I'm literally in despair at losing Roderick Hudson. His visits in the evening, for the past year, have kept me alive. They've given a point to a very dull time—a shining little silver-tip to days that seemed made of a baser metal. I don't say he's a phœnix or that he's always an angel, never a bore—but I liked to see him. Of course, however, that I shall miss him sadly is not a reason for his not going to seek his fortune. Men must work and women must weep!"

"Decidedly not!" said Rowland with a good deal of emphasis. He had suspected from the first hour of his stay that Cecilia, for all her quiet life, was in the enjoyment of some private and peculiar satisfaction, and he discovered that she found it in Hudson's lounging visits and communicative youth. Now he wondered whether, responsibly viewed, her gain in the matter were not her young friend's loss. It was evident that Cecilia was haunted here with no morbid vision of duty, and that her judgement, habitually clear under the demands of domestic economy, had made easy terms, her dull life prompting, with the joy of eye and ear. She liked her young friend just as he was; she humoured him, flattered him, laughed at him, caressed him —did everything but advise him right. It was a flirtation without the benefits of a flirtation for Roderick. She was too old to make it quite exemplary she should let him fall in love with her, which might have done him good; and it was her perversity to keep him notoriously fresh, so that the nonsense he talked might never transgress a certain

48

line. It was quite conceivable that poor Cecilia should desire to pass the time; but if one had philanthropically embraced the idea that something considerable might be made of Roderick it was impossible not to see that her friendship was not what might be called tonic. So at least Rowland reflected in the glow of an almost creative ardour. There was a later time when he would have been grateful if Hudson's susceptibility to the relaxing influence of lovely women might have been limited to such inexpensive tribute as he rendered this excellent lady. "I only wish to remind you," she went on, "that you're likely to have your hands rather full."

"I've thought of that, and I positively like the idea; liking as I do the man. I told you the other day, you know, that I was bored to feel my hands always so empty. When it first occurred to me that I might start our young friend on the path of glory I felt as if I had an unimpeachable inspiration. Then I remembered there were dangers and difficulties, and asked myself whether I had a right to drag him out of his obscurity. My notion of his really having the great gift answered the question. He is made to do the things that we are the better for having. I can't do such things myself, but when I see a young man of genius standing helpless and hopeless for want of capital, I feel—and it's no affectation of humility, I assure you—as if it would give at least a reflected usefulness to my own life to offer him his opportunity."

"In the name of the general public I suppose I ought to thank you. But I want first of all to see where my own interest comes in. You guarantee us, at any rate, I hope, all the beautiful things."

"A masterpiece a year," said Rowland cheerily, "for the next quarter of a century."

"It seems to me that we have a right to ask more—to demand that you guarantee us not only the development of the artist but the security of the man."

Rowland became grave again. "His security?"

"His moral, his sentimental security. Here, you see, all that's perfect. We are all under a tacit compact to keep him quiet. Perhaps you believe in the necessary turbulence of genius, and you intend to enjoin upon your gifted pupil the importance of cultivating his passions."

"On the contrary, I believe that a man of genius owes as much deference to his passions as any other man, but not a particle more, and I confess I have a strong conviction that the artist is better for leading a quiet life. That's what I shall preach to my gifted pupil, as you call him, by example—except that I'm unfortunately not an artist!—as well as by precept. You evidently believe," he added in a moment, "that he'll lead me a dance!"

"No, I prophesy nothing. I only think that circumstances, with our young man, have a great influence; as is proved by the fact that although he has been fuming and fretting here for the last five years he has nevertheless managed to make the best of us and found it easy, on the whole, to vegetate. Transplanted to Rome I feel sure he'll put forth some wonderful flowers. I should like vastly to see the change. You must write me about it from stage to stage. I hope with all my heart that the fruit will be proportionate to the foliage. Don't think me a bird of ill-omen; only remember that we shall consider you've really taken an engagement."

"A man should make the most of himself and be helped if he needs help," Rowland answered after a long pause. "Of course if a silk balloon is inflated very suddenly and very fast there is always the danger of its bursting. But I nevertheless approve of a certain tension of one's being. It's what a man is meant for. And then Roderick isn't a mere pretty parachute. And then too I believe in the essential good health of the sincere imagination. A man may be *all* imagination— if he *is* sincere."

"Very good, since you've thought it so wonderfully out," Cecilia said with an air of resignation that made Rowland for the moment seem to himself eager to selfishness. "We'll drink then to-day at dinner to the imagination—I mean to the good health—of our friend."

Having it much at heart to convince Mrs. Hudson of the purity of his intentions, Rowland waited upon her that evening. He was ushered into a large parlour which by the light of a couple of candles he perceived to be very meagrely furnished and very tenderly and sparingly used. The windows were open to the air of the summer night, and a circle of three persons was temporarily awed into silence by his appearance. One of these was Mrs. Hudson, who was sitting at one of the windows, empty-handed save for the pocket-handkerchief in her lap, which was held with an air of familiarity with its sadder uses. Near her, on the sofa, half-sitting, half-lounging, in the attitude of a visitor outstaying ceremony, with one long leg flung over the other and a large foot in a clumsy boot swinging to and fro continually, was a lean, sandy-haired gentleman whom Rowland recognised as the original of the portrait of Mr. Barnaby Striker. At the table, near the candles, busy with a substantial piece of needlework, sat the young person of whom he had had a moment's quickened glimpse in Roderick's studio and whom he had learned to be Miss Garland, his companion's kinswoman. The limpid penetrating gaze of this member of the group was the most effective greeting he received. Mrs. Hudson rose with a soft, vague sound of distress and stood looking at him shrinkingly and helplessly, as if sorely tempted to retreat through the open window. Mr. Striker swung his long leg a trifle defiantly. No one evidently was used to offering hollow welcomes or telling polite fibs. Rowland introduced himself; he had come, he might say, upon business.

"Yes," said Mrs. Hudson tremulously; "I know—my son has told me. I suppose it's better I should see you. Perhaps you'll take a seat."

With this invitation Rowland prepared to comply, and, turning, grasped the first chair that offered itself.

"Not that one," said a full grave voice; whereupon he perceived that a thick skein of sewing-silk had been suspended in entanglement over the back for the purpose of being wound on reels. He felt the least bit irritated at the curtness of the warning, coming as it did from a young woman whose countenance he had mentally pronounced interesting and with regard to whom he was conscious of the germ of the inevitable desire to produce a responsive interest. And then he thought it would break the ice to say something playfully urbane.

"Oh, you should let me take the chair," he answered, "and have the pleasure of holding the skein myself!"

For all reply to this sally he received a stare of undisguised amazement from Miss Garland, who then looked across at Mrs. Hudson with a glance which plainly said, "You see he's quite the insinuating foreigner we feared." The elder lady, however, sat with her eyes fixed on the ground and her two hands tightly clasped. But as regards Mrs. Hudson Rowland felt much more compassion than resentment; her attitude was not coldness, it was the instinct of fear, almost of terror. She was a small, softly-desperate woman, whose desperation gave her a false air of eagerness, just as her pale troubled face added to her apparent age. After looking at her for some minutes Rowland saw that she was still young and personable and that she must have been a very girlish bride. She had had beauty at that hour, though she probably had looked terribly frightened at the altar. Her marked refinement of line and surface seemed to tell how her son had come by his elegance, his physical finish. She wore no cap, and her auburn hair, which was of extraordinary fineness, was smoothed and confined with Puritanic precision. She was excessively shy and altogether most humble-minded; it was singular to see a woman to whom the experience of the elm-shaded life had conveyed such scanty reassurance. Rowland began immediately to like her and to feel impatient to persuade her that, as Cecilia had originally said of him, he meant well. He foresaw that she would be easy to persuade and that the right shade of encouragement—it would have to be only the right one—would probably make her pass fluttering from distrust into an oppressive extreme of confidence. But he had an indefinable sense that the person who was testing a strong young eyesight in the dim candle-light was less readily beguiled from her mysterious feminine preconceptions. Miss Garland, according to Cecilia's judgement, as Rowland remembered, had not a countenance to inspire a sculptor; but it seemed to Rowland that she might with some success hold in contemplation a man whose relation to the beautiful was amateurish. She was not pretty as the eye of habit judges prettiness, but he noted that when he had made the observation he had somehow failed to set it down against her, for he had already passed from measuring contours to tracing meanings. In Mary Garland's face there were many possible ones, and they might give him the more to think about that it was not—like Roderick's for instance—one of the quick and mobile faces over which expression flickers like a candle in a wind. They followed each other slowly, distinctly, sincerely, and you might almost have fancied that as they came and went they gave her a nameless pain. She was tall and straight and had an air of maidenly strength and decision. She had a broad forehead and dark eyebrows, a trifle thicker than those of classic beauties; her dark pupils, a trifle heavy, failed, as might be said, of publicity of expression. Her features were bravely irregular, and her mouth enabled her smile—which was the principal grace of her physiognomy—to display itself with magnificent amplitude. Rowland indeed had not yet seen this accident produced; but something assured him that when, on due cause shown, she should cease to be serious, it would be like the final rising of the plain green curtain of the old theatre on some—not very modern—comedy. She wore a scanty white dress and had a vaguely rustic, provincial air; she looked like a distinguished villager. She was evidently a girl of extreme personal force, but she lacked pliancy. She was hemming a kitchen towel with the aid of a large steel thimble. She bent her almost portentous eyes at last on the work again and let Rowland explain himself.

"I've become suddenly so very intimate with your son," he said at last, addressing himself to Mrs. Hudson, "that it seems proper I should make your acquaintance."

"Very proper," murmured the poor lady, and after a moment's hesitation was on the point of adding something more. But Mr. Striker here interposed, after a prefatory clearance of the throat.

"I should like to take the liberty, sir, of addressing you a simple question. For how long a period of time have you been acquainted with our young friend?" He continued to kick the air, but his head was thrown back and his eyes fixed on the opposite wall as if to avert themselves from the spectacle of Rowland's inevitable confusion.

"A very short time, I confess. Hardly three days."

"And yet you call yourself intimate, eh? I've been seeing Mr. Roderick daily these three years, and yet it was only this morning that I felt as if I had at last the right to say that I knew him. We had a few moments' conversation in my office which supplied the missing links in the evidence. So that now I do venture to say I'm acquainted with Mr. Roderick! But wait three years, sir, like me!" And Mr. Striker laughed with a closed mouth, and a noiseless shake of all his long person.

Mrs. Hudson smiled confusedly, at hazard; Miss Garland kept her eyes on her stitches. But it seemed to Rowland that the latter coloured a little. "Oh, in three years, of course," he said, "we shall know each other better. Before many years are over, madam," he pursued, "I expect the world to know him. I expect him to be a great man!"

Mrs. Hudson looked at first as if this could be but an insidious device for increasing her distress by the assistance of some art of comedy. Then reassured little by little by Rowland's air of conviction, she gave him an appealing glance and a timorous "Really?"

But before her visitor could respond Mr. Striker again intervened. "Do I fully apprehend your expression?" he asked. "Our young friend is to become one of our *great men*?"

"One of our great artists, I hope. Perhaps greater than any."

"This is a new and interesting view," said Mr. Striker with an assumption of judicial calmness. "We've had hopes for Mr. Roderick, but I confess that if I've rightly understood them they stopped short of towering eminence. We shouldn't have taken the responsibility of entertaining *that* idea for him. What do you say, ladies? We all feel about him here—his mother, Miss Garland, and myself—as if his merits were rather in the line of the"—and Mr. Striker waved his hand with a series of fantastic flourishes in the air—"of the light ornamental."

Mr. Striker bore his recalcitrant pupil a grudge; yet he was evidently trying both to be fair and to respect the susceptibilities of his companions. He was still unversed in the mysterious processes of feminine emotion. Ten minutes before there had been a general harmony of sombre views; but on hearing Roderick's limitations thus distinctly formulated to a stranger the two ladies mutely protested. Mrs. Hudson uttered a short faint sigh, and Miss Garland raised her eyes toward their advocate and visited him with a short cold glance.

"I'm afraid, Mrs. Hudson," Rowland pursued, evading the question of the ultimate future, "that you don't at all thank me for stirring up your son's ambition for objects that lead him so far from home. I seem to feel that I've made you my enemy."

Mrs. Hudson covered her mouth with her finger-tips and looked painfully perplexed between the desire to confess the truth and the fear of being impolite. "My cousin's no one's enemy," Miss Garland hereupon declared gently, but with the same remorseless consistency with which she had made Rowland relax his grasp of the chair.

"Does she leave that to you?" Rowland ventured to ask with a smile.

"We are inspired with none but Christian sentiments," said Mr. Striker; "Miss Garland perhaps most of all. Miss Garland," and Mr. Striker waved his hand again as if to perform an introduction which had been frivolously omitted, "is the daughter of a minister, the granddaughter of a minister, the sister of a minister."

Rowland signified, so far as he could by a gesture, that he had nothing to say against it, and the girl prosecuted her work with quite as little apparently either of embarrassment or elation at the promulgation of these facts. "Mrs. Hudson, I see," Mr. Striker continued, "is too deeply agitated to converse with you freely. She will allow me to address you a few questions. Would you kindly inform her as exactly as possible just what you propose to do with her son?"

The poor lady fixed her eyes appealingly on Rowland's face and seemed to say that Mr. Striker had spoken her desire, though she herself would have expressed it less crudely. But Rowland saw in Mr. Striker's many-wrinkled light blue eye, shrewd at once and good-natured, that he had no intention of defiance, and that he was simply pompous and conceited and sarcastically compassionate of any scheme of things in which Roderick was not a negligible quantity.

"Do, my dear madam?" demanded Rowland. "I don't propose to do anything. He must do for himself. I simply offer him the chance. He's to study, to strive, to work—very hard, I hope."

"Ah, not *too* hard, please," murmured Mrs. Hudson pleadingly, wheeling about from recent alarms at the *dolce far niente*. "He's not very strong, and I'm afraid the climate of Europe is very relaxing."

"Ah, study?" repeated Mr. Striker. "To what line of study is he to direct his attention?" Then suddenly, with an impulse of disinterested curiosity on his own account, "How do you study sculpture anyhow?"

"By looking at models and imitating them."

"At models, eh? To what kind of models do you refer?"

"To the antique, in the first place."

"Ah, the antique"—and Mr. Striker gave it the jocose intonation. "Do you hear, madam? Roderick is going off to Europe to learn to imitate the antique."

"I suppose it's all right," said Mrs. Hudson, while she twisted herself in a sort of delicate anguish.

"An antique, as I understand it," the lawyer continued, "is an image of a pagan deity, with considerable dirt sticking to it, and no arms, no nose and no clothing. A precious model, certainly!"

"That's a very good description of many," said Rowland with a laugh.

"Mercy! Truly?" asked Mrs. Hudson, borrowing courage from his urbanity.

"But a sculptor's studies, you intimate, are not confined to the antique," Mr. Striker resumed. "After he has been looking three or four years at the objects I describe——"

"He studies the living model," said Rowland.

"Does it take three or four years?" Mrs. Hudson hopelessly inquired.

"That depends upon the artist's aptitude. After twenty years a real artist is still studying."

"Oh, my poor boy!" moaned Mrs. Hudson, finding the prospect under every light still terrible.

"Now this study of the living model," Mr. Striker pursued. "Give Mrs. Hudson a sketch of that."

"Oh dear, no!" cried Mrs. Hudson shrinkingly.

"That too," said Rowland, "is one of the reasons for studying in Rome. It's a handsome race, you know, and you find very well-made people."

"I suppose they're no better made than a good tough Yankee," objected Mr. Striker, transposing his interminable legs. "The same God made us!"

55

"Surely," sighed Mrs. Hudson, but with a questioning glance at her visitor which showed that she had already begun to concede much weight to his opinion. Rowland hastened to express his assent to Mr. Striker's proposition.

Miss Garland looked up, and, after a moment's hesitation, "Are the Roman women very beautiful?" she asked.

Rowland too, in answering, hesitated; he was looking at her kindly enough. "On the whole I prefer ours," he said.

She had dropped her work in her lap; her hands were crossed upon it, her head thrown a little back. She had evidently expected a more impersonal reply and she was not satisfied. For an instant she seemed inclined to make a rejoinder, but she picked up her work in silence and drew her stitches again.

Rowland had for the second time the feeling that she judged him a person of a disagreeably sophisticated tone. He noticed too that the kitchen towel she was hemming was terribly coarse. And yet his answer had a resonant inward echo and he repeated to himself, "Yes, on the whole I prefer ours."

"Well, these models," began Mr. Striker. "You put them into an attitude, I suppose?"

"An attitude, exactly."

"And then you sit down and look at them?"

"Ah, you mustn't sit too long. You must go at your clay and try to build up something that looks like them."

"Well, there you are with your model in an attitude on one side, yourself in an attitude too, I suppose, on the other, and your pile of clay in the middle, building up, as you say. So you pass the morning. After that I hope you go out and take a walk and rest from your exertions."

"Unquestionably. But to an artist who loves his work there is no lost time. Everything he looks at teaches or suggests something."

"That's a tempting doctrine to young men with a taste for sitting by the hour with the page upturned, watching the flies buzz, or the frost melt, on the window-pane. Our young friend in this way must have laid up stores of information that I never suspected."

"It's very possible," said Rowland with an unresentful smile, "that he will prove some day the happier artist for some of those very same lazy reveries."

This theory was apparently very grateful to Mrs. Hudson, who had never had the case put for her son with such ingenious hopefulness, and who found herself disrelishing the singular situation of seeming to side against her own flesh and blood with a lawyer whose conversational tone betrayed the habit of public cross-questioning.

"My son, then," she ventured to inquire, "my son has exceptional —what you would call remarkable—powers?"

"To my sense distinctly remarkable powers."

Poor Mrs. Hudson actually smiled, broadly, gleefully, and glanced at Miss Garland as if to invite her to do likewise. But the girl's face remained as serious as the eastern sky when the opposite sunset is too feeble to make it glow. "Do you really know?" she asked, looking at Rowland.

"One can't *know* in such a matter save after proof, and proof takes time. But one can believe."

"And you believe?"

"I believe."

But even then Miss Garland vouchsafed no smile; her face became graver than ever.

"Well, well," said Mrs. Hudson, "we must hope that it's all for the best."

Mr. Striker eyed his old friend for a moment with a look of some displeasure; he saw that this was but a cunning female device for pretending still to hang back, and that, through some untraceable logic of treachery, she was now taking more comfort in the opinions of this sophistical stranger than in his own tough dogmas. He rose to his feet without pulling down his waistcoat, but with a wrinkled grin at the perfidy, let alone the inconsistency, of women. "Well, sir, Mr. Roderick's powers are nothing to me," he said, "no, nor the use he makes of them. Good or bad, he's no son of mine. But in a friendly way I'm glad to hear so fine an account of him. I'm glad, madam, you're so satisfied with the prospect. Affection, sir, you see, must have its guarantees!" He paused a moment, stroking his beard, with his head inclined and one eye half closed, looking at Rowland. The look was grotesque, but it was significant, and it puzzled Rowland more than it amused him. "I suppose you're a very brilliant young man," he went on, "very enlightened, very cultivated, quite up to the mark in the fine arts and all that sort of thing. I'm a plain practical old boy, content to follow an honourable profession in a free country. I didn't go to any part of Europe to learn my business; no one took me by the hand; I had to grease my wheels myself, and such as I am, I'm a self-made man, every inch of me! Well, if our young friend's booked for fame and fortune I don't suppose his going to Rome will stop him. But, mind you, it won't help him such a long way neither. If you've undertaken to put him through there's a thing or two you had better remember. The crop we gather depends upon the seed we sow. He may be the biggest genius of the age: his potatoes won't come up without his hoeing them. If he takes things so almighty easy as—well, as one or two young fellows of genius I've had under my eye—his produce will never gain the prize. Take the word for it of a man who has made his way inch by inch and doesn't believe that we wake up to find our work done because we have lain all night a-dreaming of it: anything worth doing is plaguy hard to do! If your young gentleman finds everything all right, and has a good time of it, and says he likes the life, it's a sign that—as I may say—you had better step round to the office and look at the books. That's all I desire to remark. No offence intended. I hope you'll have a first-rate time yourself."

Rowland could honestly reply that this seemed pregnant sense, and he offered Mr. Striker a friendly hand-shake as the latter withdrew. But Mr. Striker's rather grim view of matters cast a momentary shadow on his companions, and Mrs. Hudson seemed to feel that it necessitated between them some little friendly agreement not to be overawed.

Rowland sat for some time longer, partly because he wished to please the two women and partly because he was himself strangely beguiled. There was something touching in their worldly fears and diffident hopes, something almost terrible in the way poor little Mrs. Hudson seemed to flutter and quiver with maternal passion. She put forth one timid conversational venture after another, and asked Rowland a number of questions about himself, his age, his family, his occupations, his tastes, his religious opinions. Rowland had an odd feeling at last that she had begun to believe him very exemplary and that she might make later some perturbing discovery. He tried therefore to invent something that would prepare her to find him fallible. But he could think of nothing. It only seemed to him that Miss Garland secretly mistrusted him and that he must leave her to render him the service, after he had gone, of making him the object of a little conscientious derogation. Mrs. Hudson talked with low-voiced eagerness about her son.

"He's very lovable, sir, I assure you. When you come to know him you'll find him very lovable. He's a little spoiled, of course; he has always done with me as he pleased; but he's a dear good boy, I'm sure he's a dear good boy. And every one thinks him very attractive: I'm sure he would be noticed anywhere. Don't you think he's very handsome, sir? He's the very copy of his poor father. I had another—perhaps you have been told. He was awfully killed." And the poor little lady smiled for fear of doing worse. "He was a very fine boy, but very different from Roderick. Roderick's a little strange; he has never been an easy boy. Sometimes I feel like the goose—wasn't it a goose, dear?" and, startled by the audacity of her comparison, she appealed to Miss Garland—"The goose, or the hen, who hatched a swan's egg. I've never been able to give him what he requires. I've always thought that in more brilliant circumstances he might find his place and be happy. But at the same time I was afraid of the world for him; it was so dangerous and dreadful—so terribly mixed. No doubt I know very little about it. I never suspected, I confess, that it contained persons of such liberality as yours."

Rowland replied that evidently she had done the world but scanty justice.

"No, she always does justice," Miss Garland objected after a pause. "It's this that's so much like a fairy-tale."

"It's what, pray?"

"Why, your coming here all unannounced, unknown, so rich and so polite, and carrying off my cousin in a golden cloud."

If this was banter Miss Garland had the best of it, for Rowland fairly fell a-musing over the question of its perhaps being an acid meant to bite. Before he withdrew Mrs. Hudson made him tell her again that Roderick's powers were probably remarkable. He had inspired her with a clinging, caressing faith in his wisdom. "He will really do *beautiful* things?" she asked—"the very most beautiful?"

"I see no intrinsic reason why he shouldn't."

"Well, we shall think of that as we sit here alone," she rejoined. "Mary and I will sit here and talk about it. So I give him up," she went on as he was going. "I'm sure you'll be the best of friends to him; but if you should ever forget him or grow tired of him, if you should lose your interest in him and he should come to any harm or any trouble, please, sir, remember——" And she paused with a tremulous voice.

"Remember, my dear madam?"

"That he's all I have—that he's everything—and that it would be very terrible."

"In so far as I can help him he shall succeed," was all Rowland could say. He turned to Miss Garland to bid her good-night, and she rose and put out her hand. She was very straightforward, but he could see that if she was too modest to be bold she was much too simple to be shy. "Have *you* no injunctions to give me ?" he asked—to ask her something.

She looked at him hard, and then, even though she was not shy, she blushed. "Make him do his best," she said.

Rowland noted the full tone, the ringing depth of voice—this young woman's was a perfect contralto—with which the words were uttered. "Do you take a great interest in him ?"

"The greatest interest."

"Then if he won't do his best for you he won't do it for me." She but turned away in silence at this, and Rowland took his leave.

He walked homeward thinking of many things. The great Northampton elms interarched far above in the darkness, but the moon had risen and through scattered apertures was hanging the dusky vault with silver lamps. There seemed to Rowland something solemn in the scene in which he had just taken part. He had laughed and talked and braved it out in self-defence; but when he reflected that he was really meddling with the simple stillness of this small New England home and that he had ventured to disturb so much living security in the interest of a far-away fantastic hypothesis, he gasped, amazed at his temerity. It was true, as Cecilia had said, that for an unofficious man it was a singular position. There stirred in his mind an odd feeling of annoyance with Roderick for having so peremptorily taken possession of his nature. As he looked up and down the long vista and saw the clear white houses glancing here and there in the broken moonshine, he could almost have believed that the happiest lot for any man was to make the most of life in some such tranquil spot as that. Here were kindness, comfort, safety, the warning voice of duty, the perfect absence of temptation. And as Rowland looked along the arch of silvered shadow and out into the lucid air of the American night, which seemed so doubly vast, somehow, and strange and nocturnal, he was moved to feel that here was beauty too—beauty sufficient for an artist not to starve upon it. As he stood there lost in the darkness he presently heard a rapid tread on the other side of the road, accompanied by a loud jubilant whistle, and in a moment a figure emerged into an open gap of moonshine. He had no difficulty in recognising his young man, who was presumably returning from a visit to Cecilia. Roderick stopped suddenly and stared up at the moon, his face vividly illumined. He broke out into a snatch of song—

"The splendour falls on castle walls
And snowy summits old in story !"

And with a great musical roll of his voice he went swinging off into the darkness again as if his thoughts had lent him wings. He was dreaming of the inspiration of foreign lands—of mighty monuments and sacred sites. What a pity, after all, thought Rowland as he went his own way, that he shouldn't have a "lick" at them!

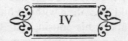

IV

It HAD been a very sage remark of Cecilia's that Roderick would change with a change in his circumstances. Rowland had telegraphed to New York for another berth on his steamer, and from the hour the answer came that youth's spirits rose to incalculable heights. He was radiant with good-humour, and his charming gaiety the evident pledge of a brilliant future. He had forgiven his old enemies and forgotten his old grievances—he seemed in every way reconciled to a world in which he was going to be important and wonderful. He was profusely jocose and suggestive, and, as Cecilia said, he had suddenly become so good that he might have been not so much beginning a Roman career as ending an earthly one. He took long walks with Rowland, who felt more and more the fascination of his surrender—a fascinated one too, in its degree—to all this complacency. Rowland returned several times to Mrs. Hudson's and found the two ladies doing their best to keep in tune with their companion's glee. Mary Garland, he thought, was succeeding better than her demeanour on his first visit had promised. He tried to have some undiverted talk with her, but her extreme reserve forced him to content himself with such response to his rather urgent overtures as might be extracted from her leaving him, very frankly, all the consciousness of them. It must be confessed, however, that if the response was vague, the satisfaction he drew from her mere colourless patience was great, and that after his second visit he kept seeing the element itself reflected in the most unlikely surfaces, the most unexpected places. It seemed strange that she should interest him so much at so slender a cost; but interest him she did, extraordinarily, and his interest had a quality altogether new to him. It made him restless and a trifle melancholy; he walked about absently, wondering and wishing. He wondered, among other things, why fate should have condemned him to make the acquaintance of a girl whom he would make a sacrifice to know better, just as he was leaving the country for years. It seemed to him that he was turning his back on a chance of happiness—happiness of a sort of which the slenderest germ should be cultivated. He asked himself whether, feeling as he did, if he had only himself to please, he would have given up his start and hung about. He had Roderick to please now, for whom disappointment would be cruel; but he took it for presumable that had there been no Roderick in the case the ship would be sailing without him. He asked the young man several questions about his cousin, but Roderick, throwing discretion to the winds on so many points, seemed to have reasons of his own for being reticent on this one. His measured answers quickened Rowland's curiosity, for the girl, with her irritating half-suggestions, had only to be a subject of guarded allusion in others to become a secret obsession. He learned from Roderick that she was the daughter of a country minister, a far-away cousin of his mother, settled in another part of the state; that she was one of half a dozen daughters, that the family had scant means, and that she had come a couple of months before to pay his mother a long visit. "It's to be a very long one now," he said, "for it's settled that she remains while I'm away."

The fermentation of beatitude in Roderick's soul reached its climax a few days before the young men were to make their farewells. He had been sitting with his friends on Cecilia's verandah, but for half an hour past he had said nothing. Lounging back against a column muffled in creepers and gazing idly at the stars, he kept chanting softly and with that indifference to ceremony for which he always found allowance, though it had nothing conciliatory but what his good looks gave it. At last, springing up, "I want to strike out hard!" he exclaimed; "I want to do something violent and indecent and impossible—to let off steam!"

"I'll tell you what to do, this lovely weather," Cecilia said. "Give a picnic. It can be as violent, it can be even as indecent, as you like, and it will have the merit of leading off our hysterics into a safe channel, as well as yours."

Roderick accepted with all affability her very practical remedy for his nervous need, and a couple of days later the picnic was given. It was to be a family party, but Roderick, in his magnanimous geniality, insisted on inviting Mr. Striker, a decision which Rowland still more genially applauded. "And we'll have Mrs. Striker too," he said, "if she'll come, to keep my mother in countenance; and at any rate we'll have Miss Striker—the divine Petronilla!" The young lady thus denominated formed, with Mrs. Hudson, Miss Garland and Cecilia, the better part of the female contingent. Mr. Striker presented himself, sacrificing a morning's work, with a magnanimity greater even than Roderick's, and foreign support was further secured in the person of Mr. Whitefoot, the young Orthodox minister. Roderick had chosen his happy valley, the feasting-place; he knew it well and had passed many a summer afternoon there, lying at his length on the grass in the shade and looking away to the blue distances, the "purple rim" of the poet, which had the wealth of the world, all the unattainable of life, beyond them. A high-hung meadow stretched on one side to a peculiarly dark wood, in which he used to say there were strange beasts and "monsters," who couldn't come out, but who put it out of the question that one should go in; and the meadow had high mossy rocks protruding through its grass and formed in the opposite direction the shore of a small lake. It was a cloudless August day; Rowland always remembered it, and the scene and everything that was said and done, with extraordinary distinctness. Roderick surpassed himself in friendly jollity, and at one moment, when exhilaration was at the highest, was seen in Mr. Striker's high white hat, drinking champagne from a broken tea-cup to Mr. Striker's health. Miss Striker had her father's light green eyes and almost his tendency to close one of them at a time for emphasis; she was dressed as if to sit for her photograph and remained for a long time with Roderick on a little promontory over-hanging the lake. Mrs. Hudson kept all day a little meek apprehensive smile. She was afraid of an "accident," though unless Miss Striker (who indeed was a little of a romp) should push Roderick into the lake it was hard to see what accident could occur. Mrs. Hudson was as neat and crisp and uncrumpled at the end of the festival as at the beginning. Mr. Whitefoot, who but a twelve-month later became a convert to Episcopacy and was already cultivating a certain sonority of private discourse, devoted himself to Cecilia. He had a little book in his pocket, out of which he read to her at intervals, lying stretched at her feet; and it was a lasting joke with Cecilia afterwards that she would never tell what Mr. Whitefoot's little book had been. Rowland had placed himself near Miss Garland while the feasting went forward on the grass. She wore a so-called gypsy hat—a little straw hat tied down over her ears, so as to cast her eyes into shadow, by a ribbon passing outside of it. When the company dispersed after lunch he proposed to her to take, in spite of Roderick's beasts and monsters, a stroll in the wood. She hesitated a moment and looked at Mrs. Hudson as if for permission to leave her. But Mrs. Hudson was listening to Mr. Striker, who sat gossiping to her with relaxed consistency, his waistcoat unbuttoned and his hat on his nose.

"You can give your cousin your society at any time," said Rowland. "But me perhaps you'll never see again."

"Why then should we attempt to be friends, if nothing is to come of it?" she asked with homely logic. But by this time she had consented and they were treading the fallen pine-needles.

"Oh, one must take all one can get," said Rowland. "If we can be friends for half an hour it's so much gained."

"Do you expect never to come back to Northampton again?" she went on with detachment.

"'Never' is a good deal to say. But I go to Europe for a long stay."

"Do you prefer that country so much to this?"

"I won't say that my preferences and reasons are *all* on one side. But I have the misfortune to be rather an idle man, and in Europe both the burden and the obloquy of idleness are less heavy than here."

She was silent for a few minutes; then at last, "In that surely we are better than Europe," she said. To a certain point Rowland agreed with her, but he demurred, to make her say more. "Wouldn't it be better," she accordingly asked, "to set at some work in order to get reconciled to America than to go to Europe just in order to get reconciled to sloth?"

"Doubtless, but you know work doesn't come to every one's hand."

"I come from a little place where it just does do that," said Mary Garland. "We all work; every one I know works. And really," she added presently, "I look at you with curiosity: you're the first unoccupied man I ever saw."

"Don't look at me too hard," Rowland laughed. "I shall sink into the earth. What's the name of your little place?"

"West Nazareth," said Mary Garland with her usual directness. "It's not so terribly small, though it's smaller than Northampton."

"I wonder whether I could find any work at West Nazareth," Rowland said.

"You wouldn't like it very much," Miss Garland declared reflectively. "Though there are far finer woods there than these. We have miles and miles of woods."

"I might chop down trees," said Rowland. "That is if you allow it."

"Allow it? Why, where should we get our firewood?" Then noticing that he had spoken jestingly she glanced at him askance, though with no visible diminution of her gravity. "Don't you know how to do anything at all? Have you no sort of profession?"

Rowland shook his head. "Absolutely none."

"What do you then do all day?"

"Nothing that would make a figure in a description. That's why, as I tell you, I'm going to Europe. There at least if I do nothing I shall see a great deal; and if I'm not a producer I shall at any rate be an observer."

"Can't we observe everywhere?"

"Certainly; and I really think that in that way I make the most of my opportunities. Though I confess," he continued, "that I often remember there are things to be seen here to which I probably have not done justice. I should like for instance to see West Nazareth."

She looked round at him, open-eyed; not apparently that she exactly supposed he was jesting, for the expression of such a desire was not necessarily facetious; but as if he must have spoken with an ulterior motive. He had spoken in fact from the simplest of motives. The girl beside him appealed, strangely, to his sense of character, and even, in her way, to his sense of beauty, and, satisfied that her quality would be very much her own, and neither borrowed nor reflected nor imposed, he wished, positively as a help for liking her better, to make her show him how little her situation had had to give her. Her second movement now was to take him at his word. "Since you're free to do as you please, why don't you go there?"

"I'm not free to do as I please now. I've offered your cousin to bear him company to Europe, he has accepted with enthusiasm, and I can't back out."

"Are you going to Europe simply for his sake?"

Rowland hesitated. "I think I may almost say so."

Mary Garland walked along in silence. "Do you mean to do a great deal for him?" she asked at last.

"What I can. But my power of helping him is very small beside his power of helping himself."

For a moment she was silent again. "You're very generous," she then simply said.

"No, I'm principally very shrewd. Roderick will repay me. It's a speculation. At first, I think," he added shortly afterwards, "you wouldn't have paid me that little compliment. You didn't believe in me."

She made no attempt to deny it. "I didn't see why you should wish to make Roderick discontented. I thought you were rather frivolous."

"You did me injustice. I don't think I'm that."

"It was because you're unlike other men—those at least whom I've seen."

"In what way?"

"Why, as you describe yourself. You have no duties, no profession, no home. You live for your pleasure."

"That's all very true. And yet I maintain I strike myself as not frivolous."

"I hope not," she said quietly. They had reached a point where the wood-path forked and put forth two divergent tracks which appeared to lose themselves, at no great distance, in a tangle of undergrowth. The young girl seemed to think the difficulty of choice between them a reason for giving them up and turning back, but Rowland thought otherwise and detected agreeable grounds for preference in the left-hand path. As a compromise they sat down on a fallen log. Looking about him, Rowland espied a curious wild shrub with a spotted crimson leaf; he went and plucked a spray of it and brought it to his companion. He had never observed it before, but she immediately called it by its name. She expressed surprise at his not knowing it; it was extremely common. He presently brought her a specimen of another delicate plant, with a little blue-streaked flower. "I suppose that's common too," he said, "but I've never seen it—or noticed it at least." She answered that this one was rare, and cast about a little before she could recall its name. At last she remembered, expressing her surprise at his having found the plant in the woods; she supposed it grew only in the marshes. Rowland complimented her on her fund of useful information.

"It's not especially useful," she answered; "but I like to know the names of plants as I do those of my acquaintances. When we walk in the woods at home—which we do so much—it seems as unnatural not to know what to call the flowers as it would be to see someone in the town with whom we shouldn't be on speaking terms."

"If there's a question of frivolity," Rowland said, "I'm sure you yourself have very little of it, unless at West Nazareth it's considered frivolous to walk in the woods and nod to the nodding flowers. Do kindly tell me a little about yourself." And to compel her to begin, "I know you come of a race of theologians," he went on.

"No," she replied, deliberating; "they're not theologians, though they're ministers. We don't take a very firm stand upon doctrine; we're practical and active rather; we haven't time to find reasons and phrases. We write sermons and preach them, but we do a great deal of hard work besides."

"And of this hard work what has your share been?"

"The hardest part—not doing anything."

"What do you call doing nothing?"

"I taught some small children their lessons once; I must make the most of that. But I confess I didn't like it. Otherwise I've only done little things at home as they turned up."

"What kind of things?"

"Oh, every kind. If you had seen my home you would understand."

Rowland would have liked to make her specify; but he took a peculiar pleasure in being felt as discreet. "To be happy, I imagine," he contented himself with saying, "you need to see results—those of your service, of your ability. You need somebody or something to expend yourself upon."

"That's not so true as it once was; now that I'm older I've developed a turn for sitting about quite shamelessly. Certainly these two months that I've been with Mrs. Hudson I've done little else. And yet I've enjoyed it. And now that I'm probably to be with her all the while that her son's away, I look forward to more with dreadful resignation."

"It's quite settled then that you're to remain with your cousin?"

"It depends upon their writing from home that I may stay. But that's probable. Only I must not forget," she said, rising, "that the ground for my doing so is that she shall not be left alone."

"I'm glad to know that I shall probably often hear about you. I assure you I shall often wonder about you!" These slightly breathless words of Rowland's were half precipitation and half prudence. They were the simple truth, and he had asked himself why he should not tell her the truth. And yet they were not all of it; her hearing the rest would depend upon the way she received this instalment. She received it not only, as he had foreseen, without the sign of a flutter or a thought of conscious grace, but with a slight movement of nervous deprecation which seemed to betray itself in the quickening of her step. Evidently if he was to take pleasure in hearing about her it would have to be a satisfaction highly disinterested. She answered nothing, and Rowland too, as he walked beside her, was silent; but as he looked along the shadow-woven wood-path what he was really facing was three interminable years of disinterestedness. He ushered them in by talking composed civility until he had brought Miss Garland back to her companions.

He saw her but once again. He was obliged to be in New York a couple of days before sailing, and it was arranged that Roderick should overtake him at the last moment. The evening before he left Northampton he went to say farewell to Mrs. Hudson. The ceremony was brief. He soon perceived that the poor little lady was in the melting mood, and as he dreaded her tears he compressed a multitude of solemn promises into a silent hand-shake and took his leave. Mary Garland, she had told him, was in the back garden with Roderick; he might go out to them. He did so, and as he drew near he heard Roderick's high-pitched voice ringing behind the shrubbery. In a moment, emerging, he found the girl leaning against a tree while her cousin stood before her and talked with great emphasis. He asked pardon for interrupting them and said he wished only to bid her good-bye. She gave him her hand, and he held it an instant without a word. "Don't forget," he said to Roderick as he turned away. "And don't, in this company, repent of your bargain."

"I shall not let him," said Mary Garland, with a nearer approach to reckless cheer than he had yet heard on her lips. "I shall see that he's punctual. He must go ! I owe you an apology for having doubted that he ought to go !" And her face, in the summer dusk, was new and vague and handsome.

Roderick was punctual, eagerly punctual, and they went. Rowland for several days was occupied with material cares and lost sight of his accepted obsession. But the questions lurking in it only slumbered and they were sharply shaken up. The weather was fine, and the two young men always sat together upon deck late into the evening. One night, towards the last, they were at the stern of the great ship, watching her grind the solid blackness of the ocean into phosphorescent foam. They talked on these occasions of everything conceivable and had the air of having no secrets from each other. But it was on Roderick's conscience that this air belied him, and he was moreover too full of his native claims for any permanent reticence.

"I must tell you something," he broke out at last. "I should like you to know it, and you'll be so glad to know it. Besides, it's only a question of time; three months hence probably you would have guessed it. I'm engaged to marry Mary Garland."

Rowland sat staring; though the sea was calm it seemed to him that the ship gave a great dizzying lurch. But in a moment he contrived to answer coherently. "Engaged to marry her! I never supposed—I never imagined—— !"

"That I was in love with her?" Roderick interrupted. "Neither did I before this last fortnight. But you came and put me into such ridiculous good-humour that I felt an extraordinary desire to spill over to some woman, and I suppose I took the nearest. Really I may say the dearest too, for Mary's a dear; you know her too little to do her justice. I myself have only been learning to know her from three months ago, and have been falling in love with her without suspecting it. It appeared when I spoke to her that she thought distinctly better of me than I supposed. So the thing was settled. I must of course make lots of money before we can marry, and it's rather awkward, certainly, to engage oneself to a girl whom one is going to leave for years the next day. We shall be condemned for some time to come to do a terrible deal of abstract thinking about each other. But I wanted her blessing and I couldn't help asking for it. Unless a man's unnaturally selfish he needs to work for someone else than himself, and I'm sure I shall run a smoother and swifter course for knowing that there's a person so good and clever and charming, to whom my success will make the grand difference, waiting at Northampton for news of my greatness. If ever I'm a dull companion and over-addicted to moping, remember in justice to me that I'm in love and that the loved object is five thousand miles away."

Rowland listened to all this with a feeling that fortune had played him an elaborately devised trick. It had lured him out into mid-ocean and smoothed the sea and stilled the winds and given him a singularly sympathetic comrade, and then it had turned and delivered him a thumping blow in mid-chest. "Yes," he said after an attempt at the usual formal congratulation, "you certainly ought to do better—with Miss Garland waiting for you at Northampton!"

Roderick, now that he had broken ground, was vivid, was natural, was delightful, and rang a hundred changes on the assurance that he was a very happy man. Then at last, suddenly, his climax was a yawn and he declared that he must tumble in. Rowland let him go alone and sat there late between sea and sky.

69

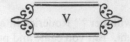

ONE WARM, still day, late in the Roman autumn, our two young men were seated beneath one of the high-stemmed pines of the Villa Ludovisi. They had been spending an hour in the mouldy little garden-house where the colossal mask of the famous Juno looks out with blank eyes from that dusky corner which must seem to her the last possible stage of a lapse from Olympus. Then they had wandered out into the gardens and were lounging away the morning under the spell, as it seemed to them, of supreme romance. Roderick declared that he would go no-where else, that after the Juno it was a profanation to look at anything but sky and trees. There was a fresco of Guercino, to which Rowland, though he had seen it on his former visit to Rome, went dutifully to pay his respects. But Roderick, though he had never seen it, declared that it couldn't be worth a fig and that he didn't care to look at ugly things. He remained stretched on his overcoat, which he had spread on the grass, while Rowland went off envying the intellectual comfort of genius, which can arrive at serene conclusions without disagreeable processes. When the latter came back his friend was sitting with his elbows on his knees and his head in his hands. Rowland, in the geniality of a mood attuned to all the stored patiences that lurk in Roman survivals, found a good word to say for the Guercino; but chiefly he talked of the view from the little belvedere on the roof of the casino, and how it looked like the prospect from a castle turret in a fairy-tale.

"Very likely," said Roderick, throwing himself back with a yawn. "But I must let it pass. I've seen enough for the present; I've reached the top of the hill. I've an indigestion of impressions; I must work them off before I go in for any more. I don't want to look at any more of other people's works for a month—not even at nature's own. I want to look, if you please, at Roderick Hudson's. The result of it all is that I'm not afraid. I can but try as well as the rest of them. The fellow who did that gazing goddess yonder only made an experiment. The other day when I was looking at Michael Angelo's Moses I was seized with a kind of exasperation, a reaction against all this mere passive enjoyment of grandeur, and, above all, against this perpetual platitude of spirit under imposed admirations. It was a rousing great success, certainly, that sat there before me, but somehow it wasn't an inscrutable mystery, and it seemed to me, not perhaps that I should some day do as much, but that at least I might do as well."

"As you say, you can but try," said Rowland. "Achievement's only effort passionate enough."

"Well then, haven't I got up steam enough ? It won't have been for want of your being a first-class stoker. It came over me just now that it's exactly three months to a day since I left Northampton. I can't believe anything so ridiculous."

"It certainly seems more."

"It seems ten years. What an exquisite ass I was so short a time ago !"

"Do you feel," Rowland asked all amusedly, "so tremendously wise now ?"

"Wise with the wisdom of the ages and the taste of a thousand fountains. Don't I look so ? Surely I haven't the same face. Haven't I different eyes, a different skin, different legs and arms ?"

"I can hardly say, because I've been too near you to catch the moments of change. But it's very likely. You're, in the literal sense of the word, more civilised. I dare say," added Rowland, "that Miss Garland would think so."

"That's not what she would call it; she would say I'm spoiled; I'm not sure she wouldn't say that I'm already hideously corrupted."

Rowland asked few questions about Mary Garland, but he always listened narrowly to his companion's voluntary observations. "Are you very sure ?"

"Why, she's a stern moralist, and she would infer from my appearance that I had become a gilded profligate." Roderick had in fact a Venetian watchchain round his neck and a magnificent Roman intaglio on the third finger of his left hand.

"Shall you feel I take a liberty," said his companion, "if I tell you I don't think you quite see her all round ?"

"For heaven's sake," cried Roderick, laughing, "don't tell me she's not a moralist ! It was for that I fell in love with her—and with security and sanity, all the 'saving clauses,' in her sweet, fresh person."

"No woman who *cares*," his friend lucidly returned, "is ever more of a moralist than she is of a partisan. If she becomes that, it's a sign she has ceased to care. I don't know whether I ever mentioned it," Rowland went on, "but I made out to my satisfaction all sorts of fine free things in Miss Garland. There's nothing at all scanted about her but her experience; everything else is large. My conviction of her is that she's very intelligent, but that she has never had a chance to prove it. Some day or other I'm sure she'll be right about everything."

"Right about everything!" Roderick cried in derision; "what a horrible description of one's future bride ! I don't ask you to be a better Catholic than the Pope. I shall be content if she's right about my interests—for 'everything,' sometimes, may happen to be hostile to *them*. But I agree with you about her turn for grim devotion. It's exactly what I built on, and, changed as I am, I'm not changed about *her*. What becomes of all our emotions, our impressions," he pursued after a long pause, "all the material of thought that life pours into us at such a rate during such a memorable three months as these ? There are twenty moments a week—a day, for that matter, some days—that seem supreme, twenty impressions that seem ultimate, that appear to form an intellectual era. But others come treading on their heels and sweeping them along, and they all melt like water into water and settle the question of precedence among themselves. The curious thing is that the more the mind takes in, the more it has space for, and that all one's ideas are like the Irish people at home who live in the different corners of a room and take boarders."

"I fancy it's our peculiar good luck that we don't see the limits of our minds," said Rowland. "We're young, compared with what we may one day be. That belongs to youth; it's perhaps the best part of it. They say that old people do find themselves at last face to face with a solid blank wall and stand thumping against it in vain. It resounds, it seems to have something beyond it, but it won't move. That's only a reason for living with open doors as long as we can."

"Open doors ?" Roderick sounded. "Yes, let us close no doors that open upon Rome. For this, for the mind, must be the most breathable air in the world—it gives a new sense to the old Pax Romana. But though my doors may stand open to-day," he presently added, "I shall see no visitors. I want to pause and breathe; I want to give the desired vision a chance to descend. I've been working hard for three months; now let my genius do the rest—the grand genius of me !"

Rowland, on his side, was not without provision for reflexion, and they lingered on in gentle desultory gossip. Rowland himself felt the need of intellectual rest, of a truce to present care for churches, statues and pictures, on even better grounds than his companion, inasmuch as he had really been living Roderick's intellectual life the past three months as well as his own. As he looked back on these animated weeks he drew a long breath of satisfaction—almost as of relieved suspense. Roderick so far had justified his confidence and flattered his perspicacity; he was giving a splendid account of himself. He was changed even more than he himself suspected; he had stepped without faltering into his birthright, and was spending money, intellectually, with the freedom of a young heir who has just won an obstructive lawsuit. His eyes still rolled and his voice quavered, doubtless, quite as when they had enlivened the summer dusk on Cecilia's verandah; but in his person generally there was an indefinable expression of experience rapidly and easily assimilated. Rowland had been struck at the outset with the instinctive quickness of his observation and his free appropriation of whatever might serve his purpose. He had not been, for instance, half an hour on English soil before he perceived that he was dressed provincially, and he had immediately reformed his style with the most unerring tact. His appetite for novelty was insatiable, and for everything characteristically foreign, as it presented itself, he had an extravagant greeting; but in half an hour the novelty had faded, he had guessed the secret, he had plucked out the heart of the mystery and was clamouring for a keener sensation. At the end of a month he offered his companion's attention a riddle that took some reading. He had caught instinctively the keynote of the general, the contrasted European order. He observed and enjoyed, he criticised and rhapsodised, but though all things interested and many delighted him, none surprised or disconcerted; he invented short cuts and was all ready for the unexpected. Witnessing the rate at which he did intellectual execution on the general spectacle of European life, Rowland felt at moments a vague dismay for his future; he was eating his cake all at once and might have none left for the morrow. But we must live as our pulses are timed, and Roderick's struck the hour very often. He was by imagination, though he never became in manner, a natural man of the world; he had intuitively, as an artist, what one may call the historic consciousness. He asked Rowland questions which this halting dilettante was quite unable to answer, and of which he was equally unable to conceive where his friend had picked up the data. Roderick ended by answering them himself, tolerably to his satisfaction, and in a short time he had almost turned the tables and become in their walks and talks the accredited fountain of criticism. Rowland took a generous pleasure in all these facilities and felicities; Roderick was so much younger than he himself had ever been. Surely youth and genius hand in hand were the most beautiful sight in the world. Roderick added to this the charm of his more immediately personal qualities. The vivacity of his perceptions, the audacity of his imagination, the picturesqueness of his phrase when he was pleased—and even more when he was displeased—his abounding good-humour, his candour, his unclouded frankness, his unfailing impulse to share with his friend every emotion and impression; all this made comradeship a high, rare communion and interfused with a deeper amenity the wanderings and contemplations that beguiled their pilgrimage to Rome.

They had gone almost immediately to Paris and had spent their days at the Louvre and their evenings at the theatre. Roderick was divided in mind as to whether Titian or Mademoiselle Delaporte were the greater artist. They had come down through France to Genoa and Milan, had passed a fortnight in Venice and another in Florence, and had now been a month in Rome. Roderick had said that he meant to spend three months in simply looking, absorbing and reflecting, without putting pencil to paper. He looked indefatigably, and certainly saw great things—things greater doubtless at times than the intention of the artist. And yet he made few false steps and wasted little time in theories of what he ought to like and to dislike. He judged instinctively and passionately, but never vulgarly. At Venice for a couple of days he had half a fit of melancholy over the pretended discovery that he had missed his way and that the only proper vestment of plastic conceptions was the colouring of Titian and the Veronese. Then one morning the two young men had themselves rowed out to Torcello, and Roderick lay back for a couple of hours watching a brown-breasted gondolier make, in high relief against the sky of the Adriatic, muscular movements of a breadth and grace that he had never seen equalled. At the end he jerked himself up, with a violence that nearly swamped the boat, to declare that the only thing worth living for was to build a colossal bronze and set it aloft in the light of a public square. In Rome his first care was for the Vatican; he went there again and again. But the old imperial and papal city altogether delighted him; only there he really found what he had been looking for from the first, the sufficient negation of his native scene. And indeed Rome is the natural home of those spirits with which we just now claimed fellowship for Roderick—the spirits with a deep relish for the element of accumulation in the human picture and for the infinite superpositions of history. It is the immemorial city of convention; and in that still recent day the most impressive convention in all history was visible to men's eyes in the reverberating streets, erect in a gilded coach drawn by four black

74

horses. Roderick's first fortnight was a high æsthetic revel. He declared that Rome made him feel and understand more things than he could express; he was sure that life must have there for all one's senses an incomparable finéness; that more interesting things must happen to one there than anywhere else. And he gave Rowland to understand that he meant to live freely and largely and be as interested as occasion demanded. Rowland saw no reason to regard this as a menace of undue surrender to the senses, because in the first place there was in almost any crudity of "pleasure," refine upon it as the imagination might, a vulgar side which would disqualify it for Roderick's favour; and because in the second the young sculptor was a man to regard all things in the light of his art, to hand over his passions to his genius to be dealt with, and to find that he could live largely enough, even quite riotously enough, without exceeding the circle of pure delights. Rowland took high satisfaction in this positive law, as he saw it, of his companion's spirit, the instinct of investing every gain of sense or soul in the enterprise of planned production. Production indeed was not always working at a clay model, but the form it sometimes took was none the less a safe one. He wrote frequent long letters to Mary Garland; when Rowland went with him to post them he thought wistfully of the fortune of the large loosely-written missives, which cost Roderick unconscionable sums in postage. He received punctual answers of a more frugal shape, written in a clear and delicate hand, on paper vexatiously thin. If Rowland was present when they came he turned away and thought of other things or tried to think. These were the only moments when his sympathy halted, and they were brief. For the rest he let the days go by unprotestingly, and enjoyed Roderick's serene efflorescence as he would have done a beautiful summer sunrise. Rome for the past month had been perfection. The annual descent of the Goths had not yet begun, and sunny leisure seemed to brood over the city.

Roderick had taken out a note-book and was roughly sketching a memento of the great Juno. Suddenly there was a noise on the gravel, and the young men, looking up, saw three persons advancing. One was a woman of middle age, with a rather grand air and a great many furbelows. She looked very hard at our friends as she passed, and glanced back over her shoulder as if to quicken the step of a young girl who slowly followed her. She had such an expansive majesty of mien that Rowland supposed she must have some proprietary right in the villa and was not just then in a permissive mood. Beside her walked a little elderly man, tightly buttoned in a shabby black coat, but with a flower in his lappet and a pair of soiled light gloves. He was a semi-grotesque figure, and might have passed for a gentleman of the old school reduced by adversity to playing cicerone to foreigners of distinction. He had little black eyes that glittered like diamonds and rolled about like balls of quicksilver, and a white moustache, cut short and as stiff as a worn-out brush. He was smiling with extreme urbanity and talking in a low mellifluous voice to the lady, who evidently was not attentive. At a considerable distance behind this couple strolled a young girl, apparently of about twenty. She was tall and slender and dressed with extreme elegance; she led by a cord a large poodle of the most fantastic aspect. He was combed and decked like a ram for sacrifice; his trunk and haunches were of the most transparent pink, his fleecy head and shoulders as white as jeweller's cotton, his tail and ears ornamented with long blue ribbons. He stepped along stiffly and solemnly beside his mistress, with an air of conscious elegance. There was something at first slightly absurd in the sight of a young lady gravely appended to an animal of these incongruous attributes, and Roderick, always quick to react, greeted the spectacle with frank amusement. The girl noticed it and turned her face full upon him; her expression was seemingly meant to enforce greater deference. It was not deference, however, that the show provoked, but startled submissive admiration; Roderick's smile fell dead, and he sat eagerly staring. A pair of extraordinary dark blue eyes, a mass of dusky hair over a low forehead, a blooming oval of perfect purity, a flexible lip just touched with disdain, the step and carriage of a tired princess—these were the general features of his vision. The young lady walked slowly, letting her long dress rustle over the gravel; the young men had time to see her distinctly before she averted her face and went away. She left a vague sweet perfume behind her as she passed.

"Immortal powers," cried Roderick, "what a vision ! In the name of transcendent perfection who is she ?" He sprang up and stood looking after her till she rounded a turn in the avenue. "What a movement, what a manner, what a poise of the head ! I wonder if she would sit to me ?"

"You had better go and ask her," said Rowland in the same spirit. "She was quite beautiful enough."

"Beautiful ? She's beauty's self—she's a revelation. I don't believe she's living—she's a phantasm, a vapour, an illusion !"

"The poodle," said Rowland, "is certainly alive."

"No, he too may be a grotesque phantom, like the black dog in *Faust*."

"I hope at least that the young lady has nothing in common with Mephistopheles. She looked dangerous."

"If beauty's the wrong thing, as people think at Northampton," said Roderick, "she's the incarnation of evil. The mamma and the queer old gentleman, moreover, are a pledge of her reality. Who are they all?"

"The Prince and Princess Ludovisi-Olimpiani and the *principessina*," suggested Rowland.

"There are no such people," said Roderick. "Besides, the little old man isn't the papa." Rowland smiled, wondering how he had ascertained these facts, and the young sculptor went on. "The old man's a Roman, a hanger-on of the mamma, a useful personage who now and then gets asked to dinner. The ladies are foreigners from some northern country; I won't say which."

"Perhaps from our neighbouring State of Maine," said Rowland.

"No, she's not an American, I'll lay a wager on that. She's a daughter of this elder world. We shall see her again, I pray my stars; but if we don't I shall have done something I never expected—I shall have had a glimpse of ideal beauty." He sat down again and went on with his sketch of the Juno, scrawled away for ten minutes, and then handed the result in silence to Rowland. Rowland uttered an exclamation of surprise and applause. The drawing represented the Juno as to the position of the head, the brow and the broad fillet across the hair; but the eyes, the mouth, the physiognomy were a straight recall of the young girl with the bedecked beast. "I've been wanting a subject," said Roderick; "there's one made to my hand! And now to tackle it!"

They saw no more of the marvellous maiden, though Roderick looked hopefully for some days into the carriages on the Pincian. She had evidently only been passing through Rome; Naples or Florence now happily possessed her, and she was guiding her fleecy companion through the Villa Reale or the Boboli Gardens with the same superb defiance of irony. Roderick went to work and spent a month shut up in his studio; he had an idea, and he was not to rest till he had embodied it. He had established himself in the basement of a huge, dusky, dilapidated old house in that long, tortuous and pre-eminently Roman street which leads, under more than one name, from the Corso to the Bridge of Saint Angelo. The black archway which admitted you might have served as the portal of the Augean stables, but you emerged presently upon a mouldy little court, of which the fourth side was formed by a narrow terrace overhanging the Tiber. Here, along the parapet, were stationed half-a-dozen shapeless fragments of sculpture, with a couple of meagre orange-trees in terra-cotta tubs and an oleander that never flowered. The unclean historic river swept beneath; behind were dusky, reeking walls, spotted here and there with hanging rags and flower-pots in windows; opposite, at a distance, were the bare brown banks of the stream, the huge rotunda of Saint Angelo, tipped with its seraphic statue, the dome of Saint Peter's and the broad-topped pines of the Villa Pamfili. The place was crumbling and shabby and sinister, but the river was delightful, the rent a trifle and everything romantic. Roderick was in the best humour with his quarters from the first, and was certain that the faculty of production would be intenser there in an hour than in twenty years at Northampton. His studio was a large empty room with a vaulted ceiling where the vague dark traces of an old fresco caused Rowland, whenever he spent an hour with his friend, to stare at it for some faint survival of floating draperies and clasping arms. Roderick had housed his personal effects economically in the same quarter. He occupied a fifth floor on the Ripetta, but he was only at home to sleep, for when he was not at work he was either lounging in Rowland's more luxurious rooms or strolling through streets and churches and gardens.

Rowland had found a convenient corner in a stately old palace close to the fountain of Trevi, and made himself a home to which books and pictures and prints and odds and ends of curious furniture gave an air of leisurely permanence. He had the habits of a collector; he spent half his afternoons ransacking the dusky magazines of the curiosity-mongers, and he often made his way in quest of a prize into the heart of impecunious Roman households which had been prevailed upon to listen —with closed doors and an impenetrably wary smile—to proposals for an hereditary "antique." In the evening often, under the lamp, amid dropped curtains and the scattered gleam of firelight upon polished carvings and mellow paintings, the two friends sat with their heads together, criticising intaglios and etchings, water-colour drawings and illuminated missals. Roderick's quick appreciation of every form of artistic beauty reminded his companion of the flexible temperament of those Italian artists of the sixteenth century who were indifferently painters and sculptors, sonneteers and engineers. When at his times of most seeing he saw the young sculptor's day pass in a single sustained flight, while his own was broken into a dozen conscious devices for disposing of the hours, and intermingled with sighs, half suppressed, some of them, for conscience' sake, over what he failed of in action and missed in possession, he felt a pang of some envious pain. But Rowland had two substantial aids for giving patience the air of contentment; he was an inquisitive reader and a passionate rambling rider. He plunged into bulky German octavos on Italian history and, during long afternoons spent in the saddle, ranged over the grassy desert that encircles Rome. As the season went on and the social groups began to constitute themselves he found that he knew a great many people and that he had easy occasion to know others. He enjoyed the quiet corner of a drawing-room beside an agreeable woman, and, though the machinery of what calls itself society seemed to him to have many superfluous wheels, he accepted invitations and made visits punctiliously, from the conviction that the only way not to be overcome by the ridiculous side of most of such observances is to take them with ordered gravity. He introduced Roderick right and left, and suffered him to make his way himself—an enterprise for which Roderick very soon displayed an all-sufficient capacity. Wherever he went he made, not exactly what is called a favourable impression, but what, from a practical point of view, is better—an ambiguous, almost a violent one. He took to evening parties as a duck to water, and before the winter was half over was the most freely and frequently discussed young man in the heterogeneous foreign colony. Rowland's theory of his own duty was to let him run his course and play his cards, only holding himself ready to point out shoals and pitfalls and administer a friendly propulsion through tight places. Roderick's manners on the precincts of the Pincian were quite the same as his manners on Cecilia's verandah; they were no manners, in strict parlance, at all. But it remained as true as before that it would have been impossible, on the whole, to violate ceremony with less of lasting offence. He interrupted, he contradicted, he spoke to people he had never seen and left his social creditors without the smallest conversational interest on their loans; he lounged and yawned, he talked loud when he should have talked low and low when he should have talked loud. Many people in consequence thought him insufferably conceited and declared that he ought to wait till he had something to show for his powers before assuming the airs of a spoiled celebrity. But to Rowland and to most friendly observers this judgement was quite beside the mark and the savour of the young man's naturalness as fine as good wine. He was prompt, spontaneous, sincere; there were so many people at dinner-tables and in studios who were not, that it seemed worth while to allow this rare specimen all possible freedom of action. If Roderick took the words out of your mouth when you were just prepared to deliver them with the most effective accent, he did it with a perfect good conscience and with no pretension of a better right to being heard, but simply because he was full to overflowing of his own momentary thought, which sprang from his lips without asking leave. There were persons waiting on your periods much more deferentially who were ten times more capable of letting you flounder, of a reflective impertinence. The young man received from various sources, chiefly feminine, enough finely-adjusted advice to have established him in life as an embodiment of the proprieties, and he received it, as he afterwards listened to criticisms on his statues, with unfaltering candour and good-humour. Here and there doubtless, as he went, he took in a reef in his sail; but he was too adventurous a spirit to be successfully tamed and he remained at most points the florid, rather strident young Virginian whose brilliant aridity had been the despair of Mr. Striker. All this was what friendly commentators (still chiefly feminine) alluded to when they spoke of his delightful freshness, and critics of harsher sensibilities (of the other sex) when they denounced his damned impertinence. His appearance re-enforced these impressions—his handsome face, his radiant unaverted eyes, his childish unmodulated voice. Afterwards, when those who loved him were in tears, there was something in all this unspotted brightness that seemed to lend a mockery to the causes of their sorrow.

Certainly, among the young men of genius who for so many ages have gone up to Rome to test their powers, none ever made a fairer beginning than Roderick. He rode his two horses at once with extraordinary good fortune; he established the happiest *modus vivendi* betwixt work and play. He wrestled all day with a mountain of clay in his studio, and chattered half the night away in Roman drawing-rooms. It all seemed part of a divine facility. He was passionately interested, he was feeling his powers; now that they had thoroughly kindled in the glowing æsthetic atmosphere of Rome the ardent young fellow should be pardoned for believing that he never was to see the end of them. He enjoyed immeasurably, after the chronic obstruction of home, the sublime act of creation. He kept models in his studio till they dropped with fatigue; he drew on other days at the Capitol and the Vatican till his own head swam with his eagerness and his limbs stiffened with the cold. He had promptly set up a life-sized figure which he called an "Adam," and was pushing it rapidly towards completion. There were naturally a great many wiseheads who smiled at his

precipitancy and cited him as one more example of Yankee crudity—
a capital recruit to the great army of those who wish to dance before
they can walk. They were right, but Roderick was right too, for the
success of his effort was not to have been foreseen; it partook really, in
the case of this particular figure, of the miraculous. He was never
afterwards to surpass the thing, to which a good judge here and there
had been known to attribute a felicity of young inspiration achieved
by no other piece of the period. To Rowland it seemed to justify
grandly the highest hopes of his friend, and he said to himself that if
he had staked his reputation on bringing out a young lion he ought now
to pass for a famous connoisseur. In his elation he travelled up to
Carrara and selected at the quarries the most magnificent block of
marble he could find, and when it came down to Rome the two young
men had a "celebration." They drove out to Albano, breakfasted
boisterously (in their respective measure) at the inn, and lounged away
the day in the sun on the top of Monte Cavo. Roderick's head was full
of ideas for other works, which he described with infinite spirit and
eloquence, as vividly as if they were ranged on their pedestals before
him. He had irrepressible reactions; things he saw in the streets, in the
country, things he heard and read, effects he found just missed or half
expressed in the works of others, wrought on his mind for provocation,
and he was terribly uneasy until in some form or other he had taken up
the glove and set his lance in rest.

The Adam was put into marble, and all the world came to see it. Of
the criticisms passed upon it this history undertakes to offer no record;
over many of them the two young men had a daily laugh for a month,
and some of the formulas of the commentators, restrictive or indulgent,
furnished Roderick with a permanent supply of humorous catchwords.
But people enough spoke flattering good sense to make the author of
the work feel as if he were already half famous. It passed formally into
Rowland's possession and was paid for as if an illustrious name had
been chiselled on the pedestal. Poor Roderick owed by that hour every
franc of the money. It was not for this, however, but because he was so
gloriously in the mood, that, denying himself all breathing-time, on the
same day he had given the last touch to the Adam, he began to shape
the rough contour of an Eve. This experiment went forward with equal
rapidity and success. Roderick lost his temper time and again with his
models, who offered but a gross degenerate image of his splendid ideal;
but his ideal, as he assured Rowland, became gradually such a fixed,
vivid presence that he had only to shut his eyes to behold an image far

more to his purpose than the poor girl who stood posturing at forty sous an hour. The Eve was finished in three months, and the feat was extraordinary, as well as the statue, which represented a creature of consummately wrought beauty. When the spring began to clasp the rugged old city in its branching arms it seemed to him that he had done a handsome winter's work and had fairly earned a holiday. He took a liberal one and lounged away at his ease the lovely Roman May. He looked very contented; with himself perhaps at times a trifle too obviously. But who could have said without good reason? He was "flushed with triumph"; this classic phrase portrayed him to Rowland's sense. He would lose himself in long reveries and emerge from them with a convulsed, refreshed face and larger motions. Rowland grudged him none of his gestures and rejoiced beyond any expression in the two guarantees of his power. He had these productions transported to his own apartment, and one warm evening in May he gave a little dinner in honour of the artist. It was small, but Rowland had meant it should be conveniently composed. He thought over his friends and chose four. They were all persons with whom he lived in a certain intimacy.

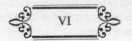

VI

ONE OF them was an American sculptor of French extraction, or remotely perhaps of Italian, for he wore like a charm, in the Roman air, his fine name of Gloriani. He was a man of forty, he had been living for years in Paris and in Rome, and he now drove an active trade in sculpture of the ingenious or sophisticated school. In his youth he had had money; but he had spent it recklessly, much of it scandalously, and at twenty-six had found himself obliged to make capital of his talent. This was quite inimitable, and fifteen years of indefatigable exercise had brought it to perfection. Rowland admitted its power, though it gave him very little pleasure; what he relished in the man was the extraordinary vivacity and frankness, not to call it the impudence, of his opinions. He had a definite, practical scheme of art, and he knew at least what he meant. In this sense he was almost too knowing. There were so many of the æsthetic fraternity who were floundering in unknown seas, without a notion of which way their noses were turned, that Gloriani, conscious and compact, unlimitedly intelligent and consummately clever, helpful only as to his own duties, and at once gracefully deferential and profoundly indifferent to those of others, had for Rowland an effect of refreshment quite independent of the character of his works. These were considered by most people to belong to a very extravagant, and by many to a thoroughly depraved type. Others found in them strange secrets of the plastic and paid huge prices for them; and indeed to be able to point to one of Gloriani's figures in the best light in your library was tolerable proof that you were not a fool. Of an art that had wandered far they freely spoke, and of a taste that was the latest fruit of time. It was the artist's opinion that there is no essential difference between beauty and ugliness; that they overlap and intermingle in a quite inextricable manner; that there is no saying where one begins and the other ends; that hideousness grimaces at you suddenly from out of the very bosom of loveliness, and beauty blooms before your eyes in the lap of vileness; that it is a waste of wit to nurse metaphysical distinctions and a sadly meagre entertainment to caress imaginary lines; that the thing to aim at is the expressive and the way to reach it is by ingenuity; that for this purpose everything may serve and that a consummate work is a sort of hotch-potch of the pure and the impure, the graceful and the grotesque. Its prime duty is to amuse, to puzzle, to fascinate, to report on a real æsthetic adventure. Gloriani's effects, elegant and strange, exquisite and base, made no appeal to Rowland as a purchaser, but the artist was such an independent spirit, and was withal so deluged with orders, that this signified nothing for their friendship. This highly modern master was a free and vivid talker, whose phrase seemed ever to have in it, if not the touch of the brush, at least the print of the expert thumb. He might have been, facially, for firmness, one of his own expensive bronzes, and when sometimes he received you at his lodging he introduced you to a lady without art of utterance whom he called Madame Gloriani—which she was not.

Rowland's second guest was also an artist, but of a very different type. His friends called him Sam Singleton; he was an American, and he had been in Rome a couple of years. He painted small landscapes, chiefly in water-colour; Rowland had seen one of them in a shop window, had liked it extremely and, ascertaining his address, had gone to see him and found him established in a very humble studio near the Piazza Barberini, where apparently fame and fortune had not yet come his way. Rowland, treating him as a discovery, bought several of his pictures; Singleton made few speeches, but was intensely grateful.

Rowland heard afterwards that when he first came to Rome he painted worthless daubs and gave no promise of talent. Improvement had come, however, hand in hand with patient industry, and his talent, though of a slender and delicate order, was now incontestable. It was as yet but scantily recognised and he had hard work to hold out. Rowland hung his little water-colours on the library wall, and found that as he lived with them he grew very fond of them. Singleton, short and spare, was made as if for sitting on very small camp-stools and eating the tiniest luncheons. He had a transparent brown regard, a perpetual smile, an extraordinary expression of modesty and patience. He listened much more willingly than he talked, with a little fixed grateful grin; he blushed when he spoke, and always offered his ideas as if he were handing you useful objects of your own that you had unconsciously dropped; so that his credit could be at most for honesty. He was so perfect an example of the little noiseless devoted worker whom chance, in the person of a moneyed patron, has never taken by the hand, that Rowland would have liked to befriend him by stealth. Singleton had expressed a yearning approval of Roderick's productions, but he had not yet met the young master. Roderick was lounging against the chimney-piece when he came in, and Rowland presently introduced him. The visitor stood as a privileged pilgrim, with folded hands, blushing, smiling and looking up as if Roderick had been himself a statue on a pedestal. He began to murmur something about his pleasure, his admiration; the desire to say something very appreciative gave him almost an air of distress. Roderick looked down at him surprised, and suddenly burst into a laugh. Singleton paused a moment and then, with an intenser smile, went on: "Well, sir, your work's most interesting, all the same!"

Rowland's two other guests were ladies, and one of them, Miss Blanchard, belonged also to the artistic fraternity. She was an American, she was young, she was pretty, and had made her way to Rome alone and unaided. She lived alone, or with no other duenna than a bushy-browed old serving-woman, though indeed she had a friendly neighbour in the person of a certain Madame Grandoni, who in various social emergencies lent her a protecting wing and had come with her to Rowland's dinner. Miss Blanchard had a small fortune, but she was not above selling her pictures. These represented generally a bunch of dew-sprinkled roses, with the dew-drops very highly finished, or else a wayside shrine and a peasant woman, with her back turned, kneeling before it. She did backs very well, but was a little weak in faces. Flowers, however, were the chief of her diet, and, though her touch was a little old-fashioned and finical, she painted them with remarkable skill. Her pictures were chiefly bought by the English. Rowland had made her acquaintance early in the winter, and as she kept a saddle horse and rode a great deal he had asked permission to be her cavalier. In this way they had become informal allies. Miss Blanchard's name was Augusta; she was slender, pale and elegant; she had a very pretty head and brilliant auburn hair, which she braided with classic simplicity. She talked in a sweet soft voice, inclined to the flower of speech scarcely less than to that of the garden, and made literary allusions. These had often a patriotic strain, and Rowland had more than once been treated to quotations from Mrs. Sigourney in the cork-woods of Monte Mario, and from Mr. Willis among the ruins of Veii. Rowland was of a dozen different minds about her, and was half surprised at times to find himself treating it as a matter of serious moment that he should like her or not. He admired her, and indeed there was something exemplary in her combination of beauty and talent, of isolation and self-support. He used sometimes to go into the little high-niched ordinary room which served her as a studio, to find her working at a panel six inches square, by an open casement, profiled against the deep blue Roman sky. She welcomed him with a meek-eyed dignity that made her seem a painted saint on a church window receiving the daylight in all her being. The breath of vulgar report passed her by with folded wings. And yet Rowland wondered why he couldn't like her better. If he failed, the reason was not far to seek. There was another woman whom he liked better, an image in his heart which gave itself small airs of exclusiveness.

On that evening to which allusion has been made, when Rowland was left alone between the starlight and the waves with the sudden knowledge that Mary Garland was to become another man's wife, he had taken after a while the simple resolution to forget her. And every day since, like a famous philosopher who wished to abbreviate his mourning for a faithful servant, he had said to himself in substance: "Remember to forget Mary Garland." Sometimes it seemed as if he were succeeding; then suddenly, when he was least expecting it, he would find her name inaudibly on his lips and seem to see her eyes meeting his eyes. All this made him uncomfortable and seemed to plant he scarce knew what ugly danger on the brow of the future. False positions were not to his taste; he shrank from imperious passions, and the idea of finding himself jealous of an unsuspecting friend could only disgust him. More than ever then the path of good manners was to forget Mary Garland, and he cultivated oblivion, as we may say, in the person of Miss Blanchard. Her fine temper, he said to himself, was a trifle cold and conscious, her purity prudish perhaps, her culture pedantic. But since he was obliged to turn the image of the girl in far New England with its face to the wall, his dull star owed him a compensation, and he had fits of angry sadness in which it seemed to him that to attest his right to sentimental satisfaction he should indulge in some defiantly incongruous passion. And what was the use, after all, of bothering about a possible which was only perhaps a dream? Even if Mary Garland had been free, what right had he to assume that he should have pleased her? The actual was good enough. Miss Blanchard had beautiful hair, and if she was a trifle old-maidish there was nothing like the conjugal tie for curing that deformity.

Madame Grandoni, who had formed with the companion of Rowland's rides an alliance which might have been called defensive on the part of the former and attractive on that of Miss Blanchard, was a thoroughly ugly old lady, highly esteemed in Roman society for her homely benevolence and her shrewd and humorous good sense. She had been the widow of a German archæologist who came to Rome in the early ages as *attaché* of the Prussian legation on the Capitoline. Her acuteness had failed her but on a single occasion, that of her second marriage. This occasion would have demanded a double dose of it, but these are by general consent not test cases. A couple of years after her first husband's death she had accepted the hand and the name of a Neapolitan music-master ten years younger than herself and with no fortune but his fiddle-bow. The union had proved a union of exasperated opposites, and the Maestro Grandoni was suspected of using the fiddle-bow as an instrument of conjugal correction. He had finally run off with a *prima donna assoluta*, who, it was commonly hoped, had given him a taste of the quality implied in her title. He was believed to be living still, but he had shrunk to a small black spot in Madame Grandoni's life, and for ten years she had not mentioned his name. She wore a light flaxen wig, which was never very artfully adjusted; but this mattered little, as she made no secret of it. She used to say, "I was not always so ugly as this; as a young girl I had beautiful golden hair, very much the colour of my wig." She had worn from time immemorial an old blue satin dress and a white crape shawl embroidered in colours; her appearance was ridiculous, but she had an interminable Teutonic pedigree, and her manners in every presence were easy and jovial, as became a lady whose ancestor had been cup-bearer to Frederick Barbarossa. Thirty years' observation of Roman society had sharpened her wit and given her an inexhaustible store of anecdote; but she had beneath her crumpled bodice a deep-welling fund of Teutonic sentiment, which she communicated only to the objects of her particular favour. Rowland had a great regard for her, and she repaid it by wishing him to offer somebody his hand, which she called his hant. She never saw him without whispering to him that Augusta Blanchard was just the somebody.

It seemed to him indeed a foreshadowing of matrimony to see Augusta Blanchard stand gracefully on his hearth-rug and bloom behind the central bouquet at his circular dinner-table. The dinner was very prosperous, and Roderick amply filled his position as hero of the feast. He had always an air of dauntless intention, but on this occasion he manifested a good deal of harmless pleasure in his glory. He drank freely and talked bravely; he leaned back in his chair with his hands in his pockets and flung open the gates of his eloquence. Singleton sat gazing and listening open-mouthed, as if Phœbus Apollo had been talking. Gloriani's fine smile showed the light of general scepticism and an evident disposition to draw Roderick out. Rowland had his apprehensions, for he knew that theory was not his young friend's strong point and that it was never fair to take his measure from his mere magnificence of speech.

"As you've begun with Adam and Eve," said Gloriani, "I suppose you're going straight through the Bible." He was one of the persons who thought Roderick delightfully fresh.

"I may make a David," said Roderick, "but I shall not try any more of the Old Testament people. I don't like the Jews; I like the big nose, as any sculptor must, but only the Christian, or still better the pagan, form. David, the boy David, is rather an exception; you can think of him and treat him as a young Greek. Standing forth there on the plain of battle between the contending armies, rushing forward to let fly his stone, he looks like a beautiful runner at the Olympic games. After that I shall skip to the New Testament. I mean to make a ripping Christ."

"You will put nothing of the Olympic games into *him*, I hope," said Gloriani.

"Oh, I shall make him very different from the Christ of tradition; more—more——" And Roderick paused a moment to think. This was the first that Rowland had heard of his so oddly described Christ.

"More rationalistic, I suppose," suggested Miss Blanchard.

"More idealistic!" cried Roderick. "The perfection of form, you know, to symbolise the perfection of spirit."

"For a companion-piece," said Miss Blanchard, "you ought—since a sculptor 'must' like the big nose—to make a Judas."

"Never! I mean never to make anything ugly. The Greeks never made anything ugly, and I'm a Hellenist; I'm not a Hebraist! I have been thinking lately of making a Cain, but I should never dream of making him ugly. He should be a very handsome fellow indeed, and he should lift up the murderous club with the beautiful movement of the fighters in the Greek friezes who are chopping at their enemies."

"There's no use trying to be a Greek," said Gloriani. "If Phidias were to come back he would recommend you to give it up—he'd send you about your business. I'm half Italian and half French, and, as a whole, an abandoned cosmopolite. What sort of a Greek should I be? I think the Judas is a capital idea for something. Much obliged to you, madam, for the suggestion. What an insidious little scoundrel one might make of him, sitting there nursing his money-bag and his treachery! There may be a great deal of interest in an ugly nose, my dear sir—especially if one has put it there."

"You mean there may be a great deal of character. Very likely," said Roderick, "but it's not the sort of character I care for. I care only for beauty of Type—there it is, if you want to know. That's as good a profession of faith as another. In future, so far as my things don't rise to that in a living way, you may set them down as failures. For me it's either that or nothing. It's against the taste of the day, I know; we've really lost the faculty to understand beauty in the large ideal way. We stand like a race with shrunken muscles, staring helplessly at the weights our forefathers easily lifted. But I don't hesitate to proclaim it—I mean to lift them again! I mean to go in for big things; that's my notion of my art. I mean to do things that will be simple and sublime. You shall see if they won't be sublime. Excuse me if I brag a little; all those Italian fellows in the Renaissance used to brag. There was a sensation once common, I'm sure, in the human breast—a kind of religious awe in the presence of a marble image newly created and expressing the human type in superhuman purity. When Phidias and Praxiteles had their statues of goddesses unveiled in the temples of the Ægean, don't you suppose there was something more than a cold-blooded, critical flutter? The thing that there was is the thing I want to bring back. I want to thrill you, with my cold marble, when you look. I want to produce the sacred terror; a Hera that will make you turn blue, an Aphrodite that will make you turn—well, faint."

"So that when we come and see you," said Madame Grandoni, "we must be sure and bring our smelling-bottles. And pray have a few sofas conveniently placed."

"Phidias and Praxiteles," Miss Blanchard remarked, "had the advantage of believing in their goddesses. I insist on believing, for myself, that the pagan mythology isn't to be explained away by a ruthless analysis, and that Venus and Juno and Apollo and Mercury used to come down in a cloud into this very city of Rome where we sit talking nineteenth-century English."

"Nineteenth-century nonsense, my dear !" cried Madame Grandoni. "Mr. Hudson may be a new Phidias, but Venus and Juno—that's you and I—arrived to-day in a very dirty cab; and were cheated by the driver too."

"But, my dear fellow," objected Gloriani, "you don't mean to say you are going to make over in cold blood those poor old academic bugbears, the prize bores of Olympus. 'Turn blue' ?—they may make us indeed ! Only Canova has so thoroughly shown them how that there's nothing left for you."

"Ah, I think I could have shown Canova how," Roderick gaily rejoined. "It won't matter a rap what you call them—you'll just know them for more than mortal. They shall be simply divine forms. They shall be Beauty; they shall be Wisdom; they shall be Power; they shall be Genius; they shall be Daring. That's all the Greek divinities were."

"That's rather depressingly abstract, you know," said Miss Blanchard.

"Cher beau jeune homme," Gloriani remarked, "there's only one thing in the world that's divine for us—which is to be twenty-five years old. You're delightfully young !"

"Isn't that indeed just it ?" Singleton echoed with a flush of sympathy across his large white forehead. "You can do anything in the world, Mr. Hudson, that you try."

"Well, there are all the Forces and Elements and Mysteries of Nature," Mr. Hudson assentingly pursued. "I mean to do the Morning; I mean to do the Night ! I mean to do the Ocean and the Mountains, the Moon and the West Wind. I mean to make a magnificent image of my Native Land."

"Your native land, your native mountains—why not say at once your native moon? You do make it shine on us!" Gloriani kindly laughed.

"I *shall*—and it will make *you* at least mad!" Roderick returned with expression. "My figures shall make no contortions, but they shall mean a tremendous deal."

"I'm sure there are contortions enough in Michael Angelo," said Madame Grandoni. "Perhaps you don't approve of him."

"Ah, why drag him in?" the young man reminiscently cried; at which they were none of them too stale of spirit to laugh. He had done, after all, some fine things.

Rowland had bidden one of the servants bring him a small portfolio of prints and had taken out a photograph of Roderick's little statue of the drinking youth. It pleased him to see his friend sitting there in radiant ardour, defending idealism against so knowing an apostle of the sophisticated, and he wished to help Gloriani to be confuted. He silently handed him the photograph.

"Bless me!" cried his guest. "Did *he* go and do this?"

"Oh, ages ago," said Roderick.

Gloriani looked at the photograph a long time and with evident admiration. "It's deucedly pretty," he declared at last. "But, my dear young friend, it's a kind of thing you positively can't keep up, you know."

"I shall do better," said Roderick.

"You'll do worse. You'll do it on purpose. This thing wasn't done on purpose. It couldn't have been. You'll have at any rate to take to violence, to contortions, to romanticism, in self-defence. Your beauty, as you call it, is the effort of a man to quit the earth by flapping his arms very hard. He may jump about or stand on tiptoe, but he can't do more. Here you jump about very gracefully, I admit; but you can't fly; there's no use trying."

"My colossal 'America' shall answer you!" said Roderick, shaking towards him a tall glass of champagne and drinking it down.

Singleton had taken the photograph and was poring over it with a little murmur of delight. "Was this done in America?" he asked.

"In a square white wooden house at Northampton Mass," Roderick answered.

"Dear old white wooden houses!" said Miss Blanchard. "Dear old Northampton, dear old 'Mass'!"

"If you could do as well as this there," said Singleton, blushing and smiling, "one might say that really you had only to lose by coming to Rome."

"Our host's to blame for that," said Roderick. "But I'm willing to risk the danger."

The photograph had been passed to Madame Grandoni, whose eye-glass had the handle of a warming-pan. "It resembles," she said, "the things a young man used to do whom I knew years ago, when I first came to Rome. He was a German, a pupil of Overbeck and a votary of spiritual art. He used to wear a black velvet tunic and a very low shirt-collar; he had a neck like a sickly crane and he let his hair grow down to his shoulders. His name was Herr Schafgans. He never painted anything so profane as a man taking a drink, for none of his people had anything so vulgar as an appetite. They were all angles and edges—they looked like diagrams of human nature. They were figures if you please, but geometrical figures. He wouldn't have agreed with Gloriani any more than you. He used to come and see me very often, and in those days I thought his tunic and his long neck infallible symptoms of genius. His talk was all of gilded aureoles and beatific visions; he lived on weak wine and biscuits and wore a lock of Saint Somebody's hair in a little bag round his neck. If he was not a Beato Angelico it was not his own fault. I hope with all my heart that Mr. Hudson will do the fine things he talks about, but he must bear in mind the history of dear Mr. Schafgans as a warning against high-flown pretensions. One fine day this poor young man fell in love with a Roman model, though she had never sat to him, I believe, for she was a buxom, bold-faced, high-coloured creature, and he painted none but pale and sickly women. He offered to marry her, and she looked at him from head to foot, gave a shrug and consented. But he was ashamed to set up his *ménage* in Rome. They went to Naples, and there, a couple of years afterwards, I saw him. The poor fellow was ruined. His wife used to beat him, and he had taken to drinking. He wore a ragged black coat and had a blotchy red face. Madame had turned washerwoman and used to make him go and fetch the dirty linen. There was nothing, unfortunately, to be done, in the 'doing-up' way, with his genius—*that* wouldn't 'wash,' and he was getting his living by painting views of Vesuvius in eruption on the little boxes they sell at Sorrento."

"Moral: don't fall in love with a buxom Roman model," said Roderick. "I'm much obliged to you for your story, but I don't mean to fall in love with any one."

Gloriani had possessed himself of the photograph again and was looking at it curiously. "Ah, you'll have been young, *par exemple*—you'll have been young!" he exclaimed with almost confessed envy. "It's the only case I've ever known of genius in the cradle."

The two sculptors continued to play with paradox after dinner, and Rowland left them at it where, in a corner of the drawing-room, the vague white presence of Roderick's Eve, above them in the shaded lamplight, might have been that of the guardian angel of the young idealist. Singleton was listening to Madame Grandoni, and Rowland took his place on the sofa near Miss Blanchard. They had a good deal of familiar desultory talk; every now and then Madame Grandoni turned round at them. Miss Blanchard at last asked Rowland certain questions about Roderick—who he was, where he came from, whether it was true, as she had heard, that Rowland had discovered him and brought him out at his own expense. Rowland answered her questions; to the last he gave a vague affirmative. Finally, after a pause, looking at him, "You're most awfully splendid, you know—to be so generous," Miss Blanchard said. The tribute was offered with extreme directness, but it brought to Rowland's sense neither delight nor confusion. He had heard something like it, and yet so unlike, before; he suddenly remembered the grave sincerity with which Mary Garland had told him he was generous while he strolled with her in the woods on the day of Roderick's picnic. They had pleased him then; now he asked Augusta Blanchard if she wouldn't have tea.

When the two ladies withdrew he went with them to their conveyance. Coming back to the drawing-room he paused outside the open door; he was struck by the group formed by the three men. They were engaged in discussion of the so admirable Eve, and the author of the figure had lifted up the lamp and was showing different parts of it to his companions. He was talking with the confidence that never failed and yet never betrayed him—the lamp-light covered his head and face. Rowland stood looking on, for the group appealed to him by its romantic symbolism. Roderick, bearing the lamp and glowing in its radiant circle, seemed the beautiful image of a genius which combined sincerity with power. Gloriani, with his head on one side, pulling his long moustache like a genial Mephistopheles and looking keenly from half-closed eyes at the lighted marble, represented art with a mixed motive, skill unleavened by faith, the mere base maximum of cleverness. Poor little Singleton, on the other side, with his hands behind him, his head thrown back and his eyes following devoutly the course of

Roderick's charming extravagance, might pass for an embodiment of aspiring candour afflicted with feebleness of wing. In all this Roderick's was certainly the *beau rôle*.

Gloriani turned to Rowland as he came up; he pointed back with his thumb to the statue, his smile half sardonic and half sympathetic. "A pretty thing—a devilish pretty thing. It's as fresh as the foam in the milk-pail. He can do it once, he can do it twice, he can do it at a stretch half a dozen times. But—but—— !"

He was returning to his former refrain; Rowland intercepted him. "Oh, he'll keep it up—you see I'm here to make him!"

Gloriani had obviously a high vision of his own consistency, and he liked interesting young men to be consistent with *that*. Roderick had taken this in with his bright clear face; he was floating on the tide of his happy magniloquence. Now, suddenly, however, he turned with a flash of irritation in his eye and demanded in a ringing voice: "In a word then you prophesy that I shall fizzle out?"

Gloriani answered imperturbably, patting him kindly on the shoulder. "My dear fellow, passion burns out, inspiration runs to seed. Some fine day every artist finds himself sitting face to face with his lump of clay, with his empty canvas, with his sheet of blank paper, waiting in vain for the revelation to be made, for the Muse to descend. He must learn to do without the Muse! When the fickle jade forgets the way to your studio, don't waste any time in tearing your hair and meditating on suicide. Come round and see me, and I'll show you how to console yourself."

"If I break down," said Roderick passionately, "I shall stay down. If the Muse deserts me she shall at least have her infidelity on her conscience."

"You've no business," Rowland interposed to Gloriani, "to talk lightly of the Muse in this company. Mr. Singleton too has received pledges from her which place her constancy beyond suspicion." And he pointed out on the wall, near by, two small landscapes by the modest water-colourist.

The sculptor examined them with deference, and Singleton himself began to laugh nervously; he was all active with hope that the great Gloriani would be pleased. "Yes, these are fresh too," Gloriani said; "extraordinarily fresh. How old are you?"

"Twenty-six, sir," said Singleton.

"For twenty-six they're famously fresh. They must have taken you a long time; you work slowly."

"Yes, unfortunately I work very slowly. One of them took me six weeks, the other two months."

"Upon my word the Muse pays you long visits." And Gloriani turned and looked from head to foot at so unlikely an object of her favours. Singleton smiled and began to wipe his forehead very hard. "Oh, you," said the sculptor—"you'll keep it up !"

A week after his dinner Rowland went into Roderick's studio and found him sitting before an unfinished piece of work with his head in his hands. He might have fancied that the fatal hour foretold by Gloriani had already of a sudden struck. Roderick rose with sombre decision, flinging down his tools. "It's no use," he said ; "I give it up!"

"What's the matter ?"

"I've struck a shallow ! I was sailing, as you may have seen, before as stiff a breeze as ever was. But for the last day or two my keel has taken to grinding the bottom."

"You've come upon a difficult bit ?" Rowland asked with a sympathetic inflexion and looking vaguely at the roughly-modelled figure.

"Oh, it's all difficult bits ! But it's not the poor old clay. The difficult bit is *here* !" And Roderick struck a blow on his heart. "I don't know what's the matter with me. Nothing comes ; all of a sudden I hate things. My old things look ugly ; everything looks asinine."

Rowland was at first, but only at first, disconcerted. He was in the situation of a man who had been riding a blood-horse at a steady elastic gallop and of a sudden felt him stumble or shy. But he bethought himself that if half the "lift" of intercourse with Roderick was his having fine nerves he himself had no right to enjoy the play of the machine—which was quite definitely what he did enjoy—without some corresponding care for it and worry about it. He immediately recognised the present hour as the very ground of his original act. He saw why he had risked it ; he felt a flood of comradeship rise in his heart which would float them both safely through the worst weather. "Ah, you're simply tired. Of course you're awfully tired," he said. "You've a right to be awfully tired."

"Do you think I've a right to be awfully tired ?" Roderick looked at him rather wanly askance.

"Unquestionably, after all you've done."

"Well, then, right or wrong, I *am* dog-tired. I really must have done a fair winter's work. I want a big change."

Rowland declared that it was certainly high time they should have a big change, time they should be leaving Rome. They would go north and travel. They would go to Switzerland, to Germany, to Holland, to England. Roderick assented, his eye brightened, and Rowland talked of a dozen things they might do. Roderick walked up and down; he seemed to have something to say which he hesitated to bring out. He hesitated so rarely that Rowland wondered and at last asked him what was on his mind. Roderick stopped before him, frowning a little.

"I've such unbounded faith in your extraordinary nature," he said, "that I believe nothing I could ever say would ever offend you."

"Well, try !"

"*Dunque*," Roderick continued, "I think my journey will do me more good if I take it alone. I needn't say I prefer your society to that of any man living. For the last six months it has been a fund of comfort. But I've a feeling that you're always expecting something of me, that you're measuring my doings by a terrifically high standard. You're watching me, my dear fellow, as my mother at home watches the tea-kettle she has set to boil, and the case is that somehow I don't want to be watched. I want to go my own way; to work when I choose and to be a fool, to be even a wretch, when I choose, and the biggest kind of either if necessary. It's not that I don't know what I owe you; it's not that we're not the best friends in the world. It's simply—it's simply—— !"

"It's simply that I bore you," said Rowland.

Roderick sounded his eyes to a depth that almost hurt him. It was as if he were probing for safety. Well, he should have it. Rowland met this long look, and then his friend laughed. "Go and amuse *your*self better too !"

Rowland grasped him by the hand. "I'll do exactly what you desire. I shall miss you, I needn't assure you, and I dare say you'll occasionally give a howl, even, for me. But I've only one request to make—that if you get into trouble of any kind whatever you'll immediately let me know."

They began their journey, however, together, crossing the Alps side by side, muffled in one rug, on the top of the Saint-Gothard coach. Rowland was going to England to pay some promised visits; his companion had no plan save to ramble through Switzerland and Germany as fancy should guide him. He had money that would outlast the summer; when it was spent he would come back to Rome and find the golden mood again awaiting him there. At a little mountain village by the way Roderick declared that he would stop; he would scramble about a little in the high places and doze in the shade of the pine forests. The coach was changing horses; the two young men walked along the village street, picking their way between dunghills, breathing the light cool air and listening to the plash of the fountain and the tinkle of cattle-bells. The coach overtook them, and then Rowland, as he prepared to mount, felt an almost overmastering reluctance.

"Say the word," he exclaimed, "and I'll stay with you."

Roderick looked almost black. "Ah, that shows you don't *really* believe in me—as distinguished from believing in yourself."

Poor Rowland flushed, hesitating but an instant. "Yes, I'm afraid there's no doubt I do believe, where you are concerned, in myself. But 'go it' then, and *buon divertimento*. Good-bye !" Standing in his place as the coach rolled away, he looked back at his friend lingering by the roadside. A great snow mountain behind Roderick was beginning to turn pink in the sunset. The slim and straight young figure waved its hat with a sort of mocking solemnity. Rowland settled himself in his place, reflecting, after all, that this was a salubrious beginning of independence. Roderick was among forests and glaciers, leaning on the pure bosom of nature. And then—and then—was it not in itself a guarantee against folly to be engaged to Mary Garland ?

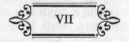

VII

ROWLAND PASSED the summer in England, staying with several old friends and two or three new. On his arrival he had it on his conscience to write to Mrs. Hudson and inform her that her son had relieved him of his tutelage. He felt that she thought of him as an incorruptible Mentor, following Roderick like a shadow, and he wished to let her know the truth. But he made the truth very comfortable and gave a detailed account of the young man's brilliant beginnings. He owed it to himself, he said, to remind her that he had not reasoned amiss, and that Roderick's present achievements were more profitable than his inglorious drudgery at Messrs. Striker and Spooner's. He was now taking a well-earned holiday and proposing to see a little of the world. He would work none the worse for this; every artist needed to take chances and seek impressions for himself. They had parted company for a couple of months, as Roderick was now a great man and beyond the need of going about with a keeper. But they were to meet again in Rome in the autumn, and then he should be able to send her more good news. Meanwhile he was very happy in what Roderick had already done—especially happy in the happiness it must have brought his mother. He ventured to ask to be kindly commended to Miss Garland.

His letter was promptly answered—to his surprise in the hand of the latter lady. The same post brought also an epistle from Cecilia. The document was voluminous, and we must content ourselves with giving an extract.

Your letter was filled with an echo of that brilliant Roman world which made me almost ill with envy. For a week after I got it I thought Northampton quite too abysmally flat. But I am drifting back again to my old deeps of resignation, and I rush to the window when any one passes with all my old gratitude for small favours. So Roderick Hudson is already a great man, and you turn out to be a great prophet? My compliments to both of you; I never saw a trick so prettily played! And he takes it all very quietly and doesn't lose his balance nor let it turn his head? You judged him then in a day better than I had done in six months, for I really never expected he would behave so properly. I believed he would do fine things, but I was sure he would intersperse them with a good many follies, and that his beautiful statues would spring up out of the midst of a dense plantation of wild oats. But from what you tell me Mr. Striker may now go and hang himself. . . . There is one thing, however, to tell you as a friend and in the way of warning. That candid soul can keep a secret, and he may have private designs on your peace of mind. What do you think of his being engaged to marry Mary Garland? The two ladies had given no hint of it all winter, but a fortnight ago, when those big photographs of his statues arrived, they first pinned them up on the wall and then trotted out into the town and made a dozen calls, announcing the great news. Mrs. Hudson did, at least; the young woman herself, I suppose, sat at home writing letters. To me, I confess, the thing was a brutal surprise. I had not a suspicion that all the while he was coming so regularly to make himself agreeable on my verandah he was quietly preferring his queer cousin to all of us. Not indeed that he was ever at particular pains to suggest he preferred *me*! I suppose he has picked up a few graces in your wonderful Rome. He must not pick up too many; if he's too possible when he comes back the young woman will count him as one of the lost. She will be a very good wife for a man of genius, and such a one as they are often shrewd enough to take. She will darn his stockings and keep his accounts, she will sit at home and trim the lamp and keep up the fire, while he studies the Beautiful in pretty neighbours at dinner-parties. The two ladies are evidently very happy and, to do them justice, very humbly grateful to you. Mrs.

Hudson never speaks of you without tears in her eyes, and I'm sure she regards you as our leading philanthropist. Verily, it's a good thing for a woman to be in love; Mary Garland has grown distinctly less plain. I met her the other night at a tea-party; she had a white rose in her hair and sang a sentimental ballad in a fine contralto voice.

Mary Garland's letter was so much shorter that we may give it entire.

MY DEAR SIR,—Mrs. Hudson, as I suppose you know, has been for some time unable to use her eyes. She requests me therefore to answer your beautiful letter of the 22nd of June. She thanks you extremely for writing and wishes me to say that she finds herself under great obligations to you. Your account of her son's progress and of the high esteem in which he is held has made her very happy, and she earnestly prays that all may go on well. He sent us a short time ago several large photographs of his two statues, taken from different points of view. We know little about such things, but they seem to us wonderfully beautiful. We sent them to Boston to be handsomely framed, and the man, on returning them, wrote us that he had exhibited them for a week in his gallery and that they had attracted great attention. The frames are magnificent, and the pictures now hang in a row on the parlour wall. Our only quarrel with them is that they make the old papering and the engravings look dreadfully shabby. Mr. Striker stood and looked at them the other day full five minutes; after which he said that if Roderick's head had been running on such things as those it was no wonder he couldn't learn to draw a deed. We lead here so quiet and monotonous a life that I am afraid I can tell you nothing that will interest you. Mrs. Hudson requests me to say that the little that might happen to us—more or less—is of small importance, as we live in our thoughts, which are fixed on her dear son. She thanks heaven he has so good a friend. Mrs. Hudson says that this is too short a letter, but I can say nothing more.

Yours most respectfully,

MARY GARLAND

It is a question if the reader will know why, but this letter gave Rowland extraordinary pleasure. He liked its shortness, almost its dryness, and there seemed to him an exquisite modesty in its saying nothing from the girl herself. He delighted in the formal address and conclusion; they pleased him as he had been pleased by the angular gesture of some maiden-saint in a primitive painting. The whole thing quickened that impression of fine feeling combined with an almost rigid simplicity which Roderick's betrothed had personally given him. Its homely stiffness showed as the direct reflexion of a life concentrated, as the writer had borrowed warrant from her companion to say, in a single devoted idea. The monotonous days of the two women seemed to Rowland's fancy to follow each other like the tick-tick of a great time-piece marking off the hours which separated them from the supreme felicity of clasping the far-away son and lover to lips sealed with the intensity of joy.

He was left to vain conjectures, however, as to Roderick's own state of mind. He knew his absent friend had scant patience for the pen and would at any time, in his own phrase, rather design a tomb than answer a note. But when a month had passed without news he began to be half anxious and half angry, and addressed the young sculptor three lines, in care of a Continental banker, begging him at least to give some sign of life. A week afterwards came an answer—brief and dated Baden-Baden. "I know I've been a great brute," Roderick wrote, "not to have sent you a word before; but really I don't know what has got into me. I've lately learned terribly well how to do nothing. I'm afraid to think how long it is since I wrote to my mother or to Mary. Heaven help them—poor patient trustful creatures ! I don't know how to tell you what I am doing or not doing. It seems all amusing enough while it lasts, but it would make a poor show as an apology and a still poorer as a boast. I found Baxter in Switzerland, or rather he found me, and he grabbed me by the arm and brought me here. I was walking twenty miles a day in the Alps, drinking milk in lonely châlets, sleeping as *you* sleep, and thinking it was all very good fun; but Baxter told me it would never do, that the Alps were 'damned rot,' that Baden-Baden was 'the cheese,' and that if I knew what was good for me I would come along with him. It is a wonderful place certainly, though, thank the Lord, Baxter departed last week, blaspheming horribly at *trente-et-quarante*. But you know all about it, and what one does—what one is liable to do. I've succumbed, in a measure, to the liabilities, and I wish I had some one here to give me a kicking. Not you—you would kick me with your boots off; you're too generous ever to do me any real good. What do you think of that for thanks ? I've fits of horrible home-sickness for my studio, and I shall be devoutly grateful when the summer is over and I can go back and potter about there. I feel as if nothing but the chisel and a sledge-hammer would satisfy me; as if in fact I could tear a figure straight out of the block even as Michael of old. There are a lot of Roman people here, English and American; I live in the midst of them and talk nonsense from morning till night. There's also some one else; and to her I don't talk sense, nor, thank goodness, mean what I say. I confess I need a month's work to take out of my mouth the taste of so many lies."

These lines brought Rowland a due perturbation; the more that what they seemed to point to surprised him. During the long stretch of their comradeship Roderick had shown so little impatience to see what was vulgarly called life that he had come to think of that possibility as a cancelled danger, and it greatly perplexed him to learn that his friend had apparently proved so pliant to opportunity. But Roderick's allusions were ambiguous, and it was possible they might simply mean that he was out of humour with idleness and mere personal success—he could so easily have so much of that—and was fretting wholesomely over his absent work. It was a very good thing certainly that tried debauchery should so particularly *not* lead him on. Nevertheless the letter needed to Rowland's mind a key: the key arrived a week later. "In common charity," Roderick wrote, "lend me a hundred pounds! I've gambled away my last franc—I've made a villainous heap of debts. Send me the money first; lecture me afterwards!" Rowland sent the money by return of post; then he proceeded, not to lecture, but to think. He hung his head—he was acutely disappointed. He had no right to be, he assured himself; but so it was. Roderick was young, impulsive, unpractised in stoicism; it was a hundred to one that he was to pay the usual vulgar tribute to folly. But his friend had regarded it as securely gained to his own belief in virtue that he was not as other foolish youths are, and that he would have been capable of looking Folly in the face, for all her bells, and passing on his way. Rowland for a while felt a sore sense of wrath. What right had a man who was engaged to that delightful girl in Northampton to behave as if his consciousness were a common blank, to be filled in with coarse sensations? Yes, distinctly, he had lost an illusion, an illusion that he had loved. He had accompanied his missive with an urgent recommendation that Baden-Baden should immediately be quitted, and with an offer to meet the young traveller at any point the latter might name. The answer came promptly; it ran as follows: "Send me another fifty pounds! I'm a bigger donkey than ever. I will leave as soon as the money comes, and meet you at Geneva. There I will tell you everything."

There is an ancient terrace at Geneva, planted with trees and studded with benches, overlooked by stately houses and overlooking the distant Alps. A great many generations have made it a lounging place, a great many friends and lovers strolled there, a great many confidential talks and momentous interviews gone forward. Here one morning, sitting on one of the battered green benches, Roderick, as he had promised, told his friend everything. He had arrived the previous evening; he looked like the battered knight who yet sports a taller plume. He made no professions of penitence, but he practised an unmitigated frankness, and his remorse might be taken for granted. He conveyed in every phrase that he had done with the flesh and the devil and was counting the hours till he should re-enter the true temple of his faith. We shall not rehearse his confession in detail; its main outline serves our turn. He had fallen in with people who really knew how to be low—which he, poor wretch, didn't, only he had thought it, in their company, a trick to be learnt. What could he do? He never read books and he had no studio; in one way or another he had to pass the time. He passed it in dangling about several very pretty women and reflecting that it was always something gained for a sculptor to sit under a tree looking at his leisure into a charming face and saying things that made it smile and play its muscles and part its lips and show its teeth. Attached to these ladies were gentlemen with wonderful names, poly-glot ambrosial gentlemen who walked about in clouds of fragrance, called him *mon cher*, sat at roulette all night and supped the next morning. Roderick had found himself in a mood for thinking them types of a high, even if a somewhat spent, civilisation. He was surprised at his curiosity, but he let it take its course. It led him to the discovery that to live with ladies almost crudely on the look-out for mementoes of friendship, even if in no more permanent form than that of expensive bouquets and of bushels of *bonbons*, and for rides in the Black Forest on shining hired horses, who expected a fellow, further, to arrange parties for the opera on nights when Patti sang and the prices were consequent, to propose light suppers at the Kursaal or drives by moon-light to the Castle, to be always arrayed and anointed and under arms for their service—that to move in such society, we say, though it might be a privilege, was a privilege with a penalty attached. But the tables made such things easy; half the Baden world lived by the tables. Roderick tried them, and found them at first a wonderful help. The help, however, was all fallacious, for he soon perceived that to seem to have money, and to have it in fact, exposed an eager and confident youth to peculiar liabilities. As his friend's narrative sailed closer Rowland was reminded of Madame de Cruchecassée in Thackeray's novel, but of a Madame de Cruchecassée mature and quasi-maternal, attached as with a horrible sincerity to her prey, and though he had listened in tranquil silence to the rest of it he found it hard not to say that all this had been, for a young man in his particular position, about as gratuitous a mistake as possible. Roderick admitted it with bitterness; and then told how much—measured simply in vulgar cash—the mistake had cost him. His luck had changed, the tables had ceased to back him, and he found himself up to his knees in debt. Every penny had gone of the solid sum which had seemed a large equivalent of those shining statues in Rome. He had been an ass, but it was not irreparable; he could make another statue in a couple of months.

Rowland looked, at this, conscientiously blank. "For God's sake," he said, "don't play such dangerous games with your facility. If you've got facility, respect it, nurse it, adore it, save it up in an old stocking —don't speculate on it." And he wondered what his companion, up to his knees in debt, would have done if there had been no good-natured Rowland Mallet to lend a helping hand. But he didn't express his curiosity in words, and the contingency seemed not to have presented itself to Roderick's imagination. The young sculptor reverted to his late adventures again in the evening, and this time talked of them more objectively, as the phrase is; with a detachment that flowered little by little into free anecdote—quite as if they had been the adventures of some other, some different, ass. He related half a dozen droll things that had happened to him, and, as if his responsibility had been disengaged by all this ventilation, wondered, with laughter, that such absurdities *could* have been. Rowland sat perfectly grave—he kept it up on principle. Then Roderick began to talk of half a dozen plastic ideas that he had in his head, and set them forth with his old inimitable touch. Suddenly, as it was relevant, he declared that his Baden doings had not been altogether fruitless, for the lady who had reminded Rowland of Madame de Cruchecassée had, poor dear, in her make-up, some wonderful, beautiful lines. Rowland at last said that such expriements might pass if one felt one was really the wiser for them. "By the wiser," he sententiously added, "I mean the stronger in reconsidered and confirmed purpose, in acquired will-power."

"Oh, don't talk about such dreadful things !" Roderick answered, throwing back his head and looking at the stars. This conversation also took place in the open air, on the little island in the rushing Rhone where Jean-Jacques, himself so far from remarkable for the control of his course, is enthroned in bronze as the genius of the spot.

"The will, it seems to me, is an abyss of abysses and a riddle of riddles. Who can answer for his properly having one? who can say beforehand that it's going in a given case to be worth anything at all? There are all kinds of uncanny underhand currents moving to and fro between one's will and the rest of one—one's imagination in particular. People talk as if the two things were essentially distinct; on different sides of one's organism, like the heart and the liver. Mine, I know—that is my imagination and my conscience—are much nearer together. It all depends upon circumstances. I believe there's a certain group of circumstances possible for every man, in which his power to choose is destined to snap like a dry twig."

"My dear man," said Rowland, "don't talk about any part of you that has a grain of character in it being 'destined.' The power to choose *is* destiny. That's the way to look at it."

"Look at it, my good Rowland," Roderick answered, "as you find most comfortable. One conviction I've gathered from my summer's experience," he went on—"it's as well to look *it* frankly in the face— is that I'm damnably susceptible, by nature, to the grace and the beauty and the mystery of women, to their power to turn themselves 'on' as creatures of subtlety and perversity. So there you have me."

Rowland, so "having" him, stared, and then strolled away, softly whistling to himself. He was unwilling to admit even tacitly that this speech had really the ominous meaning it seemed to have. In a few days the two young men made their way back to Italy and lingered a while in Florence before going on to Rome. In Florence Roderick appeared to have recovered his old innocence and his preference for the pleasures of study. Rowland began to think of the Baden episode as a bad dream, or at the worst one of the plunges, really touching bottom, that the plunger with the brine of the deep sea in his mouth doesn't need, or never has wind again, to repeat. They passed a fortnight looking at pictures and exploring for out-of-the-way remnants of fresco and carving, and Roderick exhibited all his earlier energy of appreciation and criticism. In Rome he went almost pompously to work, finishing in a month two or three small things he had left standing on his departure. He talked the most joyous nonsense about finding himself back in his old quarters. On the first Sunday following their return, at their going together in the afternoon to Saint Peter's, he delivered himself of a mystic greeting to the great church, and to the city in general, in a manner so uplifted that his voice rang quite publicly through the nave and arrested a procession of ecclesiastics on their march to the choir. He began to model a new image—a female figure of which he had said nothing to Rowland. It represented a woman leaning lazily back in her chair, with her head inclined in apparent attention, a vague smile on her lips and a pair of remarkably beautiful arms folded in her lap. With something less of its emphasised grace it would have recalled the noble statue of Agrippina in the Capitol. Rowland looked at it and was not sure he liked it. It differed singularly from anything his friend had yet done. "Who is it? what does it mean?" he asked.

"Anything you please!" said Roderick with a certain petulance. "A 'Lady conversing affably with a Gentleman.'"

Rowland then remembered that one of the Baden-Baden conversers had had wonderful "lines," and here perhaps they were. But he asked no more questions. This, after all, was a way of profiting by experience. A few days later he took his first ride of the season on the Campagna, and as he on his homeward canter was passing across the long shadow of a ruined tower he perceived a small figure at a short distance bent over a sketch-book. As he drew near he recognised Sam Singleton. The honest little painter's face was scorched to flame-colour by the light of southern suns, and borrowed an even deeper crimson from his gleeful greeting of his most appreciative patron. He was making a careful and charming sketch. On Rowland's asking him how he had spent his summer he gave an account of his wanderings which made our poor friend sigh with a sense of more contrasts than one. He had not been out of Italy, but had delved deep into the historic heart of the lovely land and gathered a wonderful store of subjects. He had rambled about among the unvisited villages of the Apennines, pencil in hand and knapsack on back, sleeping on straw and eating black bread and beans, but feasting on local colour, making violent love to opportunity and laying up a treasure of reminiscences. He took a devout satisfaction in his hard-earned results and his successful economy. Rowland went the next day by appointment to look at his sketches, and spent a whole morning turning them over. Singleton talked more than he had ever done before, explained them all, and told some honest anecdote, mainly comical and at the expense of his knowledge of "life," about the production of each.

"Dear me, how I've chattered!" he finally sighed. "I'm afraid you would rather have looked at the things in peace and quiet. I didn't know I could talk so much. But somehow I feel very happy; I feel as if I had taken a kind of stride."

"That you have," said Rowland. "I doubt whether *any* patient worker ever took a longer in the time. You must feel much more sure of yourself."

Singleton looked for some moments with great interest at a knot in the floor. "Yes," he ventured at last to acknowledge, "I feel much more sure of myself. I know better what I'm about." And his voice dropped as if he were communicating a secret which it took some courage to impart. "I hardly like to say it, for fear I should after all be mistaken. But since it strikes you, perhaps it's true. It's a great happiness; I wouldn't exchange it for a great deal of money."

"Yes, I suppose it's a great happiness," said Rowland. "I shall really think of you as living here in a state of scandalous bliss. I don't feel it's quite decent for an artist to know so well what he's about."

Singleton stared a moment, as if he supposed his visitor in earnest; then with a vision of the kindly jest he walked about the room agitating his head and shyly laughing. "And Mr. Hudson ?" he said as Rowland was going; "I hope he's as great as ever."

"He's very well—for *him*. He's back at work again."

"Ah, there's a man," cried Singleton, "who has taken his start once for all and doesn't need to stop and ask himself in fear and trembling every month or two whether he's going on. When he stops it's to rest ! And where did he spend the summer ?"

"The greater part of it at Baden-Baden."

"Ah, that's in the Black Forest," cried Singleton with profound simplicity. "They say you can make ripping studies of trees there."

"No doubt," said Rowland with a smile, laying an almost paternal hand on the little artist's stooping shoulders. "Unhappily trees are not Roderick's line. Nevertheless he tells me that at Baden he made some studies—and I gather that they were, in a manner, ripping. Come when you can, by the way," he added after a moment, "to his studio, and tell me what you think of something he has lately begun."

Singleton declared that he would come delightedly, and Rowland left him at his work.

He met a number of his last winter's friends and found that Madame Grandoni, Miss Blanchard and Gloriani had again taken up the golden thread of Roman life. The ladies gave an excellent account of themselves: Madame Grandoni had been taking sea-baths at Rimini and Miss Blanchard painting wild flowers in the Tyrol. Her complexion was somewhat browned, which was very becoming, and her flowers tossed their heads and rolled their eyes like so many little poetesses looking for rhymes. Gloriani had been in Paris and had come away in high good-humour, finding no one there in the artist-world with as long a head as his own. He came in a few days to Roderick's studio, one afternoon when Rowland was present. He examined the new figure with great deference, pronounced it tremendously *trouvé*, and abstained considerably from irritating prophecies. But Rowland fancied he observed certain signs of inward jubilation on the subtle sculptor's part, and walked away with him to learn his private opinion.

"Certainly; I liked it as well as I said," Gloriani declared in answer to Rowland's anxious query; "or rather I liked it a great deal better. I didn't say how much, for fear of making your friend angry. But one can leave him alone now, for he's coming round. I told you he couldn't keep up that flapping of his wings in the blue, and he has already come down to earth. Don't you see what I mean?"

"I don't particularly like the thing, you know," Rowland confessed.

"That's because you yourself try to sit like an angel on a cloud. This present idea of Hudson's is full of possibilities, and he'll pull some of them off; but it isn't the *sancta simplicitas* of a few months ago. He has taken his turn sooner than I supposed. What has happened to him? Has he been disappointed in love? But that's none of my business. I congratulate him on having found his feet—or at least found such a smart pair of shoes."

Roderick, however, was less to be congratulated than Gloriani had taken it into his head to believe. He was discontented with his work, he applied himself to it by fits and starts, he declared that he didn't know what was in store for him; he was turning into a man of moods. "Is this of necessity what a fellow must come to?" he asked of Rowland with a peremptory flash in his eye, a look seeming to imply that his companion had undertaken to insure him against perplexities and was not fulfilling his contract—"this damnable uncertainty when one goes to bed at night as to whether one is going to wake up in an ecstasy or in a tantrum? Have we only a season, over before we know it, in which to call our faculties our own? Six months ago I could stand up to my work like a man, day after day, and never dream of asking myself how I felt. But now, some mornings, it's the very devil to get going. My experiment looks so base when I come into the studio that I've twenty minds to smash it on the spot, and I lose three or four hours in sitting there moping and getting used to it."

Rowland said that he supposed that these changes of intellectual weather, these occasional obscurations of the mere staring sun were the lot of every poet—and what was the sculptor but the poet of the corporeal? So that the only remedy was plenty of courage and faith. And he reminded him, with a rare failure of tact perhaps, of Gloriani's having forewarned him the year before against the apparent lapse of the mere "inspired" state.

"Gloriani's a murderous mountebank!" Roderick fiercely replied. "He has got a bag of tricks and he comes with it to his studio as a conjurer comes for twenty francs to a children's party. Faugh!" He hired a horse, and began to ride with Rowland on the Campagna. This admirable exercise restored him in a measure to the appearance of felicity, but it seemed to Rowland on the whole not to stimulate his diligence. Their rides were always drawn out, and Roderick insisted on making them longer by dismounting in picturesque spots and stretching himself, in the golden air, on some mild mass of over-tangled stones. He let the Roman sky smile upon him with an intensity that his companion found more embarrassing. But in this situation he talked so much amusing nonsense that, for the sake of his company, Rowland consented to risk sunstroke and often forgot that, though in these diversions the days passed quickly, they produced neither the art of the market nor that of the temple. And yet it was perhaps by their help, after all, that Roderick secured several mornings of ardent work on his new figure and brought it forward in three or four bold jumps. One afternoon when it was practically finished Rowland went to look at it, and Roderick asked for his opinion.

"What do you think yourself?" Rowland demanded—not from pusillanimity, but from real uncertainty.

"I think it curiously, almost interestingly bad," Roderick answered. "It was false from the first; it has fundamental vices. I've shuffled them out of sight by a hocus-pocus for which I blush, but I haven't corrected them. I can't—I can't—I can't!" he cried passionately. "They stare me in the face—they're all I see!"

Rowland offered several criticisms of detail and suggested certain practical changes. But Roderick differed with him on each of these points; the thing had faults enough, but they were not *those* faults. Rowland, unruffled, concluded by saying that whatever its faults might be, he had an idea people in general would admire it.

"I wish to heaven some person in particular—but not you again, confound you!" Roderick cried—"would buy it and take it off my hands and out of my sight! What am I to do now?" he almost imperiously went on. "I haven't a blamed idea. I think of subjects, but they remain mere idiotic names. They're mere words—they're not images. What am I to do?"

Rowland was a trifle annoyed. "Be a man," he was on the point of saying, "and don't, for heaven's sake, talk in that confoundedly querulous voice!" But before he had uttered the words there rang through the studio a loud peremptory ring at the outer door.

Roderick broke into a laugh. "Talk of the devil and you seé his horns! If that's not a customer, for poetic justice, it ought to be."

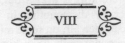

VIII

THE DOOR of the studio was promptly flung open, and a lady advanced to the threshold—an imposing voluminous person who quite filled up the doorway. Rowland immediately felt that he had seen her before, but he recognised her only when she moved forward and disclosed an attendant in the person of a little bright-eyed elderly gentleman with a bristling white moustache. Then he remembered that just a year before he and his companion had seen in the Ludovisi gardens a wonderfully beautiful girl strolling in the train of this conspicuous couple. He looked for her now, and in a moment she appeared, following her companions with the same maidenly majesty as before and leading her great snow-white poodle, who was decorated as before with motley ribbons. The elder lady offered the two young men a sufficiently gracious salute; the little old gentleman bowed and smiled with extreme deference. The young girl, without casting a glance either at Roderick or at Rowland, looked about for a chair and, on perceiving one, sank into it listlessly, pulled her poodle towards her and began to re-arrange his top-knot. Rowland saw that, even with her eyes dropped, her beauty was still dazzling.

"I trust we're at liberty to enter," said the elder lady with urbanity. "We were told that Mr. Hudson has no fixed *jour* and that we might come at any time. Let us not disturb you."

Roderick, as one of the newer lights of the Roman art-world, had not hitherto been subject to incursions from inquisitive tourists and, having no regular reception-day, was not versed in the usual arts of

Italian squire apparently divined Rowland's mute imaginings, for he stepped with a conciliatory flourish into the breach. "I've not done my duty," he remarked, "in not announcing these ladies. Madama Light, Mees Light !"

Rowland was not materially the wiser for this information, but Roderick was roused by it to the exercise of some slight civility. He altered the lighting, pulled forward two or three figures and made an apology for not having more to show. "I don't pretend to have anything of an exhibition—I'm only a novice."

"Indeed ?—a novice ! For a novice this will certainly pass," Mrs. Light declared. "Cavaliere, we've seen nothing better than this."

The Cavaliere smiled rapturously. "It's stupendous !" he murmured. "And we've been to all the studios."

"Not to all—goodness gracious !" cried Mrs. Light. "But to a number that I've had pointed out by artistic friends. I delight in studios —I should have been so happy myself to be a little quiet artist ! And if you're a novice, Mr. Hudson," she went on, "you've already great admirers. Half a dozen people have told us that yours were quite among the things to see." This amiability, however, went unanswered ; Roderick had already wandered across to the other side of the studio and was revolving about Miss Light. "Ah, he's gone to look at my beautiful daughter ; he's not the first that has had his head turned," the irrepressible lady resumed, lowering her voice to a confidential undertone ; a favour which, considering the shortness of their acquaintance, Rowland was bound to appreciate. "The artists are all crazy about her. When she goes into a studio she's fatal to the pictures. And when she goes into the ball-room what do the other women say ? Eh, Cavaliere mio ?"

"She's very very beautiful," Rowland said simply.

Mrs. Light, who through her long gold-cased glasses was looking a little at everything and at nothing as if she saw it, interrupted her random murmurs and exclamations and surveyed Rowland from head to foot. She eyed him all over ; apparently he had not been mentioned to her as a feature of Roderick's establishment. It was the challenge, Rowland felt, which the vigilant and ambitious mother of a beautiful daughter has always at her command for well-appointed young men. Her inspection in this case seemed satisfactory. "Are you also an artist ?" she inquired with an almost affectionate inflexion. It was clear that what she meant was something of this kind : "Be so good as to assure me without delay that you're really the rather manageable young man of fortune that you appear."

But Rowland answered only the formal question—not the latent one. "Dear me, no; I'm merely a poor friend of Mr. Hudson's."

Mrs. Light, with a sigh, returned to the statues and, after mistaking the Adam for a gladiator and the Eve for a gypsy, declared she could never judge of such things unless she saw them in the marble. Rowland hesitated a moment and then, speaking in the interest of Roderick's renown, said that he was the happy possessor of several of his friend's works and that she was welcome to come and see them at his rooms. She bade the Cavaliere, with alacrity, make a note of his address. "Ah, you're, for your pleasure, a protector of the arts," she said. "That's what I should like to be if I had a little money. I revel in beauty in every form. But all these people ask such monstrous prices. One must be a millionaire to think of such things, eh? Twenty years ago my husband had my portrait painted, here in Rome, by Papucci, who was the great man in those days. I was in a ball-dress, with my famous jewels and my bare shoulders and arms, which were then rather famous too—were not at any rate a *petite affaire*. The man got six hundred francs and thought he was very well treated. Those were the days when a family could live like princes in Italy for five thousand scudi a year. The Cavaliere once upon a time was a great dandy—don't blush, Cavaliere: any one can see that, just as any one can see what *I* was! Get him to tell you what he made a figure upon. The railroads have brought in the vulgarians. That's what I call it now—the invasion of the vulgarians! What are poor *we* to do?"

Rowland had begun to murmur some remedial proposition when he was interrupted by the voice of Miss Light calling across the room, "Mamma!"

"My own love?"

"This gentleman wishes to model my bust. Please speak to him about it."

The Cavaliere emitted a sound between a growl and a giggle. "Already? *Santo Dio!*" he cried.

Rowland looked round, equally surprised at the promptitude of the proposal. Roderick stood planted before the girl with his arms folded, looking at her as he would have done at the Medicean Venus. He never paid cheap compliments, and Rowland, though he had not heard him speak, could imagine the startling distinctness with which he made his request.

112

"He saw me a year ago," Miss Light went on, "and he has been thinking of me ever since." Her mode of speech was peculiar; it had a kind of studied inexpressiveness which was yet not the conscious drawl of affectation.

"I *must* make your daughter's bust—that's all, madam!" cried Roderick with warmth.

"I would rather you should make the poodle's," this young lady returned. "Is it very very tiresome? I've spent half my life sitting for my photograph, in every conceivable attitude and with every conceivable coiffure. It seems to me I've posed enough."

"My dear child," said Mrs. Light, "it may be one's duty to pose! But as to my daughter's sitting to you, sir—to a young artist whom we don't know—it's a matter that one must look at a little. It's not a favour that's to be had for the mere asking."

"If I don't make her from life," Roderick replied with energy, "I'll make her from memory, and if the thing's to be done you had better have it done as well as possible."

"Mamma hesitates," Miss Light explained, "because she doesn't know whether you mean she shall pay you for the bust or you'll pay me for the sitting. She's capable of thinking of *that*, mamma. I can assure you at least that she won't pay you a sou."

"My daughter, you forget yourself," said the poor lady with an attempt at a high tone. "Of course," she added in a moment with a change of note, "the bust would be my own property."

"Of course!" cried Roderick impatiently.

"Dearest mother," the girl interposed, "how can you carry another stone image about the world with you? Isn't it enough to drag the poor original?"

"My dear, you're talking great nonsense," Mrs. Light curtly pronounced.

"You can always get something for it," the girl pursued with the same practised innocence. "You always get something for everything. I daresay that with patience you'll still get something even for me."

Mrs. Light turned to Rowland, who was sorry for her, flushed and irritated. "She's as wicked to-day as she knows how to be, and that's saying a good deal!"

The Cavaliere grinned in silence and walked away on tiptoe with his hat to his lips, as if to leave the field clear for action. Rowland, on the contrary, wished to mediate. "You had better not refuse," he said to Miss Light, "until you've seen Mr. Hudson's things in the marble. Your mother's to come and look at some that I possess."

"Thank you; I've no doubt you'll see us. I daresay Mr. Hudson's very clever; but I don't care for modern sculpture. I can't look at it."

"You shall care for my bust, I promise you!" Roderick declared with a laugh.

"To satisfy Miss Light," said the Cavaliere, "one of the old Greeks ought to come to life."

"It would be worth his while," said Roderick, acquitting himself, to Rowland's knowledge, of his first public *madrigal*.

"I might sit to Phidias if he would promise to be very amusing and make me laugh. What do you say, Stenterello? would *you* sit to Phidias?"

"We must talk of this some other time," said Mrs. Light. "We're in Rome for the winter. Many thanks. Cavaliere, call the carriage." The Cavaliere led the way out, backing like a silver-stick, and Miss Light, following her mother, nodded, without looking at them, to each of the young men.

"Immortal powers, what a head!" cried Roderick when they were gone. "There's my fortune—on that girl's two feet."

"She's certainly very beautiful," said Rowland. "But I'm sorry you've undertaken her bust."

"And why, pray?"

"I suspect it will bring trouble."

"What kind of trouble?"

"I hardly know. They're queer people. The mamma strikes me as a good bit of an adventuress. Heaven knows what the daughter may be."

"The daughter's simply a breathing goddess," Roderick instantly returned.

"Just so. She's all the more dangerous."

"Dangerous? What will she do to me? She doesn't bite, I imagine."

"It remains to be seen. There are two kinds of women—you ought to know by this time—the safe and the unsafe. Besides, there's more than one way of biting—and I thought you had *been* bitten."

"My dear man," smiled Roderick very boldly, "with you to plaster me up——!" But he broke off—only to fall gaily a-whistling: a demonstration addressed apparently to the advent, as he had said, of his fortune.

In calling this young lady and her mamma queer people Rowland had perhaps too crudely betrayed his now alert sense for possible complications. They were so marked a variation from the monotonous troop of his compatriots that he felt much curiosity as to the sources of the change, especially since he doubted greatly whether on the whole it elevated the type. During the next week he saw the two ladies driving daily in a well-appointed landau, with the Cavaliere and the poodle in the front seat. From Mrs. Light he received a gracious salute, tempered by her native majesty; but the young girl, looking straight before her, seemed profoundly indifferent to observers. Her extraordinary beauty, however, had already made observers numerous and given the haunters of the Pincian plenty to talk about. The echoes of their commentary reached Rowland's ears; but he had little taste for raw rumour and preferred it responsibly prepared. It was so supplied him by Madame Grandoni, to whom Mrs. Light and her wonderful daughter had been from of old familiar objects.

"I've known the mamma for twenty years," said this judicious critic, "and if you ask any of the people who have been living here as long as I, you will find they remember her well. I've held the beautiful Christina on my knee when she was a little wizened baby with a very red face and no promise of beauty but those magnificent eyes. Ten years ago Mrs. Light disappeared, and was not afterwards seen in Rome, except for a few days, not long since, when she passed through on her way to Naples. Then it was you met the trio in the Ludovisi gardens. When I first knew her she was the unmarried but very marriageable daughter of an old American painter of very bad landscapes, which people used to buy from charity and use for fire-boards. His name was Savage; it used to make every one laugh, he was such a mild, melancholy, pitiful old personage. He had married a horrible wife, an Englishwoman who had been on the stage. It was said she used to beat poor Savage with his mahlstick and, when the domestic finances were low, to lock him up in his studio and tell him he shouldn't come out until he had painted half a dozen of his daubs. She had a good deal of showy beauty. She would go forth with the key in her pocket and, her beauty assisting, she would make certain people take the pictures. It helped her at last to make an English lord run away with her. At the time I speak of she had quite disappeared. Mrs. Light was then a very handsome girl, though by no means so handsome as her daughter has now become. Mr. Light was an American consul, newly appointed at one of the Adriatic ports. He was a mild, fair-whiskered young man, with some little property, and my impression

115

is that he had got into bad company at home and his family had procured him his place to keep him out of harm's way. He was at any rate clearly a gentleman. He came up to Rome on a holiday, fell in love with Miss Savage and married her on the spot. He had not been married three years when he was drowned in the Adriatic, no one ever knew how. The young widow came back to Rome, to her father, and here shortly afterwards, in the dear shadow of Saint Peter's, her little girl was born. It might have been supposed that Mrs. Light would marry again, and I know she had opportunities. But she overreached herself. She would take nothing less than a title and a fortune, and they were not forthcoming. She was admired and very fond of admiration; very vain, very worldly, very silly. She remained a pretty widow with a surprising variety of bonnets and a dozen men always in her train. Giacosa dates from this period. He calls himself a Roman, but I've an impression he came up from Ancona with her. He was *l'ami de la maison*. He used to hold her bouquets, clean her gloves and satin shoes, run her errands, get her opera-boxes, fight her battles with the shopkeepers. For this he needed courage, for she was smothered in debt. She at last left Rome to escape her creditors. Many of them must remember her still, but she seems now to have money to satisfy them. She left her poor old father here alone—helpless, infirm and unable to work. A subscription was shortly afterwards taken up among the foreigners, and he was sent back to America, where, as I finally heard, he died in some sort of asylum. From time to time, for several years, I heard vaguely of Mrs. Light as a wandering beauty at French and German watering-places. Once came a rumour that she was going to make a grand marriage in England; then we heard that the gentleman had thought better of it and left her to keep afloat as she could. She was a terribly scatter-brained creature. She pretends to be a great lady—*Dieu sait pourquoi !*—but I consider that old Filomena, my washerwoman, is in essentials a greater one. Certainly, after all, however, she has been fortunate. She embarked at last on a lawsuit about some property with her husband's family, and went to America to attend to it. She came back triumphant, with a long purse. She reappeared in Italy and established herself for a while in Venice. Then she came to Florence, where she spent a couple of years and where I saw her. Last year she passed down to Naples, which I should have said was just the place for her, and this winter she has laid siege to Rome. She seems very prosperous. She has taken a floor in the Palazzo Falconieri, she keeps her carriage, and Christina and she, between them, must have a pretty milliner's bill. Giacosa has turned up again, looking like one of those collapsed balloons, that children play with, blown out again for the occasion."

"What sort of education," Rowland attentively asked, "do you suppose the mother's adventures to have been for the daughter?"

"A strange school enough. But Mrs. Light told me in Florence that she had given her child the education of a princess. In other words, I suppose she speaks three or four languages and has read several hundred French novels. Christina, I imagine, has plenty of wit—also plenty of will. When I saw her at that same time I was amazed at her beauty, and certainly if there be any truth in faces she ought to have the soul of an angel. Perhaps she has. I don't judge her; she's an extraordinary young person. She has been told twenty times a day by her mother, since she was five years old, that she's a beauty of beauties, that her face is her fortune, that she was born for great things, and that if she plays her cards she may marry God knows whom. If she has not been quite ruined she's a very decent creature. My own impression is that, like the most interesting people always, she's a mixture of better and worse, of good passions and bad—always of passions, however; and that, whatever she is, she's neither stupid nor mean and possibly, by a miracle, not even false. Mrs. Light having failed to make her own fortune in matrimony, has transferred her hopes to her daughter and nursed them till they've become a craze. She has a hobby, which she rides in secret; but some day she'll let you see it. I'm sure that if you go in some evening unannounced you'll find her studying the tea-leaves in her cup or telling her daughter's fortune with a greasy pack of cards. She reminds me, like that, of some extravagant old woman in a novel—in something of Hoffmann or Balzac, something even of your own Thackeray. She promises the girl a prince—a reigning prince. But if Mrs. Light's a fool she can still count on her fingers, and lest considerations of state should deny her potentate the luxury of a love-match she keeps on hand a few common mortals. At the worst she would take a duke, an English lord, or even a young American with a proper number of millions. The poor woman can certainly never lie quiet, she's unacquainted with the luxury of repose. She's always building castles and knocking them down again—always casting her nets and pulling them in. If her daughter were less of a beauty her pretensions would be grotesque; but there's something in the girl, as one looks at her, that seems to make it very possible she may be marked out for one of those romantic fortunes that history now and then relates. 'Who, after all, was the Empress of the French?' Mrs. Light is for ever saying. 'And beside Christina the Empress is a dowdy ! '"

"And what does Christina say ?"

"She makes no scruple, as you know, of saying that she wouldn't mind her mother's idiocy if it wasn't for her vulgarity. What she 'thinks' goodness knows. I suspect that practically she doesn't commit herself. She's excessively proud, and holds herself fit for the highest station in the world; but she knows that her mother would make her ridiculous if anything could, and that even she herself might look awkward in making unsuccessful advances. So she remains sublimely detached and lets mamma take the risks. If the prince is captured so much the better; if he's not she need never confess to herself that even a reigning sovereign has slighted her."

"Your report's as solid," Rowland said to Madame Grandoni, thanking her, "as if it had been drawn up for the Academy of Sciences"; and he congratulated himself on having listened to it when a couple of days later Mrs. Light and her daughter, attended by the Cavaliere and the poodle, came to his rooms to look at Roderick's statues. It was more comfortable to know just with whom he was dealing.

Mrs. Light was prodigiously gracious and showered down compliments not only on the statues but on all his possessions. "Upon my word," she said, "you rich young men know how to make yourselves comfortable. If one of us poor women had half as many easy-chairs and nick-nacks we should be famously abused. It's really selfish to be living all alone in such a place as this. Cavaliere, how should you like this suite of rooms and a fortune to fill them with pictures and *bibelots* ? Christina love, look at that mosaic table. Mr. Mallet, I could almost beg it from you ! Yes, that Eve is certainly very fine. We needn't be ashamed of such a great-grandmother as that. If she was really such a beautiful woman it accounts for the good looks of some of us. Where's Mr. Roderick, whom we all the other day fell in love with— we thought him handsomer than any of his figures. Why isn't he here to be complimented ?"

Christina had remained but a moment in the chair Rowland placed for her, had given but a cursory glance at the statues, and then, leaving her seat, had begun to wander round the room—looking at herself in the mirrors, touching the ornaments and curiosities, glancing at the books and prints. Rowland's saloon was encumbered with valuable pieces, and she found plenty of occupation. Rowland presently joined her and pointed out some of the objects supposed to be interesting.

"It's an odd jumble, you know," she said frankly. "Some things are very good—some are very ugly. But I like ugly things when they have a certain look. Prettiness is terribly vulgar nowadays, and it's not every one that knows just the sort of ugliness that's amusing. However, there are more people now that are horridly knowing than not—and the only nice thing, I think, really is to be as ignorant as a fish. We *can't* be though, you or I, unfortunately, can we? we're so awfully intelligent. We're born to know and to suffer, aren't we?" With which, suddenly, she broke off. "I like looking at people's things," she then went on, turning to Rowland and resting her lovely eyes on him. "It helps you to find out their characters."

"Am I to suppose," asked Rowland smiling, "that you've arrived at any conclusions as to mine?"

"I'm rather *intriguée*; you have too many things; one seems to contradict another. You're very artistic and yet you're very prosaic; you have what is called a 'catholic' taste, and yet you're full of obstinate little prejudices and preferences which, if I knew you, I should find very tiresome. I don't think I like you."

"You make a great mistake," laughed Rowland. "I assure you I'm worth liking."

"Yes, I'm probably wrong, and if I knew you I should find out I was wrong, and that would irritate me and make me dislike you more. So you see we're necessarily enemies."

"No, I don't at all object to *you*."

"Worse and worse; for you certainly will never get any good of me."

"You're very discouraging then."

"I'm fond of facing the truth, though some day you'll deny even that. Where's the young man of genius?" she pursued—"whom I'm not, in spite of my mother, in love with!"

"You mean my friend Hudson? He's represented by these beautiful works."

Miss Light looked for some moments at the objects in question. "Yes," she said, "they're not so silly as most of the things we've seen. They've no beastly chic, and yet they're beautiful."

"You describe them perfectly," said Rowland. "They're beautiful, and yet they've no beastly chic. That's it!"

"If he'll promise to put no beastly chic into my bust I've a mind to let him make it. A request made in those terms deserves to be granted."

"In what terms?"

"Didn't you hear him? 'Mademoiselle, you almost come up to

one of my dreams. I must model your bust.' That *almost* should be rewarded ! He's like me, he likes to face the truth. No, I'm not in love with him, but I think we should get on together."

The Cavaliere approached Rowland to express the pleasure he had derived from his splendid collection. His smile was exquisitely bland, his attitude seemed to call attention to its exemplary correctness. But he gave Rowland an odd sense of looking at an elaborate waxen image adjusted to perform certain gestures and emit certain sounds. It had once contained the marvellous machinery of a spirit too, but some accident had apparently befallen that part of the mechanism, to the cost of the perfect imitation of life. Nevertheless, Rowland reflected, there are more graceless things than the mere motions and passes of a very old civilisation—the civilisation that had given this personage his inexhausted impetus never having struck him as so immemorially old. The Cavaliere also had spirit enough left to desire to speak a few words on his own account and call Rowland's attention to the fact that he was not after all a hired cicerone, but an ancient Roman gentleman. Rowland felt sorry for him; he hardly knew why. He assured him in friendly fashion that he must come again, that his house was always at his service. The Cavaliere took it with perfect delicacy. "You do me too much honour," he murmured. "If you'll allow me—it's not impossible !"

Mrs. Light meanwhile had prepared to depart. "If you're not afraid to come and see two quiet little women we shall be most happy ! We have no statues nor pictures—we have nothing but each other. Eh, darling ?"

"I beg your pardon," said Christina.

"Oh, and the Cavaliere," added her mother.

"The poodle, please !" cried the girl.

Rowland glanced at the Cavaliere; he was smiling more blandly than ever.

Our friend presented himself a few days later, as civility demanded, at Mrs. Light's door. He found her living in one of the stately houses of the Via dell' Angelo Custode and rather to his surprise was told she was at home. He passed through half a dozen rooms and was ushered into an immense saloon, at one end of which sat the mistress of the establishment with a piece of embroidery. She received him very graciously and then, pointing mysteriously to a large screen which was unfolded across the embrasure of one of the deep windows, "I'm mounting guard, you see !" she said. Rowland looked interrogative, whereupon she beckoned him forward and motioned him to step beyond the screen. He obeyed and for some moments stood gazing. Roderick, with his back turned, stood before an extemporised pedestal, ardently shaping a formless mass of clay. Before him sat Christina Light, in a white dress, with her shoulders bare, her magnificent hair twisted into a classic coil, her head admirably carried. Meeting Rowland's gaze she smiled a little, only in the depths of her blue-grey eyes, without moving. She looked divinely fair.

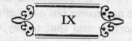

IX

THE BRILLIANT Roman winter came round again, and the whole sense of it entered still more deeply into Rowland's spirit. He grew intimately, passionately fond of all Roman sights and sensations, and to breathe the air that formed their medium and assured them their quality seemed to him the only condition on which life could be long worth living. He could not have defined nor explained the nature of his relish, nor have made up the sum of it by adding together his calculable pleasures. It was a large, vague, idle, half-profitless emotion, of which perhaps the most pertinent thing that might be said was that it brought with it a relaxed acceptance of the present, the actual, the sensuous—of existence on the terms of the moment. It was perhaps for this very reason that, in spite of the charm which Rome flings over one's mood, there ran through Rowland's meditations an undertone of melancholy natural enough in a mind which finds its horizon sensibly limited— even by a magic circle. Whether it be that one tacitly concedes to the Roman Church the monopoly of a guarantee of immortality, so that if one is indisposed to bargain with her for the precious gift one must do without it altogether; or whether in an atmosphere so heavily weighted with echoes and memories one grows to believe that there is nothing in one's consciousness not predetermined to moulder and crumble and become dust for the feet and possible malaria for the lungs of future generations—the fact at least remains that one parts half willingly with one's hopes in Rome and misses them only under some very exceptional stress of circumstance. For this reason it may perhaps be said that there is no other place in which one's daily temper has so mellow a serenity, and none at the same time in which acute attacks of depression are more intolerable. Rowland had found in fact a perfect response to his prevision that to live in the lap of the incomparable sorceress was an education to the senses and the imagination; but he sometimes wondered whether this were not a questionable gain in case of one's not being prepared to ask no more of consciousness than they could give. His growing submission to the mere insidious actual, which resembled somehow the presence of an extravagant, flattering visitor, questionably sincere, seemed sometimes to pivot about by a mysterious inward impulse and look his conscience in the face. "But afterwards . . .?" it brought out with a long interrogative echo; and he could give no answer but a shy affirmation that there was no such thing as to-morrow and that to-day was uncommonly fine. He often felt heavy-hearted; he was sombre without knowing why; there were no visible clouds in his heaven, but there were cloud-shadows on his mood. Shadows projected they often were, without his knowing it, by an undue apprehension that things might after all not go so ideally well with Roderick. When he caught himself fidgeting it vexed him, and he rebuked himself for taking the case unduly hard. If Roderick chose to follow a crooked path, it was no fault of his; he had given him, he would continue to give him, all that he had offered him —friendship, sympathy, counsel, patience. He had not undertaken to make him over.

If Rowland felt his roots striking and spreading in the Roman soil, Roderick also affected him as having flung all questions to the winds. More than once he heard him declare that he meant to live and die within the shadow of Saint Peter's and that he cared little if he should never again draw breath in American air. "For a man of my temperament Rome is the only possible place," he said; "it's better to recognise the fact early than late. So I shall never go home unless I'm absolutely forced."

"What's your idea of 'force'?" asked Rowland, who had noticed from far back the unalloyed respect that he entertained for his temperament. "It seems to me you've an excellent reason for going home some day or other."

"Ah, you mean my engagement?" Roderick answered with unaverted eyes. "Oh yes, of course there's always that funny fact to be reckoned with. I call it funny, poor dear little fact," he went on, "because it savours so of Northampton Mass., and because Northampton Mass. seen from here somehow is so funny. To work Mount

Holyoke and Mount Tom into the same picture—the same picture of one's life as the Pincian and the Palatine—is rather a job. But Mary had better come out here. Even at the worst I've no intention of giving up Rome for six or eight years, and a union deferred for that length of time would be too absurd."

"Miss Garland could hardly leave your mother alone," Rowland judiciously observed.

"Oh, of course my mother should come ! I think I must suggest it in my next letter. It will take her a year or two to make up her mind to it, but if she consents it will brighten her up. It's too small and too starved a life over there even for a person who asks—asks, what do I say ? insists on—so little here below as my mother. It's hard to imagine," Roderick added, "any change *in* Mary being a change for the better; but I suppose there's no crime in seeing the profit of a change *for* her. She would undertake, I daresay, not to be altered by it, in any essential way, enough to make a scandal. One's never so good, I suppose, but that one can improve."

Rowland took in for a moment the tone of this, and he felt fifty words in answer to it rise to his lips. But he ended by pronouncing only a few and none of them those that had at first risen. "If you wish your mother and Miss Garland to come, hadn't you better go home and bring them ?"

"Ah, my dear man, I like the way you talk of my going 'home' ! The more I should 'go' the less of that sacred name there would be about it—so that not really to *become* homeless I had better keep my distance. At present, moreover," Roderick pursued, "it would just exactly break the charm. I'm just beginning to profit, to get accustomed to—well, to not being accustomed; just beginning, that is, to live into my possibilities. Northampton Main Street—even for three days again—has become, I think, my principal *im*possibility."

It was reassuring to hear that Roderick in his own view was but "just beginning" to spread his wings, and Rowland, if he had had any forebodings, might have suffered them to be modified by this declaration. This was the first time since their meeting at Geneva that the youth had mentioned his cousin's name, but the ice being broken he indulged for some time afterwards in frequent allusions to his betrothed, which always had an accent of scrupulous, of almost studied, consideration. An uninitiated observer, hearing him, would have imagined her to be a person of a certain age—possibly an affectionate maiden aunt—who had once done him a kindness which he highly appreciated;

perhaps presented him with a cheque for a thousand dollars. Rowland noted the difference between his present frankness and his reticence during the first six months of his engagement, and sometimes wondered whether it were not rather an anomaly that he should expatiate more largely as the happy event receded. He had wondered over the whole matter first and last in a great many different ways—he had looked at it in all possible lights. There was something that mocked any sense of due sequences in the fact of his having fallen in love with his cousin. She was not, as Rowland conceived her, the "type" that, other things being what they were, would most have touched him, and the mystery of attraction and desire, always so baffling if seen only from without, quite defied analysis here. Just why it was that Roderick should not in consistency have received his impression his comrade would have been at a loss to say; but the conviction must have been largely grounded in a tacit comparison between himself and the accepted suitor. Roderick and he were as different as two men could be, and yet Roderick had taken it into his head to mark with the seal of prospective possession a woman at whose disposition he himself had been keeping, from the moment of his first meeting her, a secret fund of strange alacrities. That if Rowland Mallet happened to be very much struck with the merits of Roderick's mistress the irregularity here was hardly Roderick's, was a view of the case to which our virtuous hero did scanty justice. There were women, he said to himself, whom it was every one's business to fall in love with a little—women beautiful, brilliant, artful, easily interesting. Miss Light, for instance, was one of these; every man who spoke to her did so, if not in the language, at least with something of the agitation, the terror or the hunger, of a lover. There were other women—they might have great beauty, they might have small; their discussable beauty was not what had most to do with it— whose triumphs in this line were rare, but immutably permanent. Such a one conspicuously was Mary Garland. By the law of probabilities it had been unlikely she should exert the same charm for each of them, and was it not possible therefore that the charm for Roderick had been simply the circumstance of sex, the accident of nearness, the influence of youth, sympathy, kindness—of the present feminine in short— enhanced indeed by the advantage of an expressive countenance? The charm for Rowland, on the other hand, by this subtle sophistry—*the* charm! was the mysterious, individual, essential woman. There was indeed an element in the glamour working so well for his friend that he was obliged fairly to allow for, but which he forbore to linger upon;

the rather important attraction, namely, of reciprocity. As to the girl's being herself in love, and showing it, and commending herself by the indubitable tribute, this was a side of the matter from which he averted his head for delicacy, as he conceived, but for a delicacy not pleasantly painless. He wouldn't for the world have asked himself—and he quite noted it—how "far" Mary had gone; gone toward creating Roderick's flattered state by showing him first that she was smitten. He confined himself only to judging that the young man was not irresistibly flattered now, and to feeling that Miss Garland was as living a presence in his own world as she had been five days after he left her. He drifted, under these deep discretions indeed, nearer and nearer to the conviction that at just that crisis any other girl would have answered Roderick's supposedly sentimental needs as well. Any other woman verily would do so still ! Roderick had confessed as much to him at Geneva in saying that he had been taking at Baden-Baden the measure of his susceptibility.

His extraordinary success in modelling the bust of the beautiful Miss Light was pertinent evidence of the quantity of consciousness of the great feminine fact always at his service for application and discrimination. She sat to him repeatedly for a fortnight, and the work was rapidly finished. On one of the last days Roderick asked Rowland to come and give his opinion as to what was still wanting; for the sittings had continued to take place in Mrs. Light's apartment, the studio being pronounced too damp for the fair model. When Rowland presented himself Christina, still in her white dress, with her shoulders bare, was standing before a mirror to readjust her hair, the arrangement of which on this occasion had apparently not met the young sculptor's approval. He stood beside her directing the operation with an emphatic ring that struck Rowland as denoting a considerable advance in intimacy. As this visitor entered Christina was losing patience. "Do it yourself then!" she cried, and with a rapid movement unloosed the great coil of her tresses and let them fall over her shoulders.

They were magnificent, and with her perfect face dividing their rippling flow she looked like some immaculate saint of legend being led to martyrdom. Rowland's eyes presumably betrayed his admiration, but her own showed no vulgar perception of anything she was so little concerned with. If Christina was a coquette, as the remarkable timeliness of this incident might have suggested, her coquetry had the highest finish.

125

"Hudson has the luck to be a sculptor, in his way," Rowland remarked with gaiety; "but it comes over me that if I were only a painter——!"

"Thank goodness you're not !" said Christina. "I'm having quite enough of this minute inspection of my charms."

"My dear young man, hands off !" cried Mrs. Light as she came forward and seized her daughter's hair. "Christina love, I'm more surprised than I can say."

"Is it indelicate?" Christina asked. "I beg Mr. Mallet's pardon."

Mrs. Light gathered up the dusky locks and let them fall through her fingers, glancing at her visitor with a significant smile. Rowland had never been in the East, but if he had attempted to make a sketch of an old slave-merchant calling attention to the "points" of a Circassian beauty he would have depicted such a smile as Mrs. Light's. "Mamma's not really shocked," added Christina in a moment, as if she had guessed her mother's by-play. "She's only afraid that Mr. Hudson may have injured my hair and that, *per conseguenza*, I shall fetch a lower price."

"You unnatural child!" cried mamma. "You deserve that I should make a fright of you!" And with half a dozen skilful passes she twisted the tresses into a single picturesque braid, placed high on the head and producing the effect of a coronet.

"What does your mother do when she wants to do you justice?" Rowland inquired, observing the admirable line of the girl's neck and shoulder.

"I do her justice when I say she says very atrocious things. What's one to do with such a horrible handful?" Mrs. Light demanded.

"Think of it at your leisure, Mr. Mallet," said Christina, "and when you've discovered something let us hear. But I must tell you that I shall not willingly believe in any remedy of yours, for you have something in the expression of your face that particularly provokes me to make the remarks my mother so inconsolably deplores. I noticed it the first time I saw you. I think it's because your face is so broad. For some reason or other broad faces exasperate me; they fill me with a kind of *rabbia*. Last summer at Carlsbad there was an Austrian count with enormous estates and some great office at court. He was very attentive—seriously so; he was really very far gone. *Cela ne tenait qu'à moi!* But I couldn't; he was impossible. He must have measured from ear to ear at least a yard and a half. And he was tow-coloured too, which made it worse—almost as fair as Stenterello—though of course Stenterello's face, like his conversation, is full of point. So I said to him frankly: 'Many thanks, Herr Graf; your uniform's magnificent, but your face is too fat.' "

"I'm afraid that mine also," said Rowland with a smile, "seems just now to have assumed an unpardonable latitude."

"Oh, I take it you know very well that we're hunting for a husband and that none but tremendous swells need apply. Surely before these gentlemen, mamma, I may speak freely; they're so perfectly disinterested. Mr. Mallet won't do, because, though he's rich, he's not rich enough. Mamma made that discovery the day after we went to see you, moved to it by the promising look of your furniture. I hope she was right, eh? Unless you have millions, you know, you needn't apply."

"You reduce me to the sense of beggary," said Rowland.

"Oh, some better girl than I will decide some day, after mature reflection, that, on the whole, you yourself add something to your fortune. Mr. Hudson of course is nowhere; he has nothing but his genius and his extraordinary *beaux yeux*."

Roderick had stood looking at Christina intently while she delivered herself, softly and slowly, of this surprising nonsense. When she had finished she turned and confronted him; their eyes met and he blushed a little. "Let me be your modeller, and he who can may be your husband!" he said abruptly.

Mrs. Light, while her daughter talked, had been adding a few touches to the arrangement of her hair. "She's neither so silly nor so vicious as you might suppose," she said to Rowland with dignity. "If you'll give me your arm we'll go and look at the bust."

"Does that most represent silliness or vice—unless they come to the same thing?" Christina demanded when they stood before it.

Rowland transferred his glance several times from the portrait to the original. "It represents a young lady whom I shouldn't pretend to judge off-hand."

"She may be a fool, but you're not sure. Many thanks! You've seen me half a dozen times. You're either very slow or I'm very deep."

"I'm certainly slow," said Rowland. "I don't expect to make up my mind about you in less than six months."

"I give you six months if you'll promise then a perfectly frank opinion. Mind, I shall not forget; I shall insist upon a judgement."

"Well, though I'm slow I'm tolerably judging," said Rowland— "and I'm tolerably brave. So look out!"

127

Christina considered the bust with a sigh. "I'm afraid, after all," she said, "that there's very little wisdom in it save what the artist has put there. Mr. Hudson looked particularly wise while he was working; he scowled and growled, but he never opened his mouth. It's very kind of him not to have represented me yawning."

"If I had felt obliged to talk a lot of rubbish to you," Roderick candidly said, "the thing wouldn't have been a tenth so good, and I should have been a great deal more fatigued."

"Is it good, after all? Mr. Mallet's a famous connoisseur; hasn't he come here to pronounce?" the girl went on.

The bust was in fact a very happy performance—Roderick had risen to the level of his subject. It was thoroughly a portrait—not a vague fantasy executed on a graceful theme, as the busts of pretty women in modern sculpture are apt to be. The resemblance was close and firm; inch matched with inch, item with item, grain with grain, yet all to fresh creation. It succeeded by an exquisite art in representing without extravagance something that transcended and exceeded. Rowland, however, as we know, was not fond of exploding into superlatives, and after examining the piece he contented himself with suggesting two or three alterations of detail.

"Ah, how can you be so cruel?" demanded Mrs. Light with rich reproachfulness. "It's surely a wonderful thing!"

"Rowland knows it's a wonderful thing," said Roderick, smiling. "I can tell that by his face. The other day I finished something he thought really bad, and he looked very differently from this."

"How *can* Mr. Mallet look?" asked Christina.

"My dear Rowland," said Roderick, "I'm speaking of my poor listening lady. You looked as if you had on a pair of tight boots."

"Ah, my child, you'll not understand that!" cried Mrs. Light. "You never yet had a pair that were small enough."

"It's a pity, Mr. Hudson," said Christina gravely, "that you couldn't have introduced my feet into the bust. But we can hang a pair of satin shoes round the neck."

"I nevertheless like your finished portraits, Roderick," Rowland observed, "better than your rough sketches. This is a great commemoration of a great subject. Miss Light, you may really be proud!"

"Thank you, Mr. Mallet, for the permission," returned the girl.

"I'm dying to see it in the marble—I make it out in a kind of violet velvet niche," said Mrs. Light.

"Placed there on the mosaic table and under the Sassoferrato!"

Christina went on. "We have a Sassoferrato, you know, from which we're inseparable—we travel with our picture and our poodle. I hope you keep well in mind, Mr. Hudson, at all events, that you've not a grain of property in your work and that if mamma chooses she may have it photographed and the copies sold in the Piazza di Spagna at five francs apiece without your having a sou of the profits."

"Amen!" said Roderick. "It was so nominated in the bond. My profits are here!" And he tapped his forehead.

"It would be prettier if you said *here*!" And Christina touched her heart.

"My precious child, how you do run on!" murmured Mrs. Light.

"It's Mr. Mallet's effect on me," the girl answered. "I can't talk a word of sense so long as he's in the room. I don't say that to make you go," she added; "I say it simply to justify myself."

"The noble art of self-defence!" said Rowland.

Roderick declared that he must get at work and requested Christiana to take her usual position, and Mrs. Light proposed to her visitor that they should adjourn to her boudoir. This was a small room, hardly more spacious than a recess, opening out of the drawing-room and having no other issue. Here, as they entered, on a divan near the door, Rowland perceived the constant Cavaliere, with his arms folded, his head dropped upon his breast and his eyes closed.

"Sleeping at his post!" laughed Rowland.

"That's a punishable offence," rejoined Mrs. Light sharply. She was on the point of calling him in the same tone when he suddenly opened his eyes, stared a moment and then rose with a smile and a bow.

"Excuse me, dear lady," he said. "I was overcome by the—the great heat!"

"Nonsense, Cavaliere!" cried the lady; "you know we're perishing here with the cold! You had better go and cool yourself in one of the other rooms."

"I obey, dear lady," said the Cavaliere; and with another salutation to Rowland he departed, walking very discreetly on his toes. Rowland outstayed him but a short time, his appetite for Mrs. Light's conversation being small; he found nothing very inspiring in her frank intimation that if he chose he might become a favourite. He was disgusted with himself for pleasing her; he repudiated any such intention. In the courtyard of the palace he overtook the Cavaliere, who had stopped at the porter's lodge to say a word to this functionary's little girl. She was a young lady of very tender years and she wore a very dirty pinafore. He had taken her up in his arms to sing her an infantine rhyme, while she stared at him with big deep Roman eyes. On seeing Rowland he put her down with a kiss, then stepped forward with a conscious grin, an unresentful admission that he was sensitive both to infant beauty and to ridicule. Rowland began to pity him again; he had taken his dismissal from the drawing-room so meekly.

"You don't keep your promise to come and see me. But please don't forget it. I want you to tell me about Rome thirty years ago."

"Thirty years ago? Ah, dear sir, Rome is Rome still; a place where strange things happen! But happy things too, since I have your renewed permission to call. You do me too much honour. Is it in the morning or in the evening that I should least intrude?"

"Take your own time, Cavaliere; only come some time. I depend upon you," said Rowland.

The Cavaliere thanked him with formal obeisance. To old Giacosa too he felt that he was, in Roman phrase, sympathetic; but the idea of pleasing this extremely reduced gentleman was not disagreeable to him.

Miss Light's bust stood for a while on exhibition in Roderick's studio, and half the foreign colony came to see it. With the completion of his work, however, Roderick's visits at the Palazzo Falconieri by no means came to an end. He spent half his time in Mrs. Light's drawing-room and began to be talked about as "attentive" to Christina. The success of the bust restored his equanimity, and in the garrulity of his good-humour he suffered Rowland to see that she was just now the object uppermost in his thoughts. Rowland, when they talked of her, was rather listener than speaker; partly because Roderick's tone admitted of few openings, and partly because, when his companion laughed at him for having called her unsafe, he for some reason lacked presence of mind to defend himself. The impression remained with our friend that she was unsafe; that she was a complex, wilful, passionate creature who might easily draw down a too confiding spirit into some strange underworld of unworthy sacrifice, not unfurnished with traces of others of the lost. And yet these elements in her were in themselves an appeal to curiosity, and she struck him not only as preying possibly thus on the faith of victims, but as ready to take on occasion her own life in her hand. Roderick, in the glow of that renewed admiration provoked by the fixed attention of portrayal, was never weary of descanting on the extraordinary perfection of her beauty.

"I had no idea of it," he said, "till I began to look at her with an eye to reproducing line for line and curve for curve. Her face is the most exquisite piece of modelling that ever came from creative hands. Not a line without meaning, not a hair's-breadth that's not admirably finished. And then her divine mouth—it might really be that of a goddess ! It's as if a pair of lips had been shaped just *not* to utter all the platitudes and all the pretences." Later, after he had been working for a week, he was to declare that if the girl had been inordinately plain she would still be the most wonderful of women and the best conceivable company. "I've quite forgotten her beauty," he said, "or rather I've ceased to perceive it as something distinct and defined, something independent of the rest of her. She's all one, and all impossibly interesting."

"What does she do—what does she say that's so remarkable ?" Rowland asked.

"Say ? Sometimes nothing—sometimes everything. She's never the same, and you never know how she'll be. And it's not for a pose—it's because there are fifty of her. Sometimes she walks in and takes her place without a word, without a smile, gravely, stiffly, as if it were an awful bore. She hardly looks at me, and she walks away without even glancing at my work. On other days she laughs and chatters and asks endless questions and pours out the most irresistible nonsense—is really most extraordinarily droll. She's a creature of moods ; you can't count upon her ; she keeps one's expectation, she keeps one's nerves, on the stretch : she's as far from *banal* as it's possible to be. And then, bless you, my dear man, she has seen, compared with you and me, for instance, so remarkably much of the world. She says the most astounding things."

"What sort of things ?" Rowland wonderingly asked.

It made his friend hesitate. "I can scarcely think of a specimen that wouldn't too much shock you !"

"It's altogether a singular type of young lady," said Rowland after the scene I have sketched. "It may be a charm, but it's certainly not the orthodox charm of marriageable maidenhood, the charm of the 'nice girl' or the 'dear girl' as we have been accustomed to know those blest creatures. Our American girls are accused of being more forward than any others, and this wonderful damsel is nominally an American. But it has taken twenty years of Europe to make her what she is. The first time we saw her I remember you called her the product of an effete civilisation, and certainly you were not far wrong."

"Well, you see, she has an atmosphere," said Roderick in a tone of high appreciation.

"Young unmarried women should be careful not to have too much," his companion sagely risked.

"Ah, you don't forgive her for hitting you so hard ! A man ought to be flattered when such a girl as that takes so much notice of him."

"A man's never flattered at a beautiful woman's not liking him," said Rowland.

"Are you sure she doesn't like you ? That's to the credit of your humility. A fellow of more vanity might, on the evidence, persuade himself that he was positively in favour."

"He would have also then," laughed Rowland, "to be a fellow of remarkable ingenuity." He asked himself privately how the deuce Roderick reconciled it to his conscience to think so much more of the girl he was not engaged to than of the other. But it amounted almost to arrogance in poor Rowland, you may say, to pretend to know how often Roderick thought of Mary Garland. He wondered gloomily, at any rate, whether for men of his friend's large easy power there was not an ampler moral law than for narrow mediocrities like himself, who, yielding Nature a meagre interest on her investment (such as it was), had no reason to expect from her this affectionate laxity as to their accounts. Was it not a part of the eternal fitness of things that Roderick, while rhapsodising about Christina Light, should have it at his command to look at you with eyes of the most guileless and unclouded blue and to shake off your musty imputations by a toss of his romantic brown locks? Or else had he, in fact, no conscience to speak of ? Fortunate mortal either way !

Our friend Gloriani came, among others, to congratulate Roderick on his model and what he had made of her. "Devilish pretty through and through !" he said as he looked at the bust. "Capital handling of the neck and throat; lovely work on the facial muscles and extraordinary play, extraordinary elegance of life, everywhere. Your luck's too hateful, but you oughtn't to have let her off with the mere sacrifice of her head. There would be no end to be done with the whole inimitable presence of her. If I could only have got hold of her I would have pumped every inch of her empty. What a pity she's not a poor Trasteverina whom we might have for a franc an hour ! I've been carrying about in my head for years an idea for a creature as fine as a flower-stem and yet as full as a flame, but it has always stayed there for want of a tolerable model. I've seen my notion in bits, but in her I see it whole. As soon as I looked at her I said to myself, 'By Jove, there's my idea in the flesh !'"

"What's the name of your idea?" Roderick asked.

"Don't take it ill," said Gloriani. "You know I'm the very deuce for observation. The name of my idea is the name of the young woman— what was *hers*?—who pranced up to the king her father with a great bloody head on a great gold tray."

"Salome, daughter of Herodias?"

"Exactly, and of Herod, king of the Jews."

"Do you think Miss Light looks then like a Jewess?"

"No, he only thinks," Rowland interposed, "that Herodias must much have resembled Miss Light—unless indeed he also sees our young woman with *your* head on her charger."

"Ah," Gloriani laughed, "it isn't a question of Hudson's 'head'!"

If Roderick had taken it ill, this likening of the girl he so admired to the *macabre* maiden of the Christian story (which resentment was not probable, since we know he thought Gloriani an ass and expected little truth of him), he might have been soothed by the candid incense of Sam Singleton, who came and sat for an hour in the very prostration of homage before both bust and artist. But Roderick's attitude in regard to this worshipper was one of undisguised though friendly amusement; as indeed there was oddity enough in the little water-colourist's gasps and glares and other fond intensities, which had ever some lapse of intelligibility for their climax. "Ah, don't envy our friend," Rowland said to Singleton afterwards, on his expressing with a small groan of depreciation of his own paltry performances his sense of the brilliancy of Roderick's talent. "You sail nearer the shore, but you sail in smoother waters. Be contented with what you are, and paint me another picture."

"Oh, I don't envy Hudson anything he possesses," Singleton said, "because to take anything away would spoil his beautiful completeness. 'Complete,' that's what he is; while we little clevernesses are like half-ripened plums, only good eating on the side that has had a glimpse of the sun. Nature has made him so, and fortune confesses to it! He's himself in person such a subject for a painter—a Pinturicchio-figure, isn't he? come to life; he has more genius than any one, and as a matter of course the most beautiful girl in the world comes and offers to feed him with her beauty. If that's not completeness where shall one look for it?"

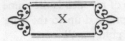

X

ONE MORNING, going into Roderick's studio, Rowland found the young sculptor entertaining Miss Blanchard—but entertaining her, as it were, quite at her own expense. She ministered, for him, to irritation, and he had never climbed to her sky-parlour with the exclamatory herd at large —exclamatory over her petals and dewdrops. He had once quoted Tennyson against her:

> "And is there any moral shut
> Within the bosom of the rose?"

"In all Miss Blanchard's roses you may be sure there is a moral," he had said. "You can see it sticking out its head, and if you go to smell the flower it scratches your nose." But on this occasion she had come with a propitiatory gift—introducing her friend and countryman Mr. Leavenworth. Mr. Leavenworth was a tall, expansive, bland gentleman, with a carefully-brushed whisker and a spacious, fair, well-favoured face, which seemed somehow to have more room in it than was occupied by a smile of superior benevolence, so that (with his smooth white forehead) it bore a certain resemblance to a large parlour with a very florid carpet, but without mural decoration. He held his head high, talked impressively, and told Roderick within five minutes that he was a widower travelling to distract his mind, and that he had lately retired from the proprietorship of large mines of borax in the Middle West. Roderick supposed at first that under the influence of his bereavement he had come to order a tombstone; but observing the extreme benevolence of his address to Miss Blanchard he credited him with a judicious prevision that on the day the tombstone should be completed a monument of his inconsolability might appear mistimed. Mr. Leavenworth, however, was disposed to give an Order—to give it with a capital letter.

"You'll find me eager to patronise our indigenous talent," he said. "You may be sure that I've employed a native architect for the large residential structure that I'm erecting on the banks of the Ohio. I've sustained a considerable loss; but are we not told that the office of art is second only to that of religion? That's why I have come to you, sir. In the retreat that I'm preparing, surrounded by the memorials of my wanderings, I hope to recover a certain degree of tone. They're doing what they can in Paris for the fine effect of some of its features; but the effect I have myself most at heart will be that of my library, filled with well-selected and beautifully-bound authors in groups relieved from point to point by high-class statuary. I should like to entrust you, can we arrange it, with the execution of one of these appropriate subjects. What do you say to a representation, in pure white marble, of the idea of Intellectual Refinement ?"

"Whose idea, sir ?" Roderick asked. "Your idea ?"

But as at this question, and especially at a certain sound in it, Mr. Leavenworth looked a little blank, Miss Blanchard artfully interposed. "I wish I could induce Mr. Hudson to think he might perhaps do something with mine !"

It immediately relieved the tension and made Mr. Hudson consider her with great gravity. "If your idea resembles your personal type, Miss Blanchard, I quite *see* my figure. I close with you on Intellectual Refinement, Mr. Leavenworth, if this lady will sit for us."

Miss Blanchard demurred; the tribute might be ironic; and there was ever afterwards a reflexion of her uncertainty in her opinion of Roderick's genius. Mr. Leavenworth responded that, with all deference to Miss Blanchard's beauty, he desired something less breathingly actual— more monumentally impersonal. "If I were to be the happy possessor of a likeness of Miss Blanchard," he added, "I shouldn't wish it in the form of a cold symbol."

He spoke as if the young woman's charms might compromise the chastity of his conception, but Roderick, after an instant, imperturbable, had drawn him into deep waters. Rowland, nervously conscious of this, appealed meanwhile to the judicious Augusta. "Who's your pompous friend ?"

"A very worthy man. The architect of his own fortune—which is magnificent. One of nature's gentlemen !"

This was nobly sufficient, but Rowland turned in vague unrest to the bust of Miss Light. Like every one else in Rome by this time, Miss Blanchard had an opinion on that young woman's beauty, and, after her own fashion, she expressed it in a quotable phrase. "She looks half like a Madonna and half like a *ballerina* !"

Mr. Leavenworth and Roderick arrived, however, under Rowland's anxious eyes, at an understanding that testified not a little on the part of each to the power nobly to unbend, and the young master, with a habit he had of finally coming round, in a rush of indifferent generosity, from some first crude challenge to patience—a habit that Rowland, whom it had caused to forgive him many things, had known himself privately to pronounce irresistible—the young master good-naturedly promised to do his best to rise to his client's conception. "His conception be hanged!" Roderick exclaimed none the less after Mr. Leavenworth had departed. "His conception is sitting on an india-rubber cushion with a pen in her ear and the lists of the stock-exchange in her hand. It's a case for doing, of course, exactly as one likes—yet how *can* one like, by any possibility, anything that such a blatant humbug as that possibly can? It's as much as one can do to like his awful money. I don't think," our young man added, "that I ever before swallowed anything that wanted so little to go down, and I'm doubtless on my way now to any grovelling you please."

Mrs. Light meanwhile had fairly established herself in Roman society. "The dear God knows how," Madame Grandoni said to Rowland, who had mentioned to her several evidences of the lady's prosperity; "but a door is forced, of course, only as a heavy piece of furniture is moved—you shut your eyes and you push hard. A month ago she knew no one but her washerwoman, and now I'm told that the cards of Roman princesses are to be seen on her table. *Che vuole?* She has opened her booth at the fair; she has her great natural wonder to show, and she beats her big drum outside. Her big drum is her *piano nobile* in a great palace, her brilliant equipage, her marvellous bonnets, her general bedizenment, and the phenomenon in the booth is her wonderful daughter. Christina's a better 'draw' than the two-headed calf or the learned pig. She's spending a lot of money, and you'll see that in two or three weeks she'll take upon herself to open the season by giving a magnificent ball. Of course it's Christina's beauty that floats her. People go to see her because they're curious."

"And they go again because they're wonderstruck," said Rowland.

"To whom do you say it? Hasn't she drawn even *me*? She came to see me of her own free will the other day, and for an hour she was deeply interesting. I think she's an actress, but she believes in her part while she's playing it. She had taken it into her head to believe she was very unhappy, and she sat there, where you're sitting, and told me a tale of her miseries which brought tears to my eyes. She cried profusely— she cries as naturally as possible. She said she was weary of life and that she knew no one but me she could speak frankly to. She must speak or she should go mad. She sobbed as if her heart would break.

I assure you it's well for you susceptible young men that you don't see her when she sobs. She said in so many words that her mother was an infamous woman. Heaven knows what she meant—unless perhaps only that Mrs Light makes debts she knows she can't pay. She said the life they led was horrible; that it was monstrous a poor girl should be dragged about the world to be sold to the highest bidder. She was meant for better things; she could be perfectly happy without those dreadfulnesses. It was not money she wanted. I might not believe her, but she really cared for serious things—for the good, the beautiful and the true. Sometimes she thought of taking poison."

"What did you say to that ?"

"I recommended her to come and see me instead. I would help her about as much and I was on the whole less unpleasant. Of course I could help her only by letting her talk herself out, and kissing her and patting her beautiful hands, and telling her that if she would be very patient and brave and quiet and clever, and sit very tight—in short exercise all the cardinal virtues—there would be something good for her in the end. About once in two months I expect her to reappear on the same errand, and meanwhile quite to forget my existence. I believe I melted to the point of telling her that I would find her some kind, quiet, respectable husband, and even one with a decent fortune; but she declared, almost with fury, that she was sick of the very name of husbands, which she begged I would never mention again. And in fact it was a rash offer; for I'm sure that there's not a man of the kind that might really make a woman happy but would be afraid to marry a young person of her particular distinction. Looked at in that way she's certainly very much to be pitied, and, indeed, altogether, though I don't think she either means all she says or, by a great deal, says all she means, I feel very sorry for her."

Rowland met the two ladies about this time at several entertainments and looked at Christina with a kind of imaginative *attendrissement*. He suspected more than once that there had been a passionate scene between them about coming out, and he wondered what arguments Mrs. Light had found effective. But Christina's face told no tales, and she moved about, beautiful and silent, looking absently over people's heads, barely heeding the men who pressed about her, and suggesting somehow that the soul of a world-wearied mortal had found its way into the blooming body of a goddess. "Where in the world has Miss Light been before she's turned twenty-one," observers with pretensions to earnestness asked, "to have left all her illusions behind ?" And the general verdict was that, though she was incomparably beautiful, she was too disconcertingly indifferent. She was scarcely even vain enough. Young ladies who were *not* indifferent, and yet sometimes perhaps not beautiful either, were free to reflect that she was "not at all liked."

It would have been difficult to guess, all the same, how they reconciled this conviction with a variety of contradictory evidence and in especial with the spectacle of Roderick's inveterate devotion. All Rome might behold that he at least "liked" Christina Light. Wherever she appeared he was either awaiting her or immediately followed her. He was perpetually at her side, trying apparently to preserve some broken thread of talk, the fate of which was, to judge by her face, profoundly immaterial to the young lady. People in general smiled at the radiant good faith of the handsome young sculptor, and asked each other if he really supposed flowers of that rarity to be pluckable by mere geniuses who happened also to be mere Americans. But although Christina's deportment, as I have said, was one of high inexpressiveness, Rowland had drawn from Roderick no suspicion that he suffered from active cruelty, and he was therefore surprised at an incident that occurred one evening at a large musical party. Roderick, as usual, was not in a state of effacement, and on the ladies' taking the chairs which had been arranged for them he immediately placed himself beside Christina. As most of the gentlemen were standing his position made him as conspicuous as Hamlet at Ophelia's feet. Rowland was leaning somewhat apart, against the chimney-piece. There was a long solemn pause before the music began, and in the midst of it Christina rose, left her place, came the whole length of the immense room, with every one looking at her, and stopped before him. She was neither pale nor flushed; she had a dim smile.

"Will you do me a favour?"

"A thousand!"

"Not now, but at your earliest convenience. Please remind Mr. Hudson that he's not in a New England village, that it's not the custom in Rome to address one's conversation exclusively, night after night, to the same poor girl, and that——"

The music broke out with a great blare and covered her voice. She made a gesture of impatience, and Rowland offered her his arm and led her back to her seat.

The next day he repeated her words to Roderick, in whom they produced mere unabashed amusement. "Oh, the charming 'cheek' of her! She does everything that comes into her head."

"Had she never asked you before not to talk to her so much?" Rowland inquired.

"On the contrary, she has often said to me, 'Mind you now, I forbid you to leave me. Here comes that beast of a So-and-so.' She cares as little about the custom of the country as I do. What could be a better proof than her walking up to you with five hundred people looking at her? Is that, for beautiful watched girls, the custom of the country?"

"Why then should she take such a step?"

"Because as she sat there the notion took her. That's reason enough for her. I've imagined she wishes me well, as they say here—though she has never distinguished me in such a way as that."

Madame Grandoni had foretold the truth; Mrs. Light a couple of weeks later convoked all Roman society to a brilliant ball. Rowland went late and found the staircase so encumbered with flower-pots and servants that he was a long time making his way into the presence of the hostess. At last he approached her as she stood making curtsies at the door with her daughter by her side. Some of Mrs. Light's curtsies were very low, for she had the happiness of receiving a number of the social potentates of the Roman world. She was rosy with triumph, to say nothing of a less metaphysical cause, and was evidently vastly contented with herself, with her company and with all the omens and portents. Her daughter was less overtly jubilant and distributed her greetings with impartial frigidity. But if Christina was awfully detached, as they said, her detachment gave the greater relief to her magnificent beauty. Dressed simply in vaporous white relieved with half a dozen white roses, the perfection of her features and of her person, and the mysterious depth of her expression, seemed to glow with the white light of a splendid pearl. She recognised no one individually and made her salutations slowly, gravely, with her eyes on the ground. Rowland felt sure, however, that for himself her obeisance was subtly overdone, but he sighed patiently, as for the worrying whim of it, and reflected as he passed on that if she disliked him, which was all such minor ironies could mean, he had nothing to reproach himself with. He walked about, had a few words with Miss Blanchard, who, with a fillet of cameos in her hair, was leaning on the arm of Mr. Leavenworth, and at last came upon the Cavaliere Giacosa, modestly stationed in a corner. The little gentleman's coat-lappet was decorated with an enormous bouquet, and his neck encased in a voluminous white handkerchief of the fashion of thirty years ago. His arms

139

were folded and his eyelids, before the glittering scene, contracted, though you saw through them the answering glitter of his intensely dark vivacious pupil. He immediately embarked on an elaborate apology for not having yet manifested as he felt it his sense of the honour Rowland had done him.

"I'm always on service with these ladies, you see, and that's a duty to which one wouldn't willingly be faithless an instant."

"Evidently," said Rowland, "you're a very devoted friend. Mrs. Light, in her situation, is very happy to be able so to depend on you."

"We are old friends," the Cavaliere gravely said. "Very good friends. I knew the signora many years ago, when she was the prettiest woman in Rome—or rather in Ancona, which is even better. The beautiful Christina now is perhaps the very greatest beauty in Europe."

"There's nothing more probable."

"Very well, sir, I taught her to read; I guided her little hands to touch the piano." And at these faded memories the Cavaliere's eyes glowed with an old Roman fire. Rowland half expected him to proceed with a flash of long-repressed passion, "And now—and now, sir, they treat me as you observed the other day !" But he only looked out at our friend hard from among his wrinkles, and seemed to remark instead, as with the social discipline of a thousand years, "Oh, I say nothing more. I'm neither so vulgar nor so shallow as to complain !"

Evidently the Cavaliere was both deep and delicate, and Rowland could but repeat his respectful tribute. "You're a devoted friend."

"Eh, *che vuole*? I'm a devoted friend. A man may do himself justice after twenty years !"

Rowland after a pause made some remark about the beauty of the ball. It was very brilliant.

"Stupendous !" said the Cavaliere solemnly. "It's a great day. We have four Roman princes, to say nothing of others." And he counted them over on his fingers and held up his hand triumphantly. "And there she stands, the girl to whom I—I, Giuseppino Giacosa—taught her alphabet and her piano-scales; there she stands in all her grace, and *les grands de la terre* come and do her homage. Here, in his quiet corner, her old master permits himself to be proud."

"It's very friendly and very charming of him," Rowland benevolently said.

The Cavaliere drew his lids a little closer, but strange things came through. "It's very natural, signore—at the same time that it's very idiotic too. Christina's at any rate a *brava ragazza*; she remembers my

140

little services. Here comes, however," he added in a moment, "the young Prince of the Belle-Arti. I'm sure he has bowed lowest of all."

Rowland looked round and saw Roderick moving slowly across the room and casting about him his usual high light of contemplation. He presently joined them, nodded familiarly to the Cavaliere and immediately put to Rowland the largest "Have you seen her?"

"I've seen Miss Light," Rowland answered on a smaller scale. "She's looking remarkably well."

"I'm intoxicated with her beauty!" Roderick continued so loud that several persons turned round.

Rowland saw that he was flushed, and laid a hand on his arm, which he felt tremble. "If you'll go straight away with me I'll keep you company anywhere."

"Go straight away?" cried Roderick almost angrily. "Don't you suppose I intend to dance with her?"

The Cavaliere had been watching him attentively; he gently took possession of the other arm. "Softly, softly, dear young man. Let me speak to you as a father."

"Oh, speak even as a mother and I really shall not mind it!"

"Be very reasonable then and go away."

"Why the devil should I go away?"

"Because you're too charmingly in love," said the Cavaliere.

"I might as well be in love here as in the streets."

"Carry your love as far as possible from that young woman. She'll never listen to you—she can't."

"She 'can't'?" demanded Roderick. "She's not the sort of person —she's the very last—of whom you may say that. She can if she will. She does as she chooses."

"Up to a certain point. Beyond it—*niente*!" And the Cavaliere's two forefingers made a wonderful airy sign. "It would take too long to explain; I only beg you to believe that if you think you can pretend to Miss Light you prepare for yourself *de mauvais draps*. Have you a princely title? have you a princely fortune? No? Then you're not her affair."

And the Cavaliere folded his arms again, like a man who has done his duty. Roderick wiped his forehead and looked askance at Rowland; he seemed to be guessing his thoughts, and it might have been imaginable that they made him colour. But he smiled blandly and, addressing the Cavaliere, "I'm much obliged to you for the information," he gracefully declared. "Now that I've obtained it, let me tell you that

141

I'm no more in love with Miss Light than my friend here is. He perfectly knows that. I admire her—yes, immensely. But that's no one's business but my own, and though I have, as you say, neither a princely title nor a princely fortune, I mean to suffer neither that draw back nor those who can boast of its opposite to diminish my right."

"If you're not in love, my dear young man," said the Cavaliere with his hand on his heart and an apologetic smile, "*meno male*. But let me entreat you as an affectionate old busybody to keep a watch on your sensibility. You're young, you also are admirably beautiful; you have a brilliant genius and a generous heart. But—I may say it almost with authority—you're not our young lady's 'fate.'"

Whether Roderick were in love or not, he was nettled by what apparently seemed to him too insistent a negation of an inspiring possibility. "You speak as if she had made her choice!" he answered. "Without pretending to confidential information on the subject, I'm very sure she has done nothing of the sort."

"No, but she must make it soon," said the Cavaliere. And raising his forefinger, he laid it against his under lip. "She must choose very great things. And she will!"

"She'll do exactly as her inclination prompts. She'll marry the man who pleases her, if he hasn't a dollar. I know her better than you."

The Cavaliere turned perhaps a little paler than usual, but he smiled more urbanely. "No, no, *caro signorino*, you don't know her better than I. You've not watched her day by day for twenty years. I too have admired her. She *is* a *brava ragazza*; she has never said an unkind word to me; the blessed Virgin be thanked! But she must have a great position and a brilliant destiny; they've been marked out for her and she'll submit. You had better believe me; it may save you some rash expense."

"I shall see what I shall see." But Roderick's serenity was strained.

"Then you'll tell me. But I retire from the discussion," the Cavaliere added. "I've no wish to provoke you to attempt to prove to me that I'm a *vieille bête*. You're already *très-monté*."

"No more than is natural to a man who in an hour or so is to dance a *cotillon* with a divinity."

"A *cotillon*? has she promised?"

Roderick patted the air as for pity of those who pretended to guess the terms of the understanding of two such intimates. "You'll see what *you* will see!"

The Cavaliere gave an exaggerated shrug. "You'll make a great many mourners!"

"What a mourner won't he have made already!" Rowland silently echoed. This was evidently not the first time that reference had been made between Roderick and the Cavaliere to the young man's possible illusion, and Roderick had failed to consider it the simplest and most natural course to say in three words to the vigilant little gentleman that there was no cause for alarm—his fancy was not free. Rowland hoped, obscurely, that his reticence had some basis of tact that was not immediately apparent; then he turned away with a vague pang: there was something insecure, so to say, in the basis of Roderick's radiance. The tide was setting to the regions of supper, and he drifted with it to the door. The crowd at this point was dense, and he was obliged to wait for some minutes before he could advance. At last he felt his neighbours dividing behind him and, looking about, he saw Christina pressing her way forward alone. She was noticing no one, and save for the fact of her being so at her ease one wouldn't have supposed she was in her mother's house. As she recognised Rowland she beckoned and, taking his arm, motioned him to lead her to the quarter of the spread tables. She said nothing till he had forced a passage and they stood somewhat isolated.

"Take me into the most out-of-the-way corner you can find," she then began, "and get me somewhere a piece of bread."

"Nothing more? There seems to be everything conceivable."

"A simple roll. Nothing more, on your peril. Only bring something for yourself."

It seemed to Rowland that the embrasure of a window (embrasures in Roman palaces are deep) was a retreat sufficiently obscure for Christina to execute whatever design she might have contrived against his equanimity. A roll, after he had found her a seat, was easily procured. As he presented it he remarked that, frankly speaking, he was at a loss to understand why she should have selected for the honour of so great an attention a poor man who could do so little to please her.

"Ah yes, of course I dislike you!" said Christina. "To tell the truth I had forgotten it. There are so many people here whom I dislike more that when I caught your eye just now you seemed an intimate friend. But I've not come into this corner to talk nonsense," she went on. "You mustn't think I always do, eh?"

"I've never heard you do anything else," said Rowland sturdily, having decided that he would keep only on the broad highroad with her.

"Very good. I like your frankness. It's quite true. You see I'm a strange girl, and rather bold and bad. *D'abord*, I'm frightfully egotistical. Don't flatter yourself you've said anything very clever if you ever take it into your head to tell me so. I know it much better than you. So it is; I can't help it. I'm tired to death of myself; I would give all I possess to get out of myself; but somehow at the end I find myself so vastly more interesting than nine-tenths of the people I meet. If a person wished to do me a favour I would say to him: 'I beg you with tears in my eyes to interest me. Be a brute, if necessary, to do it; only be something positive and strong—something that in looking at I can forget my detestable self!' Perhaps that's nonsense too. If it is I can't help it either. I can only apologise for the nonsense that I know to be such, and that I talk—oh, for more reasons than I can tell you! I wonder whether, if I were to try you, you'd understand me."

"I'm afraid I should never understand," said Rowland, as if for her edification, "why a person on a good—or call it perhaps a bad—occasion can willingly talk nonsense."

"That proves how little you know about women. But I like your hearty directness. When I told you the other day, with my usual rudeness to every one, that you bored me so, I had an idea you were more formal—how do you say it?—more *guindé*. I'm very capricious. To-night I like you better."

"Oh, I'm not at all *guindé*," said Rowland gravely.

"I beg your pardon then for thinking so. Now I've an idea that you'd make a faithful friend; an intimate friend—a friend to whom one could tell everything. For such a friend what wouldn't I give, don't you see?"

Rowland looked at her in stirred, yet in quite self-possessed, speculation. Was this a sincere yearning or only an equivocal purpose? Her beautiful eyes looked divinely candid; but then, if candour was beautiful, beauty, and *such* beauty, somehow carried questions so far! "I hesitate to recommend myself out and out for the office," he said, "but I believe that if you were to depend upon me for anything that a friend may do I should not be found wanting."

"Very good. One of the first things one asks of a friend is to judge one not by isolated acts, but by one's whole conduct. I care for your opinion—I don't know why."

"Nor do I, I confess!" Rowland laughed.

"What do you think of this affair?" she went on as if his confession didn't matter.

144

"Of your ball? Why, it's a very grand affair."

"It's horrible—that's what it is. It's a mere rabble. There are people here whom I never saw before, people who were never asked. Mamma went about inviting every one, asking other people to invite any one they knew, doing anything to have a crowd. I hope she's satisfied. It's not my doing. I feel weary, I feel angry, I want to cry, I want to bite. I've twenty minds to escape into my room and lock the door and let mamma s'en tirer as she can. By the way," she added in a moment, without a visible reason for the jump, "can you tell me something to read?"

Rowland stared at the disconnectedness of the question.

"Can you recommend me some books?" she repeated. "I know you literally have some. I've no one else to ask. We never see one in our lives—where should we, and why? We make debts for clothes and champagne, but we can't spend a sou on our poor benighted minds. And yet, though you may not believe it, I really like things that are *for* the mind."

"I shall be most happy to lend you any books," Rowland said. "I'll pick some out to-morrow and send them to you."

"No nasty novels then, please, if you don't mind. I'm tired of nasty novels—at one time I read several. I never was a bit looked after in *that* way. I can at all events imagine situations for myself beyond any in fiction—above all in our poor *bête* English. Some good poetry, if there is such a thing nowadays, and some memoirs and histories and books of facts."

"You shall be served. Your taste agrees with my own."

She was silent a moment, looking at him. Then suddenly, "Tell me something about Mr. Hudson," she exclaimed. "You're very, very great friends?"

"Oh yes," said Rowland; "we're very, very great friends."

"Tell me about him. *Allons!* Begin."

"Where shall I begin? You know him for yourself."

"No, I don't know him; I don't find him so easy to know. Since he has finished my bust and begun to come here disinterestedly, he has grown a great talker. He says very fine things; but does he mean all he says?"

"Few of us do that."

"You do, I imagine. You ought to know, for he tells me you discovered him." Rowland was silent, and Christina continued: "Do you consider him very, very, *very* clever?"

"Very, very, *very*."

"His talent's really distinguished?"

"So it seems to me."

"In short, he's a great genius?"

"Yes, call him a great genius."

"And you found him vegetating in a little village and took him by the hand and set him on his feet in Rome?"

"Is that the popular legend?" Rowland asked.

"Oh, you needn't be modest. There was no great merit in it; there would have been none at least on my part in the same conditions. Great geniuses are not so common, and if I had discovered one in the wilderness I should have brought him out in the market-place to see how he would behave. It would be excessively amusing. You must find it so to watch Mr. Hudson, eh? Tell me this: do you think he's going to be a *real* swell, a *big* celebrity, have his life written, make his fortune, and immortalise—as the real ones *do*, you know—the people he has done busts of and the women he has loved?"

"Well, that's a large order," said Rowland. "I don't prophesy, but I've good hopes."

Christina was silent. She stretched out her bare arm and looked at it a moment absently, turning it so as to see—or almost to see—the dimple in her elbow. This was apparently a frequent gesture with her; Rowland had already observed it. It was as coolly and naturally done as if she had been alone before her toilet-table. "So he's one of the glories-to-be!" she suddenly resumed. "Don't you think I ought to be extremely flattered to have one of the glories-to-be perpetually hanging about? He's the first such young lion I ever saw, but I should have known he was not a common mortal. There's something strange about him. To begin with he has no manners. You may say that it's not for me to blame him, since I've none myself. That's very true, but the difference is that I can have them when I wish to (and very charming ones too; I'll show you some day); whereas Mr. Hudson will never, never, never arrive—and thank God after all—at the least little *tenue*. For somehow one sees he's a gentleman. He seems to have something urging, driving, pushing him, making him restless and defiant. You see it in his eyes. They're the finest, by the way, I ever saw. When a person has such eyes you forgive him his bad manners. I suppose they represent what's called the sacred fire."

Rowland made no answer except to ask her in a moment if she would have another roll. She merely shook her head and went on—

146

"Tell me how you found him. Where was he—how was he?"

"He was in a place called Northampton Mass. Did you ever hear of it? He was studying law. I don't say he was learning it."

"It appears it was something horrible, eh?"

"Something horrible?"

"This little village. No society, no pleasures, no beauty, no interest."

"You've received a false impression. Northampton isn't so gay as Rome, but Roderick had some charming friends."

"Tell me all about them. Who were his charming friends?"

"Well, there was my cousin, through whom I made his acquaintance—a delightful woman."

"Young—pretty?"

"Yes, a good deal of both. And very clever."

"Did he make love to her?"

"Not in the least."

"Well, who else?"

"He lived with his mother. She's quite the best of women."

"Ah yes, I know all that one's mother is. But she does not count as society. And who else?"

Rowland hesitated. He wondered whether Christina's insistence were the result of a general interest in Roderick's antecedents or of a particular suspicion. He looked at her; she was looking at him a little askance, waiting for his answer. As Roderick had said nothing about his engagement to the Cavaliere it was probable that with this object of his admiration he had not been more explicit. And yet the thing was announced, it was public; the other person concerned was happy in it, proud of it. Rowland, thinking of the other person, felt a kind of vicarious resentment. But he kept silence a moment longer. He deliberated intently.

"What in the world are you frowning at?" said Christina.

"There was some one else—quite his principal friend; the young lady to whom he's engaged."

Christina stared, raising her eyebrows. "Ah, Mr. Hudson's engaged?" she said very simply. "Is she interesting, is she pretty?"

"Very interesting, I think, as engaged to *him*," Rowland meant to practise great brevity, but in a moment he found himself saying: "And I also call her handsome."

"Ah, then you like her, too? You must be glad of that, and so must he," Christina went on. "But why don't they marry?"

"Roderick's waiting till he can afford it."

Christina slowly put out her arm again and looked at the dimple in her elbow. "Ah, *il y a ça?* He never told me."

Rowland perceived at this moment that the people about were ebbing back to the ball-room, and immediately afterwards he saw Roderick making his way to themselves. The young man stood the next moment before Miss Light.

"I don't claim that you've promised me the cotillon," he said, "but I consider you've given me hopes which warrant the confidence that you'll dance it with me."

Christina looked at him a moment. "Certainly I've made no promises," she said. "It seemed to me that, as the daughter of the house, I should keep myself free and let it depend on circumstances."

"Then I very earnestly entreat you." And the pressure was still more in the tone than in the words.

Christina rose and began to laugh. "You say that very well, but the Italians do it better."

This assertion seemed likely to be put to the proof, as Mrs. Light now hastily approached leading rather than led by a tall, slim, brown young man whose face was like a prize-design and whose race was vivid in his type. "My precious love," she cried, "what a place to hide in! We've been looking for you for twenty minutes; I've chosen a cavalier for you—and chosen well!"

The young man disengaged himself, made a ceremonious bow, clasped his two hands and murmured with an ecstatic smile, "May I venture to hope, dear signorina, for the honour of your hand?"

"It would be fine if you mightn't!" said Mrs. Light. "The honour's for us!"

Christina hesitated but a moment, then swept the young man a curtsey as profound as his own salutation. "You're very kind, Prince, but you're too late. I've just accepted!"

"Ah, *voyons*, my own darling!" murmured—almost moaned—Mrs. Light.

Christina and Roderick exchanged a single glance—a glance caught by Rowland and which attested on the part of each something of a new consciousness. She passed her hand into his arm; he tossed his ambrosial locks and led her away.

A short time afterwards Rowland saw the young man she had rejected leaning against a doorway. His countenance, constructed and regular, was yet as heavy as if it had been, for brow, nose and mouth, all cornice, column and basement. A portrait-figure of some

148

Renaissance court where poison was used, his rather lustreless part there would have been to die of it. But he was distinguished and bored; he fingered his young moustache broodingly, as if it had been the relic of an ancestor, and looked up nostalgically at the rococo mythological world of the fine old florid ceiling. The creatures there would have indeed been more his company and his "form," Rowland thought, than the modern polyglot crowd. Rowland espied the Cavaliere Giacosa hard by and, having joined him, asked him the young man's name.

"Oh, he's a *pezzo grosso*! A rich Neapolitan. Prince Casamassima."

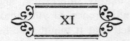

XI

ONE DAY on entering Roderick's lodging (not the modest rooms on the Ripetta which he had first occupied, but a much ampler apartment on the Corso) Rowland found a letter on the table addressed to himself. It was from Roderick and consisted of but three lines. "I'm gone to Frascati—for meditation. If I'm not at home on Friday you had better join me." On Friday he was still absent, and Rowland went out to Frascati. Here he found his friend living at the inn and spending his days, according to his own account, lying under the trees of Villa Mondragone and reading Ariosto. He was melancholy, almost morose; his subjects of "meditation" seemed not to have been happy. Nothing especially pertinent to our narrative had passed between the two young men since Mrs. Light's ball save a few words bearing on a passage of that entertainment. Rowland had informed Roderick the next day that he had told Miss Light of his engagement, and had added: "I don't know whether you'll thank me, but it's my duty to let you know it. Miss Light perhaps has already done so."

Roderick stared hard an instant, his colour rising. "Why should I not thank you? I'm not ashamed of my engagement."

"As you had not spoken of it yourself I thought you might have a reason for not having it known."

"A man doesn't gossip about such a matter with strangers," Roderick rejoined; and the ring of irritation was in his voice.

"With strangers—no!" said Rowland smiling.

Roderick continued his work; but, after a moment, turning round with a frown, "If you supposed I had a reason for being silent, pray why should you have spoken?" he demanded.

"I didn't speak idly, my dear man. I weighed the matter first, and promised myself to let you know immediately afterwards. It seemed to me Miss Light had better have it in her head that your faith and honour are pledged."

"The Cavaliere then has put it into yours that I'm making love to her?"

"No; in that case I shouldn't have spoken to her first."

"Do you mean then that she's making love to *me*?"

"This is what I mean," said Rowland after a pause. "She finds you fitfully but unmistakably interesting, and she's pleased, even though she may feign indifference, at your finding her more continuously so. I said to myself that it might save her some little waste of imagination to know without delay that you're not at liberty to become indefinitely interested in other women."

"You seem to have taken the measure of my liberty with extraordinary minuteness," Roderick observed.

"You must do me justice then. I'm the cause of your separation from Miss Garland, the cause of your being exposed to influences and opportunities here that she hardly even dreams of. How could I ever meet her again," Rowland continued with much warmth of tone, "if at the end of it all she should find herself short?"

"I had no idea she had made such an impression on you. You're too anxious and, I really think, too zealous. I take it she didn't really request you to look after her affairs."

"If anything happens to you I'm accountable. You must understand that."

"That's a view of the situation I can't accept—in your own interest no less than in mine. It can only make us both very uncomfortable. I know all I owe you; I feel it: you know that. But I'm not a small boy nor a country lout any longer, and whatever I do I do with my eyes open. When I do well the merit's my own; if I do ill the fault's my own. The idea that I make you nervous is not to be borne. Dedicate your nerves to some better cause, and believe that if Miss Garland and I have a quarrel we shall settle it between ourselves."

Rowland had found himself wondering shortly before whether possibly his brilliant young friend were without a conscience; now it dimly occurred to him that he was without that indispensable aid to completeness, a feeling heart. Rowland, as we have already intimated, was a man of moral passion, and no small part of that motive force had been spent in this adventure. There had been from the first no protestations of friendship on either side, but Rowland had implicitly offered everything that belongs to friendship, and Roderick had to every appearance as deliberately accepted it. Rowland indeed had taken an exquisite satisfaction in his companion's easy, inexpressive assent to his interest in him. "Here's an uncommonly fine thing," he said to himself; "a nature all *unconsciously* grateful, a man in whom friendship does the thing that love alone generally has the credit of —knocks the bottom out of pride." His reflective judgement of his companion, as time went on, had indulged in a great many irrepressible vagaries; but his affection, his sense of something in the other's whole personality that appealed to his tenderness and charmed his understanding, had never for an instant faltered. He listened to Roderick's last words, and then he smiled as he rarely smiled—with bitterness.

"I don't at all like your telling me I'm meddlesome. If I hadn't been meddlesome I should never have cared a fig for you."

Roderick flushed deeply and thrust his modelling-tool up to the handle into the clay. "Say it outright—as you want to. You've been an awful fool to believe in me."

"I don't want to say it, and you don't honestly believe I do," said Rowland, all in patience. "It seems to me I'm really very good-natured even to reply to such nonsense."

Roderick sat down, crossed his arms and fixed his eyes on the floor. Rowland looked at him for some moments; it seemed to him that he had never so clearly perceived him as all strangely and endlessly mixed —with his abundance and his scarcity, his power to charm and his power to hurt, the possibilities of his egotism, the uncertainties of his temper, the delicacies of his mind. It would have made him quite sick, however, to think that on the whole the values in such a spirit were not much larger than the voids, and he was so far from having ceased to believe in it that he felt just now more than ever that a fine moral agitation, adding a zest to life, is the inevitable portion of those who, themselves unendowed, yet share romantically the pursuits of the inspired. Rowland, who had not a grain of genius either to make one say he was an interested reasoner or to enable one to feel that he could afford a dangerous theory or two, adhered to his conviction of the essential salubrity of genius. Suddenly he felt a rush of pity for his companion, whose beautiful faculty of production was thus a double-edged instrument, susceptible of being dealt in back-handed blows at its possessor. Genius was priceless, beneficent, divine, but it was also at its hours capricious, sinister, cruel; and natures ridden by it, accordingly, were alternately very enviable and very helpless. It was not the first time he had had a sense of Roderick's standing passive in the clutch of his temperament. It had shaken him as yet but with a half good-humoured wantonness; but henceforth possibly it meant to handle him more roughly. These were not times, therefore, for a friend to have a short patience.

"When you err you say the fault's your own," he said at last. "It's because your faults are your own that I heed them."

Rowland's voice, when he spoke with feeling, had an extraordinary amenity. Roderick sat staring a moment longer at the floor, then he sprang up and laid his hand affectionately on his friend's shoulder. "You're the best man in the world," he said, "and I'm a vile brute. Only," he added, in a moment, "*you don't understand me!*" And he looked at him out of such bottomless depths as might have formed the element of a shining merman who should be trying, comparatively near shore, to signal to a ruminating ox.

Rowland's own face was now a confession of his probably being indeed too heavy to float in such waters. "What is it now? Explain."

"Oh, I can't explain!" cried Roderick impatiently, returning to his work. "I've only one way of expressing my deepest feelings—it's this." And he swung his tool. He stood looking at the half-wrought clay for a moment and then flung the instrument down. "And even this half the time plays me false!"

Rowland felt that his irritation had not subsided, but he nevertheless risked, for a decent consistency's sake, the words he had had on his conscience from the beginning. "We must do what we can and be thankful," he said. "And let me assure you of this—that the practice of your talent will never see you out of one kind of difficulty only just to expose you to another."

Roderick pressed his hand to his forehead with vehemence, and then shook it in the air despairingly; a gesture that had of late become frequent with him. "No, no, it's no use; you don't understand me. But I don't blame you. You can't!"

"You think it *will* then?" said Rowland, to whom it had suddenly occurred that he sincerely might.

"I think that when you expect a man to produce beautiful and wonderful works of art you ought to allow him a certain freedom of action, you ought to give him a long rope, you ought to let him follow his fancy and look for his material wherever he thinks he may find it. A mother can't nurse her child unless she follows a certain diet; an artist can't bring his visions to maturity unless he has a certain experience. You demand of us to be imaginative, and you deny us the things that feed the imagination. In labour we must be as passionate as the inspired sibyl; in life we must be as regular as the postman and as satisfactory as the cook. It won't do, you know, my dear chap. When you've an artist to deal with you must take him as he is, good and bad together. I don't say they're pleasant creatures to know or easy creatures to live with; I don't say they satisfy themselves any better than other people. I only say that if you want them to produce you must let them conceive. If you want a bird to sing you mustn't cover up its cage. Shoot them, the poor devils, drown them, exterminate them, if you will, in the interest of public morality: it may be morality would gain—I daresay it would. But if you suffer them to live, let them live on their own terms and according to their own inexorable needs!"

"I've no wish whatever either to shoot you or to drown you," Rowland perhaps a little infelicitously laughed. "Why defend yourself with such very big guns against a warning offered you altogether in the interest of your freest development? Do you really mean that you've an inexorable need of an intimate relation with Miss Light?— a relation as to the felicity of which there may be differences of opinion, but which can't, at best, under the circumstances, be called innocent. Your last summer's adventures were more so! As for the terms on which you're to live, I had an idea you had arranged them otherwise."

"I've arranged nothing—thank God! I don't pretend to arrange. I'm young and ardent and inquisitive, and I'm interested in that young woman. That's enough. I shall go as far as the interest leads me. I'm not afraid. Your genuine artist may be sometimes half a madman, but he's never even half a coward!"

"I see; it's a speculation. But suppose that in your speculation you should come to grief artistically as well as—what shall I say?—more intimately."

"Well then, I must take life as it comes—I can't always be arranging grand bargains. If I'm to fizzle out, the sooner I know it the better. Sometimes I half suspect it. But let me at least go out and reconnoitre for the enemy, and not sit here waiting for him, cudgelling my brains for ideas that won't come!"

Do what he would, Rowland could not think of Roderick's theory of the fell play of experiment, especially as applied in the case under discussion, as anything but a pernicious illusion. But he saw it was vain to discuss the matter, for inclination was powerfully on his friend's side. He laid his two hands on his shoulders, held him hard, with troubled eyes, then shook a mournful head and turned away.

"I can't work any more," said Roderick. "You put an end to *that*. I'll go and stroll on the Pincian." And he tossed aside his blouse and prepared himself for the street. As he was arranging his necktie before the glass something occurred to him that made him thoughtful. He stopped a few moments later, as they were going out, with his hand on the door-knob. "You did from your own point of view an indiscreet thing, you know, to tell Miss Light of my engagement."

Rowland faced him in a manner which was partly a protest, but also partly a recognition.

"If she's the particular sort of vampire you seem to take her for," Roderick added, "you've only given her an incentive."

"And that's the girl you propose to devote yourself to?" his companion cried.

"Oh, I don't say it, mind! I only say—well, I say that the next time you mean to render me a service it will be safest for you to give me notice beforehand!"

It was perfectly characteristic of Roderick that a fortnight later he should have let his friend know that he depended upon him for society at Frascati as freely as if no irritating topic had ever been discussed between them. Rowland thought him generous, and he had at any rate a liberal faculty of forgetting that he had given you any reason to be displeased with him. It was equally characteristic of Rowland that he complied with his friend's summons without a moment's hesitation. His cousin Cecilia had once told him that he was too credulous to have a right to be kind. She put the case with too little favour, or too much, as the reader chooses; it is certain at least that he gave others, as a general thing, the benefit of any doubt, reserving for himself the detriment. Nothing happened, however, to suggest to him that he was deluded in thinking that Roderick's secondary impulses were the prompt saving ones, and that his nature as a mixed whole tasted distinctly more of its sweet than of its bitter parts. The wind had dropped, at all events, for the time, round the young man's head, even if the cloud had not lifted; he was lazy, listless and detached, but he had never been so softly submissive. Winter had begun by the calendar, yet the weather was divinely mild, and the companions took long slow strolls on the hills and lounged away the mornings in the villas. The villas at Frascati make infinitely for peace and are rich in the romantic note. Roderick, as he had said, was meditating, and if a masterpiece was to come of his meditations Rowland could hold his breath for it with the best will in the world. But Roderick let him know from the first that he was in a miserably sterile mood, and, cudgel his brains as he would, could think of nothing that would serve for the statue he was to make for Mr. Leavenworth.

"It's worse out here than in Rome," he said, "for here I'm face to face with the dead blank of my mind. There I couldn't think of anything either, but there I found things that helped me to live without thought." This was as free a renewed tribute to forbidden fruit as could have hoped to pass; it seemed indeed to Rowland surprisingly free—a lively instance of his friend's disassociated manner of looking, as might have been said, at the time of day. Roderick was silent sometimes for hours, with a vague anxiety in his face and a new fold between his even eyebrows; at other times he restlessly talked, though in a fitful, musing monologue. Rowland could have felt it his duty at moments to offer to feel his pulse; he wondered if he hadn't symptoms of fever. Roderick had taken a great fancy to Villa Mondragone, and used to pay it florid compliments as they strolled, in the winter sunshine, on the great terrace which looks toward Tivoli and the iridescent Sabine hills. He carried his volume of Ariosto in his pocket and took it out every now and then to spout passages to his companion. He was as a general thing very little of a reader; but at intervals he would take a fancy to one of the classics and nose over it as for the flowers. He had picked up Italian without study, and gave it a wonderful sound, though in reading aloud he ruined the sense of half his admirations and felicities. Rowland, who pronounced badly but understood everything, once said to him that Ariosto was not the poet for a man of his craft; a sculptor should above all make a companion of Dante. So he gave him a fine old copy of the *Inferno*, a high rarity, one of his portable treasures, and advised him to make it familiar. Roderick took it responsively—perhaps he should find it tonic; but he had renounced it the next day: he had found it horribly depressing.

"A sculptor should model as Dante writes—you're right there," he said. "But when his genius is in eclipse Dante's a dreadfully smoky lamp. By what perversity of fate," he went on, "has it come about

155

that I find myself a sculptor at all? A sculptor's such a confoundedly special genius; there are so few subjects he can treat, so few things in life that bear upon his work, so few moods in which he himself is inclined to it." (It may be noted that Rowland had heard him a dozen times affirm the flat reverse of all this.) "If I had only been a painter—a little, quiet, docile, matter-of-fact painter like our friend Singleton—I should only have to open my Ariosto here to find a subject, to find colour and attitudes, stuffs and composition; I should only have to look up from the page at that mouldy old fountain against the blue sky, at that cypress alley wandering away like a procession of priests in couples, at the crags and hollows of the Sabines there, to find my picture begun. Best of all would it be to be Ariosto himself or one of his brotherhood. Then everything in nature would give you a hint, and every form of beauty be part of your stock. You wouldn't have to look at things, only to say—with tears of rage half the time —'Oh yes, it's wonderfully pretty, but what the devil can I do with it?' But a sculptor now, come! That's a pretty trade for a fellow who has got his living to make, and yet is so damnably constituted that he can't work, on the one hand, unless the trumpet really sounds, and can't play, on the other, either at working or at anything else, while he's waiting for its call. You can't model the serge-coated cypresses, nor those mouldering old Tritons and all the sunny sadness of that dried-up fountain; you can't put the light into marble—the lovely, caressing, consenting Italian light that you get so much of for nothing. Say that a dozen times in his life a man has a completely plastic vision—a vision in which the imagination recognises a real, valid subject and the subject reacts on the imagination. It's a renumerative rate of production, and the intervals are convenient!"

One morning as the young men were at their ease on the sun-warmed grass at the foot of one of the slanting pines of the Villa, Roderick gave himself up to a free and beautiful consideration of the possible mischances of genius. "What if the watch should run down," he asked, "and you should lose the key? What if you should wake up some morning and find it stopped—inexorably, appallingly stopped? Such things have been, and the poor devils to whom they happened have had to grin and bear it. The whole matter of genius is a mystery. It bloweth where it listeth, and we know nothing of its mechanism. If it gets out of order we can't mend it; if it breaks down altogether we can't set it going again. We must let it choose its own pace and hold our breath lest it should lose its balance. It's dealt out in different doses, in big cups and little, and when you have consumed your portion it's as *naïf* to ask for more as it was for Oliver Twist to ask for more porridge. Lucky for you if you've got one of the big cups; we drink them down in the dark and we can't tell their size until we tip them up and hear the last gurgle. Those of some men last for life: those of others for a couple of years. I say, what are you grinning at?" he went on as in the best possible faith. "Nothing is more common than for an artist who has set out on his journey on a high-stepping horse to find himself all of a sudden dismounted and invited to go his way on foot. You can number them by the thousand—the people of two or three successes; the poor fellows whose candle burnt out in a night. Some of them groped their way along without it, some of them gave themselves up for blind and sat down by the wayside to beg. Who shall say that I am not one of these? Who shall assure me that my credit is for an unlimited sum? Nothing proves it, and I never claimed it; or if I did, I did so in the mere boyish joy of shaking off the dust of my desert. If you believed so, my dear fellow, you did it at your own risk. What am I, what are the best of us, but a desperate experiment? Do I more or less idiotically succeed—do I more or less sublimely fail? I seem to myself to be the last circumstance it depends on. I'm prepared, at any rate, for a fizzle. It won't be a tragedy, simply because I shan't assist at it. The end of my work shall be the end of my life. When I've played my last card I shall cease to care for the game. I'm not making vulgar threats of the dagger or the bowl; for destiny, I trust, won't make me further ridiculous by forcing me publicly to fumble with them. But I have a conviction that if the hour strikes *here*," and he tapped his forehead, "I shall disappear, dissolve, be carried off in a something as pretty, let us hope, as the drifted spray of a fountain; *that's* what I shall have been. For the past ten days I've had the vision of some such fate perpetually swimming before me. My mind is like a dead calm in the tropics, and my imagination as motionless as the blighted ship in the 'Ancient Mariner'!"

Rowland listened to this outpouring, as he often had occasion to listen to Roderick's flights of eloquence, with a number of mental restrictions. Both in gravity and in gaiety he said more than he meant, and you did him simple justice if you privately concluded that neither the glow of purpose nor the chill of despair was of so intense a strain as his gift for expression implied. The moods of an artist, his exaltations and depressions, Rowland had often said to himself, were like the pen-flourishes a writing-master makes in the air when he begins to set his copy. He may bespatter you with ink, he may hit you in the eye, but he writes a magnificent hand. It was nevertheless true that at present poor Roderick showed grave symptoms of a general breakage of his springs. As to genius held or not held on the precarious tenure he had sketched, Rowland had to confess himself too much of an outsider to argue. He secretly but heavily sighed; he wished his companion had had a trifle more of little Sam Singleton's pedestrian patience. But then was Sam Singleton a man of genius? He answered that such questions struck him as idle, even inane; that the proof of the pudding was in the eating; that he knew nothing about bringing dead things back to life again, but that you might sometimes pull a man out of bed who wouldn't get up. "Don't worry about your mood," he prosaically pleaded, "and don't believe there's any calm so utter that your lungs can't ruffle it with a breeze. If you've pressing business to attend to don't wait to settle the name and work out the pedigree of the agent you despatch on it: tumble to work somehow and see what it looks like afterwards."

"I've a prejudice against tumbling, anywhere," Roderick rejoined; "the pleasure of motion for me is in seeing where I go. If I don't see I don't move—that is, I but jump up and down in the same place. In other words I'm an ass unless I'm an angel. You should talk to Gloriani: he's an ass all the while, only an ass for a circus, who can stand on his hind legs and fire off pistols. But you're right," he added after a while; "this is unprofitable talk, and it makes my head ache. I shall take a nap and see if I can dream of a bright idea or two."

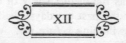

XII

HE TURNED his face upward to the parasol of the great pine, closed his eyes and in a short time forgot his hard argument. January though it was, the mild stillness seemed to vibrate with faint midsummer sounds. Rowland sat vaguely attentive; he wished that for their common comfort the paste of Roderick's composition had had a certain softer ductility. It was like something that had dried to colour, to brilliancy; but hadn't it also dried to brittleness? Suddenly, to his musing sense, the soft atmospheric hum was overscored with distincter sounds. He heard voices beyond a mass of shrubbery at the turn of a neighbouring path. In a moment one of them began to seem familiar, and an instant later a large white poodle emerged into view, slowly followed by his mistress. Miss Light paused on seeing Rowland and his companion; but though the former perceived he was recognised she gave him no greeting. Presently she walked directly toward him; and then, as he rose and was on the point of rousing Roderick, she laid her finger on her lips and motioned him to forbear. She stood looking at the deep peace of Roderick's sleep.

"What delicious oblivion!" she said. "Happy man! Stenterello" —and she pointed to his face—"wake him up!"

The poodle extended a long pink tongue and began to lick Roderick's cheek.

"Why," asked Rowland, "if he's happy?"

"Oh, I want companions in misery! Besides, I want to show off my dog." Roderick roused himself, sat up and unconfusedly stared. By this time Mrs. Light had approached, walking with a gentleman on each side of her. One of these was the Cavaliere Giacosa, the other was Prince Casamassima. "I should have liked to lie down on the grass and go to sleep," Christina added. "But it would have been unheard of."

"Oh, not quite," said the Prince in English, with a fine acquired distinctness. "There was already a Sleeping Beauty in the Wood!"

"Charming!" cried Mrs. Light. "Do you hear that, my dear?"

"When the Prince says a brilliant thing it would be a pity to lose it," said the girl. "Your servant, sir!" And she smiled at him with a grace that might have reassured him if he had thought her compliment ambiguous.

Roderick meanwhile had risen to his feet, and Mrs. Light began to exclaim on the oddity of their meeting and to set forth how, the day being lovely, she had been charmed with the idea of spending it in the country. And who would ever have thought of finding Mr. Mallet and Mr. Hudson asleep under a tree?

"Oh, I beg your pardon; I was very wide awake," said Rowland.

"Don't you know that Mr. Mallet's Mr. Hudson's sheep-dog?" asked Christina. "He was mounting guard to keep away the wolves."

"To indifferent purpose, madam!" said Rowland, indicating to Mrs. Light her daughter.

"Is that the way you spend your time?" Christina demanded of

Roderick. "I never yet happened to learn what men were doing when they supposed women were not watching them, but it was something vastly below their reputation."

"When, pray," said Roderick, smoothing his ruffled locks, "are women not watching them?"

"We shall give you something better to do at any rate. How long have you been here? It's an age since I've seen you. We consider you as an old inhabitant, and expect you to play host and entertain us."

Roderick said that he could offer them nothing but to show them the great terrace and its view; and ten minutes later the little group was assembled there. Mrs. Light was extravagant in her satisfaction; Christina looked away at the Sabine mountains in silence. The Prince stood by, frowning at the raptures of the elder lady.

"This is nothing," he said at last. "My word of honour. Have you seen the terrace at San Gaetano?"

"Ah, that *merveille*," murmured Mrs. Light amorously. "I suppose it's magnificent!"

"It's four hundred feet long, and paved with marble. And the view is a thousand times more beautiful than this. You see far away the blue, blue sea and the little smoke of Vesuvio!"

"Christina, love," cried Mrs. Light forthwith, "the Prince has a terrace four hundred feet long, all paved with marble!"

The Cavaliere gave a little cough and began to wipe his eye-glass.

"Stupendous!" said Christina. "To go from one end to the other the Prince must have out his golden coach." This was apparently an allusion to one of the other items of the young man's grandeur.

"You always laugh at me," said the Prince. "I know no more what to say."

She looked at him with a sad smile and shook her head. "No, no, dear Prince, I don't laugh at you. Heaven forbid! You're much too serious an affair. I assure you I feel your importance. What did you inform us was the value of the hereditary diamonds of the Princess Casamassima?"

"Ah, you're laughing at me yet!" said the young man, who had turned rather pale and stiff.

"It doesn't matter," Christina went on. "We've a note of it; mamma writes all those things down in a little book!"

"If you're laughed at, dear Prince, at least it's in company," said Mrs. Light caressingly; and she took his arm as if to combat his possible displacement under the shock of her daughter's sarcasm. But the Prince looked heavy-eyed at Rowland and Roderick, to whom the girl was turning, as if he had much rather his lot were cast with theirs.

"Is the villa inhabited?" Christina asked, pointing to the vast melancholy structure that rises above the terrace.

"Not privately," said Roderick. "It's occupied by a Jesuits' college for little boys."

"Can women go in?"

"I'm afraid not." And Roderick was struck with the picture. "Fancy the poor little devils looking up from their Latin declensions and seeing Miss Light shine down on them!"

"I should like to see the poor little devils, with their rosy cheeks and their long black gowns, and when they were pretty I shouldn't scruple to kiss them. But if I can't have that amusement I must have some other. We mustn't stand planted on this enchanting terrace as if we were a row of flower-pots. We must dance, we must feast, we must do something romantic, poetic. Mamma has arranged, I believe, that we're to go back to Frascati to lunch at the inn. I decree that we lunch here and send the Cavaliere back there to get the provisions! He can take the carriage, which is waiting below."

Miss Light carried out this programme with a high, light hand. The Cavaliere was summoned, and he stood to receive her commands, uncovered and his eyes cast down, as if she had been a princess addressing her major-domo. She, however, took him with friendly grace by his button-hole and called him a dear good old Family Friend for being always so obliging. Her spirits had risen with the occasion and she talked irresistible nonsense. "Bring the best they have," she said, "no matter if it ruins us! And if the best is very bad it will be all the more amusing. I shall enjoy seeing Mr. Mallet try to swallow it for propriety's sake. Mr. Hudson will say out like a man that it's horrible stuff and that he'll be choked first. Be sure you bring a dish of macaroni; the Prince must have the diet of the Neapolitan nobility. But I leave all that to you, my poor dear Family Friend; you know what's good, and you get it so cheap. Only be sure, above all, you bring a guitar. Mr. Mallet will play us a tune, I'll dance with Mr. Hudson, and mamma will pair off with the Prince, of whom she is so fond!"

And as she concluded her recommendations she patted her discreet old servitor tenderly on the shoulder. He gave Rowland a covert look charged with reminders—"Didn't I tell you she's as good as she's clever, and as clever as she's beautiful?"

The Cavaliere returned with zealous speed, accompanied by one of the servants of the inn, who bore a basket containing the materials of a rustic luncheon. The porter of the villa was easily induced to furnish a table and half a dozen chairs, and the repast when set forth was pronounced a perfect success; not so good as to fail of an amusing disorder, nor yet so bad as to defeat the proper function of repasts. Christina continued to display the most charming animation and compelled Rowland to reflect privately that, think what one might of her, the harmonious gaiety of so splendid a creature would not have been an impression to be missed. Her good-humour was contagious. Roderick, who an hour before had been descanting on madness and suicide, commingled his laughter with her lightest sallies; Prince Casamassima stroked his young moustache and found a fine cool smile for everything; his neighbour, Mrs. Light, who had Rowland on the other side, made the friendliest confidences to each of the young men, and the Family Friend contributed to the general hilarity by the solemnity of his attention to his plate. As for Rowland, the spirit of kindly mirth prompted him to propose the health of this useful personage. A moment later he wished he had held his tongue, for although the toast was drunk with demonstrative goodwill the Cavaliere received it with a brief dignity of deprecation which suggested to Rowland that his diminished gentility but half relished honours that savoured possibly of patronage. To perform punctiliously his mysterious duties toward the two ladies, and to elude or to baffle observation on his own merits —this clearly exhausted the Family Friend's modest ambition. Rowland perceived that Mrs. Light, who was not always remarkable for tact, seemed to have divined his humour on this point. She touched her lips with her glass, but she said nothing gracious and she immediately gave another direction to the talk. The old man had brought no guitar, so that when the feast was over there was nothing to hold the little group together. Christina wandered away with Roderick to another part of the terrace; the Prince, whose smile had vanished, sat gnawing the head of his cane near Mrs. Light, and Rowland strolled apart with the Cavaliere, to whom he wished to address a friendly word of apology for the light he had played a moment over his preferred obscurity. The Cavaliere was a mine of information upon all Roman places and people; he told Rowland a number of curious anecdotes of which the ancient villa was more or less the subject. "If history could always be taught in this fashion !" thought Rowland. "It's the ideal—strolling up and down on the very spot commemorated, hearing out-of-the-way anecdotes from deeply indigenous lips." At last, as they passed, Rowland observed the mournful physiognomy of Prince Casamassima, and glancing towards the other end of the terrace saw that Roderick and Christina had disappeared from view. The young man was sitting upright in an attitude, apparently habitual, of ceremonious rigidity; but his lower jaw had fallen and was propped up with his cane, and his dull dark eye was fixed upon the angle of the villa which had just eclipsed Miss Light and her companion. His features kept the odd rigour of their symmetry, and his expression was vacuous; but there was a lurking delicacy in his face which seemed to tell you that nature had been making Casamassimas for a great many centuries, and, though she adapted her mould to circumstances, had learned to mix her material to an extraordinary fineness and to perform the whole operation with a kind of insolent art. The Prince was stupid, Rowland suspected, but he imagined he was amiable, and he saw that, with his dim aspirations and alarms, he felt himself in charge of the very highest interests. Rowland touched his companion's arm and pointed to the melancholy nobleman.

"Why in the world doesn't he go after her and insist on being noticed ?"

"Oh, he's very proud !" said the Cavaliere.

"That's all very well, but a gentleman who cultivates a passion for that young lady must be prepared to make sacrifices."

"He thinks he has already made a great many. He comes of a very great family—a race of princes who for endless generations have sought brides only with some correspondence of name and condition. But he's—what do you call it ?—very hard hit, and he would certainly stretch the point for Christina."

"Then it's she who won't stretch *her* point ?"

"Ah, she's very proud too!" The Cavaliere was silent a moment, as if he were measuring the propriety of freedom. He seemed to have formed a high opinion of Rowland's discretion, for he presently continued: "It would be a great match, for she brings him neither a name nor a fortune—nothing but her wit and her beauty. But *questa ragazza* will receive no favours; I know her too well. She would rather have her beauty blasted than seem to care about the marriage, and if she ever accepts the Prince it will be only after she has kept him for months on his knees."

"But she does care about it," said Rowland, "and to bring him to his knees she's working upon his jealousy by pretending to be interested in my friend Hudson. If you said more you would say that, eh?"

The Cavaliere's sagacity exchanged a glance with Rowland's. "By no means. Christina's a *drôle de fille*. She has many romantic ideas. She would be quite capable of interesting herself seriously in a remarkable young man like your friend and doing her utmost to discourage a splendid suitor like the Prince. She would act sincerely and she would go very far. But it would be unfortunate for the remarkable young man," he added after a pause, "for at the last she'd go back!"

"A *drôle de fille* indeed."

"She would accept the more brilliant *parti*. I can answer for it."

"And what would be the logic of her proceeding?"

"She would be forced. There would be circumstances, conditions, necessities, *des raisons majeures*. I can't tell you more."

"But this implies that the rejected suitor would come back to *her*. He might grow tired of waiting."

"Oh, this one's good for almost anything. Look at him now." Rowland obeyed, and saw that the Prince had left his place by Mrs. Light and was moving restlessly to and fro between the villa and the parapet of the terrace. Every now and then he consulted his watch. "In this country, you know," said the Cavaliere, "a young lady never goes walking alone with a *beau jeune homme*. It seems to him very strange."

"It must seem to him monstrous, and if he overlooks it he must be very much in love."

"Oh, he'll overlook it. He's just what you say."

"Who is this exemplary lover then; what is he?"

"A Neapolitan; of one of the oldest houses in Italy. He's a prince in your English sense of the word; unlike most of his countrymen, even of the highest pretensions, he has a princely fortune, coming mostly from his great Sicilian property. He's very young; he's only just of age; he saw the signorina last winter in Naples. He fell in love with her from the first, but his family interfered, and an old uncle, a high ecclesiastic, a Cardinal probably of the next batch, hurried up to Naples, seized him and locked him up. Meantime he has passed his majority, and *s'il ne fait pas de bêtises* he won't have, in the exercise of his freedom, any one but himself to consider. His relations are moving heaven and earth to prevent his marrying Miss Light, and they've sent us word that he forfeits this, that and the other if he takes his wife out of a certain line. I've investigated the question and I find this is but a fiction to frighten us. He's perfectly untrammelled; but the estates are such that it's no wonder they wish to keep them in their own hands. It's a rare case, among *us*, of unencumbered property. The Prince has been an orphan from his third year; he has therefore had a long minority and made no inroads upon his fortune. Besides, he's very prudent and shrewd; I'm only afraid that some day he'll pull the purse-strings too tight. All these years his affairs have been in the hands of his reverend uncle, a man of wonderful head, who has managed them to perfection—paid off mortgages, planted forests, opened up mines. It is now a magnificent fortune; such a fortune as with his name would justify the young man in pretending to any alliance whatsoever. And he lays it all at the feet of that little person who's wandering in yonder *boschetto* with a penniless artist."

"He's certainly a phœnix of princes! The signora must be in the seventh heaven."

The Cavaliere looked imperturbably grave. "The signora has a high esteem for his personal merit."

"Well, his personal merit," Rowland returned with a smile; "what name do you give to *it*?"

"Eh, Prince Casamassima's a real *gran' signore*! He's a very good young man. He's not brilliant nor witty, but he won't let himself be made a fool of. He's a faithful son of the Church—and it's lucky for our friends that they too are children of the great Mother. He's as you see him there: a young man without many ideas, but with a very firm grasp of a single one—the conviction that Prince Casamassima is a very great person, that he greatly honours any young lady by asking for her hand, and that things are going very strangely when the young lady turns her back upon him. The poor young man's terribly puzzled. But I whisper to him every day, 'Pazienza, Signor Principe!'"

"So you firmly believe," said Rowland in conclusion, "that Miss Light will accept him just in time not to lose him?"

"I count upon it. She would fill a great position too perfectly to miss her destiny."

"And you hold that nevertheless, in the meanwhile, in allowing any sort of voice about it to my friend Hudson, she will have been acting in good faith?"

The Cavaliere lifted his shoulders a trifle, and gave an inscrutable smile. "Eh, caro signore, our young lady's very romantic!"

"So much so, you intimate, that she'll eventually give way in consequence not of a change of sentiment, but of a mysterious outward pressure?"

"If everything else fails, there's that resource. But it will *be* mysterious, as you say, and you needn't try to guess it. You won't make it out."

"It will be something then at least by which Miss Light will suffer?"

"Not too much, I hope."

"And the remarkable young man? I understand you that there necessarily *can* be nothing but disappointment in store for the infatuated youth who loses his heart to her?"

The Cavaliere hesitated. "He had better," he said in a moment, "go and pursue his studies in Florence. There are very fine antiques in the Uffizi."

Rowland presently joined Mrs. Light, toward whom her noble companion had not yet retraced his restless steps. "That's right," she said; "sit down here; I've something serious to say to you. I'm going to talk to you as a friend. I want your assistance. In fact, you *must* help me; it's your duty. Look at that unhappy young man."

"Yes, he seems unhappy."

"He's just come of age, he bears one of the greatest names in Italy, and owns one of the greatest properties, and he's pining away with love for my daughter."

"So the Cavaliere tells me."

"It's none of the Cavaliere's business," said Mrs. Light sharply. "Such information should come from me. The Prince is pining, as I say; he's consumed, he takes it very hard. It's a real Italian passion: I know what that means!" And she rolled an eye which seemed to commune with the vividness of her own annals. "Meanwhile, if you please, my daughter's hiding in the woods with your dear friend Mr. Hudson. I could cry with rage."

"If things are as bad as that," said Rowland, "it seems to me that you should find nothing easier than to despatch the Cavaliere to bring the guilty couple back."

"Never in the world! My hands are tied. Do you know what my wretch of a girl would do? She would tell the Cavaliere to go about his business—heaven forgive her!—and send me word that if she had a mind to she would roam the woods till midnight. Fancy the Cavaliere coming back and delivering such a message as that before the Prince!

Think of a sane young woman making a mess of such a fortune ! He would marry her to-morrow at six o'clock in the morning."

"It's certainly very sad," said Rowland.

"That costs you little to say ! If you had left your precious young meddler to vegetate in his native village you would have saved me a world of worry."

"Ah, you marched into the jaws of danger," said Rowland. "You came and knocked at poor Hudson's door."

"In an evil hour ! I wish to goodness you would talk with him."

"I talk with him a great deal. He's wonderful," said Rowland, "to talk with."

"I wish then that in common consideration you would take him away. You have plenty of money. Do me a favour. Take him to travel. Go to the East—go to Timbuctoo. Then, when my daughter *has* accepted her destiny and is settled to it," Mrs. Light added in a moment, "he may come back if he chooses !"

"Does she really care for him ?" Rowland abruptly asked.

"The deuce knows whom she really cares for—even to me who have so known and so watched her she's a living riddle. She has ideas of her own, and theories and views and inspirations, each of which is the best in the world until another is better. She's perfectly sure about each, but they are fortunately so many that she can't be sure of any one very long. They may last all together, none the less, long enough to dish the Prince's patience, and if that were to happen I don't know what I should do. I should be the most miserable of women. It would be too cruel, after all I have suffered to make her what she is, to see the labour of years blighted by mere wicked perversity. For I can assure you, sir," Mrs. Light declared, "that if my daughter *is* the gifted creature you see, I deserve some of the credit of the creation."

Rowland promptly remarked that this was obvious, for he saw that the poor woman's irritated nerves required the comfort of some accepted overflow and he assumed designedly the attitude of a person impressed by her sacrifices. She told him then the story of her efforts, her hopes, her dreams, her presentiments, her disappointments, in this exalted cause of Christina's capture of a prize—such a prize as would really be the crown of such a fabric of visions. It was a wonderful rigmarole of strange confidences, and while it went on the Prince continued to pass to and fro, stiffly and solemnly, like a pendulum marking the time allowed for the young lady to come to her senses. Mrs. Light evidently at an early period had gathered her maternal and social appetites together into a sacred parcel, to which she said her prayers and burnt incense—which she treated generally as a sort of fetish. These things had been her religion; she had none other, and she performed her devotions bravely and cheerily, in the light of day. The poor old fetish had been so caressed and manipulated, so thrust in and out of its niche, so passed from hand to hand, so dressed and undressed, so mumbled and fumbled over, that it had lost by this time much of its early freshness and seemed a rather battered and disfeatured divinity. But it was still brought forth in moments of trouble, to have its tinselled petticoat twisted about and be set up on its altar. Rowland observed that Mrs. Light had at the service of her tawdry ideal a conscience that worked in the most approved and most punctual fashion; she considered that she had been performing a pious duty in bringing up Christina to carry herself, "marked" very high and in the largest letters, to market; and when the future looked dark she found consolation in thinking that destiny could never have the heart to deal a blow at so deserving a person. It made almost as much and as comically for the topsy-turvy as if he had seen the good stout lady herself stand on her head.

"I don't know whether you believe in presentiments," said Mrs. Light, "and I don't mind if you think they're rubbish. I've had one for the last fifteen years, and if people have often laughed at it they've never laughed me out of it. It has been everything to me; I couldn't have lived without it. One must believe in something, hang it ! It came to me in a flash, when Christina was five years old. I remember the day and the place as if it were yesterday. She was a very ugly baby— I give you *that* for a remarkable fact; for the first two years I could hardly bear to look at her, and I used to spoil my own looks with crying about her. She had an Italian nurse who was very fond of her and insisted that she would grow up pretty. I couldn't believe her, I used to contradict her, and we were for ever squabbling. I was just a little foolish in those days—surely I may say it now—and I was very fond of being amused. If my daughter was ugly, at least it was not that she resembled her mamma; I had, I don't mind telling you, no lack of amusement. People accused me, I believe, of neglecting my little girl; if I ever did I've made up for it since. One day I went to drive on the Pincio—I was in very low spirits. A certain person—I needn't name him—had trifled with a confidence—a confidence that I had in short placed: oh my dear, but *placed* ! While I was there he passed me in a carriage, driving with a horrible woman who had made trouble

I should be really very nervous. Even in such a position she would hold her head very high, and if anything should happen to her she would make no concessions to the popular fury. The best thing, if one would be prudent, seems to be a nobleman of the highest possible rank short of belonging to a reigning stock. There you see one striding up and down, looking at his watch and counting the minutes till my daughter reappears !"

Rowland listened to all this with a large compassion for the heroine of the tale. What an education, what a history, what a school of character and of morals ! He looked at the Prince and wondered whether he too had heard Mrs. Light's story. If he had he was a brave man. "I certainly hope you'll nail him," he said to Mrs. Light. "You've played a dangerous game with your daughter; it would be a pity not to win. But there's hope for you yet; here she comes at last !"

Christina reappeared as he spoke these words, strolling beside her companion with the same Olympian command of the air, as it were, not less than of the earth, with which she had departed. Rowland imagined that there was a faint pink flush in her cheek which she had not carried away with her, and there was certainly a light in Roderick's eyes that he had not seen there for a week.

"Bless my soul, how they're all looking at us !" she cried as they advanced. "One would think we were prisoners of the Inquisition !" And she paused and glanced from the Prince to her mother and from Rowland to the Cavaliere, and then threw back her head and burst into far-ringing laughter. "What is it, pray ? Have I been very improper ? Am I ruined for ever ? Dear Prince, you're looking at me as if I had committed the unpardonable sin !"

"I myself," said the Prince, "would never have ventured to ask you to walk with me alone in the country for an hour !"

"The more fool you, dear Prince—as I should say if I were vulgar and rude. Our walk has been awfully interesting. I hope you, on your side, have enjoyed each other's society."

"My dear daughter," said Mrs. Light, taking the arm of her predestined son-in-law, "I shall have something serious to say to you when we reach home. We'll go back to the carriage."

"Something serious ! Decidedly it *is* the Inquisition. Mr. Hudson, stand firm and let us agree to make no confessions without conferring previously with each other ! They may put us on the rack first. Mr. Mallet I see also," Christina added, "has something serious to say to me !"

171

Rowland had been looking at her with the shadow of his lately-stirred pity in his eyes. "Possibly," he said. "But it must be some other time."

"I'm always, you know, at your service. I see our innocent gaiety is gone. And I only wanted to be amiable ! Try to go in for an artless ease ! It's very discouraging. Cavaliere, you alone don't look as if you wanted to bite me; from your old dear stupid face, at least, there's no telling what you think. Give me your arm and take me away."

The party took its course back to the carriage, which was waiting in the grounds of the villa, and Rowland and Roderick bade their friends farewell. Christina threw herself back in her seat and closed her eyes; a manœuvre for which Rowland imagined the Prince was grateful, as it enabled him to look at her without seeming to depart from his attitude of distinguished disapproval.

Rowland found himself roused from sleep early the next morning to see Roderick standing before him dressed for departure, his bag in his hand. "I'm off," he said—"I'm for work again. An idea has come to me, by a miracle, and I must try to set it up while I *have* it. Addio !" And he went by the first train. Rowland followed at his ease.

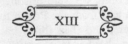

XIII

ROWLAND WENT very often to the Coliseum; he had established with this monument and with its exuberance of ruin, in those days all un-trimmed, a relation of the tenderest intimacy. One morning, about a month after his return from Frascati, as he was strolling across the vast arena, he observed a young woman seated on one of the fragments of stone which are arranged along the line of the ancient parapet. It seemed to him that he had seen her before, but he was unable to give her a frame. Passing her again he perceived that one of the little red-legged French soldiers who were at that time on guard there had made her the object of an irresistible military advance. She smiled upon him with a radiance, and Rowland recognised the address (it had ever pleased him) of a certain comely Assunta who sometimes opened the door for Mrs. Light's visitors. He wondered what she was doing alone in the Coliseum, and put it together that she had admirers as well as her young mistress, but that, being without the same domiciliary conveniences, she was using this massive heritage of her Latin ancestors as hall of audience. In other words she had an appointment with her lover, who would do well from present appearances not to delay. It was a long time since Rowland had mounted to the upper tiers of the great circus, and, as the day was splendid and the distant views promised to be particularly clear, he determined to give himself this pleasure. The custodian unlocked the great wooden wicket, and he climbed through the winding shafts where the eager Roman crowds had pressed and surged, not pausing till he reached the highest accessible stage. The views were as fine as he had supposed; the lights on the Sabine mountains had never so seemed the very blurs of the scroll of history. He lingered, he gazed to his satisfaction; then he began to retrace his steps. In a moment he paused again on an abutment somewhat lower, from which the glance dropped dizzily into the deep vast cup. There are accidents of ruggedness in the upper portions of the Coliseum which offer a very fair imitation of the large excrescences on some Alpine face. In those days a multitude of delicate flowers and sprays of wild herbage had found a friendly soil in the hoary crevices, and they bloomed and nodded as on the shoulders of a mountain. Rowland was turning away when he heard a sound of voices rise from below. He had but to step slightly forward to find himself overlooking two persons who had seated themselves on a narrow ledge in a sunny corner. They had apparently an eye to extreme privacy, but they had not observed that their position was commanded by the abutment on which Rowland stood. One of these high climbers was a lady, thickly veiled, so that even if he had not been placed directly above her he could not have made out her face. The other was a young man whose face he also missed, but who presently gave a toss of clustered locks that was equivalent to a master's signature. A moment's reflexion satisfied him of the identity of the lady. He had been unjust to poor Assunta, sitting patient in the gloomy arena; she had not come to it on her own errand. Rowland's discoveries made him hesitate and delay. Should he retire as softly as possible, or should he call out a friendly good-morning? While he was debating he found himself hearing his friends' words, which availed to make him unwilling to retreat, and yet rendered awkward the disclosure of a position that must have kept him an auditor.

"If what you say is true," said Christina with her silvery clearness of tone—it made her words rise with peculiar distinctness to Rowland's ear—"you're simply as weak as any other *petit jeune homme*. I'm so sorry! I hoped—I really believed—you were strong."

"No, I'm not weak," Roderick returned with vehemence; "I maintain I'm not weak! I'm incomplete perhaps; but I can't help that. Incompleteness is a matter of the outfit. Weakness is a matter of the will."

"Incomplete then be it, since you hold to the word. It's the same thing," Christina went on, "so long as it keeps you from splendid achievement. Is it written then that I shall really never know what I've so often dreamed of?"

"What then have you dreamed of?"

"A man whom I can have the luxury of respecting!" cried the girl with a sudden flame. "A man whom I can admire enough to make me know I'm doing it. I meet one, as I've met more than one before, whom I fondly believe to be cast in a bigger mould than most of the vulgar human breed—to be large in character, great in talent, strong in will. In such a man as that, I say, one's weary imagination at last may rest; or may wander if it will, but with the sense of coming home again a greater adventure than any other. When I first knew you I gave no sign, but you had struck me. I observed you as women observe, and I fancied you had the sacred fire."

"Before heaven I believe I have!" Roderick broke out.

"Ah, but so very little of it! It flickers and trembles and sputters; it goes out, you tell me, for whole weeks together. From your own account it doesn't much look as if you'd take either yourself or any one else very far."

"I say those things sometimes myself," came in Roderick's voice, "but when I hear you say them they make me feel as if I could scale the skies."

"Ah, the man who's strong with what I call strength," Christina replied, "would neither rise nor fall by anything I could say! I'm a poor weak woman; I've no strength myself, and I can give no strength. I'm a miserable medley of vanity and folly. I'm silly, I'm ignorant, I'm affected, I'm false. I'm the fruit of a horrible education sown on a worthless soil. I'm all that, and yet I believe I have one merit. I should know a great character when I saw it, and I should delight in it with a generosity that would do something toward the remission of my sins. For a man who should really give me a certain feeling—I have never had it, but I should know it when it came—I would send Prince Casamassima and his millions to perdition. I don't know what you think of me for saying all this; I suppose we have not climbed up here under the skies to play propriety. Why have you been at such pains to assure me, after all, that you are a little man and not a great one, a weak one and not a strong? I innocently imagined at first that your eyes—because they're so beautiful—declared you strong. I think they declare nothing but just their beauty. That *would* be enough—if you were a being like me. But I want some one so much better than myself! Your voice, at any rate, *caro mio*, condemns you; I always wondered at it; it's not the voice of a conqueror!"

"Give me something to conquer," Roderick answered, "and when I say that I thank you from my soul, my voice, whatever you think of it, shall speak the truth!"

Christina for a moment said nothing, and Rowland was now too interested to think of moving. "You pretend to such devotion," she went on, "and yet I'm sure you have never really chosen between me and that person in America."

"Do me the great favour not to speak of her," Roderick almost groaned.

"Why not? I say no ill of her, and I think all kinds of good. I'm certain she is a far better girl than I, and far more likely to make you happy."

"This is happiness, this present palpable moment," said Roderick; "though you *have* such a genius for knowing what will be most odious to me."

"It's greater happiness than you deserve then! You've never chosen, I say; you've been afraid to choose. You've never really looked in the face the fact that you're false, that you've broken your faith. You've never looked at it and seen that it was hideous and yet said 'No matter, I'll brave the penalty, I'll bear the shame.' You've closed your eyes; you've tried to stifle remembrance, to persuade yourself that you were not behaving so badly as you seemed to be, that there would be some way, after all, of doing what you liked and yet escaping trouble. You've faltered and dodged and drifted, you've gone on from accident to accident, and I'm sure that at this present moment you can't tell what it is you really wish."

Roderick was sitting with his knees drawn up and bent and his hands clasped round his legs. He dropped his head, resting his forehead on his knees.

Christina went on with a sort of infernal pitiless calm. "I believe that really you don't greatly care for your friend in America any more than you do for me. You're one of the men who care only for themselves and for what they can make of themselves. That's very well when they can make something great, and I could interest myself in a man of extraordinary power who should wish to turn all his passions to account. But if the power should turn out to be, after all, rather ordinary? Fancy feeling one's self ground in the mill of a third-rate talent! If you've doubts about yourself I can't reassure you; I've too many doubts myself about everything in this weary world. You've gone up like a rocket in your profession, they tell me; are you going to come down like the stick? I don't pretend to know; I repeat frankly what I've said before—that all modern sculpture seems to me vulgar, and that the only things I care for are some of the most battered of the antiques of the Vatican. No, no, I can't reassure you; and when you tell me—with a confidence in my discretion of which certainly I'm duly sensible—that at times you feel terribly scant, why, I can only answer, 'Ah then, my poor friend, I'm afraid you *are* scant!' The language I should like to hear from a person offering me his career is that of a confidence that would knock me down."

Roderick raised his head, but said nothing; he seemed to be making with his companion some long, deep, dumb exchange. The result of it was that he flung himself back at last with an incoherent wail. Rowland, admonished by the silence, had been on the point of turning away, but was arrested by a sudden gesture on Christina's part. She pointed a moment into the blue air, and Roderick followed the direction of her gesture.

"Is that little flower we see outlined against the dark niche," she asked, "as intensely blue as it looks through my veil?" She spoke apparently with the amiable design of directing the conversation into a less painful channel.

Rowland, from where he stood, could see the flower she meant—a delicate plant of radiant hue, which sprouted from the top of an immense fragment of wall some twenty feet from their place.

Roderick turned his head and looked at it without answering. At last glancing round, "Put up your veil!" he said; and then on the girl's complying: "Does it look as blue now?"

"Ah, what a lovely colour!" she murmured as she leaned her head to one side.

"Should you like to have it?"

She stared a moment, then laughed as if in spite of herself.

"Should you like to have it?" he repeated in a ringing voice.

"Don't look as if you would eat me up," she answered. "Do you suppose I want you to get it for me ?"

Roderick rose to his feet and stood looking at the little flower. It was separated from the ledge on which he stood by a rugged surface of vertical wall which dropped straight into the dusky vaults behind the arena. Suddenly he took off his hat and flung it behind him. Christina then sprang to her feet.

"I'll get it for you," he said.

She seized his arm. "Are you crazy ? Do you mean to kill yourself ?"

"I shall not kill myself. Sit down !"

"Pardon me. Not till you do !" And she grasped his arm with both hands.

Roderick shook her off and pointed with a violent gesture to her former place. "Go there !" he harshly cried.

"You can never, never !" she pleaded with clasped hands. "I do entreat you."

Roderick turned and looked at her, and then in a voice which Rowland had never heard him use, a voice which roused the echoes of the mighty ruin, "Sit down !" he thundered. She hesitated a moment, after which she sank to the ground and buried her face in her hands.

Rowland had seen all this and he saw what followed. He saw Roderick clasp in his left arm the jagged corner of the vertical partition on which he proposed to try his experiment, then stretch out his leg and feel for a resting-place for his foot. Rowland had measured with a hard stare and a dry throat the possibility of his holding on, and pronounced it uncommonly small. The wall was garnished with a series of narrow projections, the remains apparently of a brick cornice supporting the arch of a vault which had long since collapsed. It was by lodging his toes on these loose brackets, and grasping with his hands at certain mouldering protuberances on a level with his head, that Roderick intended to proceed. The relics of the cornice were utterly worthless as a support. Rowland's sharpened sense had made sure of this, and yet for a moment he had hesitated. If the thing were possible he felt a sudden high bold relish of his friend's attempting it. It would be finely done, it would be gallant, it would have a sort of ardent authority as an answer to Christina's sinister *persiflage*. But it was not possible ! Rowland left his place with a bound and scrambled down a near flight of steps, and the next moment a stronger pair of hands than Christina's were laid upon Roderick's shoulders.

He turned, staring, pale and angry. Christina rose, pale and staring too, but beautiful in her wonder and alarm. "My dear young idiot," said Rowland, "I'm only preventing you from doing a very foolish thing. That's an exploit for spiders, not for young sculptors of promise."

Roderick wiped his forehead, looked back at the wall; he closed his eyes as if with a rush of retarded dizziness. "I won't resist you," he said. "But I've made *you* do as I told you," he added, turning to Christina. "Am I weak now?"

She had recovered her composure; she looked straight past him and addressed Rowland. "Be so good as to show me the way out of this horrible place!"

He helped her back into the corridor; Roderick followed after a short interval. Of course, as they were descending the steps, came questions for Rowland to meet, also more or less surprise. Where had he come from? how happened he to have appeared just at that moment? Rowland answered that he had been rambling overhead and that, looking out of an aperture, he had seen a gentleman preparing to undertake a preposterous gymnastic feat and a lady swooning away in consequence. Interference seemed in order, and he had made it as prompt as possible. Roderick was far from hanging his head as might become a man who had been caught in the perpetration of an extravagant folly; but if he held it more erect than usual our friend believed that this was much less because he had made a show of personal daring than because he had triumphantly proved to Christina that, like a certain person she had dreamed of, he too could speak the language of decision. Christina descended to the arena in silence, apparently occupied with her own thoughts. She betrayed no sense that the sequestered nature of her interview with Roderick might have invited an explanation; she appeared tacitly to assume that Rowland would have seen stranger things in New York. The only evidence of her recent agitation was that on being joined by her maid she declared that she was unable to walk home—she must have a carriage. A fiacre was found resting in the shadow of the Arch of Constantine, and Rowland suspected that after she had got into it she disburdened herself under her veil of a few natural tears.

Rowland had played eavesdropper to so good a purpose that he might justly have omitted the ceremony of denouncing himself to Roderick. He preferred, however, to let him know that he had overheard a portion of his talk with Christina.

"Of course it seems to you," Roderick said, "a proof that I'm hopelessly infatuated."

"Your companion seemed to me to know very well how to handle you," Rowland returned. "She was twisting you round her finger. I don't think she exactly meant to defy you; but your preposterous attempt to pluck the flower was a proof that she could go all lengths in the way of making a fool of you."

"Yes," said Roderick meditatively; "she's quite wiping her feet on me."

"And what do you expect to come of it?"

"Not a thousand a year." And Roderick put his hands into his pockets and looked as if he were considering the most colourless fact in the world.

"And in the light of your late interview, what do you make of your young lady?"

"If I could tell you that, it would be plain sailing. But she'll not tell me again that I'm a muff."

"Are you very sure you're much stronger than she was willing to allow?"

"I may be as weak as a cat, but *she* shall never dare—she shall never *care*—to say it!"

Rowland said no more until they reached the Corso, when he asked his companion whether he were going to his studio.

Roderick started out of an absence and passed his hands over his eyes. "Oh no, I can't settle down to work after such a scene as that. I was not afraid of breaking my neck then, but I feel in a devil of a shake now. I'll go—I'll go and sit in the sun on the Pincio!"

"Promise me this first," said his companion very solemnly, "that the next time you meet Miss Light it shall be on the earth and not in the air!"

Since his return from Frascati Roderick had been working doggedly at the statue ordered by Mr. Leavenworth. To Rowland's eye he had made a very fair beginning, but he had himself insisted from the first that he liked neither his subject nor his patron, and that it was impossible to feel any warmth of interest in a work on which the baleful shadow of Mr. Leavenworth was to rest. It was all against the grain; he wrought without love. Nevertheless after a fashion he wrought, and the figure grew beneath his hands. Miss Blanchard's friend was ordering works of art on every side, and his purveyors were in many cases persons with whom Roderick declared it was an infamy to be associated. There had been famous tailors, he said, who declined to make you a coat unless you should get the hat you were to wear with it from an artist of their own choosing, and it struck him that he had an equal right to exact that his statue should not form part of the same system of ornament as the "Pearl of Perugia," a picture by an American aspirant who had, in Mr. Leavenworth's opinion, an eye for colour scarcely matched since Titian. As a liberal customer, Mr. Leavenworth used to drop into Roderick's studio to see how things were getting on and give a friendly hint or exert an enlightened control. He would seat himself squarely, plant his gold-topped cane between his legs, which he held very much apart, rest his large white hands on the head, and enunciate the principles of spiritual art—a species of fluid wisdom which appeared to rise in bucketfuls, as he turned the crank, from the well-like depths of his moral consciousness. His benignant and imperturbable pomposity gave Roderick the sense of suffocating beneath an immense feather-bed, and the worst of the matter was that the good gentleman's placid vanity had a surface from which the satiric shaft rebounded. Roderick admitted that in thinking over the tribulations of struggling genius the danger of dying of too much attention had never occurred to him.

The deterrent effect of the episode of the Coliseum was apparently of long continuance: if Roderick's nerves had been shaken his hand needed time to recover its steadiness. He cultivated composure upon principles of his own; by frequenting entertainments from which he returned at four o'clock in the morning and lapsing into habits which might fairly be called irregular. He had hitherto made few friends among the artistic fraternity; chiefly because he had taken no trouble about it and because, further, there was in his demeanour an elastic independence of the favour of his fellow-mortals which made social advances on his own part peculiarly necessary. Rowland had told him —on grounds that worthy might have been at a loss to defend—that he ought to fraternise a trifle more with his colleagues, and he had always answered that he had not the smallest objection to fraternising; let his colleagues arrive ! They arrived on rare occasions, and Roderick was not punctilious about returning their visits. He declared there was not one of them the fruits of whose genius gave him the least desire to delve in the parent soil. For Gloriani he professed a consistent contempt, and having been once to look at his wares never crossed his threshold again. The only one of the fraternity for whom by his own admission he cared a straw was small Singleton; but he took the more diverted view of this humble genius whenever he encountered him, and quite forgot his existence in the intervals. He had never been to see him, but Singleton edged his way from time to time timidly into Roderick's studio, and opined with characteristic modesty that brilliant fellows like Hudson might consent to receive homage but could hardly be expected to render it. Roderick never acknowledged applause, and apparently failed to follow with any curiosity the footsteps of appreciation. And then his taste as to company was never to be foretold. There were very good fellows who were disposed to cultivate him, but who bored him to crying out, and there were others beyond even the wide bounds of Rowland's charity with whom he appeared to delight to rattle. He gave the most fantastic reasons for his likes and dislikes. He would declare he thirsted for the blood of a man with a flat nose, and he would explain his unaccountable fancy for some competitor wholly featureless by telling you that he had an ancestor who in the thirteenth century had walled up his wife alive. "I like to talk to a man whose ancestor has walled up his wife alive," he would say. "You may not see the charm of it, and think my poor gentleman a dull dog. It's very possible; I don't ask you to admire him. But he appeals to me—I mean that fact about him does: it sets him off. The old fellow, the rude forefather, left her for three days with her face exposed, and placed a looking-glass opposite to her, so that she could see, as he said, if her gown was a fit!"

His accessibility to odd association had led him to acquaintance with a number of people outside of Rowland's well-ordered circle, and he made no secret of their being very queer fish. He formed an intimacy, among several, with a strange character who had come to Rome as an emissary of one of the Central American republics, to drive some ecclesiastical bargain with the papal government. The Pope had given him the cold shoulder, but since he had not prospered as a diplomatist he had sought compensation as a man of the world, and his great flamboyant curricle and negro lackeys were for several weeks one of the striking ornaments of the Pincian. He spoke a queer jargon of Italian, Spanish, French, English, American, humorously relieved with scraps of ecclesiastical Latin, and to those who inquired of Roderick what he found to interest him in so "dreadful" a type, the latter would reply, looking at his interlocutor with his lucid blue eyes, that he had a beautiful freedom of mind. The two had gone together one night to a ball given by a lady of some renown in the Spanish colony, and very late, on his way home, Roderick came up to Rowland's rooms, in the windows of which he had seen a light. Rowland was going to bed, but Roderick flung himself into an arm-chair and chattered for an hour. The friends of the tropical envoy were as amusing as himself, and very much in the same line. The mistress of the house had worn a yellow satin dress and gold heels to her slippers, and at the close of the entertainment had sent for a pair of castanets, tucked up her petticoats and danced a fandango, while the gentlemen sat cross-legged on the floor. "It was awfully low," Roderick said; "all of a sudden I perceived it and bolted. Nothing of that kind ever amuses me to the end; before it's half over it bores me to death; it makes me sick. Hang it, why can't a poor fellow enjoy things in peace ? My illusions are all broken-winded; they won't carry me twenty paces. I can't laugh and forget; my laugh dies away before it begins. Your friend Stendhal writes on his book-covers (I never got further) that he has seen too early in life *la beauté parfaite*. I don't know how early he saw it; I saw it before I was born—in another state of being. I can't describe it positively; I can only say I don't find it anywhere now. Not at the bottom of champagne glasses; not, strange as it may seem, in that extra half-yard or so of shoulder that some women have their ball-dresses cut to expose. I don't find it at noisy supper-tables where half a dozen ugly men with pomatumed heads are rapidly growing uglier still with heat and wine; nor when I come away and walk through these squalid black streets and go out into the Forum and see a few old battered stone posts standing there like gnawed bones stuck into the earth. Everything's mean and dusky and shabby, and the men and women who make up this so-called brilliant society are the meanest and shabbiest of all. They have no real spontaneity; they are nothing but parrots and popinjays. They have no more dignity than so many grasshoppers. Nothing is good but one !" And he jumped up and stood looking at one of his wrought figures, which shone vaguely across the room in the dim lamplight.

"Yes, do tell us," said Rowland, "what to hold on by !"

"Those things of mine were pretty devilish good," he answered. "But my idea was so much better—and that's what I mean !"

Rowland said nothing. He was willing to wait for Roderick to complete the circle of his metamorphoses, but he had no desire to officiate as chorus to the play.

"You think I've the 'cheek' of the devil himself," the latter said at last, "coming up to moralise at this hour of the night ! You think I want to throw dust into your eyes, to put you off the scent. That's your eminently rational view of the case."

"Pardon my not taking any view at all," said Rowland.

"You've given me up then?"

"No, I've merely suspended judgement. I'm waiting."

Roderick looked at him a moment. "What are you waiting for?"

Rowland made an angry gesture. "Oh miserable, oh merciless youth! When you've hit your mark and made people care for you, you shouldn't twist your weapon about at that rate in their vitals. Allow me to say I'm sleepy. Good night!"

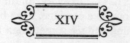

XIV

IT HAPPENED some days later that, on a long afternoon ramble, Rowland took his way through one of the quiet corners of the Trastevere. He was particularly fond of this part of Rome, though he could hardly have expressed the sinister charm of it. As you pass away from the dusky swarming purlieus of the Ghetto you emerge into a region of empty, soundless, grass-grown lanes and alleys, where the shabby houses seem mouldering away in disuse and yet your footstep brings figures of startling Roman type to the doorways. There are few monuments here, but no part of Rome seemed more oppressively historic, more weighted with a ponderous past, more blighted with the melancholy of things that had had their day. When the yellow afternoon sunshine slept on the sallow battered walls and lengthened the shadows in the grassy courtyards of small closed churches the place acquired a strange fascination. The church of Saint Cecilia has one of these sunny waste-looking courts; the edifice seems abandoned to silence and the charity of chance devotion. Rowland never passed it without going in, and he was generally the only visitor. He entered it now, but he found that two persons had preceded him, both of whom were women. One was at her prayers at one of the side-altars; the other was seated against a column at the upper end of the nave. Rowland walked to the altar and paid in a momentary glance at the clever statue of the saint in death in the niche beneath it the usual tribute to the charm of polished ingenuity. As he turned away he looked at the person seated and recognised Christina Light. Seeing that she perceived him he advanced to speak to her.

She was sitting in a listless manner, her hands in her lap; her attitude spoke of weariness, and her walking-dress, in its simplicity, of the desire to escape observation. When he had greeted her he glanced back at her companion and recognised the faithful Assunta.

Christina found a smile to note this movement. "Are you looking round for Mr. Hudson? He's not here, I'm happy to say."

"If he were here one might understand," said Rowland. "This is a strange place to meet you alone."

"It's just the place to meet me. People call me a strange girl, and I might as well have the comfort of it. I came to take a walk; that, by the way, is part of my strangeness. I can't loll all the morning on a sofa and sit perched all the afternoon in a carriage. I get horribly restless; I must move; I must do something and see something. Mamma suggests a cup of tea. Meanwhile I put on an old dress and half a dozen veils, I take Assunta under my arm and we start on a pedestrian tour. It's a bore that I can't take the poodle, but he attracts attention. We trudge about everywhere; there's nothing I like so much. I hope you congratulate me on the simplicity of my tastes."

"I congratulate you on your great sense. To live in Rome and not to walk about would, I think, be poor pleasure. But you're terribly far from home, and I'm afraid you're rather tired."

"A little—enough to sit here a while."

"Might I offer you my company while you rest?"

"If you'll promise to amuse me. I'm in dismal spirits."

Saying he would do what he could, Rowland brought a chair and placed it near her. He was not in love with her; he disapproved of her; he distrusted her; and yet he felt it a rare and expensive privilege to watch her, and he found her presence in every way important and momentous. The background of her nature had a sort of landscape largeness and was mysterious withal, emitting strange, fantastic gleams and flashes. Waiting for these was better sport than some kinds of fishing. Moreover it was not a disadvantage to talk with a girl who forced one to make sure of the sufficiency of one's wit; it was like having in one's bank-book after "wild" drafts: it settled the question of one's balance.

Assunta had risen from her prayers and, as he took his place, was coming back to her mistress. But Christina motioned her away. "No, no; while you're about it say a few dozen more! Pray for *me*," she added in English. "Pray that I say nothing silly. She has been at it half an hour; I envy her volubility !"

"One envies good Catholics many things," said Rowland with conscious breadth.

"Oh, speak to me of that ! I've been through that too, though I'm not so much a good Catholic as a bad one. Mamma's what I call a good one—*ecco* ! There was a time when I wanted immensely to be a nun; it was not a laughing matter. It was when I was about sixteen years old. I read the *Imitation* and the Life of Saint Catherine; I fully believed in the miracles of the saints and I was dying to have one of my own—little of a saint as I was ! The least little accident that could have been twisted into a miracle would have carried me straight into the cloister. I had for three months—positively—the perfect vocation. It passed away, and as I sat here just now I was wondering what has become of it."

Rowland had already been sensible of something in this young lady's tone which he would have described as an easy use of her imagination, and this epitome of her religious experience failed to strike him as an authentic text. But it was no disfiguring mask, since she herself was evidently the foremost dupe of her inventions. She had a fictitious history in which she believed much more fondly than in her real one, and an infinite capacity for extemporised reminiscence adapted to the mood of the hour. She liked to carry herself further and further, to see herself in situation and action; and the vivacity and spontaneity of her character gave her really a starting-point in experience, so that the many-coloured flowers of fiction that blossomed in her talk were perversions of fact only if one couldn't take them for sincerities of spirit. And Rowland felt that whatever she said of herself might have been, under the imagined circumstances; energy was there, audacity, the restless questioning soul. "I'm afraid I'm sadly prosaic," he said, "for in these many months now that I've been in Rome I've never ceased for a moment to look at the Faith simply from the outside. I don't see an opening as big as your finger-nail where I could creep into it !"

"What do you believe ?" asked Christina, looking at him. "Do you believe anything at all ?"

"I'm very old-fashioned. I believe in the grand old English Bible."

"'English'—— ?"

"American then," Rowland smiled.

She let her beautiful eyes wander a while, and then gave a small sigh. "You're much to be envied !"

"Oh 'envied'—— !" And Rowland fairly sounded bitter.

"Yes, you have rest."

"You're too young to envy anybody anything."

"I'm not young; I've never been young ! My mother took care of that. I was a little wrinkled old woman at ten."

"I'm afraid," said Rowland in a moment, "that you're fond of overloading the picture."

She looked at him a while in silence. "Do you wish to win my eternal gratitude ? Prove to me that I'm better than I suppose."

"I should have first to know what you really suppose."

She shook her head. "It wouldn't do ! You would be horrified to learn even the things I imagine about myself, and shocked at the knowledge of evil displayed in my very mistakes."

"Well, then," said Rowland, "I'll ask no questions. But, at a venture, I promise you to catch you some day in the act of doing something very good."

"Are you too trying to flatter me ? I thought you and I had fallen from the first into rather a truth-speaking vein."

"Oh, I've not given it up," said Rowland; and he determined, since he had the credit of homely directness, to push his advantage further. The opportunity seemed excellent. But while he was hesitating how to begin, his companion said, bending forward and clasping her hands in her lap : "Please tell me about your faith."

"My faith—— ?"

"The faith you said just now you have."

"Tell you about it ?" Rowland looked cold. "Never in the world !"

She flushed a little. "Is it such a mighty mystery it can't be put into words or communicated to my inferior mind ?"

"Such things—one's way of meeting, morally, the mystery of the universe—lie very deep down, at the bottom of one's trunk. One can't always put one's hand on them in a moment."

"Then of what use are they ?" Christina asked; "a folded squashed garment that one never wears ? Deep convictions, it seems to me," she said, "should be eloquent and aggressive. They should wish to make converts, to persuade and illumine, to take possession !"

"Isn't it true, rather, that the deeper they are the more they take the colour of one's general disposition ? I'm not aggressive, and certainly I'm not eloquent."

"Well, I'm sure I shouldn't greatly care for anything you might say," Christina rejoined. "It would certainly, after all, be half-hearted. You're not in the least satisfied."

"How do you know that?"

"Oh, I'm an observer!"

"No one's satisfied with everything, I suppose—but I assure you I complain of nothing."

"So much the worse for your honesty. To begin with, you're in love."

"You wouldn't have me complain of that!"

"And it doesn't go well. There are grievous obstacles. So much I know. You needn't protest; I ask no questions. You'll tell no one—me least of all. Why does one never see you?"

"Why, if I come to see you," said Rowland, deliberating, "it wouldn't be, it couldn't be, for a trivial reason—because I had not been for a month, because I was passing, because I admire you. It would be because I should have something very particular to say. I haven't come because I've been slow in making up my mind to say it."

"You're simply cruel then," the girl declared. "Something particular, in this ocean of inanities? In common charity, speak!"

"I doubt whether you'll like it."

"Oh, I hope to goodness it's not some tribute to my charms!" Christina wailed.

"It may be called a tribute to your reasonableness. That's one of your charms, you know. You perhaps remember that I gave you a hint of it the other day at Frascati."

"Has it been hanging fire all this time? Then let it off—no matter with what bang. I promise not to stop my ears."

"It relates to my friend Hudson." And Rowland paused. She was looking at him expectantly; her face gave no other sign. "I'm rather disturbed in mind about him. He seems to me at times not quite to have found his feet." He paused again, but Christina said nothing. "The case is simply this," he went on. "It was by my advice, you see, that he gave up his work at home and went in for the artist's, went in for *this*, life. I made him burn his ships, I brought him to Rome, I launched him into the world, and I've undertaken to answer to—to his mother for his doing well. It's not such smooth sailing as it might be, and I'm inclined to put up prayers for fair winds. If he's to succeed he must work—very quietly and very hard. It's not news to you, I imagine, that Hudson's a great admirer of yours."

Christina remained silent; she turned away her eyes with an air, not of confusion, but of deep deliberation. Violent frankness had, as a general thing, struck Rowland as the keynote of her system, but she had more than once given him a suggestion of an unfathomable power of calculation, and her silence now had for him vaguely something charged and ominous. He had of course rather sounded his scruples before deciding to make to an unprotected girl, for the needs of a cause—and not *her* cause, but his very own—the point that another man was in a state about her: the thing too much resembled, superficially, risking the disturbance of her peace. But he was clear that even rigid discretion is not bound to take such a person at more than her own estimate, and Christina presently reassured him as to the limits of her susceptibility. "Mr. Hudson's mad about me," she simply said.

Rowland flinched a trifle. Then, "Am I," he asked, "from this point of view of mine, to be glad or sorry?"

"I don't understand you."

"Why, is Hudson to be happy or unhappy?"

She hesitated a moment. "You wish him to be great in his profession? And for that you consider that he must be happy in his life?"

"Decidedly. I don't say it's a general rule, but I think it's a rule for him."

"So that if he were very happy he would become very great?"

"He would at least do himself justice."

"And by that you mean a great deal?"

"A great deal."

Christina sank back in her chair and rested her eyes on the cracked and polished slabs of the pavement. At last she looked up. "You've not forgotten, I suppose, that you told me he was engaged to be married?"

"By no means."

"He's still engaged then?"

"To the best of my belief."

"And yet you desire that, as you say, he should be made happy by something I can do for him?"

"What I desire is this—that your great influence with him should be exerted for his good, that it should help him and not retard him. Understand me well. You probably know that your admirers, your victims, have rather a hapless time of it. I can answer for two of them. You don't know your own mind very well, I imagine, and as you like being admired the poor devil on whom you have cast your spell has to pay all the expenses. Since we're really being frank I wonder whether I mightn't say the great word."

"You needn't; I know it. I'm a beastly low flirt."

"No, not a 'low' one, rather a high one, since I'm making an appeal to your intelligence and your generosity. I'm pretty sure you can't imagine yourself marrying my friend."

"There's nothing I can't imagine. That's my difficulty."

Rowland's brow contracted impatiently. "*I* can't imagine it then !"

Christina flushed faintly; then very gently, "I'm not so bad as you think," she said.

"It's not a question of badness; it's a question of whether the conditions don't make the thing an extreme improbability."

"Worse and worse. I can be bullied then—or bribed ?"

"You're not so candid as you pretend to be. My feeling's simply this," Rowland went on. "Hudson, as I understand him, doesn't need, as an artist, the stimulus of strong emotion, of precarious passion. He's better without it; he's emotional and passionate and precarious enough when left to himself. The sooner passion's at rest therefore the sooner he'll settle down to work, and the fewer emotions he has that are mere emotions and nothing more the better for him. If you cared for him enough to marry him I should have nothing to say; I should never venture to interfere. But I greatly guess you don't, and therefore I suggest most respectfully that you leave him alone."

"If I leave him alone he'll go on like a new clock, eh ?"

"He'll do better. He'll have no excuses, no pretexts."

"Oh, he makes me a pretext, does he ? I'm much obliged !" cried Christina with a laugh. "What's he doing now ?"

"I can hardly say. He's like a very old clock indeed. He's moody, desultory, idle, irregular, fantastic."

"Heavens, what a list ! And it's all poor me ?"

"No, not all. But you're a part of it, and I turn to you because you're a more tangible, sensible, responsible cause than the other things."

Christina raised her hand to her eyes and bent her head thoughtfully. Rowland was puzzled to measure the effect of his venture; she rather surprised him by her mildness. At last, without moving, "If I were to marry him," she asked, "what would have become of his *fiancée* ?"

"I'm bound to suppose that she would have become extremely unhappy."

Christina said nothing more, and Rowland, to let her make her reflexions, left his place and strolled away. Poor Assunta, sitting patiently on a stone bench and unprovided on this occasion with military consolation, gave him a bright frank smile which might have been construed as an expression of regret for herself and of intelligence for her mistress. Rowland presently seated himself again near that young woman.

"What do you think of your friend's infidelity to that person in the little place?" she asked with a sudden look at him.

"I don't like it."

"Was he very much in love with her?"

"He requested the favour of her hand. You may judge."

"Is she also poor?"

"Yes, she's also poor."

"Is she very much in love with him?"

"I know her too little to say."

She paused again and then resumed. "You've settled in your mind then that I'll never seriously listen to him?"

"I shall think it unlikely until the contrary's proved."

"How shall it be proved? How do you know what passes between us?"

"I can judge of course only from appearances; but, like you, I am an observer. Hudson has not at all to me the air of the lucky lover."

"If he has a bad air there's a good reason. His bad air's his bad conscience. One must hope so at least. On the other hand, simply as a friend," she continued gently, "you think I can do him no good?"

The humility of her tone, combined with her beauty as she made this remark, was inexpressibly touching, and Rowland had an uncomfortable sense of being put at a disadvantage. "There are doubtless many good things you might do if you had proper opportunity," he said. "But you seem to be sailing with a current which leaves you little leisure for quiet benevolence. You live in the whirl and hurry of a world into which a poor artist can hardly find it to his advantage to follow you."

"In plain English I'm odiously frivolous. You put it very generously."

"I won't hesitate to say all my thought," said Rowland. "For better or worse you seem to me to belong both by character and by destiny to what is called the world, the 'great,' the dangerous, the delightful world. You're made to ornament it magnificently—you're made to charm it irresistibly. You're not made to be an artist's wife."

"I see. But even from your point of view that would depend upon the artist. Extraordinary talent might take him into the wonderful place you speak of."

Rowland smiled. "That's very true."

"If, as it is," Christina continued in a moment, "you take a low view of me—no, you needn't protest !—I wonder what you would think if you knew certain things."

"What things do you mean ?"

"Well, for example, how I was brought up. I've had a horrid vulgar life. There must be some good in me, since I've perceived it, since I've turned and judged my circumstances."

"My dear Miss Light !" Rowland murmured remonstrantly.

She gave an almost harsh little laugh. "You don't want to hear ! You don't want to have to think about that !"

"Have I a right to ? You needn't justify yourself."

She turned upon him a moment the quickened light of her beautiful eyes, then fell to musing again. "Is there not some novel or some play," she asked at last, "in which a beautiful wicked woman who has ensnared a young man sees his father come to her and beg her to let him go ?"

"I seem to remember many—and that the wicked woman generally weeps and makes the sacrifice."

"Well, I'll try at least to weep. But tell me," she continued, "shall you consider—admitting your proposition—that in ceasing to be nice to Mr. Hudson, so that he may go about his business, I do something magnanimous, heroic, sublime, something with a fine name like that ?"

Rowland, elated with the prospect of gaining his point, was about to reply that she would deserve the finest name in the world; but he instantly suspected that this tone wouldn't please her. Besides, it wouldn't express his meaning. "You do something I shall greatly respect," he contented himself with saying.

She made no answer and in a moment she beckoned to her maid. "What have I to do to-day ?" she asked.

Assunta meditated. "Eh, it's a very busy day ! Fortunately I've a better memory than the signorina," she said, turning to Rowland. She began to count on her fingers, "We've to go to the Piè di Marmo to see about those laces that were sent to be washed. You said also that you wished to say three sharp words to the Buonvicini about your pink dress. You want some moss rosebuds for to-night, and you won't get them for nothing ! You dine at the Austrian Embassy, and that Frenchman's to powder your hair. You're to come home in time to receive, for the signora gives a dance. And so away, away till morning!"

"Ah, yes, the moss roses !"—Christina rose to this vision. "I must have a great lot—at least a hundred. Nothing but buds, eh ? You must sew them in a kind of immense apron down the front of my dress. Packed tight together, eh? It will be delightfully barbarous. And then twenty more or so for my hair. They go very well with powder; don't you think so?" And she turned to Rowland. "I'm going *en Pompadour*."

"Going where?"

"To the Spanish Embassy, or whatever it is."

"All down the front, signorina? *Dio buono!* You must give me time!" Assunta cried.

"Yes, we'll go!" And she left her place. She walked slowly to the door of the church, looking at the pavement, and Rowland couldn't have guessed if she were thinking of her apron of moss rosebuds or of her opportunity for a spiritual flight. Before reaching the door she turned away and stood gazing at an old picture, indistinguishable with blackness, over an altar. At last they passed out into the court. Glancing at her in the open air Rowland was startled; she might have been weeping like the wicked women of the plays. They had lost time, she said, and they must hurry; she sent Assunta to look for a coach. She remained silent a while, scratching the ground with the point of her parasol, and then at last, looking up, she thanked Rowland for his confidence in her "reasonableness." "It's really very comfortable to be expected to do something good, after all the horrid things one has been used to doing—instructed, commanded, coerced to do. I'll think over what you've said to me." In that deserted quarter coaches are rare, and there was some delay in Assunta's procuring one. Christina talked of the church, of the picturesque old court, of that strange decaying corner of Rome. Rowland was perplexed; he was ill at ease. At last the cab arrived, but she waited a moment longer. "So, decidedly," she suddenly asked, "I can only hurt him?"

"You make me feel very brutal," said Rowland.

"And he's such a fine fellow that it would be really a great pity, eh?"

"I shall praise him no more," Rowland said.

She turned away quickly, but she lingered still. "Do you remember promising me, soon after we first met, that at the end of six months you would tell me definitely what you thought of me?"

"It was a foolish promise."

"You gave it. Bear it in mind. I shall think of what you've said to me. Farewell." The two women stepped into the carriage and it rolled away. Rowland stood for some minutes looking after it, and then went his way with a sigh. If this expressed general mistrust he ought three days afterwards to have been reassured. He received by the post a note containing these words—

"I've done it. Begin to respect me !

"C. L."

To be perfectly satisfactory, indeed, the note required a commentary. Calling that evening upon Roderick, he found one in the information offered him at the door by the old serving-woman—the startling information that the signorino had gone to Naples.

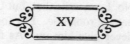

ABOUT A month later Rowland addressed to his cousin Cecilia a letter of which the following is a portion.

"... So much for myself; yet I tell you but a tithe of my own story unless I let you know how matters stand with poor Hudson, for he gives me more to think about just now than anything else in the world. I need a good deal of courage to begin this chapter. You warned me, you know, and I made rather light of your warning. I've had all kinds of hopes and fears, but hitherto, in writing to you, I've resolutely put the hopes foremost. Now, however, my pride has forsaken me, and I should like hugely to give expression to a little comfortable despair. I should like to say, 'My dear wise cousin, you were right and I was wrong; you were a shrewd observer and I was a meddlesome donkey !' When I think of a certain talk we had about the 'salubrity of genius' I feel my ears tingle. If what I've seen is salubrity give me raging disease. I'm pestered past bearing; I go about with a chronic heart-ache; there are moments when I could shed salt tears. There's a pretty portrait of your dear dull kinsman. I wish I could make you understand; or rather I wish you could make *me*. I don't understand a jot; it's a hideous, mocking mystery; I give it up. I don't in the least give it up, you know; I'm incapable of giving it up. I sit holding my head by the hour, racking my brain, wondering what to invent. You told me at Northampton that I took the thing too lightly; you'd tell me now perhaps that I take it too hard. I do, altogether; but it can't be helped. Without flattering myself I may say that I'm cursed with sympathy—I mean as an active faculty, the last of fond follies, the last of my own. Wiser men, before this, would have cast their worries to the winds and settled that the *bel enfant* of my adoption must lie on his bed as he has made it. Some people perhaps would even say I'm making my ado about nothing, that I'm crying out before I'm hurt, or at least before *he* is; and that in short I've only to give him rope and he'll tire himself out. He tugs at his rope, however, much too hard for me to hold it comfortably. I certainly never pretended the thing was anything but an experiment; I promised nothing, I answered for nothing; I only said that the case was hopeful and it would be a shame not to give him a chance. I've done my best, and if the machine's running down I've a right to stand aside and let it rattle. Amen, amen ! No, I can write that, but I can't feel it. I can't be just; I can only be insanely romantic. I'm too abjectly fond of the hapless youth; I can never give him up. As for understanding him, that's another matter; nowadays I don't believe even you would. One's intelligence sometimes really ceases to serve one over here, and I'm in the way of seeing more than one quaint specimen of human nature. Roderick and Miss Light, between them ! . . . Haven't I already told you about Miss Light ? Last winter everything was perfection. Roderick struck out bravely, did really great things—proved himself, as I supposed, sound all through. He was strong, he was first-rate; I felt perfectly secure, and paid myself the most fulsome compliments. We had passed at a bound into the open sea and left danger behind. But in the summer I began to be uneasy, though I succeeded in keeping down alarm. When he came back to Rome, however, I saw that the tide had turned and that we were close upon the rocks. It's in fact another case of Ulysses and the Sirens; only Roderick refuses to be tied to the mast. He's the most extraordinary being, the strangest mixture of the clear and the obscure. I don't understand so much power—because it *is* power—going with so much weakness, such a brilliant gift being subject to such lapses. The poor fellow isn't *made* right, and it's really not his fault; Nature has given him his faculty out of hand and bidden him be hanged with it. It's as if she had shied her great gold brick at him and cried 'Look out for your head !' I never knew a creature harder to advise or assist when he's not in the mood for listening. I suppose there's some key or other to his tangle, but I try in vain to find it; and yet I can't believe our stars so cruel as simply to have turned the lock and thrown the key away. He makes a notorious fool of me, and if he tires out my temper he doesn't my attention. Sometimes I think he hasn't a grain of conscience and sometimes I find him all too morbidly scrupulous. He takes things at once too easy and too hard—it depends on what they are—and has found means to be both loose and rigid, indifferent and passionate. He has developed faster even than you prophesied, and for good and evil alike he takes up a formidable space. There's too much of him for me, at any rate. Yes, he *is* hard; there's no mistake about that. He's inflexible, he's brittle; and though he has plenty of spirit, plenty of soul, he hasn't what I call a heart. He has something that Miss Garland took for one, and I suppose her a judge. But she judged on scanty evidence. He has something that Christina Light, here, makes believe at times that she takes for one, but she's no judge at all. I think it established that in the long run egotism (in too big a dose) makes a failure in conduct: is it also true that it makes a failure in the arts ? . . . Roderick's standard is immensely high; I must do him that justice. He'll do nothing beneath it, and while he's waiting for the vision to descend his imagination, his nerves, his senses must have something to amuse them. This is my elegant way of breaking it to you that he has taken to riotous living and has just been spending a month at Naples—a city where amusement is actively cultivated—in very bad company. Are they all like that, all the men of genius ? There are a great many artists here who hammer away at their trade with exemplary diligence; in fact I'm surprised at their success in reducing the matter to a virtuous habit; but I really don't think that one of them has his exquisite quality of talent. The talent's there, it's the application that has broken down. Nothing comes out of the bottle; he turns it upside down; it refuses to flow. Sometimes he declares it's empty— that he has done all he was made to do. This I consider great nonsense; but I would nevertheless take him on his own terms if it were only I that am concerned. But I keep thinking of those two praying, trusting neighbours of yours, and I feel like a bad bungler when I don't feel like a swindler. If his working mood came at its intervals, fixed ones, I'd willingly wait for it and keep him on his legs somehow or other between; but that would be a sorry account to present to *them* ! A few years of this sort of thing, moreover, would effectually settle the question. I wish, heaven forgive me, that he were less of a genius and more of a charlatan. He's too confoundedly all of one piece; he won't throw overboard a grain of the cargo to save the rest. Fancy him thus with all his brilliant personal charm, his handsome head, his careless step, his look as of a nervous nineteenth-century Apollo, and you'll understand that there's mighty little comfort in seeing him spoil on the tree. He was extremely perverse last summer at Baden-Baden, but he finally pulled together and for some time was steady. Then he began to knock about again and at last toppled over. Now, literally, he's lying prone. He came into my room last night miserably the worse for liquor. I assure you it didn't amuse me. . . . About Miss Light it's a long story. She's one of the great beauties of all time and worth coming barefoot to Rome, like the pilgrims of old, to see. Her complexion, her eyes, her step, the planting and the mass of her dusky tresses, may have been seen before in a goddess on a cloud or a nymph on a Greek gem, but never in a mere modern girl. And you may take this for truth, because I'm not in love with her. On the contrary I sometimes quite detest her. Her education has been simply infernal. She is corrupt, perverse, as proud as a potentate, and a coquette of the first magnitude; but she's intelligent and bold and free, and so awfully on the lookout for sensations that if you set rightly to work you may enlist her imagination in a good cause as well as in a bad. The other day I tried to bring it over to my side. I happened to have some talk with her to which it was possible to give a serious turn, and I boldly broke ground and begged her to suffer my poor friend to go in peace. After leading me rather a dance—in conversation—she consented, and the next day, with a single word, she packed him off to Naples to drown his humiliation in poisonous waters. I've come to the conclusion that she's more dangerous in her virtuous moods than in her vicious, and that she probably has a way of turning her back which is the most maddening thing in the world. She's an actress, she couldn't forgo doing it with a flourish, and it was just the flourish that made it work wrong. I wished her of course to let him down easy; but she must have the curtain drop on an attitude, and her attitudes don't in the least do for inflammable natures. . . . Roderick made an admirable bust of her at the beginning of the winter, and a dozen women came rushing to him to be done, *mutatis mutandis*, in the same style. They were all great ladies and ready to take him by the hand, but he told them all their faces didn't interest him *pour deux sous* and sent them away vowing his destruction."

At this stage of his long burst of confidence Rowland had paused and put by his letter. He kept it three days and then read it over. He was disposed thereupon to destroy it, but he decided finally to keep it, in the hope that it might strike a spark of useful suggestion from the flint of Cecilia's good sense. We know he had a talent for taking advice. And then it might be, he reflected, that his cousin's answer would throw some light on Mary Garland's present vision of things. In his altered mood he added a few lines.

"I unburdened myself the other day of this monstrous load of anxiety; I think it did me good, and I now let it stand. I was in a melancholy muddle and was trying to lash myself out of it. You know I like discussion in a quiet way, and there's no one with whom I can have it as quietly as with you, most abysmal of cousins. There's a sharp old lady here with whom I often confer and who talks very much to the point. But Madame Grandoni has disliked Roderick from the first, and if I were to take her advice I would wash my hands of him. You would laugh at me for my long face, but you would do that in any circumstances. I'm half ashamed of my letter, for I've a faith in our friend that's deeper than my doubts. He was here last evening, talking about the Naples Museum, the Aristides, the bronzes, the Pompeian frescoes, with such a beautiful intelligence that doubt of the ultimate future seemed blasphemy. I walked back to his lodging with him, and he was as mild as midsummer moonlight. He has that ineffable something that charms and convinces; my last word about him shall not be a harsh one."

Shortly after sending his letter, going one day into his friend's studio, he found Roderick suffering the honourable torture of a visit from Mr. Leavenworth. The young man submitted with extreme ill grace to being bored, and he was now evidently in a state of high exasperation. He had lately begun a representation of a *lazzarone* lounging in the sun; an image of serene, irresponsible, sensuous life. The real lazzarone, he had admitted, was a vile fellow; but the ideal lazzarone—and his own had been subtly idealised—was the flower of a perfect civilisation.

Mr. Leavenworth had apparently just transferred his spacious gaze to the figure. "Something in the style of the Dying Gladiator?" he sympathetically observed.

"Oh no," said Roderick seriously, "he's not dying, he's only drunk."

"Ah, but intoxication, you know," Mr. Leavenworth rejoined, "is not a proper subject for sculpture. Sculpture shouldn't deal with transitory attitudes."

"Lying dead drunk's not a transitory attitude. Nothing's more permanent, more sculpturesque, more monumental."

"An entertaining paradox," said Mr. Leavenworth, "if we had time to exercise our wits upon it. I remember at Florence an intoxicated figure by Michael Angelo which seemed to me a deplorable aberration of a great mind. I myself touch liquor in no shape whatever. I have travelled through Europe on cold water. The most varied and attractive lists of wines are offered me, but I brush them aside. No cork has ever been drawn at my command."

"The movement of drawing a cork calls into play a very 'pretty set of muscles," said Roderick. "Jolly to make a figure in that position."

"A Bacchus realistically treated? My dear young friend, never trifle with your lofty mission. Spotless marble seems to me false to itself when it represents anything less than Conscious Temperance—'the golden mean' in all things." And while Mr. Leavenworth threw back his head, squared his shoulders and heaved his torso, as if to exorcise the spirit of levity, his attention broke again like a slow wave, this time on a marble replica of the bust of Christina. "An ideal head, I presume," he went on; "a fanciful representation of one of the pagan goddesses—a Diana, a Flora, a naiad, a dryad? I often regret that our American artists should not boldly break with those artificial appellations."

"She's neither a naiad nor a dryad," said Roderick, "and her appellation's as good as yours or mine."

"You call her——?" Mr. Leavenworth blandly inquired.

"Christina Light," Rowland interposed in charity.

"Ah, our great American beauty? Not a pagan goddess—an American Christian maiden. Yes, I've had the pleasure of conversing with Miss Light. Her conversational powers are not quite what one might have expected, but her beauty's of a high order. I observed her the other evening at a large party where some of the proudest members of the European aristocracy were present—duchesses, princesses, countesses and others distinguished by similar titles. But for beauty, grace and elegance our young countrywoman left them all nowhere. What woman can compare with a refined and cultivated American lady? The duchesses the other night had no attractions for my eyes; they looked coarse and bold and sensual. It seemed to me that the tyranny of class distinctions must indeed be terrible when such countenances could inspire admiration. You see more beautiful girls in an hour on Broadway than in the whole tour of Europe. Miss Light now, on Broadway, would excite no particular remark."

"Oh, damn Broadway!" Roderick murmured.

Mr. Leavenworth stared as if this were unpatriotic; then he resumed almost severely: "I suppose you've heard the news about our lovely compatriot."

"What news?" Roderick had stood with his back turned, fiercely poking at his *lazzarone*; but at Mr. Leavenworth's last words he faced quickly about.

"It's the news of the hour, I believe. Miss Light is admired by the highest people here. They tacitly recognise her superiority. She has had offers of marriage from *very* prominent people—as such people go in this part of the world. I was extremely glad to hear it and to learn that they had mostly been left sighing. She has not been dazzled by their titles and pedigrees and pretensions, by their gilded coronets. She has judged them simply as real men, and by that measure has found them wanting. One of them, however, a young Neapolitan prince, I believe, has, after a long probation, succeeded in making himself acceptable. Miss Light has at last smiled upon him and the engagement has just been announced. I'm not generally a retailer of the gossip of the passing hour, but the fact was alluded to an hour ago by a lady to whom I had been presented, and subjects of interest seem scarcely numerous enough in Europe, to dispense with the aid of these conversational futilities, therefore suffered myself to be—as I may say—impressed. Yes, I regret that Miss Light should ally herself with a purely conventional character. Americans should stand by each other. If she wanted a brilliant match we could have organised it for her. If she wanted a fine bright fellow— a specimen of clean comfortable *white* humanity—I would have undertaken to find him for her without going out of my native State. And if she wanted a big fortune I would have found her twenty that she would have had hard work to make an impression on; money right there in convertible securities—not tied up in fever-stricken lands and worm-eaten villas. What's the name of the young man? Prince Cantimasher or some such thing!" It was well for Mr. Leavenworth that he was fond of listening to his own correct periods; for the current of his eloquence floated him past the short, sharp, startled cry with which Roderick greeted his anecdote. The young man stood looking at him with parted lips and an excited eye. "The position of woman," he imperturbably resumed, "is certainly a very degraded one in these countries. I doubt if a European princess commands the *true* respect which in our country is exhibited to the obscurest females. The civilisation of a country should be measured by the deference shown to the weaker sex. Judged by that standard, where are they over here?"

Though Mr. Leavenworth had not observed Roderick's emotion it was not lost upon Rowland, who was making sundry uncomfortable reflexions upon it. He saw that it had instantly become one with the acute irritation produced by the poor gentleman's large inevitable oratory, and that an explosion of some sort was imminent. Mr. Leavenworth, with calm unconsciousness, proceeded to fire the mine.

"And now, please, for *my* Creation!" he said with the same grandiloquence, demanding by a gesture the discovery of the muffled mass that, standing somewhat apart, had represented for some time past the young sculptor's partial response to his encouraging order.

Roderick stood looking at him a moment with concentrated rancour and then strode to the indicated object and twitched off the sheet. Mr. Leavenworth settled himself into his chair with an air of flattered proprietorship and scanned the unfinished image. "I can conscientiously express myself as gratified with the general conception," he said. "The figure has considerable majesty and the countenance wears a fine open expression. The cerebral development, however, strikes me as not sufficiently emphasised. Our subject being, as we called it—didn't we? —Intellectual Refinement, there should be no mistaking the intellect, symbolised (wouldn't it be?) by an unmistakably thoughtful brow. The eye should instinctively seek the frontal indications. Couldn't you strengthen them a little?"

Roderick, for all answer, tossed the sheet back over the statue. "Oblige me, sir," he said, "I beg you to oblige me. Never mention that thing again."

"Never mention it? Why, my dear sir—— !"

"Never mention it. It's a base fraud."

"Base? My grand conception?"

"Yours indeed!" cried Roderick. "It's none of mine. I disown it."

"Disown it if you please," said Mr. Leavenworth, now sternly enough, "but finish it first!"

"I would much rather smash it!" Roderick returned.

"This is petulant folly, sir. You must keep your engagements."

"I made no engagement. A sculptor isn't a tailor, and I didn't measure you for a pair of trousers. Did you ever hear of inspiration? Mine's dead! And it's no laughing matter. You yourself killed it."

"I—I—killed your inspiration?" cried Mr. Leavenworth with the accent of righteous wrath. "You're a very ungrateful young man! My desire has been that you should feel yourself encouraged and so far *as* possible inspired."

"I appreciate your kindness, and I don't wish to be uncivil. But your interest is somehow fatal to me. I object to your interest. I can't work for you."

"I call this gross ill-humour, my good sir !" said Mr. Leavenworth, as if he had found the damning word.

"Oh, I'm in a perfectly infernal humour !" Roderick now quite cheerfully answered.

"Pray, sir, is it produced by my inopportune allusion to Miss Light's marriage ?"

"It's produced by your inopportune everything. I don't say that to offend you; I beg your pardon if it does. I say it by way of making our rupture complete and irretrievable."

Rowland had stood by in silence, but he now interfered. "Listen to me well," he said, laying his hand on Roderick's arm. "You're standing on the edge of a very deep sea. If you suffer this accident to put you out, you take your plunge. It's no matter at all that you don't like your work; it's no matter at all—if he'll magnanimously allow me to say so —that you don't even like Mr. Leavenworth: to whom it certainly isn't any matter either ! You'll do the wisest thing you ever did if you muster the resolution *not* to chuck up a commission so definitely accepted. Make the effort necessary at least for finishing your job. Then destroy what you've done, if you like; but finish it first and see. I speak only the truth."

Roderick looked at him with eyes that regret for impossibility made almost tender. "You too ?" he simply said.

He felt he might as well attempt to squeeze water from a polished crystal as hope to move him. He turned away and walked into the adjoining room with a sense of sickening helplessness. In a few moments he came back and found that Mr. Leavenworth had departed —he really hoped with due superiority. Roderick was sitting with his elbows on his knees and his head in his hands. Rowland made one more attempt. "You won't mind me the least little bit ?"

"Be so good as not to mind *me* !"

"There's one more point: that you should make and keep a resolve not to go back—for the present at least—to Mrs. Light's."

"I shall go back this evening."

"That too is fatal folly."

"Well," Roderick smiled, "when one's a fatalist as well as a fool——!"

"You talk like a slave, not like a free agent."

"Why then do you make me talk ?"

Rowland meditated a moment. "Are your fatalism and your folly prepared to lose you the best friend you have ?"

Roderick looked up; he still smiled. "I defy them to rid me——!"

His best friend clapped on that gentleman's hat and strode away; in a moment the door sharply closed.

XVI

THIS OBSCURE hero walked hard for a couple of hours. He passed up the Corso, out of Porta del Popolo and into Villa Borghese, of which he made a complete circuit. The keenness of his irritation subsided, but it left an intolerable weight on his heart. When dusk had fallen he found himself near the lodging of his friend Madame Grandoni. He frequently paid her a visit during the hour which preceded dinner, and he now ascended her unillumined staircase and rang at her relaxed bell-rope with an especial desire for diversion. He was told that for the moment she was occupied, but that if he would come in and wait she would presently be with him. He had not sat musing in the firelight for five minutes when he heard the jingle of the door-bell and then a rustle and a murmur in the hall. The door of the little parlour opened, but before the visitor appeared he had recognised her voice. Christina Light swept forward, preceded by her poodle and almost filling the narrow room with the train of her dress. She was coloured here and there by the flickering firelight.

"They told me you were here," she simply said as she took a seat.

"And yet you came in? It was very brave," Rowland returned.

"You're the brave one, when one thinks of it! The padrona's to come?"

"I've already waited some minutes; I expect her from moment to moment."

"Meanwhile we're alone?" And she glanced at the duskier background.

"Unless Stenterello counts," said Rowland.

"Oh, he knows my secrets—unfortunate brute!" She sat silent a while, looking into the firelight. Then at last, glancing at Rowland, "*Voyons!* Say something pleasant!" she exclaimed.

"I've been very happy to hear of your engagement."

"Oh, I don't mean that! I have heard that so often, only since

202

breakfast, that it has lost all sense. I mean some of those unexpected charming things that you said to me a month ago at Saint Cecilia's."

"I didn't please you then," said Rowland. "I was afraid I hadn't."

"Ah, such things occur to you ? Then why haven't I seen you since?"

"Really I don't know." And he hesitated for an explanation. "I think I must have called—but you've never been at home."

"You were careful to choose the wrong times. You have a way with a poor girl ! You sit down and state to her that she's a person with whom a respectable young man can't associate without contamination; your friend's a very superior person, you're very careful of his morals, you wish him to know none but nice people, and you beg me therefore to desist. You request me to take these suggestions to heart and to act upon them as promptly as possible. They're not particularly flattering to my vanity. Vanity, however, is a sin, and I listen submissively, with an immense desire to be just. If I have many faults I know it in a general way, and I try, on the whole, to do my best. '*Voyons*,' I say to myself, 'it isn't particularly charming to hear oneself made out a pig, but it's worth thinking over; there's probably a good deal of truth in it and at any rate we must be as good a girl as we can. That's the great point ! And then here's a magnificent chance for humility. If there's doubt in the matter, let the doubt count against oneself. It's what Saint Catherine did, and Saint Theresa, and all the others, and they're said to have had in consequence the most ineffable joys. Let us go in for a little ineffable joy.' I tried it; I swallowed my rising sobs, I made you my curtsey, I determined I wouldn't be spiteful, nor passionate, nor vengeful, nor anything that's supposed to be particularly feminine and that *ces dames*, now saints in heaven, wouldn't have been. I was a better girl than you made out—better at least than you thought; but I would let the difference go, and do magnificently right lest I should not do right enough. I thought of it a great deal for six hours, when I know I didn't seem to be thinking, and then at last I did it. *Santo Dio!*"

"My dear Miss Light, my dear Miss Light !" her companion rather vaguely pleaded.

"Since then," the young girl went on, "I've been waiting for the ineffable joys. But they're dividends, on my speculation, that haven't yet begun to come in."

"Pray, listen to me !" Rowland began.

"Nothing, nothing, nothing has come of it. I've passed the dreariest month of my life."

"You're a very terrible young woman," Rowland remarked.

"What do you mean by that?"

"A good many things. We'll talk them over. But first forgive me if I really wounded you."

She looked at him a moment, hesitating, and then thrust her hands into her muff. "That means nothing. Forgiveness is between equals, and you don't regard me as your equal."

"How do you make it out?"

Christina rose and moved for a moment about the room. Then turning suddenly, "You don't believe in me!" she cried; "not a grain! I don't know what I wouldn't give to *force* you to believe in me!"

Rowland sprang up, protesting, but before he had time to go far one of the scanty *portières* was raised and Madame Grandoni came in, pulling her wig straight. "You shall believe in me yet, you know," Christina murmured as she passed towards her hostess.

Madame Grandoni turned tenderly to her young friend. "I must give you a very solemn kiss, my dear; you're the heroine of the hour. You've really accepted him, eh?"

"So they say!"

"But you ought to know best."

"I don't know—I don't care!" She stood with her hand in Madame Grandoni's, but looking askance at Rowland.

"That's a pretty state of mind," said the old lady, "for a young person who's going to be so great."

Christina shrugged her shoulders. "Every one expects me to go into ecstasies over my greatness. Could anything be more vulgar? Let others do the gloating. Mamma will do any amount. Will you let me stay to dinner?"

"If you can dine on black bread and onions. But I imagine you're expected at home."

"Nothing's more certain. Prince Casamassima dines there *en famille*. I'm not of his family yet!"

"Do you know you're very wicked?" the old lady asked. "I've half a mind not to keep you."

Christina dropped her eyes reflectively. "I wish awfully you'd let me stay," she said. "If you want to cure me of my wickedness you must be very patient and kind with me. It will be worth the trouble. You must show confidence in me." And she gave Rowland another look. Then suddenly, in a different tone, "I don't know what I'm saying!" she wailed. "I'm weary and dreary; I'm more lonely than ever; I wish I were dead!" The tears rose to her eyes, she struggled with them an instant and buried her face in her muff; but at last she burst into uncontrollable sobs, flinging herself on Madame Grandoni's neck. This shrewd woman gave Rowland a significant nod and a little shrug over the young girl's beautiful bowed head, and then led Christina tenderly away into the adjoining room. Rowland, left alone, stood there for an instant, intolerably puzzled, face to face with Miss Light's poodle, who had set up a sharp unearthly cry of sympathy with his mistress. Rowland vented his confusion in dealing a rap with his stick at the animal's unmelodious muzzle, and rapidly quitted the house. He saw Mrs. Light's carriage waiting at the door, and heard afterwards that Christina had gone home to dinner.

A couple of days later he went for a fortnight to Florence. He had twenty minds to leave Italy altogether, and at Florence he could at least more freely decide upon his future movements. He felt deeply, incurably disgusted. Reflective benevolence stood prudently aside for the time, touching the source of his irritation with no softening side-lights. It was the middle of March, however, and by the middle of March, in Florence, the spring is already warm and deep. He had an infinite taste for the place and the season, but as he strolled by the Arno and paused here and there in the great galleries they failed to bring balm to his ache. He was sore at heart, and as the days went by the soreness rather deepened than healed. He had a complaint against fortune and, good-natured as he was, his good-nature itself now took up the quarrel. He had tried to be wise, he had tried to be kind, he had engaged in an estimable enterprise; but his wisdom, his kindness, his labour had all been thrown back in his face. He was intensely disappointed, and his disappointment for a while burned hot. The sense of wasted time, of wasted hope and faith, kept him constant company. There were times when the beautiful things about him only exasperated his pain. He went to the Pitti Palace, and Raphael's Madonna of the Chair seemed in its soft serenity to mock him with the suggestion of unattainable repose. He lingered on the bridges at sunset and knew that the light was enchanting and the mountains divine, but there seemed something horribly invidious and unwelcome in the fact. He felt himself, in a word, a man cruelly defrauded and naturally bent on revenge. Life owed him, he thought, a compensation and he should be restless and resentful till he should find it. He knew—or seemed to know—where he should find it; but he hardly told himself, thinking of it under mental protest, as a man in want of money may think of funds that he holds in trust. In his melancholy meditation the idea of something better than all this, something that might softly, richly interpose, that might reconcile him to the future, that might freshen up a vision of life tainted with staleness—the idea, in fine, of compensation in concrete form found itself remarkably resembling a certain young woman in America, shaped itself sooner or later into the image of Mary Garland.

Very odd, you may say, that at this time of day Rowland should still be brooding over a girl of no brilliancy, of whom he had had a bare glimpse two years before; very odd that an impression should have fixed itself so sharply under so few applications of the die. It is of the very nature of such impressions, however, to show a total never represented by the mere sum of their constituent parts. One night he couldn't sleep; his thought was too urgent; it kept him pacing his room. His windows were on the Arno, and as they stood open the noise of the river came in; it would have taken little more to make him go down into the street. Towards morning he flung himself into a chair; though he was wide awake he was now less a prey to agitation. It seemed to him that he saw his idea from the outside, that he judged it and condemned it, and it stood still there all distinct and with a strange face of authority. During the day he tried to keep it down; but it fascinated, haunted, at moments quite frightened him. He tried to amuse himself, paid visits, resorted to several violent devices for diverting his thoughts. If he had been guilty on the morrow of some misdeed the persons he had seen that day would have testified that he had talked incoherently and had not seemed himself. He felt, certainly, very much somebody else; long afterwards, in retrospect, he used to perceive that during those days he had been literally *beside* himself—even as the ass, in the farmer's row of stalls, may be beside the ox. His uncanny idea persisted; it clung to him like a sturdy beggar. The sense of the matter, roughly expressed, was that if Roderick were really going, as he himself had phrased it, to fizzle out, one might help him on the way—one might smooth the *descensus Averni*. For forty-eight hours there swam before Rowland's eyes a vision of the wondrous youth, graceful and beautiful as he passed, plunging like a diver into a misty gulf. The gulf was destruction, annihilation, death; but if death had been decreed why shouldn't the agony be at least brief? Beyond this vision there faintly glimmered another, as in the children's game of the magic lantern a picture is superposed on the white wall before the last one has quite faded. It represented Mary Garland standing there with eyes in which the horror seemed slowly, slowly to expire, and hanging motionless hands which at last made no resistance when his own offered to take them. When of old a man was burnt at the stake it was cruel to have to be present; but, one's presence assumed, it was charity to lend a hand, to pile up the fuel and make the flames do their work quickly and the smoke muffle up the victim. And it didn't diminish the charity that this was perhaps an obligation especially felt if one had a reversionary interest in something the victim was to leave behind.

One morning in the midst of all this Rowland walked heedlessly out of a florid city gate and found himself on the road to Fiesole. It was a day all benignant; the March sun felt like May, as the English poet of Florence says; the thick-blossomed shrubs, the high-climbing plants that hung over the walls of villa and *podere* flung their odorous promise into the warm still air. He followed, our friend, the winding, mounting lanes; lingered as he got higher beneath the rusty cypresses, beside the low parapets, where you look down on the charming city and sweep the vale of the Arno; reached the small square before the cathedral and rested a while in the massive, dusky church; then, climbing higher, pushed up to the Franciscan convent poised on the very apex of the great hill. He rang at the little gateway; a shabby, senile, red-faced brother admitted him, a personage almost maudlin with the milk of human kindness. There was a dreary chill in the chapel and the corridors, and he passed rapidly through them into the delightfully steep and tangled old garden which runs wild over the forehead of the mountain. He had been there before, he came back to it as to a friend. The garden hangs in the air, and you ramble from terrace to terrace and wonder how it keeps from slipping down, in full consummation of its dishonour and decay, to the nakedly romantic gorge beneath. It was just noon at Rowland's visit, and after roaming about a while he flung himself on the sun-warmed slab of a mossy stone bench and pulled his hat over his eyes. The short shadows of the brown-coated cypresses above him had grown very long, later on, and yet he had not passed back through the convent. One of the monks, in a faded snuff-coloured robe, came wandering out into the garden, reading a greasy little breviary. Suddenly he approached the bench on which Rowland had stretched himself and paused for respectful interest. Rowland was still in possession, but seated now with his head in his hands and his elbows on his knees. He seemed not to have heard the sandalled tread of the good brother, but as the monk remained watching him he at last looked up. It was not the ignoble old man who had admitted him, but a pale, gaunt personage, of a graver and more ascetic and yet of a charitable aspect. Rowland's face might have borne for him the traces of extreme trouble; something he appeared mildly to consider as he kept his finger in his little book and folded his arms picturesquely across his breast. Was his attitude, as he bent his sympathetic Italian eyes, the mere accident of his civility or the fruit of an exquisite spiritual tact? To Rowland, however this might have been, it appeared a sort of offer of ready intelligence. He rose and approached the monk, laying his hand on his arm.

"My brother," he said, "did you ever see the Devil in person?"

The *frate* gazed gravely and crossed himself. "Heaven forbid, my son!"

"He was here," Rowland went on, "here in this lovely garden, as he was once in Paradise, half an hour ago. But have no fear; I drove him out." And he stooped and picked up his hat, which had rolled away into a bed of cyclamen in vague suggestion of a positive scrimmage.

"You've been tempted, *figlio mio*?" asked the friar tenderly.

"Hideously!"

"And you've resisted—and conquered!"

"I believe I've conquered."

"The blessed Saint Francis be praised! It's well done. If you like we'll offer a mass for you."

Rowland hesitated. "I'm not of your faith."

The *frate* smiled with dignity. "That's a reason the more."

"But it's for you then to choose. Shake hands with me," Rowland added; "that will do as well; and suffer me as I go out to stop a moment in your chapel."

They shook hands and separated. The *frate* crossed himself, opened his book and wandered away in relief against the western sky. Rowland passed back into the convent and paused long enough in the chapel to look for the alms-box. He had had what is vulgarly called a great scare; he believed very poignantly, for the time, in Beelzebub and felt an irresistible need to subscribe to any institution that might engage to keep him at a distance.

The next day he returned to Rome and the day after that went in search of Roderick. He found him on the Pincian with his back turned to the crowd and his eyes to the beauty of the sunset. "I went to Florence," he said, "and I thought of going further; but I came back on purpose to give you another piece of advice. You decline decidedly to leave Rome?"

"Oh, my boy, rather !"

"The only chance I then see of a revival of your sense of responsibility to—to those various sacred things you've forgotten is in sending for your mother to join you here."

Roderick stared. "For my mother ?"

"For your mother—and for Miss Garland."

Roderick still stared; and then, slowly and faintly, his face flushed. "For Mary Garland—for my mother ?" he repeated. "Send for them ?"

"Answer me now a question," Rowland simply pursued, "which I've long forborne, out of delicacy, to ask you. Your engagement still holds ?"

"'Holds' ?" Roderick glared. "Holds what ?"

"Well, some residuum of what it originally did. If you were to see your intended you would perhaps be able to judge."

Roderick thought. "Do you mean by that that if *you* see her you may be better able to squash me ?"

Rowland winced at this—he flushed; but he bore up. "I should in the light of that speech, even if I hadn't already, as it seems to me, other lights, regard you as a very sick man. I can't imagine that if Miss Garland knew *how* sick she shouldn't at once feel that her place is at your side."

Roderick looked at him for some time darkly and askance. "Is there more in this than meets the eye ?"

"More—— ?"

"I mean is it a deeper scheme than my poor wit can fathom ?"

Rowland had come back to Rome with his patience reinstated, but these words gave it again a mortal chill. "Heaven forgive you !" he none the less resolutely answered. "My idea shouldn't surely be beyond your comprehension—though it ought, I think, to be beyond your suspicion. I've tried to befriend you, to help you, to inspire you with confidence, and I've failed. I took you from your mother and that young lady, and it seems to me my duty to restore you to their hands. That's all I have to say."

He was going, but Roderick forcibly detained him. It would have been but a rough way of expressing the case to say that one could never know what particular reaction any touch of that young man would produce. It had happened more than once that when deservedly hit hard he had received the blow with a noble mildness. On the other hand he had often resented the lightest taps. The secondary effect of

Rowland's present admonition seemed reassuring. "I beg you to wait," he said, "to forgive that shabby speech and to let me think it over." And he walked up and down and publicly considered. At last he stopped; the reign of all reason was in his face. It was like the sudden light of a golden age to come. "How strange it is that the simplest arrangements are the last to suggest themselves!" And he broke into easy laughter. "To see Mary Garland's just what I want. And my mother—my mother can't hurt me now!"

"You'll write then?"

"I'll cable. They must come at whatever cost. Striker can arrange it all for them."

In a couple of days he told Rowland that he had received a telegraphic answer to his message, informing him that the two ladies were to sail immediately for Leghorn in one of the small steamers then plying between that port and New York. They would arrive therefore in less than a month. Rowland passed this month of expectation in no great riot of relief. His suggestion had had its source in the deepest places of his charity; but there was something intolerable in the thought of the pain to which the possible event might subject creatures so little forearmed. They had scraped together their scanty funds and embarked at twenty-four hours' notice upon the dreadful sea, only to be handed over at the end to an element still more capable of betraying them. He could but promise himself to be their stubborn even if disdained support. Preoccupied as he was, he could still observe how expectation, with Roderick, took a form which seemed singular even among his characteristic singularities. If redemption—the brilliant youth appeared to reason—was to arrive with his mother and his affianced bride, these last moments of error should be worth redeeming. He only idled, but he idled with intensity. He laughed and whistled and went often to Mrs. Light's; though Rowland could but wonder to what issue events had brought his relations with Christina. The month ebbed away, and our friend daily expected to learn that he had gone to Leghorn to meet the ship. No such report came, however, and late one evening, not having seen him for three or four days, he stopped at his lodging to make sure of his absence. A cab was standing in the street, but as it was a couple of doors off he hardly heeded it. The hall at the foot of the staircase was dark, like most Roman halls, and he paused in the open doorway on hearing the advancing footstep of a person with whom he wished to avoid a collision. While he did so he heard another footstep behind him and, turning round, found that

Roderick himself had just overtaken him. At the same moment a woman's figure advanced from within, into the light of the street-lamp, and a face, half startled, looked at him out of the darkness. He gave a cry—it was the face of Mary Garland. Her attention flew past him to Roderick, and in a second a startled exclamation broke from her own lips. It made him turn again, turn to see Roderick stand there strange and pale, apparently trying to speak, yet producing no sound. His lips were parted and his attitude foolish, the attitude, unmistakably, of a man who has drunk too much. Then Rowland's eyes met Miss Garland's again, and her own, which had rested a moment on Roderick's, were formidable.

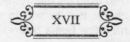

XVII

How it occurred that Roderick had failed to be at Leghorn at the moment of his mother's arrival was never to be clearly set forth; for he undertook at no moment any elaborate explanation of his fault. He never indulged in professions (touching personal conduct) as to the future, or in remorse as to the past; and as he would have asked no praise if he had travelled night and day to embrace Mrs. Hudson as she set foot on shore, he made (in Rowland's presence at least) no apology for having left her to come in search of him. It was to be said that, thanks to an unprecedented fine season, the voyage of the two ladies had been surprisingly rapid, and that, according to common probabilities, if Roderick had left Rome on the morrow (as he declared that he had intended) he would still have had a day or two of waiting at Leghorn. Rowland's silent inference was that Christina Light had beguiled him into letting the time slip, and it was accompanied with a tacit inquiry as to the degree of her direct malice. Her interesting friend had told her, presumably, that his mother and his cousin were about to arrive; and it was pertinent to remember hereupon that she was a person of wayward motions. Rowland possessed himself more easily meanwhile of the recent history of the two troubled pilgrims. Mary Garland's wish, at Leghorn, on finding they were left to their own devices, had been to telegraph to Roderick and await an answer, for she was not unaware that they had rather stolen a march. But Mrs.

Hudson's maternal heart had taken the alarm. Roderick's sending for them at all was, to her imagination, a confession of some pernicious ill, some visitation, probably, of malignant disease, and his not being at Leghorn a proof of the worst; an hour's delay was therefore cruel both to herself and to him. She insisted on immediate departure, and, unversed as they were in strange tongues and systems, they had somehow floundered along. Reaching Rome late in the evening and knowing nothing of inns, they had got into a cab and proceeded to Roderick's lodging. At the door poor Mrs. Hudson's trepidation had overcome her, and she had sat paralysed and weeping in the vehicle. Mary had bravely gone in, groped her way up the dusky staircase, gained Roderick's door and, with the assistance of such acquaintance with the local idiom as she had culled from a phrase-book during the calm hours of the voyage, learned from the old woman who had her cousin's household economy in charge that he was in the best of health and spirits and had gone forth a few hours before, his hat on his ear, *per divertirsi*.

These things Rowland learned during a visit paid the ladies the second evening of their stay. Mrs. Hudson spoke of them with great abundance and repetition and with an air of clinging confidence which told her visitor that he was now enshrined in her innermost faith. But her fright was over, though she was still catching her breath a little, like a person dragged ashore out of waters uncomfortably deep. She was exquisitely astray about everything, and appealed more than ever to correction and precaution. Before her companion he was distinctly conscious that he quaked. He wondered extremely what was going on in this young lady's mind, what had been her silent commentary on the incidents of the night before. He wondered all the more because he immediately perceived that she was now a person changed, and changed not to her disfigurement. She was older, easier, lighter; she had, as would have been said in Rome, more form. She had thus, he made out, more expression, facial and other, and it was beautifully as if this expression had been accumulating all the while, lacking on the scene of her life any channel to waste itself. It was like something she had been working at in the long days of home, an exquisite embroidery or a careful compilation, and she now presented the whole wealth of it as a kind of pious offering. Rowland felt almost instantly—he could hardly have said why; it was in her voice, in her tone, in the air—that a different principle governed her manner of regarding him. She built on him now absolutely; whether or no she liked him she believed in his solidity. He felt that during the coming weeks he should need to be solid. Mrs. Hudson was at one of the smaller hotels, and her sitting-room was frugally lighted by a couple of candles. He made the most of this dim illumination for some quest of the afterglow of that frightened flash from Mary's eyes the night before. It had been but a flash, for what provoked it had instantly vanished. Rowland, on this occasion, seeing the high delinquent instantly measure his peril, had mutely applauded the art of his recovery. If he had been drinking the quick consciousness sobered him; he had collected his wits with inimitable grace. The next moment, with a ringing jovial cry, he was folding the girl in his arms, and the next after he was beside his mother's cab, half smothered in her sobs and caresses. Rowland had recommended an hotel close at hand and had then discreetly retired. Roderick was at that time "playing up" to them all brilliantly, and Mary Garland's face was serene. It was clear now, twenty-four hours later; but her vision had none the less flared there for its minute. What had become of it? It had dropped down deep into her memory and was lying there for the present in the shade. From one day to another, Rowland yet said to himself, it would hold up its head, would begin to watch and listen, would rise again and confront him. Meanwhile he made the most of the hours—he passed them in the consciousness of being near her. The two ladies had passed the day indoors, resting, reacting, recovering. The younger, Rowland suspected, was not quite so spent as she suffered it to be assumed. She had remained with Mrs. Hudson to attend to her personal wants, which the latter seemed to think, now that she was in a foreign land with a southern climate and a Catholic religion, would forthwith become very complex and formidable, though as yet they had simply resolved themselves into a desire for a great deal of tea and for a certain extremely familiar old black and white shawl across her feet as she lay on the sofa. But the sense of novelty was evidently strong upon Mary and the light of expectation in her eye. She was restless and excited; she moved about the room and went often to the window; she took everything in; she watched the Italian servants as they came and went; she had already had a long colloquy with the French chambermaid, who had published her views on the Roman question; she noted the small differences in the furniture, in the cookery, in the sounds that came in from the street. She might have been an exceptionally fine specimen-islander of an unclassed group, brought home by a great navigator and treatable as yet mainly by beads and comfits. Rowland was sure she observed to good purpose, that she only needed opportunity, and that she would gather impressions in clusters as thick as the purple bunches of a vintage. He wished immensely he might have a hand in the work; he wished he might show her Rome. That of course would be Roderick's office, but he promised himself at least to take advantage of off-hours.

"It behoves you to appreciate your good fortune, you know," he permitted himself to say. "To be young and eager, and yet old enough and wise enough to discriminate and reflect, and to come to Italy for the first time—that's one of the greatest pleasures life has to offer. It's but right to remind you of it, so that you may make the most of your chances and not accuse yourself later of having wasted the precious season."

Mary looked at him with her large smile and went to the window again. "I expect to enjoy it. Don't be afraid; I'm not wasteful."

"I'm afraid we're not so very qualified, you know," said Mrs. Hudson. "We're told that you must know so much, that you must have read so many books. Our taste has not highly been cultivated. When I was a young lady at school I remember I had a medal with a pink ribbon for 'proficiency in ancient history'—the seven kings, or is it the seven hills? and Quintus Curtius and Julius Cæsar, and—and that period, you know. I believe I have my medal somewhere in a drawer now, but I've forgotten all about the kings. After Roderick came to Italy we tried to pursue a course. Last winter Mary used to read *Corinne* to me in the evenings, and in the mornings she used to read another book to herself. What was it, Mary, that book that was so long, you know—in fifteen volumes?"

"It was Sismondi's *Italian Republics*," Mary honestly answered.

Rowland showed, for all his precautions, an amusement; whereat the girl coloured. "And did you push quite through?"

"Yes, and began another—a shorter one—Roscoe's *Leo the Tenth*."

"Did you find them interesting?"

"Oh yes."

"Do you like history?"

"Some of it."

"That's a woman's answer! And do you like art?"

She paused a moment. "I think I've never seen any—except Roderick's. Of course I've liked *that*."

"Ah, that proves nothing!" Rowland freely declared. "You must try other people's."

"I'm sure she'll only want to try," Mrs. Hudson interposed. "You've

214

great advantages now, my dear, with Roderick and Mr. Mallet," she said to Mary. "No young lady can ever have had greater. You come straight to the highest authorities. Roderick, I suppose, will show you the practice of art, and Mr. Mallet, perhaps, if he will be so good, will show you the theory. As an artist's wife you ought to know something at least about that."

"One learns a good deal about it here by simply living one's life," said Rowland; "by going and coming about one's daily avocations."

"Dear, dear, how wonderful that we should be here in the midst of it !" murmured Mrs. Hudson. "To think of art being out there in the streets ! We didn't see much of it last evening as we drove from the station. But the streets were so dark, and we shouldn't have known, at any rate, where to look. Now, however, we're quite ourselves, and Mary, I think, is really enjoying the revulsion."

"Oh, I'm all right," this young woman replied; and she wandered again to the window, as if the very largeness of their case defied expansion.

Roderick came in at this moment and kissed his mother, and then went over and joined her companion. Rowland sat with Mrs. Hudson, who evidently had a word she deemed important for his private ear. She followed her son with intensely earnest eyes.

"I wish to tell you, sir," she said, "how deeply indebted, how very grateful, what a happy mother I am ! I feel I owe you *all* of it. To find my poor boy so handsome, so prosperous, so elegant, so famous—and ever to have doubted of you ! What must you think of me ? You're our guardian angel; it's what Mary and I call you."

Rowland felt himself wear in answer to this speech an anxiously impenetrable face. He could only murmur that he was glad she found Roderick looking well. He had of course promptly asked himself if it wouldn't be his best line to give her a word of warning—turn the handle of the door through which, later on, disappointment and its train might enter. But he had determined to say nothing and simply to wait for Roderick to find effective inspiration in the eyes now so deeply resting on him. It was even to be supposed he was actually looking for it; he remained some time at the window with his cousin. But at last he turned away and came over to the fire with the first fine cloud already on his brightness. In what wrong place had the poor girl happened to touch him ? She presently followed him, and for an instant Rowland observed her watch him as if he struck her as strange. "Strange enough," thought their companion, "he may seem to her if he will !" Roderick looked at his friend with a vague peremptory pressure, a sign to him that he too must really mount to the breach. "Heaven help us all !" Rowland tacitly groaned; "are they already giving on his nerves ?"

"To-morrow, of course, we must begin to put you through the mill," Roderick said to his mother. "And be it hereby known to Mallet that we count upon him to turn the wheel."

"I will do as you please, my son," said Mrs. Hudson. "So long as I have you with me I don't care where I go. We must not take up too much of Mr. Mallet's time."

"His time's inexhaustible; he has nothing under the sun to do. Can you dream, Rowland, of anything more delirious than our company ? If you had seen the big hole I've been making in his life ! Where will you go first ? You have your choice—from the Scala Santa to the Cloaca Maxima."

"Let us take things in order," said Rowland. "We will go first to Saint Peter's church. Miss Garland, I hope you're impatient to see Saint Peter's church."

"I should like to go first to Roderick's studio," Miss Garland declared.

"It's a very horrid, nasty, depressing place, my studio," said Roderick. "But do whatever in the wide world you like."

"Yes, we must see your beautiful things before we can look contentedly at anything else," said Mrs. Hudson.

"I have no beautiful things," said Roderick. "You may see a dozen ghosts of dead dreams. What makes you look so——? But how is it you *do* look ?"

This inquiry was abruptly addressed to his mother, who in response glanced appealingly at Mary, and raised a startled hand to her smooth hair.

"No, it's your dear old face. What has come over it in my absence ? It has got something in it, you know," he said, with quite a flicker of interest, to Rowland.

"It must have in it all the fond prayers she has been putting up for you," Mary gravely suggested.

"Oh, I don't suppose it represents the trace of orgies ! But whatever it is, mammy, it's a great improvement; it makes you a very good face —very interesting, very decent, very solemn. It has two or three rare tragic lines in it; something might be done with it." And Roderick held one of the candles near the poor lady's head.

She was covered with confusion. "My son, my son," she said with dignity, "I don't understand you."

In a flash all his old alacrity had come to him. "I suppose a man may admire his own lovely mother ! If you please, ma'am, you'll sit to me for that beautiful head. I see it, I see it ! I'll make something that a queen can't get done for her."

Rowland respectfully urged her to assent; he saw Roderick was in the vein and he calculated on the spot, with one of his own odd flights, that this might lead to the masterpiece of the young sculptor's life. It was such a chance for "sincerity"—the very sincerity, immortal now, of the early Tuscans. Mrs. Hudson gave her promise at last, after many inarticulate protests and a fond request that she might be allowed to keep her knitting.

Rowland returned, the next day, with plenty of zeal for the part his friend had assigned him. It had been arranged that they should drive to Saint Peter's, and Roderick, whose sky had again cleared, watched his mother, in the carriage, on the way, with a fine mixture of filial and professional interest. Mrs. Hudson looked up ruefully at the high, sinister houses and grasped the side of the barouche as if she were launched in deep seas. Rowland sat opposite to Miss Garland, who appeared for the time totally oblivious of her companions. From the moment the carriage left the hotel she sat gazing wide-eyed and absorbed at the objects about them. If Rowland had felt more reckless he might have made a joke, or even a greater affair, of the dead weight of this tribute to the magic of Rome, the most candid, in a manner, that he had ever seen paid. From time to time he told her the name of a place or a building, and she nodded without looking at him. When they emerged into the great square between Bernini's colonnades she laid her hand on Mrs. Hudson's arm and sank back in the carriage, staring up at the golden immensities. Within the high doors at last Roderick gave his arm to his mother, and Rowland constituted himself the guide of the younger lady. He walked with her slowly everywhere, making the entire circuit and telling her all he knew, trying to tell her all he felt. This was no small matter, but she listened attentively, keeping her eyes on the dome. For Rowland himself it had never had such consecrating power; even, as might be, of the hushed human passions beneath it. He felt, in this promotion of its effect, almost as if he had designed it and had a right to be proud of it. He left Mary Garland awhile on the steps of the choir, where she had seated herself to rest, and went to join their companions. Mrs. Hudson was watching a circle of tattered *contadini* kneel before the image of Saint Peter. The fashion of their tatters fascinated her; she stood gazing at them in terrified pity and could be induced to look at almost nothing else. Rowland went back to Mary and sat down beside her.

"Well, what do you think of Europe?" he amicably asked.

"I think it's dreadful!" she presently brought out.

"Dreadful?"

"I feel so strangely—I could almost cry."

"How is it then you feel?"

"So sorry for the poor little past that seems to have died here in my heart in an hour!"

"But surely you're pleased—you're interested."

"I'm overwhelmed. Here in a single hour everything's changed. It's as if a wall somewhere about me had been knocked down at a stroke. Before me lies an immense new world, and it makes the old one, the little narrow familiar conceited one I've always known, seem pitiful."

"But you didn't come to Rome to walk backward, to keep your eyes fastened on what you left. Forget it, turn away from it, give yourself up to this."

"I should like nothing better. But as I sat here just now, looking up at that golden mist in the dome, I seemed to see in it the vague shapes of certain people and things at home. To enjoy so much beauty and wonder is to break with the past—I mean with one's poor old own. And breaking's a pain."

"Don't mind the pain, and it will cease to trouble you. Enjoy, enjoy; it's your duty. Yours especially."

"Why mine especially?" the girl asked.

"Because I'm so convinced that you've a mind formed to do justice to everything interesting and beautiful. You're extremely intelligent."

"You don't know," she simply said.

"In that matter one feels. I really think I know better than you. I don't want to seem patronising, but I see in you a capital subject for development. Give yourself the best company, trust yourself, let yourself go."

She looked away from him for some moments, down the gorgeous vista of the great church. "But what you say," she said at last, "means *change*."

"Change for the better," Rowland insisted.

"How can one tell? As one stands one knows the worst. It seems to me very frightful to develop," she went on.

"One is in for it in one way or another, and one might as well do it with a good grace as with a bad. Since one can't escape life it's better to take it by the hand."

"Is this what you call life?" she presently asked.

"What do you mean by 'this'?"

"What's around us—all this splendour, all Rome; pictures, ruins, statues, beggars, monks."

"It's not all of it, but it's a large part of it. All these things are impregnated with life; they're the results of an immemorial, a complex and accumulated, civilisation."

"'Immemorial, complex, accumulated'—ah, those are words I'm afraid of."

"There may be better ones for what I mean," Rowland smiled; "but I don't believe it's in you to be *really* afraid of anything. Don't at any rate conclude on that point just yet. Wait till you've tested your courage. While you wait you'll see an immense number of very beautiful things—things that you're made to understand. They won't leave you as they found you; then you can judge. Don't tell me I know nothing about your understanding. I've a right to count upon it."

Mary gazed a while aloft into the dome. "I'm not sure I understand *that*." And she nodded upwards.

"I hope at least that at a cursory glance it pleases you. You needn't be afraid to tell the truth. What strikes some people," Rowland said, "is that it's so disconcertingly small."

"Oh, it's large enough; it will do for me. There are things in Rome, then," she added in a moment, turning and looking at him, "that are quite supremely beautiful?"

"Lots of them."

"Some of the most beautiful things in the world?"

"Unquestionably."

"What are they? which things have most beauty?"

"That's according to taste. I should say the antique sculpture."

"How long will it take to see it all; to know at least something about it?"

"You can see it all, as far as mere seeing goes, in a fortnight. But to know it is a thing for one's leisure. The more time you spend with it the more you care for it." After a moment's hesitation he went on:

"Why should you grudge time? It's all in your way, since you're to be an artist's wife."

"Oh, I've thought of that," she said. "It may be that I shall always live here—among the most beautiful things in the world."

"Very possibly. I should like to see you ten years hence."

"I daresay that many things will by that time have come to me, and I certainly hope it. But I'm nevertheless sure——!"

"Of what?" he asked as she paused.

"That for the most part I shall be quite stupidly unaltered by them. I ask nothing better than to believe the fine things you say about my understanding, but even if they're true it won't matter. I shall be what I was made, what I am now—a young woman from the very heart of New England. The fruit of a civilisation as different as possible from this so strangely-mixed Roman."

"I'm delighted to hear it. The heart of New England's an excellent basis."

"Perhaps if you show me anything more you'll grow rather tired of my basis. Therefore I warn you."

"I'm not frightened. I should like extremely to make a request of you. Be what you are, what you like, what you must—be your very worst. But *do*, sometimes, as I tell you."

If Rowland was not frightened neither perhaps was his companion; but she brought their talk to an end as if not to make this promise. She proposed they should join the others.

Mrs. Hudson spoke under her breath; she could not be accused of the want of reverence often attributed to the crude heretic in the great Catholic temples. "Mary dear," she whispered, "suppose we had to kiss that dreadful brass toe. If I could only have kept our door-knocker at Northampton as bright as that! I think it's heathenish, but Roderick says he thinks it's sublime."

Roderick had evidently grown a trifle perverse. "It's sublimer than anything that *your* religion asks you to do!"

"Surely our religion sometimes gives us very difficult duties," said Mary.

"The duty of sitting in a whitewashed meeting-house and listening to a nasal Puritan! I admit that's difficult. But it's not sublime. I'm speaking of ceremonies, of magnificent forms. It's in my line, you know, to make much of magnificent forms. I think this a very interesting case of a grand form. Couldn't you do it?" he demanded, looking at his cousin.

She looked back at him intently and then shook her head. "I think not !"

"Why not ?"

"I don't know. I couldn't !"

During this little discussion our four friends were standing near the venerable image of the *genius loci*, and a squalid, savage-looking peasant, a tattered ruffian of the most orthodox Italian aspect, had been performing his devotions before it. He turned away crossing himself, and Mrs. Hudson gave a little shudder of horror.

"After that," she murmured, "I suppose he thinks he's as good as any one ! And here's another. Oh, what a beautiful person !"

A young lady had approached the sacred effigy after having wandered away from a group of companions. She kissed the brazen toe, touched it with her forehead and, turning round to face our friends, presented herself to Rowland as Christina Light. He took account of this indication that she had suddenly begun again to *pratiquer* religiously, for it was but a few weeks before that she had treated him to a passionate profession of indifference. Had she already taken up the duties laid down by decorum for a Princess Casamassima ? While Rowland was mentally asking these questions she had drawn nearer—she was moving toward the great altar. But at first she had not taken in our group.

Mary Garland had been watching her. "You told me," she said gently to Rowland, "that Rome contained some of the most beautiful things in the world. This surely is one of them !"

At this moment Christina's eye met Rowland's, and before giving him any sign of recognition she glanced rapidly at his companions. She saw Roderick, but without expression of it; she looked at Mrs. Hudson, she looked at Mary Garland. At Mary she looked with attention, with penetration, from head to foot, the slow pace at which she advanced making it possible. The next thing, as if she had perceived Roderick for the first time, she broke into a friendly, a radiant smile. In a moment he was at her side. She stopped, and he stood talking to her; she continued to look at Mary.

"Why, Roderick knows her !" cried Mrs. Hudson in an awestruck whisper. "I suppose she was some great princess."

"She is—almost !" said Rowland. "She's the most beautiful girl in Europe, and Roderick has modelled her."

"'Modelled'——? Dear, dear !" murmured Mrs. Hudson, as if aghast at some vision of a new freedom. "What a very strange bonnet !"

"She has very strange eyes," said Mary, turning away.

The two ladies, with Rowland, took their way towards the door of the church. On their way they passed Mrs. Light and the Cavaliere, and Rowland informed his companions of the relation in which these personages stood to Roderick's young lady.

"Think of it, Mary !" said Mrs. Hudson. "What splendid people he must know ! No wonder he found Northampton rather mild."

"I like the wise little old gentleman," said Mary.

"Why do you call him wise ?" Rowland asked, struck with the observation.

"Because I think I'm learning what wisdom *is*."

As they approached their egress they were overtaken by Roderick, whose interview with Miss Light had left in his face a traceable after-glow. "So you're acquainted with princesses ?" said his mother, softly, as they passed into the portico.

"Miss Light isn't a princess !" he rather dryly returned.

"But Mr. Mallet says so," urged Mrs. Hudson, disappointed.

"I meant that she's going to be," said Rowland.

"It's by no means certain that she's even going to be !" Roderick answered.

"Ah then," Rowland laughed, "I give it up !"

XVIII

RODERICK CAME almost immediately back to his idea that his mother should sit to him at his studio for her portrait, and Rowland ventured to add another word of urgency. If Roderick's idea had really taken hold of him it was an immense pity his inspiration should be wasted; inspiration had become in these days too rare a visitor. It was arranged therefore that for the present, during the mornings, Mrs. Hudson should place herself at her son's service. This involved but little sacrifice, for the good lady's appetite for antiquities was diminutive and bird-like, the usual round of galleries and churches fatigued her, and she was glad to purchase immunity from sight-seeing by a regular afternoon drive. It became natural in this way that as Mary Garland had her mornings free Rowland should feel it no more than civil to offer himself as a guide. He could scarce find it in his heart to accuse Roderick of neglect of that function, united to him though the girl might be by a double bond; for it was natural that the inspirations of a man of genius should be both capricious and imperious, and on what plan had he ever started moreover but on that of diligence and claustration? Yet he wondered how Mary felt, as the young man's promised wife, on being so summarily handed over to another man to be entertained. However she might feel he was still certain he should learn very little about it. There had been between them none but indirect allusions to her intended marriage; and Rowland had no desire to discuss it more largely, for he had no quarrel with matters as they stood. They wore the same delightful aspect through the lovely month of May, and the ineffable charm of Rome at that period seemed but the radiant sympathy of nature with his happy opportunity. The weather was divine; each particular morning, as he walked from his lodging to Mrs. Hudson's modest inn, had a particular blessing on it. The elder lady had usually gone off to the studio, and he found Mary sitting alone at the open window, turning the leaves of some book of artistic or antiquarian reference that he had given her. She was always eager, alert, responsive; she had always her large settled smile, which reminded him of some clear ample "sparc-room," some expectant guest-chamber, as they said in New England, with its windows up for ventilation. She might be grave by nature, she might be sad by circumstance, she might have secret doubts and pangs, but she was essentially young and strong and fresh—able to respond to any vivid appeal. Her response was not a random chatter, but it was full of intention. It was not amusement and sensation she coveted, but knowledge—facts that she might noiselessly lay away, piece by piece, in the fragrant darkness of her serious mind, so that under this head at least she should not be a perfectly portionless bride. She never merely pretended to understand; she let things go, with her arrested concession, at the moment; but she watched them on their way over the crest of the hill, and when her attention seemed not likely to be missed it went hurrying after them and ran breathless at their side and begged them for the secret. Rowland took a high satisfaction in observing that she never mistook the second-best for the best and that when she stood in great presences she recognised the importance of the occasion. She said many things that he thought very happy—that is if they meant certain other things that they perhaps didn't, and meant *all* of those. This point he usually tried to ascertain; but he was obliged to proceed cautiously, for the effect of her so suddenly-quickened vision of a more mixed order than she had ever dreamt of was to make her see everything as mixed, and cross-examination, by that law, as necessarily ironic. She wished to know just where she was going—what she should gain or lose. This was partly on account of the purity and rigidity of a mind that had not lived with its door ajar upon the high-road of cosmopolite chatter, for passing phrases to drop in and out at their pleasure, but that had none the less looked out, ever, from the threshold, for any straggler on the "march of ideas," any limping rumour or broken-winged echo of life, that would stop and be cherished as a guest. It was even more perhaps because she was aware of a sort of growing self-respect, a sense of devoting her consciousness not to her own ends, but to those of another whose career would be high and splendid. She had been brought up to think a great deal of "nature" and nature's innocent laws; but now Rowland had talked to her ingeniously of the need of man's spirit to refine upon them, her fresh imagination had responded, and she was following this mystic clue into retreats where the intellectual effort gave her a well-nigh tragic tension. She wished to be very sure, to take only the best, knowing it to be the best. Her desire to improve herself struck him at moments as almost grim, and not the less so that the fruits of the process for which his aid was indispensable were so little to be served at any table of his. She might have been originally as angular as he had, on the other scene, positively liked her for being; but who was to say now what mightn't result for her from the cultivation of a motive for curves? "Oh, exquisite virtue of circumstance," her companion admirably mused, "that takes us by the hand and leads us forth out of corners where perforce our attitudes are a trifle contracted, and beguiles us into testing unsuspected faculties!" She would develop, evidently, right and left, and to the top of her capacity; and he would have been at the bottom of it all. But that was where he would remain, essentially and obscurely: all taken for granted, merely for granted, as a good cellar, with its dusky supporting vaults, is taken for granted in a sound house.

They went a great deal to Saint Peter's, and Mary easily recognised that to climb the long low yellow steps, beneath the huge florid façade, and then, pushing the ponderous leathern apron of the door, find oneself a mere sentient point in that brilliant immensity, was an act that had its way of remaining a thrill. In those days the hospitality of the Vatican had not been curtailed, and it was an easy and delightful matter to pass from the gorgeous church to the solemn company of the antique marbles. Here it was that communication for our friends found its best allies; here Rowland, mounting a mild æsthetic hobby or two, might amble down long perspectives as with the ring of silver hoofs on marble floors. He discovered that she made notes of her likes and dislikes in a new-looking little pocket-book, and he wondered to what extent she reported his own discourse. These were hours of grave felicity. The galleries had been so cold all winter that Rowland had been an exile from them; but now that the sun was already scorching in the great square between the colonnades, where the twin fountains flashed almost fiercely, the comparative chill of the image-bordered vistas was as tonic as the breath of antiquity. The great herd of tourists had almost departed, and the couple often felt themselves for half an hour at a time in sole and tranquil possession of the beautiful Braccio Nuovo. Here and there was an open window, where they lingered and leaned, looking out into the warm dead air, over the towers of the city, at the soft-hued historic hills, at the stately, shabby gardens of the palace, or at some sunny empty grass-grown court lost in the heart of the labyrinthine pile. They went sometimes into the chambers painted by Raphael, and of course paid their respects to the Sistine Chapel; but Mary's evident preference was to linger among the marbles. Once, when they were standing before that noblest of sculptured portraits, the so-called Demosthenes of the Braccio Nuovo, she made the only spontaneous allusion to her plighted faith that had yet fallen from her lips. "I'm so glad that Roderick's a sculptor—like the man who did *that*. Glad, I mean, that he's not a painter." And then when Rowland had asked her the reason of her gladness: "It's not that painting's not fine, but that sculpture's so much finer. It's work for men!"

Rowland tried at times to make her talk about herself, but in this she had little skill. Since she thus struck him as older, as much older, more pliant to social uses than when he had seen her at home, he wished to make her tell him how her interval had been occupied. He had begun by exaggerating to her, even, the degree in which he found her different. "It appears then," she said, "that, after all, one can grow even in our hard air."

"Unquestionably. You may there, by taking thought, add the famous cubit. But you must take a great deal of thought. Your growth then," he went on, "was unconscious? You didn't watch yourself and water your roots?"

225

She paid no heed to his question. "I'm willing to grant," she said, "that Europe's richer than I supposed; and I don't admit that I had thought of it stupidly. But you must admit that America *has* a drop for the thirsty."

"I have not a fault to find with the country that produced *you*."

"It produced me without a strain of its resources. And yet you want me to change," she said: "to assimilate Europe, I suppose you'd call it."

"I've felt that desire only on general principles. Shall I tell you what I feel now? If America has made you thus far, why not let America finish you? I should like to ship you back without delay and see what becomes of you. If that sounds uncivil I admit there's a cold intellectual curiosity in it."

She shook her head. "The charm's broken; the thread's snapped! I prefer to remain here."

Invariably, when he was inclined to make of some chance of their talk a direct application to herself, she wholly failed to assist him; she let the application, no matter how awkwardly for him, lie where it had fallen. Once, with a spark of ardent irritation, he told her she was very secretive. At this she coloured a little, and he said that in default of any larger confidence it would at least be a satisfaction to make her confess to that charge. But even this satisfaction she denied him, and his only revenge was in risking, two or three times afterwards, an allusion to her duplicity that was violent enough for a joke. He told her that she was both abysmal and tortuous and he wound up on one occasion by pronouncing her labyrinthine. "Very good," she answered almost indifferently, "and now please remind me again—I have forgotten it—of what you said an 'architrave' was."

It was on the occasion of her asking him a question of this kind that he charged her—still by way of pleasantry, but in a tone in which, had she been curious in the matter, she might have detected a spark of restless ardour—with having an insatiable avidity for facts. "You're always snatching at useful instruction," he said; "you'll never consent to any disinterested conversation."

She frowned a little, as she always did when he arrested their talk upon something personal. But this time she assented; she confessed she was eager for items. "One must make hay while the sun shines. I must lay up a store against dark days. After all, I can't believe that I shall spend my life here."

He knew he had divined her real motive; but he felt that if he might have said to her—what it seemed impossible to say—that fortune possibly had a bitter disappointment in store for her, she would have been capable of answering immediately, after the first sense of pain: "Say then I'm laying up resources for solitude !"

But all the accusations were not his own. He had been waiting once while they talked—they were differing and arguing a little—to see whether she would take her forefinger out of her *Murray*, into which she had inserted it to keep her place. It would have been hard to say why this point interested him, for he had not the slightest real fear she would ever turn priggish. The simple human truth was that Rowland was jealous of science. In preaching art and history to her he had slighted again the good cause that he might never, never plead. Suddenly sinking, at any rate, the question of his lessons or of her learning, she faced him very frankly and began to frown. At the same time she let the *Murray* slide to the ground, and he was so charmed with this circumstance that he made no movement to pick it up.

"You're awfully inconsistent, Mr. Mallet, you know," she said.

"Oh, nothing so makes for good relations as inconsistency."

"Not of your elaborate kind. That first day we were in Saint Peter's you said things that inspired me. You bade me plunge into all this. I was all ready; I only wanted a little push; you gave me a great one; here I am up to my neck ! And now, instead of helping me to swim, you stand on the shore—the shore of superior information—and fling pebbles at me !"

"Pebbles, my dear young lady ? They're life-preservers. I must have played my part very ill."

"Your part ? What's your part supposed to have been ?"

He hesitated a moment. "That of usefulness pure and simple."

"I don't understand you !" she said; and picking up her guide-book she fairly buried her nose in it.

That evening he made her a speech which she perhaps understood as little. "Do you remember my begging you the other day to do occasionally as I told you ? It seemed to me you tacitly consented."

"Very tacitly !"

"I've never yet really presumed on your consent. But now I should like you to do this: whenever you catch me in the act of what you call flinging pebbles, ask me the meaning of some architectural term. I shall know what you mean—a word to the wise !"

There came a morning that they spent among the ruins of the

Palatine, that sunny chaos of rich decay and irrelevant renewal, of scattered and overtangled fragments, half excavated and half identified, known as the Palace of the Cæsars. Nothing in Rome is more interesting than this confused and crumbling garden, where you stumble at every step on the disinterred bones of the past; where damp frescoed corridors, relics possibly of Nero's Golden House, serve as gigantic bowers, and where in the springtime you may sit on a Latin inscription in the shade of a flowering almond and admire the composition of the Campagna. The day left a deep impression on Rowland's mind, partly owing to its intrinsic sweetness and partly because his companion on this occasion let some book of reference she had brought with her lie unopened for an hour and asked several questions which had no connection with Consuls or Cæsars. She had begun by saying that it was coming over her, after all, that Rome was a ponderously sad place. The sirocco was gently blowing, the air was heavy, she was tired, she looked pale and grave.

"Everything," she said, "seems to insist that all things are vanity indeed. If one has something good to do I suppose one feels a certain strength within one to say otherwise. But if one has nothing it's surely depressing to live year after year among the ashes of things that once were mighty. If I were to remain here I should either become permanently 'low,' as they say, or I would take refuge in some practical occupation."

"And what occupation would be your idea?"

"I would open a school for those beautiful little beggars, though I'm sadly afraid I should never bring myself to scold them."

"I've no practical occupation," said Rowland, "and yet I've kept, I think, from growing absolutely limp."

"I don't call you at all unoccupied," Mary Garland declared.

"It's very good of you. Do you remember our talking about that at Northampton?"

"During that walk in the woods? Perfectly. Has your coming abroad succeeded for yourself as well as you hoped?"

"I think I may say that it has turned out as well as I expected."

"Are you very happy?"

"Don't I look so?"

"So it seems to me. But"—and she hesitated a moment—"I imagine you look happy whether you're so or not."

"I'm like that ancient comic mask that we saw just now in yonder excavated fresco; I'm made to grin."

"Shall you come back here next winter?" she went on without heed of this.

"Very probably."

"Are you settled for ever?"

"'For ever' is a long time. I live only from year to year."

"Shall you never marry?"

Rowland gave a laugh. "'For ever'—'never'! You go in for big figures. I've taken no monastic vow."

"Shouldn't you like to have a home?"

"You mean in the American sense?" And then as she seemed to wonder: "Some one to share it with? Oh yes, I should like it immensely."

To this she made no rejoinder; but presently she asked: "Why don't you write a book?"

Rowland laughed—this time more freely. "A book! What book should I write?"

"A history; something about art or antiquities."

"I've neither the learning nor the talent."

She made no attempt to contradict him; she simply said she had supposed otherwise. "You ought, at any rate," she continued in a moment, "to do something for yourself."

"For myself? I should have supposed that if ever a man seemed to live for himself—— !"

"I don't know how it seems," she interrupted—"to careless observers. But we know—we know that you've lived—a great deal for *us*." Her voice trembled slightly, and she brought out the last words with a little jerk.

"She has had that speech on her conscience," thought Rowland; "she has been thinking she owed it to me, and it seemed to her that now was her time to make it and have done with it."

She went on in a way which confirmed these reflexions, speaking with due solemnity. "You ought to be made to know very well what we all feel. Mrs. Hudson tells me she has told you what she feels. Of course Roderick has expressed himself. I've been wanting to thank you too; I do, most sincerely."

Rowland made no answer; his face at this moment might have resembled the tragic mask more than the comic. But Mary was not looking at him; she had opened her eternal explanatory volume.

In the afternoon she usually drove with Mrs. Hudson, but Rowland frequently saw her again in the evening. He was apt to spend half an hour in the little sitting-room at the hôtel-pension on the slope of the Pincian, and Roderick, who dined regularly with his mother, was present on these occasions. Rowland saw him little at other times, and for three weeks no observations passed between them on the subject of Mrs. Hudson's advent. To Rowland's vision, as the weeks elapsed, the benefits to proceed from the presence of the two ladies remained shrouded in mystery. Roderick's reflecting surface exhibited, for the time, something of a blur. He was preoccupied with his progress on his mother's portrait, which was taking a very happy turn; and often when he sat silent, with his hands in his pockets, his legs outstretched, his head thrown back and his eyes on vacancy, it was to be supposed that his fancy was hovering about the half-shaped image in his studio, exquisite even in its immaturity. He said little, but his silence was no necessary sign of disaffection, for he clearly liked again, almost as he had liked it as a boy, in convalescence from measles, to lounge away the hours in an air so charged with feminine service. He was not alert, he suggested nothing in the way of excursions (Rowland was the prime mover in such as were attempted), but he conformed, passively at least, to the tranquil temper of the two women, and made neither harsh comments nor sombre allusions. Rowland wondered whether he had, after all, done his friend injustice in denying him the sentiment of duty. He refused invitations, to Rowland's knowledge, in order to dine at the sordid little table-d'hôte; wherever his spirit might be he was present in the flesh with religious constancy. Mrs. Hudson's felicity betrayed itself in a remarkable tendency to finish her sentences and wear her best black silk gown. Her tremors had trembled away; she was like a child who discovers that the shaggy monster it has so long been afraid to touch is an inanimate terror compounded of straw and sawdust, and that there may even be a gay impunity in tickling the absurd nose. As to whether the love-knot of which Mary Garland had the keeping still held firm, who should pronounce? The young woman, as we know, wore no such favour on her sleeve. She always sat at the table, near the candles, with rather a strenuous-looking piece of needlework. This was the attitude in which Rowland had first seen her, and he thought, now that he had seen her in several others, that, even when maintained with perhaps too deep a discretion, it was not the least becoming.

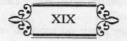

XIX

THERE CAME at last a couple of days during which Rowland was unable to go to the hotel. Late in the evening of the second Roderick appeared at his lodgings. In a few moments he announced that he had finished the bust of his mother.

"And it's ripping, you know," he declared. "It's quite my high-water mark."

"I'm delighted to hear it," Rowland replied. "Never again talk to me about your inspiration being dead."

"Why not? This may be its last kick! I feel very tired. But the thing isn't too nauseating, though I do say it. They tell us we owe so much to our parents. Well, I've paid the debt with interest!" He walked up and down, the purpose of his visit evidently still hung fire. "There's one thing more I want to say," he presently resumed. "I feel as if I ought to tell you." He stopped before his companion with his head high and his face as clear as a beach at the ebb. "Your invention's a failure!"

"My invention?" Rowland repeated.

"Bringing out my mother and Mary."

"A failure?"

"It's no use! They don't help me."

Rowland had believed he had no more surprises for him; but that hero had himself a wide-eyed stare.

"They bore me to death," Roderick went on.

"Oh, oh!" cried Rowland.

"Listen, listen," said his friend with perfect gentleness. "I'm not complaining of them; I'm simply stating a fact. I'm very sorry for them; I'm greatly disappointed."

"Have you given them a fair trial?"

"Shouldn't you call it that? It seems to me I've been sublime."

"You've done very well. I've been building great hopes on it."

"I've done too well—that's just what's the matter with me. After the first forty-eight hours my own hopes collapsed. But I determined to fight it out; to stand within the temple; to let the spirit of the Lord

231

descend. Do you want to know the result? Another week of it and I shall begin to hate them. I shall want to poison them."

"Miserable boy!" Rowland groaned. "They're the most touching, most amiable of women."

"Very likely. But they mean no more to me than a piano means to a pig."

"I can say this," said Rowland in a moment. "I don't pretend to understand the state of your relations with Miss Garland."

Roderick shrugged his shoulders and let his hands drop at his sides. "She thinks all the world of me. She likes me as if I were good to eat. She's saving me up, cannibal-fashion, as if I were a big feast. That's the state of my relations." He smiled strangely.

"Have you broken off your engagement?"

"Broken it off? You can't break off a star in Orion. You can only," Roderick explained, "let it alone."

His friend waited a little. "Have you absolutely no affection for her?"

He placed his hand on his heart and held it there a moment. "Dead —dead—dead!"

"I wonder," Rowland presently observed, "if you really know what a charming girl she is. She's an awfully charming girl."

"Evidently—or I should never have cared for her."

"She has completely ceased then to interest you in any way?"

"Oh, don't force a fellow to say base things!"

"Well, I can only say that you don't know what you're giving up." Roderick gave a quickened glance. "Do *you* know so well?"

"You must admit that you've allowed me time to find out."

Roderick smiled almost sympathetically. "Well, you haven't wasted it!"

Rowland's thoughts were crowding upon him fast. If Roderick was resolute why should he be gainsaid? If Mary was to be sacrificed why in *that* way try to save her? There was another way; it only needed a little presumption to make it possible. Rowland tried to summon presumption to his aid; but whether it should come or not it was to find a particular consideration there before it. This presence consisted but of three words—only they were cogent. "For *her* sake—for *her* sake," it dumbly murmured; and Rowland resumed his argument. "I don't know what I wouldn't do," he said, "rather than that Miss Garland should be disappointed." He heard himself grotesquely use this term—which might have applied to a shopgirl.

"There's one thing, you know," Roderick answered with an odd earnestness. "She is very very plucky."

"Well then if she's plucky, believe that with a longer chance, a better chance, she won't be too discouraged to endeavour to regain your affection."

"Do you know what you ask then?" Roderick demanded. "That I shall make love to a girl I hate?"

"You *hate*?"

"As her lover I should mortally hate her. Do you really urge my marrying a woman who would bore me to death? I shouldn't be long in letting her know it, and then, pray, where would the poor thing be?"

Rowland walked the length of the room a couple of times and stopped suddenly. "Go your way then. Say all this to *her*, not to me."

"To her? Why, I'm afraid of her, don't you see? I want you to help me."

"My dear chap," said Rowland with a strained smile, "I can't help you any more."

Roderick frowned, hesitated a moment and then took his hat. "Oh, well," he said, "I'm not so afraid of her as all that!" And he turned as if to depart.

"Stop!" cried Rowland as he laid his hand on the door.

Roderick paused and stood waiting, but only half patient.

"Come back; sit down there and listen to me. Of anything you say in your present state of mind you'll live, I'm certain, very bitterly to repent. You don't know what you really think, you don't know what you really feel. You don't know your own mind, you don't do justice to Miss Garland. All this is impossible here, where your conditions for it are of the worst. You're blind, you're deaf, you're under a spell. To break it you must leave Rome."

"Leave Rome? Rome was never so dear to me."

"That's not of the smallest consequence. Leave it to-morrow."

"And where shall I go?"

"Go to some place where you may be alone with your mother and your cousin."

"Alone? You'll not come?"

"Oh yes—if you ask it of me."

Roderick, inclining his head a little, looked at his friend askance. "I don't understand you, you know," he said. "I think I really wish you liked Mary either a little less or a little more."

Rowland felt himself flush, but he tried to keep his words from reflecting it. "You put it to me that I'm to 'help' you, but on these present terms I can do nothing. If on the other hand you'll leave your question exactly as it is for a couple of months, and meanwhile leave Rome, leave Italy, I'll do what I can to ease you off in the event of your then still wishing to be liberated."

"I must do without your help then, really," Roderick replied. "Your terms are impossible. I'll leave Rome at the time I've always intended— at the end of June. My rooms and my mother's are taken till then; all my arrangements are made accordingly. We'll go at our settled time— not before."

"You're not candid," said Rowland. "Your real reason for staying has nothing to do with your rooms."

Roderick after an instant took this for what it was worth. "Well, if I'm not candid it's for the first time in my life. Since you know so much about my real reason, let me hear it. No, stop !" he suddenly added, "I won't trouble you. You're right—I've an underhand motive. On the twenty-fourth of the month Christina Light's to be married. As I take an immense interest in all that concerns her it's an occasion on which I wish to be present."

"But you said the other day at Saint Peter's that it was by no means certain such an event would now take place."

"Apparently I was wrong. I'm told the invitations are going out."

Rowland felt it would be vain to remonstrate and that his only resource was to make the best bargain possible. "If I offer no further opposition to your waiting for—what you want to wait for, will you promise, meanwhile and afterwards, for a certain period, to abide by my judgement, to be very quiet and very good and say and do nothing that may give alarm to Miss Garland ?"

"For a certain period ? For what period ?" Roderick promptly demanded.

"Ah, don't screw me down so ! Don't you understand that I've taken you away from her, that I suffer for it in every corner of my mind, and that I must do what I can to give you back ?"

"Do what you can then," said Roderick, throwing out and dropping his arms. "Do what you can, my dear man, by all means." He stood there an instant limpidly, beautifully passive—the image of some noble and incurable young spendthrift winding up a slightly sordid interview with his disagreeably lucid but quite trusty man of business. Then he gave his friend his hand firmly, as if in sanction of the latter's freedom of action—after which they separated.

His bust of his mother, whether or no it were a discharge of what he called the filial debt, was at least a most interesting thing. Rowland, at the time it was finished, met Gloriani one evening, and this confident critic was eager for news of it. "I'm told our high-flying friend has really come down to earth. He has been doing a queer little old woman."

"A queer little old woman!" Rowland exclaimed. "My dear sir, she's Hudson's admirable mother."

"All the more reason for her being queer! It's a thing for terra-cotta, eh?"

Rowland hesitated but a moment. "If there were a big enough piece in the world it would be a thing for ivory."

His friend looked doubtful. "Oh, ivory begs the question. Why not fine gold? It was described to me at all events as a charming piece of quaintness; a little demure, thin-lipped old lady with her head on one side and the prettiest wrinkles in the world—a sort of fairy god-mother."

"Go and see it and judge for yourself," Rowland said.

"No, I seem to make out I've been 'sold.' It must be quite the other thing, the *vieux jeu*, domestic detail, button-holes and hairpins for the *campisanti*. I wish the perverse young wretch would let me save him!"

But a day or two later Rowland met him again in the street and, as they were near, proposed they should adjourn to Roderick's studio. He consented, and on entering they found the young master of the scene. Roderick had from the first, as we know, never "grovelled" before the less frequent of his guests, and his noble detachment varied to-day by no perceptible shade. But his great *confrère*, like the truth-lover he really was, cared nothing for his manners; he cared only for the question of his value. The bust of Mrs. Hudson touched Gloriani as he was seldom touched; the beauty of it bloomed like a flower that had grown in the night. The poor lady's small, neat, timorous face had certainly no great character, but Roderick had presented its sweetness, its mildness, its minuteness, its still maternal passion, with the most unerring art. The truth was all tenderness, the tenderness all truth. Gloriani stood taking this in while Roderick wandered away into the neighbouring room.

"I give it up!" he said at last. "I don't understand it."

"But you like it?" Rowland insisted.

"Like it? It's a pearl of pearls. Tell me this," his companion added; "has he a special worship for her, is he one of your sons in a thousand?" And he gave Rowland almost a hard look.

"Why, she adores the ground he treads on," said Rowland, smiling.

"I take that for an answer! But it's none of my business. Only if I, in his place, being suspected of having—what shall I call it?—a cold and corrupt heart, had risked that look of love, oh, oh! I should be called a pretty lot of names. Charlatan, *poseur*, *arrangeur*! But he can do as he chooses! My dear young man, I know you don't like me," he went on as Roderick came back. "But it's a pity to waste your time on that, because you're strong enough never to think of me again. You're strong all round and everywhere."

Roderick even at this scarce departed from his dryness. "I'm sorry to differ from you, but I'm hopelessly weak."

Well, his visitor still allowed for his arrogance. "I told you last year that you wouldn't keep it up. I was a great ass. You *will* keep it up."

"I beg your pardon—I won't!" retorted Roderick.

"Though I'm a great ass all the same, eh? Well, call me what you will, so long as you turn out this sort of thing. I don't suppose it makes any particular difference to you, but I shall rejoice, for myself, to have made this sign of how largely I count on you."

Roderick stood looking at him with a strange rigour. It turned slowly to a flush, and two glittering angry tears filled his eyes. It was the first time Rowland had ever seen them there; he saw them but once again. Poor Gloriani, he was sure, had never in his life spoken with less of the mocking spirit; but a profession of faith came wrongly, somehow, at such a moment, for Roderick's nerves. He turned away with his imprecation scarce suppressed. Gloriani was ever trying to get near life, but life now baffled him. "What's the matter with him?" he asked with simplicity.

Rowland gave a sad smile and touched his forehead. "Genius—too much of it!"

"Ah, one mustn't have it so badly as that!" But Gloriani sent another parting, lingering look at the bust. "It's as cool as a draught of the *acqua Marcia*—and as pretty as the plash of it. He *is* to be counted on. But I'm glad, since his spirit's so high, that mine's a poorer thing. It makes," he explained with a laugh as he looked for Roderick to wave him good-bye and saw his back still turned, "it makes a more sociable studio!"

Rowland had purchased, as he supposed, temporary peace for Mary Garland; but his own spirit, in these days, was given over to the elements. The ideal life had been his general purpose, but the ideal life could only go on very real legs and feet, and the body and the extremities somehow failed always to move in concert. The days passed, but brought with them no official invitation to Christina Light's wedding. He occasionally met her, and he occasionally met Prince Casamassima; but the two were always separate: they were apparently taking their happiness in the inexpressive and isolated manner proper to people of social eminence. Rowland continued to see Madame Grandoni, for whom he felt a confirmed esteem. He had always talked to her with comfortable candour, but now he made her the confidant of his innermost worries. Roderick and Roderick's concerns had been a common theme with him, and it was in the natural course to talk of Mrs. Hudson's arrival and Mrs. Hudson's companion. In respect to certain equivocations, however, that he had not been ashamed to practise in regard to this young lady, she lost no time in putting his case for him in a nutshell. "At one moment you tell me the girl's plain," she said; "the next you tell me she's lovely. I'll call on them, I'll invite them. But one thing's very clear; you're in love with her down to the ground." Rowland, for all answer, glanced round to see that no one heard her, and it was odd to him that he should so like her saying it.

"More than that," she added, "you've been in love with her these two years. There was that certain something about you—— ! I knew you were of what we Germans call a subjective turn of mind; but you had a twist of it more than was natural. Why didn't you tell me at once ? You would have saved me a great deal of trouble. And poor Augusta Blanchard too !" With which Madame Grandoni produced, for their consumption, a colloquial plum. Miss Blanchard and Mr. Leavenworth were going to make a match; the young lady had been staying for a month at Albano, and as Mr. Leavenworth had been dancing attendance the event was a matter of course. Rowland, who had been lately reproaching himself with a failure of attention to Augusta's doings, made some such observation.

"But *you* didn't find it so," his hostess objected—"I mean when you, on your side, were so kind to her without seeming to care that it might have committed you. It was a matter of course perhaps that Mr. Leavenworth, who seems to be going about Europe with the sole view of picking up furniture for his 'home,' as he calls it, should think Miss

Blanchard a very handsome *morceau*; but it was not a matter of course —or it needn't have been—that she should be willing to become a sort of superior table-ornament. She would have accepted you in a jiffy if you had tried."

"You're supposing the insupposable," said Rowland. "She never gave me a particle of encouragement."

"What would you have had her do? The poor girl did her best, and I'm sure that when she surrendered to Mr. Leavenworth she was thinking of quite another gentleman."

"She thought of the pleasure her marriage would give him."

"Aye, pleasure indeed! She's a thoroughly good girl, but she has her little grain of feminine spite as well as the rest. Well, he's richer than you, and she will have what she wants; but before I forgive you I must wait and see this new arrival—what do you call her?—Miss Garlant of the Back Woods. If I like her very much I'll forgive you; if I don't I shall always bear you a grudge."

Rowland answered that he was sorry to forfeit any advantage she might offer him, but that his exculpatory passion for Miss Garland of the Back Woods was a figment of her fancy. Miss Garland of the Back Woods—he declared he liked that title—was engaged to another man. He himself had no claim.

"Well then," said Madame Grandoni, "if I like her we'll have it that you *ought* to be what you say—perhaps mendaciously—that you're not. If you fail in this it will be a double misdemeanour. The man she has accepted doesn't care a straw for her. Leave me alone and I'll tell her what I think of the man she hasn't!"

As to Christina Light's marriage Madame Grandoni could say nothing positive. The maiden had of late made her several flying visits, in the intervals of the usual pre-matrimonial shopping and dress-fitting; she had spoken of the event with a toss of her head, as a matter which with a wise old friend who viewed things in their essence she needn't pretend to treat as a solemnity. It was for Prince Casamassima to do that. "It's what they call a marriage of reason," she once had said. "That means, you know, a marriage of madness."

"What have you managed for her—since you must have managed something—in the way of advice?" Rowland asked.

"Very little, but that little has been a good word for the Prince. I know nothing of the mysteries of the young lady's heart. It may be a gold-mine, but at any rate it's at the bottom of a very long shaft. The marriage in itself, however, is an excellent marriage. It's not only 'great,' but it's good. I think Christina's quite capable of giving it some wrong turn, of spoiling somehow its beauty; but there's no position in the world that would be sacred to her. The Prince is an irreproachable young man; there's nothing against him, nothing inconvenient about him but that his name *is*, in his opinion, something to live up to. It's not often, I fancy, that a personage wearing it has been put through his paces at this rate. No one knows the wedding-day; the cards of invitation have been printed half a dozen times over with a different date; each time Christina has destroyed them. There are people in Rome who are furious at the delay; they want to get away; they're in a dreadful fright about the fever-season, but they're dying to see the wedding, and if the day were fixed they would make their arrangements to wait for it. I think it very possible that after having kept them for a month and been the cause of a dozen cases of malaria, Christina will be married at sunrise by an old friar—in Romeo and Juliet fashion—and with simply the legal witness."

Rowland brooded a while. "I feel as if we had still to reckon with her."

"Do you mean," his friend asked, "that she may even yet run away with Mr. Hudson?"

It was more than he had meant, but it had struck him the next minute as not perhaps more than might be. "I'm prepared for anything!"

"Do you mean that Mr. Hudson's ready?"

"Do you think *she* is?" Rowland asked.

"I think they're a precious pair—and yet that one hasn't said all when one says, as I have so often done, that she likes drama, likes theatricals—what do you call them?—histrionics, for their own sweet sake. She's certain to do every now and then something disinterested and sincere, something for somebody else than herself. She needs to think well of herself; she knows a fine character easily when she meets one; she hates to suffer by comparison, even though the comparison be made by herself alone; and when the figure she makes, to her own imagination, ceases to please or to amuse her she has to do something to smarten it up and give it a more striking turn. But of course she must always do that at somebody's expense—not one of her friends but must sooner or later pay, and the best of them doubtless the oftenest. Her attitudes and pretences may sometimes worry one, but I think we have most to pray to be guarded from her sincerities. Those are the prickles, after all, that she most turns upon her mother—and that she will turn yet upon her husband. But we mustn't, all the same," Madame Grandoni concluded, "give her up. Don't *you* !" she said with some emphasis to Rowland.

"Oh *me* !" he simply sighed: "I'm prickle-proof !"

His sagacious friend came the next day to call on the two ladies from Northampton. She carried their shy affections by storm and made them promise to drink tea with her on the evening of the morrow. Her visit was an epoch in the life of poor Mrs. Hudson, who did nothing but make sudden desultory allusions to her for the next thirty-six hours. "To think of her being a foreigner !" she would exclaim after much intent reflexion over her knitting; "she speaks the language as if she were driving her own carriage—and with her whip well up in her hand, don't you think ?" Then in a little while: "She wasn't so much dressed as you might have expected. Did you notice how easy it was in the waist ? I wonder if that's the fashion ?" Or "She's very old to wear a jaunty hat; I should never dare to wear a jaunty hat !" Or "Did you notice her hands ?—very pretty hands for such a stout person. A great many rings, but nothing very handsome. I suppose they're handed down." Or "She's certainly not handsome, but she looks wonderfully clever. I wonder why she doesn't have something done to her teeth." Rowland also received a summons to Madame Grandoni's tea-drinking, and went betimes, as he had been requested. He took a fond interest, which he would have been at a loss to defend, in Mary Garland's first appearance, as he felt it to be, on any social, certainly on any critical, stage. The two ladies had arrived with Roderick, easily "interesting" but irrecoverably vague, in attendance. Miss Blanchard was also present, escorted by Mr. Leavenworth, and the party was completed by a couple of dozen artists of both sexes and various nationalities. It was a friendly and lively concourse, like all Madame Grandoni's parties, and in the course of the evening there was some excellent music. People often played and sang for her who were not in general to be heard for the asking. She was herself a superior musician, and singers found it a privilege to perform to her accompaniment. Rowland conversed with various persons, but for the first time in his life his charity deserted its post and his attention flagrantly strayed: they were rejoicingly conscious of but one young woman, who filled for him, though all by no motion of her own, the part of heroine of the occasion. Madame Grandoni had said that he sometimes spoke of this person as pretty and sometimes as plain; to-night if he had had occasion to describe her type he would recklessly have pronounced it "rich." It was as if she had somehow put lights in her dim windows and you could hear somewhere behind them the tuning of mystic fiddles. She was dressed more than he had ever seen her; it was becoming and gave her an importance, all attaching, for the eye. Two or three persons were apparently witty people, for she sat listening to them with her brilliant natural smile. Rowland, from an opposite corner, reflected that he had never varied in his appreciation of Miss Blanchard's classic contour, but that somehow to-night it impressed him hardly more than an effigy stamped on a bad modern medal. Roderick could not be accused of rancour, for he had approached Mr. Leavenworth with unstudied familiarity and, lounging against the wall with hands in pockets, held him evidently under the spell of the good gentleman's not quite being able to decide as to the biggest hat, as it were, that his dignity could put on. Now that he had done him an impertinence the young man apparently found him less intolerable. Mr. Leavenworth stood stirring his tea and silently opening and shutting his mouth, without looking at his interlocutor; he might have been a large drowsy dog snapping at flies. Rowland had found it agitating to be told Miss Blanchard would have married him for the asking, and he would have felt embarrassment in going to speak to her if he hadn't worked it out so well, in the interval, from memory, that he hadn't really trifled with her. The facile side of a union with Miss Blanchard had never been present to his mind; it had struck him as a thing, in all ways, to be compassed with a great effort, and he had not even renounced the effort: he had never come, he felt, so near it. He had half an hour's talk with her; a farewell talk, as it seemed to him—a farewell not to a real illusion, but to the idea that for him, in the matter of committing himself for life, grim thought, there could ever be a motive that wouldn't ache like a wound. Such a pressure would resemble that of the button of an electric bell kept down by the thumb—prescribing definite action to stop the merciless ring. He congratulated Miss Blanchard upon her engagement, and she received his good wishes as if he had been a servant, at dinner, presenting the potatoes to her elbow. She helped herself in moderation, but also all in profile. He had wished to be decent, but he felt the chill and his zeal relaxed, while he fell a-thinking that a certain natural ease in a woman was the most delightful thing in the world. There was Christina Light, who had decidedly too much, and there was Miss Blanchard, who had decidedly too little, and there was Mary Garland, who had decidedly the right amount. He went to Madame Grandoni in an adjoining room, where she was pouring out tea. "I'll make you an excellent cup," she said, "because I've forgiven you."

He looked at her, answering nothing; but he swallowed his tea with great gusto and a wait for more—more of everything; by all of which she could know he was gratified. In a moment he intimated that in so far as he had sinned he was now quite square with his conscience, but Madame Grandoni had already forgotten.

"The Back Woods then," she said, "grow such interesting plants? I like your young lady—she's not a bit *banal*. And yet she escapes it so quietly—not, as they sometimes do, by standing on her head. I think that if she'll let me make a friend of her I shan't bore her either. I have a *flair*—oh yes, in spite of Augusta, Augusta Victoria as I now call her—for the chance of their boring *me*. Miss Garlant, you deep creature, defies at any rate your account of her."

"She's unfortunately plain," said Rowland, laughing and re-enforcing his account; "very simple and artless and ignorant——"

"But thoroughly neat and respectable!"—his old friend took him up. "Which, being interpreted, means, 'She's very handsome, very subtle, very clever, and has read hundreds of volumes on winter evenings in the country.'"

"You're a veritable sorceress," Rowland made answer; "you frighten me away." As he was turning to leave her there rose above the hum of voices in the drawing-room the sharp grotesque note of a barking dog. Their eyes met in a glance of intelligence.

"There's the veritable sorceress!" Madame Grandoni declared. "The sorceress and her necromantic poodle!" And she hastened back to the post of hospitality.

Rowland, accompanying her, found Christina Light erect in the middle of the drawing-room and looking about in perplexity. Her poodle, sitting on his haunches and gazing at the company, had apparently been expressing a sympathetic displeasure at the absence of a welcome. But in a moment Madame Grandoni had come to the girl's relief and Christina had tenderly kissed her.

"I had no idea," the young woman began while she surveyed the assembly, "that you had such a lot of grand people, or I would never have come in. The servant said nothing; he took me for an *invitée*. I came to spend a neighbourly half-hour; you know I haven't many left! It was too dismally dreary at home. I hoped I should find you alone and I brought Stenterello to play with the cat. Since I'm here, at any rate, I beg you to let me stay. I'm not dressed, but am I very hideous ? I'll sit in a corner and no one will notice me. My dear sweet lady, do let me stay ! Only, why in the world didn't you ask me ? I never have been to a little party like this. They must be very charming. No dancing—tea and conversation ? No tea, thank you; but if you could spare a biscuit for Stenterello; a sweet biscuit, please. Really, why didn't you ask me ? Do you have these things often ? Madame Grandoni, it's very unkind !" And the girl, who had delivered herself of the foregoing succession of sentences in her usual low, cool, penetrating voice, uttered these last words with a certain tremor of feeling. "I see," she went on; "I do very well for balls and great banquets, but when people wish to have a cosy, friendly, comfortable evening, they leave me out with the big flower-pots and the gilt candlesticks."

"I am sure you're welcome to stay, my dear," said Madame Grandoni, "and at the risk of displeasing you I must confess that if I didn't invite you it was because you *are*, in effect, so grand for small occasions and you come, as it were, so dear. Your dress will do very well, with its fifty flounces, and there's no need of your going into a corner. Indeed since you're here I propose to have the glory of it. You must remain where my people can see you."

"They're evidently determined to do that by the way they stare. Do they think I've come to dance a *tarantella* ? Who are they all; do I know them ?" And lingering in the spacious centre, with her arm passed into Madame Grandoni's, she let her eyes wander slowly from group to group; all groups of course observing her. Standing in the little circle of lamplight with the hood of an Eastern burnous shot with silver threads falling back from her beautiful head, while one hand gathered its voluminous shimmering folds and the other played with the silken top-knot on the uplifted head of her poodle, she was a figure radiantly romantic and might have suggested an extemporised *tableau vivant*. Rowland's position made it becoming for him to speak to her without delay. As she looked at him he saw that, judging by the light of her beautiful eyes, she was in a humour to a specimen of which she had not yet treated him. In a simpler person he would have called it a great and direct kindness, but in this young lady's deportment the flower was apt to be one thing and the perfume another. "Tell me about these people," she went on again: "I had no idea there were so many people in Rome I've not seen. What are they all talking about ? It's all very clever, I suppose, and quite beyond me. There's Miss Blanchard detaching herself as usual against the darkest object she can find. She would find means to make the Great Desert resemble a photographer's studio. But she's too much like a head on a postage-stamp. And there's that nice little old lady in black, Mrs. Hudson. What a dear little woman for a mother! *Comme elle est proprette !* And the other, the *fiancée*, of course she's here. Ah, I see !" She paused; she was looking intently at Mary Garland. Rowland measured the sincerity of her glance and suddenly acquired a conviction. "I should like so much to know her !" she said, turning to Madame Grandoni. "She has a charming face; I'm sure she's the nicest person here. I wish very much you would introduce me. No, on second thoughts I would rather you didn't. I'll speak to her bravely myself, as a friend of her—what do you call it in English ?—her *promesso sposo*." Madame Grandoni and Rowland exchanged glances of baffled conjecture, and Christina flung off her burnous, crumpled it together and, with uplifted finger, tossing it into a corner, gave it in charge to her poodle, who straightway proceeded to squat on it with upright vigilance. Christina crossed the room with the step and smile of a ministering angel and introduced herself to the young lady from Northampton. She had once told Rowland that she would show him some day how awfully civil she knew how to be, and was now redeeming her promise. Rowland, watching her, saw Mary Garland rise slowly in response to her greeting and look at her with serious deep-gazing eyes. The almost dramatic opposition of these two keenly interesting girls touched him with a nameless apprehension, and after a moment he preferred to turn away. In doing so he noticed Roderick, who, standing planted on the train of a lady's dress, was watching the same passage with undisguised earnestness. There were several more pieces of music; Rowland sat in a corner and listened to them. When they were over the company began to take leave, Mrs. Hudson among the number. Rowland saw her come up to Madame Grandoni, clinging shyly to Mary Garland's arm. Mary looked a little as if she had just jumped, rather dangerously, to save her life or her honour, from some great height. The two ladies, he gathered, had appealed tacitly to Roderick, but Roderick now had his back turned. He had approached Christina, who, with an absent air, was sitting alone, where she had taken her place near her innocent rival to watch the guests pass out of the room. Her face, like Mary's, showed a vague afterglow, but only as an intenser radiance. Hearing Roderick's voice she looked up at him sharply; then silently, with a single quick gesture, she motioned him away. He obeyed her and came and joined his mother in bidding good-night to Madame Grandoni. Christina in a moment met Rowland's eyes and immediately beckoned him to come to her. He was familiar with her peremptory way and was not particularly surprised. She made a place for him on the sofa beside her; he wondered what was coming now. He was not sure it was not a mere fancy, but it seemed to him that he had never seen her look just as she was looking then. There was a high mildness, a sweetness of humility in it which threw into relief the rare nature, the strange life and play, of her beauty. "How many more metamorphoses," he asked himself, "am I to be treated to before we have done?"

"I want to tell you," said Christina, "I've such a beautiful impression of Miss Garland. Aren't you glad?"

"Quite overjoyed, madam," Rowland returned.

She kept her eyes on him. "Ah, I see you don't believe a word of it!"

"Is it so hard to believe?"

"Not that people in general should admire her, but that I should. I'm not good enough—that's what you feel. But I want to tell you; I want to tell some one; I can't tell Miss Garland herself. She regards me already as a horrid false creature, and if I were to express to her frankly what I think of her I should simply disgust her. She would be quite right; she has Repose, and from that point of view I and my doings must seem monstrous. Unfortunately I haven't Repose—ah, what wouldn't I give for it! I'm trembling now; if I could ask you to feel my arm you'd see. But I want to tell you that I admire Miss Garland more than any of the people who call themselves her friends —except of course you. Oh, I know that! To begin with she's extremely handsome and she hasn't the least idea of it. Now that by itself, you know——!"

"She's not generally thought handsome," Rowland conscientiously said.

"Evidently! That's the vulgarity of the taste of the rabble. Her head has great character, great natural style. If a woman's not to scream out from every pore that she has an appearance—which is a most awful fate—quite the best thing for her is to carry *that* sort of dark lantern. On occasion she can flash it as far as she likes. She'll not be thought pretty by people in general and desecrated as she passes by the stare of every vile wretch who chooses to thrust his nose under her bonnet; but a certain number of intelligent people will find it one of the delightful things of life to look at her. That lot's as good as another. And then your friend has every virtue under heaven."

"You found that out soon," Rowland laughed.

"How long did it take *you*? I found it out before I ever spoke to her. I met her the other week in Saint Peter's; I knew it then. I knew it—do you want to know how long I've known it?"

"Really," said Rowland, "I didn't mean to cross-examine you."

"Do you remember mamma's ball in December? We had some talk and you then mentioned her—not by name. You said but three words, but I saw you admired her and I knew that if you admired her she must have every virtue under heaven. That's what you require."

"Upon my word," he declared, "you make three words go very far!"

"Oh, Mr. Hudson has also spoken of her."

"Ah, that's better!" said Rowland.

"I don't know. He doesn't like her."

"Has he told you so?" The question left Rowland's lips before he could stay it—which he would have done on a moment's reflexion. Christina looked at him intently. "Not in so many words," she said at last. "That would have been dishonourable, wouldn't it? But I know it from my knowledge of him. He doesn't like perfection; he's not bent on being so awfully safe and sound in his likings; he's willing to risk something! Poor dear man, he risks too much!"

Rowland was silent; he didn't care for the thrust, but he was profoundly mystified. Christina beckoned to her poodle, and the dog marched stiffly across to her. She gave a loving twist to his rose-coloured top-knot and bade him go and fetch her burnous. He obeyed, gathered it up in his teeth and returned with great solemnity, dragging it along the floor.

"I do her justice. I do her full justice." She wonderfully kept it up. "I like to say that, I like to be able to say it. She's full of intelligence and courage and devotion. She doesn't do me a grain of justice; but that's no harm—I mean above all no harm to *her*. There's something so noble in the aversions of a good woman!"

"If you would give Miss Garland a chance," said Rowland, "I'm sure she would be glad to be your friend."

"What do you mean by a chance? She has only to take it. I told her I liked her immensely, and she glared as if I had said something disgusting. She looks magnificent when she glares—like a Medusa crowned not with snakes but with a tremor of doves' wings." Christina rose with these words and began to gather her mantle about her. "I don't often like women—small blame to me," she went on. "In

246

fact I generally detest 'em. But I should like to know that one well.
I should like to have a friendship with her; I have never had one;
they must be very delightful, good safe friendships. But I shan't have
one now—not if she can help it! Ask her what she thinks of me;
see what she'll say. I don't want to know; keep it to yourself. It's too
sad. So we go through life. It's fatality—that's what they call it, isn't
it? We make the most inconvenient good impression on people we
don't care for; we inspire with loathing those we do. But I appreciate
her, I do her justice; that's the most important thing. It's because
I've after all a lot of imagination. She has none. Never mind; it's her
only fault. Besides, imagination's not a virtue—it's a vice. I do her
justice; I understand very well." She kept softly murmuring and
looking about for Madame Grandoni. She saw the good lady near
the door and put out her hand to Rowland for good-night. She held
his hand an instant, fixing him with her eyes, by the living splendour
of which he was momentarily dazzled. "Yes, I do her justice," she
repeated. "And you do her more; you would lay down your life for
her." With this she turned away and before he could answer she
left him. She went to Madame Grandoni, grasped her two hands
and held out a forehead to be kissed. The next moment she was gone.

"That was a happy accident!" said Madame Grandoni. "She
never looked so beautiful and she made my little party brilliant."

"Beautiful verily!" Rowland answered. "But it was no accident."

"What was it then?"

"It was a plan. She wanted to see Mary Garland. She knew she
was to be here."

"How so?"

"By Roderick evidently."

"And why did she wish to see her?"

"Heaven knows! I give it up."

"Ah, the bold bad girl!" Madame Grandoni sighed.

"No," said Rowland; "don't say that now. She's too beautiful."

"Oh, you men—the best of you!"

"Well then," cried Rowland, "she's too good!"

THE OPPORTUNITY presenting itself the next day, he failed not, as you may imagine, to ask Mary Garland what she thought of Christina. It was a Saturday afternoon, the time at which the beautiful marbles of the Villa Borghese are thrown open to the public. Mary had told him that Roderick had promised to take her to see them with his mother, and he joined the party in the splendid Casino. The warm weather had left so few strangers in Rome that they had the place to almost themselves. Mrs. Hudson had confessed to an invincible fear of treading even with the help of her son's arm the polished marble floors, and was sitting patiently on a stool, with folded hands, looking shyly here and there at the undraped paganism around her. Roderick had sauntered off alone with an irritated brow which seemed to betray the conflict between the instinct of observation and the perplexities of circumstance. His cousin was astray in another direction, and if Rowland caught her with her eyes on the catalogue he explained it as a sign of her system of concealing anxieties. He joined her, and she presently dropped for him on a divan and rather wearily closed her eternal red handbook. Then he asked her abruptly how Christina had pleased her.

She started the least bit at the question, and he felt she had been thinking of Christina. "I don't like her !" she dryly said.

"What do you think of her ?"

"I think she's false." It quite rang out.

"But she wished to please you; she tried," Rowland rejoined in a moment.

"She wished above all to please herself!"

He was silent again, held a moment by a strange intensity of thought. Yes, this young woman would never be anything but unjust to the other one, and that though neither had a vulgar soul. And he saw the attitude in Mary as immutable for ever, and Christina was interesting, and Mary would be wrong. He himself could take it thus and yet not "mind." How little with her there, verily, he minded ! This came and went in fifty seconds—leaving all the rest, however, not less distinct. He knew that his companion knew, by that infallible sixth sense of a woman who loves, how the beautiful strange girl she had seen for the first time at Saint Peter's (since when she had asked no question about her) had possibly the power to do her a definite wrong. To what extent she had the will remained of course ambiguous, and last night's interview had somehow, by a perverse process, only proved an omen of ill. It was in these conditions equally unbecoming for Rowland to depreciate or to defend Christina, and he had to content himself with simply having verified the latter's own assurance that she had made a bad impression. He tried to talk of indifferent matters—about the statues and the frescoes; but to-day plainly the quest of elegant knowledge on Mary's part had folded its wings. Curiosity of another sort had taken its place. She was longing, he was sure, to break ground again on the subject of Christina; but she found a dozen reasons for hesitating. Her questions would imply that Roderick had not treated her with confidence; for information on this point should properly have come from himself. They would imply that she was jealous, and to betray her jealousy was intolerable to her pride. For some minutes, as she sat pressing the brilliant pavement with the point of her umbrella, it was to be supposed that her pride and her anxiety held an earnest debate. At last anxiety won.

"About Miss Light then," she asked; "do you know her very well?"

"I can hardly say that. But I've seen her repeatedly."

"Do you like her very much?"

"Yes and no. I think I'm sorry for her."

Mary had spoken with her eyes on the pavement. At this she looked up. "Sorry for her? Why?"

"Well—she's unhappy."

"What are her miseries?"

"Well—she has a horrible mother and has had a wretched bringing-up."

For a moment Mary was still. Then "Isn't she very beautiful?" she asked.

"Don't you think so?"

"That's measured by what men think! She's extremely clever too."

"Oh yes—speaking as men think!"

"She has beautiful dresses."

"Any number of them."

"And beautiful manners."

"Yes—sometimes."

"And plenty of money."

"Money enough apparently."

"And she's enormously admired."

"Oh, enormously."

"And she's to marry a grandee."

"So they say."

Mary rose and turned to rejoin her companions, commenting these admissions with a pregnant silence. "Poor Miss Light !" she at last simply said. But it went, as for her ironic purpose, very far.

Late the next evening his servant brought him the card of a visitor. He was surprised at so nocturnal a call, but it may be said that when he read the inscription—Cavaliere Giuseppe Giacosa—he recognised the working of events. He had had an unnamed prevision of some sequel to the apparition at Madame Grandoni's—which the Cavaliere would have come to usher in.

He had come evidently on a portentous errand. He was as pale as some livid old marble mask into which he might have suggested that a pair of polished agate eyes had been for an occasion inserted. Prodigiously grave, he might have been the bearer of a *cartel*, had not his deep deference to his host and to the latter's general situation been clearly again his first need.

"You've more than once done me the honour to invite me to call upon you, and I'm ashamed of my long delay. But my time for many months has been particularly little my own." Rowland assented, ungrudgingly, fumbled for some Italian correlative of "Better late than never," begged him to be seated and offered him a cigar. The Cavaliere sniffed imperceptibly the fragrant weed and then declared that if his entertainer would allow him he would reserve it for consumption at another time. It was not a case, clearly, for hanging up smoke-wreaths. "I must confess," he said, "that even now I come on business not of my own—or my own at least only in a secondary sense. I've been despatched as an ambassador—an envoy extraordinary, I may say—by my dear friend Mrs. Light."

"If I can in any way be of service to Mrs. Light I shall much rejoice," Rowland found himself a little recklessly articulating.

"Well then, dear sir, Casa Light's in high commotion. The povera signora's in great trouble, in terrible trouble." For a moment Rowland expected to hear that the povera signora's trouble was of a nature that a loan of five thousand francs would assuage. But the Cavaliere was more interesting even than that. "Miss Light has committed a great crime; she has plunged a dagger into the heart of her mother."

"A dagger——?"

The Cavaliere nervously patted the air. "I speak strongly—one must: *che vuole?* She has broken off her marriage."

"Broken it off?"

"Short! She has turned the Prince out of the house." And the good gentleman, with this report, folded his arms and, straight at his friend, looked strange, the strangest, things. A mocking little light of pride might have glimmered in his decent despair.

Rowland greeted the news with a gasp, and there sounded in his ears the sinister click as of a fitting together of bad pieces. She had been too plausible to be honest. Without being able to trace the connexion, he yet instinctively associated her present rebellion with her meeting of Mary. Sinister it thus suddenly showed, her exhibition of eager mildness at Madame Grandoni's, and all the uneasiness she had then stirred in him came back with a chill. Yes, it was clearer than it was obscure, and he recognised in the stroke now startling him the hand armed to deal some blow at Miss Garland's small remnant of security. So it hung before him, portentous and ugly. If she had not seen Mary she would have let things stand, but she had seen her and she had acted. It was monstrous indeed to suppose that she could have sacrificed so brilliant a fortune to a mere movement of jealousy, to a calculation of quite futile effects, to a desire to create for the poor girl some poisonous alarm. Yet he remembered his first impression of her; she was "dangerous," and she had measured in each quarter the penetration of her announced rupture. She hovered there for him as tasting *that* strength in it. If the question had been of her penetrating, *he*, verily, was penetrated, and it made him long, for a minute that was as sharp as a knife-edge, to denounce her to her face. But of course all he could say to his visitor was that he was extremely sorry, though indeed he was not surprised.

"You're not surprised?"

"With Miss Light everything's possible. Isn't that true?"

Another ripple seemed to play an instant in the current of the old man's irony, but he made no answer. "It was a magnificent marriage," he said at last. "I have my reserves about a great many people, but I had none about the Signor Principe."

"I should judge him indeed a very honourable young man," said Rowland.

"Eh, young as he is he's made of the old stuff. And now perhaps he's blowing his brains out. He's the last of his house; it's a great house. But Miss Light will have made it, for the nonce, feel very small."

"Is that what she has *wanted* to do?"

The Cavaliere's smile was like the red tip of a cigar seen for a few seconds in the dark. "You've observed Miss Light with attention," he said, "and this brings me to my errand. Mrs. Light has a high opinion of your wisdom, of your kindness, and she has reason to believe you've great influence with her daughter."

"I—with her daughter? Not a grain!"

"That's possibly your modesty. Mrs. Light believes that something may yet be done and that our young lady will listen to you as to no one. She begs you therefore to come and see her before it's too late."

"But all this, my dear Cavaliere, is none of my business," Rowland objected. "I can't possibly in such a matter take the responsibility of advising Miss Light."

The Cavaliere fixed his eyes for a moment on the floor, in brief but intense reflexion. Then looking up, "Unfortunately," he said, "she has no man near her whom she respects. She has no father."

"And such a finished fool of a mother!" Rowland gave himself the satisfaction of exclaiming.

The Cavaliere was so pale that he could not easily have turned paler; yet it seemed for a moment that his dead complexion blanched. "Eh, signore, such as she is the mother appeals to you. A very handsome woman—dishevelled, in tears, in despair, literally undressed, uncombed and refusing food." Rowland reflected a moment, not on the attractions of Mrs. Light in the guise evoked by the Cavaliere, but on the relief he should find in bringing home to Christina her damnable need of making mischief.

"I must add," said the Cavaliere, "that Mrs. Light desires also to speak to you on the subject of Mr. Hudson."

"She believes Mr. Hudson connected with this step of her daughter's?"

"Intimately. He must be got out of Rome."

"Mrs. Light then must get an order from the Pope to remove him. It's not in my power."

The Cavaliere showed his intelligence. "Mrs. Light's equally helpless. She would leave Rome to-morrow, but nothing will induce Christina to budge. An order from the Pope would do nothing. A bull in council would do nothing."

"She's really," said Rowland, "a terrible explosive force."

But the Cavaliere rose—he responded more coldly. "She has a great spirit—the very greatest." And it seemed to Rowland that her great spirit, for mysterious reasons, gave him more pleasure than the distressing use she made of it gave him pain. He was on the point of charging him with his inconsistency when the good gentleman took himself up. "But if the marriage can be saved it *must* be saved. It's a beautiful marriage. It *will* be saved."

"Notwithstanding Miss Light's great spirit to the contrary ?"

"Miss Light, notwithstanding her great spirit, will come round again to her duty."

"And will the Signor Principe come round ?"

"I warrant him !"

"Well, then," said Rowland, "heaven grant our prayer !"

"Oh, we must help heaven !" And with Rowland's promise to present himself on the morrow at Casa Light his visitor departed. He left our friend revolving many things : Christina's magnanimity, Christina's perversity, Roderick's contingent fortune, Mary Garland's certain misery and the Cavaliere's own fine ambiguities.

Rowland's present vow obliged him to disengage himself from an excursion which he had arranged with the two ladies at the inn. Before going to Casa Light he repaired in person to that establishment. He found Roderick's mother seated with tearful eyes, staring at an open note that lay in her lap. At the window hovered Mary, who turned on him as he entered a gaze both anxious and confident. Mrs. Hudson quickly rose and came to him, holding out the note.

"In pity's name what's the matter with my boy ? If he's ill I entreat you to take me to him !"

"He's not ill, to my knowledge," Rowland said. "What have you there ?"

"A note—a most dreadful thing. He tells us we're not to see him nor to think of him for a week. If I could only go to his room ! But I'm afraid, I'm afraid !"

"I imagine there's no need of going to his room. What's the occasion, may I ask, of his note ?"

"He was to have gone with us on this drive to—what is the place ? —to Cervara. You know it was arranged yesterday morning. In the evening he was to have dined with us. But he never came, and this morning arrives this awfulness. Oh dear, I'm so nervous. Would you mind reading it ?"

Rowland took the note and glanced at its half-dozen lines. "I mustn't go to Cervara," they ran; "I have something else to do. This will occupy me perhaps a week, so you won't see me. Don't talk about me too much and don't miss me. Learn not to miss me. I bless you both, but I know what I need and must insist on my conditions.—R.H."

"Why, it means," Rowland explained, "that he has taken up a fresh piece of work and that it's all-absorbing. That's very good news." This explanation was not sincere, but he had not the courage not to offer it as a stop-gap. And he found he needed all his courage to support it, for Mary had left her place and approached him, formidably unsatisfied.

"He never works in the evening," said Mrs. Hudson. "Can't he come for five minutes? Why does he write such a cruel cold note to his poor mother—to poor Mary? What have we done that he acts so strangely? It's this wicked, infectious, heathenish place!" And the poor lady's suppressed mistrust of the Eternal City broke passionately out. "Oh, dear Mr. Mallet," she went on, "I'm sure it's this poisonous air, that the fever's on him and that he's already delirious."

"I'm very sure it's not that," Mary distinctly protested.

She was still fixing Rowland, so that his eyes met hers and his own glance wandered away. This made him angry, and to carry off his confusion he pretended to be looking meditatively at the floor. After all, what had *he* to be ashamed of? For a moment he was on the point of making a clean breast of it, of crying out "Good ladies, I abdicate; I can't help you!" But he checked himself; he felt so impatient to have his three words with Christina. He grasped his hat. "I'll see what it is and let you know." And then he was glad he had not abdicated, for as he turned away he glanced again at Mary and saw that, though her face was full of apprehensions, it was not hard and accusing, but charged with appealing friendship.

He went straight to Roderick's apartment, deeming this, at an early hour, the safest place to seek him. He found him in his sitting-room, which had been closely darkened to keep out the heat. The carpets and rugs had been removed, the floor of speckled concrete was bare and lightly sprinkled with water. Here and there, over it, certain strongly-odorous flowers had been scattered. Roderick was lying on his divan in a white dressing-gown, staring at the frescoed ceiling. The room was deliciously cool and filled with the moist sweet fragrance of the circumjacent roses and violets. These were somehow "quaint" notes, yet Rowland hardly felt surprised.

"Your mother was greatly alarmed at your note," he said, "and I came to satisfy myself that, as I believed, you're not ill."

Roderick lay motionless except that he slightly turned his head towards his friend. He was smelling a large white rose, which he continued to present to his nose. In the darkness of the room he looked exceedingly pale, but his beautiful eyes quite shed a light. He let them rest for some time on Rowland, lying there like a Buddhist in an intellectual swoon, a deep dreamer whose perception should be slowly ebbing back to temporal matters. "Oh, I'm not ill," he said at last. "I've never been better in my life."

"Your note, nevertheless, and your announced absence, have very naturally alarmed your mother. I advise you to go to her directly and reassure her."

"Go to her? Going to her would be worse than staying away. Staying away at present is a kindness." And he inhaled deeply his huge rose, looking up over it at Rowland. "My presence, in fact, would be indecent."

"Indecent? Pray explain."

"Why, you see, as regards Mary Garland. I'm disgustingly happy. Doesn't it strike you? You ought to agree with me. You wish me to spare her feelings; I spare them by staying away. Last night I heard something——"

"I heard it too," Rowland said with a high intention of dryness. "And it's in honour of this piece of news that you've taken to your bed in this fashion?"

"Extremes meet! I can't get up for joy."

"May I inquire how you heard what has given you such pleasure? From Miss Light herself?"

"By no means. It was brought me by her maid, who's in my service as well."

"The Prince's loss then is to such a certainty your own gain?"

"I don't talk about certainties. I don't want to be arrogant. I don't want to offend the immortal gods. I'm keeping very quiet and behaving, I maintain, as a gentleman should. But I can't help my deep peace. I shall wait a while. I shall bide my time."

"And then?"

"And then the most interesting person in the world—in my world —will confess to me that when she threw overboard her Prince she remembered that I adore her."

"I feel bound to tell you," was in the course of a moment Rowland's

255

response to this speech, "that I'm now on my way to Mrs. Light's."

"I congratulate you—I envy you," Roderick imperturbably remarked.

"Mrs. Light has sent for me to remonstrate with her daughter, with whom she has taken it into her head that I have an influence. I don't know to what extent I shall remonstrate, but I give you notice I shall not speak in your interest."

Roderick looked at him for a moment with a lazy radiance. "Pray don't !" he simply answered.

"You deserve I should tell her you're a very shabby fellow."

"My dear Rowland, the comfort with you is that I can so beautifully trust you. You're incapable of doing anything the least tiny bit indelicate."

"You mean to lie here then smelling your roses and nursing your visions and leaving your mother and Miss Garland to eat their hearts out ?"

"Can I go and flaunt my felicity in their faces ? Wait till I get used to it a trifle. I've done them a villainous wrong, but I can at least forbear to add insult to injury. I may be the biggest donkey, or the blackest monster, in Rome, but for the moment I have taken it into my head to be glad to be alive. I shouldn't be able to keep it from them; my being glad, or even my being alive, on such a basis, would mortally scandalise them. So I lock myself up as a dangerous character."

"Well, I can only hope that your gladness may not grow less or your danger greater."

Roderick closed his eyes again and sniffed at his rose. "God's will be done !"

On this Rowland left him and repaired directly to Mrs. Light's. This afflicted lady hurried forward to meet him. Since the Cavaliere's visit to Rowland she had taken a reef, as the saying is, in her distress, but she was evidently still in high agitation and she clutched Rowland by his two hands as if in the ship-wreck of her hopes he were her single floating spar. Rowland greatly pitied her—so respectable is sincerity of sorrow. She too was in the blighting circle of her daughter's contact, and this exposure, shared with the others who were more interesting, almost gave her, with the crudity of her candour, something of their dignity.

"Speak to her, plead with her, don't leave her till you've moved her !" she cried, pressing and shaking his hands. "She'll not heed *us*, no more than if we were a pair of running fountains. Perhaps she'll listen to you; she always liked you."

"She always disliked me," said Rowland. "But that doesn't matter now. I've come here simply because you sent for me—not because I can help you. I can't advise your daughter."

"Oh, if you think I'm going to take that from you——! You *must* advise her; you shan't leave this house *till* you've advised her!" the poor woman passionately retorted. "Look at me in my misery and refuse to help me! You needn't be afraid, I know I'm a fright, I haven't an idea what I've on. If this goes on she and I may both as well turn scarecrows. If ever a woman was desperate and heartbroken, such a woman speaks to you now! I can't begin to tell you. To have nourished a serpent, sir, all these years! To have lavished one's self upon a viper that turns and stings her own devoted mother! To have toiled and prayed, to have pushed and struggled, to have eaten the bread of bitterness and gone through fire and water—and at the end of all things to find myself at this pass! It can't be, it's too cruel, such things don't happen, the Lord don't allow it. I'm a religious woman, sir, and if the Saints above don't know all about me it isn't my fault. But hadn't they, with their own very hands, just given me their reward? I would have lain down in the dust and let her walk over me; I would have given her the eyes out of my head if she had taken a fancy to them. No, she's a cruel, wicked, heartless, unnatural girl! I speak to you, Mr. Mallet, in my dire distress, as to my *only* friend. There isn't a creature here that I can look to— not one of them all that I have faith in. But I always thought everything of *you*. I said to Christina the first time I saw you that you were a perfect gentleman, a real one—different enough from some I could name! Come, don't disappoint me now! I feel so terribly alone, you see; I feel what a nasty hard heartless world it is that has come and devoured my dinners and danced to my fiddles and yet that hasn't a word to throw to me in my trouble. The mere money I've spent, all round, to *do* it—I could speak of that too if I cared!"

While this high tide was flowing Rowland had had time to look round the room and to see the Cavaliere sitting in a corner, like a major-domo on the divan of an ante-chamber, pale, rigid, inscrutable. "I have it at heart to tell you," he said, "that if you consider my friend Hudson——"

Mrs. Light gave a toss of her head and hands. "Oh, it's not that! She told me last night to bother her no longer with Hudson. Hudson, forsooth! She didn't care a button for Hudson. I almost wish she did; then perhaps one might understand it. But she doesn't care for anything in the wide world except to do her own hard wicked will and to crush me and shame me with her cruelty."

"Ah then," said Rowland, "I'm as much at sea as you, and my presence here's an impertinence. I should like to say three words to Miss Light on my own account. But I must wholly decline to talk to her about the Prince. This is simply impossible."

Mrs. Light burst into angry tears. "Because the poor boy is a prince, eh? because he's of a great family and has an income of millions, eh? That's why you begrudge him and stand off from him and won't lift a finger for him. I knew there were vulgar people of that way of feeling, but I didn't expect it of *you*. Make an effort, Mr. Mallet; rise to the occasion; forgive the poor darling his advantages. Be just, be reasonable! It's not *his* fault, and it's not mine. Pray, hasn't he human feelings and isn't he horribly suffering? He's the best, the truest, the kindest young man in Italy and the most correct and cultivated and incapable of a thought——! If he were standing here in rags I would say it all the same. The man first—the money afterwards: that was always my motto—ask the Cavaliere. What do you take me for? Do you suppose I would give Christina to a *vicious* person? do you suppose I would sacrifice my precious child, little comfort as I have in her, to a man against whose character a syllable could be breathed? Casamassima's only too good, too innocently good; he's a saint of saints; his word is his word and he understands nothing else. There isn't such another in the length and breadth of Europe. What he has been through in this house not a common peasant would endure. Christina has treated him as you wouldn't treat a dog. He has been dealt with as if to see how much of it he would take. He has been driven hither and thither till he didn't know where he was. He has stood there where you stand—there, with his name and his millions and his devotion—as white as your handkerchief, with hot tears in his eyes and me ready to go down on my knees to him and say 'My own sweet Prince, I could kiss the ground you tread on, but it isn't decent that I should allow you to enter my house and expose yourself to these horrors again.' And he would come back, and he would come back, and go through it all again, and take all that was given him, and only want the girl the more. He opened himself to me as he might to his mother in heaven, and it's not too much to say that we lived through everything together. He used to beg my own forgiveness for her worst caprices. What do you say to that? I seized him once and kissed him hard, I verily did! To find that and to find all the rest with it, and to believe that luck was at last, in spite of everything, on my side, and then to see it dashed away before my eyes and to stand here helpless—oh, it's a fate I hope you may ever be spared!"

"It would seem then that in the interest of Prince Casamassima himself I ought to refuse to interfere," Rowland presently said.

Mrs. Light looked at him hard, slowly drying her eyes. The magnificence of her woe gave her a kind of majesty, and Rowland for the moment felt ashamed of the somewhat grim humour of his observation. "Very good, sir," she said. "I'm sorry your heart isn't so tender as your conscience. My compliments to your conscience! It must give you great happiness. Of course it's your own affair. Since you fail us we're indeed driven to the wall. But I've fought my own battles before and have never *really* lost courage, so I don't see why I should break down now. Cavaliere, come here!" That personage rose at her summons and stood impenetrably at attention. He had shaken hands with Rowland in silence. "Mr. Mallet refuses to say a word," Mrs. Light went on. "Time presses, every minute's precious. God only knows what that poor boy may be doing. If at this moment a truly clever woman should get hold of him it wouldn't matter if she were a fright: it would be her grand chance. It's horrible to think of."

The Cavaliere fixed his eyes on Rowland, and his expression, which the night before had been singular, was now extraordinary in its mixture of fine anxiety—an anxiety that seemed to plead against the young man's reluctance—and of some emotion of a bearing less calculable. Suddenly and vaguely Rowland felt the presence of a new active element in the situation that had been made a drama somehow by Christina's having been made, so all generically, a heroine. It was as if a subordinate performer had suddenly advanced to the footlights. He looked from their companion to Mrs. Light, whose tears had been succeeded by a grand air of detachment.

"If you could bring yourself," the Cavaliere said with all his grave rich unction and with the effect, in his fine Roman voice, as of a round-hand copy set for a pupil, "if you could bring yourself to address a few words of solemn remonstrance to Miss Light you would perhaps do more for us than you know. You would save several persons a great deal of pain. This gracious lady here first and then Christina herself. Christina in particular. Me too, I might take the liberty to add!"

Rowland felt these words, after an instant, press upon his heart as with a repetition of discreet and intense finger-taps. To the personage so urbanely sounding them his imagination had from the first all benevolently attached itself, and they now seemed a supreme manifestation of the mysterious obliquity of his life. On the spot something sharply occurred to him; it was something very odd and it stayed his glance from again turning to Mrs. Light. His idea embarrassed him, and to carry off his embarrassment he repeated that it was folly to suppose *his* counsel would have any weight with their young friend.

The Cavaliere stepped forward and laid two fingers, as for positive emphasis of the effect Rowland had already figured, on his interlocutor's breast. "Do you wish to know the truth of the case ? You're the only man whose words she ever repeats."

Rowland was moving from one new light to another. "I'll say then what I can !" By this time he had again caught Mrs. Light's conscious eyes, which appeared to accuse him for an instant of possible defection.

"If you fail," she said sharply, "there's something else we can do. But for God's sake be straight !"

She had hardly spoken when the sound of a short sharp growl caused the company to turn. Christina's pompous poodle stood in the middle of the great drawing-room with his nose raised as if to sniff conspiracy. He had preceded his mistress as the sharpest of scouts, and she now slowly advanced from a neighbouring place.

"You will be so good as to listen to Mr. Mallet," her mother promptly rang out, "and to reflect carefully on what he says. I suppose you'll admit that *he's* disinterested. In half an hour you shall hear from me again !" And her retreat with her companion might have been the march of a squad that has changed guard.

Christina looked hard at Rowland, but offered him no greeting. She was very pale, and, strangely enough, it at first seemed to Rowland that her beauty was in eclipse. But he recognised more than ever that its shadows were as fine as its lights and that attempted discussion would always have it to reckon with. "Why have you come here at this time ?" she asked.

"Your mother sent for me in pressing terms, and I was very glad to have an opportunity to speak to you."

"Have you come to help me or to worry me ?"

"I've as little power to do one as I've desire to do the other. I came in great part to ask you a question. First, is your determination absolutely taken ?"

Christina's two hands had been hanging clasped in front of her; she separated them and flung them apart by an admirable gesture.

"Would you have done this if you had not seen a certain person?"

"What person?"

"The young lady you so much admire."

She looked at him with quickened attention; then suddenly, "This is really interesting," she exclaimed. "Let us see what's in it." And she flung herself into a chair and pointed to another.

"You don't answer my question," Rowland said.

"You've no right that I know of to ask it. But it's very intelligent— it puts such a lot into it. Into my having seen her, I mean." She paused a moment; then with her eyes on him, "She helped me certainly," she went on.

"Provoked you, you mean, to hurt her—through Roderick?"

For a moment she deeply coloured, and he had really not intended to force the tears to her eyes. A cold clearness, however, quickly forced them back. "I see your train of reasoning, but it's really all wrong. I meant no harm whatever to Miss Garland; I should be extremely sorry to cause her any distress. Tell me that, since I assure you of that, you believe it."

"How am I to tell you," he asked in a moment, "that I don't?"

"And yet your idea of an inward connexion between our meeting and what has happened since corresponds to something that *has* been, for me, an inward reality. I took into my head, as I told you," Christina continued, "to be greatly struck with Miss Garland (since that's her sweet name!) and I frankly confess that I was tormented, that I was moved to envy, call it, if you like, to jealousy, by something I found in her. There came to me there in five minutes the sense of her character. *C'est bien beau*, you know, a character like that, and I got it full in the face. It made me say to myself, 'She in my place would never marry Gennaro—no, no, no, never!' I couldn't help coming back to it, and I thought of it so often that I found a kind of inspiration in it. I hated the idea of being worse than she—of doing something that she wouldn't do. I might be bad by nature, but I needn't be by reflexion. The end of it all was that I found it impossible not to tell the Prince that I was his very humble servant, but that decidedly I couldn't take him for mine."

"Are you sure it was only of Miss Garland's character that you were jealous," Rowland asked, "and not of her affection for her cousin?"

"*Sure* is a good deal to say. Still, I think I may do so. There are two

261

reasons; one at least I can tell you. Her affection has not a shadow's weight with Mr. Hudson! Why then should one resent it?"

"And what's the other reason?"

"Excuse me; that's my own affair."

Rowland felt himself puzzled, baffled, charmed, inspired. "I've promised your mother," he presently went on, "to do my best on behalf of the Prince."

She shook her head sadly. "The Prince needs nothing you can say for him. He's a magnificent *parti*. I know it perfectly."

"You know also of your mother's deep disappointment?"

"Her disappointment's demonstrative. She has been abusing me for the last twenty-four hours as if I were the vilest of the vile"—a statement to which the purity of the girl's beauty gave a high dramatic value. "I've failed of respect to her at other times, but I've not done so now. How is it failing of respect to have found out at last, once for all, and with terrible trouble and pain, by how much too little I care for the person she wishes to force upon me—by how much too much I *don't* care for him? I tried—I've been trying for months—I went as far as I could. And I liked what he offered me, liked it immensely—if I could have had it without *him*. But to let him think he pleased or satisfied me too—or ever would—that deception struck me finally as too base. I know, I feel in all my bones, nevertheless, what I give up; so that to be clear—clear about my innermost feeling of all, and about that only—hasn't been, I assure you, child's play. I was looking for inspiration, if you like; and I found it—well, I found it," she went on, "where I could. Shall I tell you?" she demanded with sudden ardour; "will you understand me? It was on the one side the world, the splendid, beautiful, powerful, interesting world. I know what that is; I've tasted of the cup; I like its sweetness. Ah, if I chose, if I should let myself go, if I should fling everything to the winds, the world and I would be famous friends. I know its merits, and I think without vanity it would feel mine. You should see some fruits of the alliance. I should like to be a grandee—the Prince is, among many wonderful things, hereditary *Grand d'Espagne*—and I think I should be a very good one; I would play my part well. I'm fond of luxury, I'm fond of a great society, I'm fond of being looked at, I thrill with the idea of high consideration. Mamma, you see, has never had *any*. There I am in all my native horror. I'm corrupt, corrupting, corruption! Ah, what a pity that couldn't be too! Mercy of heaven!" Her voice had a convulsion; she covered her face with her hands and sat motionless. Rowland saw that an intense agitation, hitherto successfully repressed, underlay her fine pretence of finality, and he could easily believe her battle had been fierce. She rose quickly and turned away, walked a few paces and stopped. In a moment she was before him again, her air confessing at once to her pride and her humility. "But you needn't think I'm afraid !" she said. "I've chosen, and I shall hold to it. I've something here, here, *here* !" and she patted her heart. "It's my own. I shan't part with it. Is it what you call in Boston one's higher self ? I don't know; I don't care ! It's bigger and brighter than the Casamassima diamonds—every one of which, if you please, I've seen and handled and adored."

"You say that certain things are your own affair," Rowland presently rejoined; "but I must nevertheless make an attempt to learn what all this means—what it promises for my friend Hudson. Is there any hope for him ?"

"This is a point I can't discuss with you minutely. I like him very much."

"Would you marry him if he were to ask you ?"

"He *has* asked me."

"And if he should ask again ?"

"I shall marry no one just now."

"Roderick," said Rowland, "has been wonderfully affected. He appears much exalted."

"He knows then of my rupture ?"

"He's making a great holiday of it."

Christina pulled her poodle towards her and began to retouch his beauty. "I like him very much," she repeated; "much more than I used to. Since you told me all that about him at Saint Cecilia's I've felt a great friendship for him. *Il n'est ni banal ni bête*; and then there's nothing in life he's afraid of. He's not afraid of failure; he's not afraid of ruin or death."

Rowland had a stare—he indeed had a chill—for this singular description. "Oh, he's a romantic figure !"

"A romantic figure, yes; the most romantic I've ever met, I think— and with the charm of coming, so oddly, from your awful country. There are things in one to which it makes him quite sharply appeal."

"Yet your mother," Rowland objected, "told me just now that you say you don't care a button for him."

"Very likely ! I meant as an *amoureux*. One doesn't want a lover one pities, and one doesn't want—of all things in the world—a husband who's a picturesque curiosity. The Prince himself is, in his own way, almost that. I should like Mr. Hudson as something else. The world's idea of possible relations, either for man or woman, is so poor—there would be so many nice free ones. I wish he were even my brother, so that he could never talk to me of marriage. Then I could adore him. I would nurse him, I would wait on him and save him all disagreeable rubs and shocks. I'm much stronger than he, and I would stand between him and the world. Indeed with Mr. Hudson for my brother I should be willing to live and die an old maid."

"Have you ever expressed to him these sentiments?"

"I daresay. I've chattered to him like a magpie. If you wish I'll put it to him formally—so he'll know *à quoi s'en tenir*."

"There's nothing I could wish less!" Rowland promptly replied. "The one thing I ask of you is to let him alone."

"Good," said the girl. "I make a note of it."

He was lingering there, weighing one impression against another, weighing sympathy against suspicion and feeling it sink the scale, when the curtain of a distant doorway was lifted and Mrs. Light passed across the room. She stopped half-way and rather grimly took in our interlocutors. Sniffing the air for the powder of the battle, she perhaps too much missed the scent as she moved away with a passionate toss of her drapery. Rowland's previous impression came back to him: he saw her somehow possessed of some obscure and odious, some wholly ungenerous advantage, a means of influence too base to be used save under sharp coercion. She might, to his fancy, at that moment, have had this furbished weapon concealed in the folds of her not particularly fresh wrapper. Christina, meanwhile, had really for the time been soaring aloft, to his vision, and though in such flights of her moral nature—the energy of which now affected him as real—there was a certain painful effort and tension of wing, it was none the less piteous to imagine her being rudely jerked down to the base earth. She would need all her magnanimity for her own contest, and there was grossness in his making other demands upon it.

He took up his hat. "You asked a while ago if I had come to help you. If I knew how I might help you I should be particularly glad."

She stood a moment thinking. Then at last looking up: "You remember your promising six months ago to tell me what you should finally think of me? I should like you to tell me now."

Ah, this pressed the spring, and his inward irony, for himself, gave a hum! Madame Grandoni had insisted on the fact that she was an actress, and this little speech seemed a glimpse of the cothurnus. She had played her great scene, she had made her point, and now she had her eye at the hole in the curtain and she was watching the house. But she blushed as she guessed his fine comment, and her blush, which was beautiful, carried off her betrayal. He turned his back. There was a great chain of rooms in Mrs. Light's apartment, the pride and joy of the hostess on festal evenings, through which the departing visitor passed before reaching the door, and in one of the first of these he found himself waylaid and arrested by the distracted mistress of the house.

"Well, well?" she cried, seizing his arm. "Has she listened to you—have you moved her?"

"Hadn't you better, dear madam," Rowland rather ruefully asked, "leave the poor girl alone? She's doing—for herself, I mean—the best she can."

"For herself?" the wretched woman shrieked. "Is *that* what I asked you to find out?—as if we didn't know enough about it! Pray, what is she doing for me and for *him*?—and what have *you* been doing for either of us?" And then as he had nothing but his blankness to show her she turned upon him with fury. "I believe you came, perfidiously, but to back her up, and you're conspiring with her to kill me."

Rowland tried for a moment, with small taste for the job, to appease her unreason and persuade her that if she would stay her wrath she might gain something by patience. This however, too visibly, was a counsel of perfection, and she broke away from him in undiminished disgust, leaving him to come an instant later upon the Cavaliere, who was sitting with his elbows on his knees and his head in his hands, so buried in thought that he had to call him before he roused himself. The poor gentleman's eyes then charged themselves heavily with his question, but Rowland could again only throw up his hands. "Mrs. Light, all the same, seems to have an idea she can still do something; so that if you believe in Mrs. Light's idea—— !"

The Cavaliere stood a moment in deep gloom. "I always believe in Mrs. Light's ideas. It's a magnificent marriage. The girl should be reasonable."

"Ah," Rowland sighed, "if you've a way to make her *that*—— !"

"It will make her either that——"

"Or it will dish you altogether?" Rowland asked as he hesitated.

The old man's face probed a moment the consciousness from which this question had sprung. "Pray for her, dear sir," he at last simply said.

"I'll pray for *you*, Cavaliere," Rowland answered as he went.

He had become aware of Mrs. Light's renewed approach and he slipped straight away. Yes, it was after this some providential support to her vague coadjutor that he found himself most invoking.

XXI

OF RODERICK meanwhile he saw nothing; but he immediately went to Mrs. Hudson and assured her that her son was in even exceptionally good health and spirits. After this he called again on his two country-women, but as Roderick's absence continued he was able neither to dispense much comfort nor to feign much conviction. Mary's tense smoothness—a serenity with a surface like slippery ice and from which any vain remark rebounded with its heels in the air—seemed to him an image of his own state of mind. He was deeply depressed, he felt a real storm in the wind and wished it would come and wash away their troubles. On the afternoon of the third day he pushed into Saint Peter's, in whose vast clear element the hardest particles of thought ever infallibly entered into solution. From a heartache to a Roman rain there were few contrarieties the great church did not help him to forget. He had wandered there for half an hour when he came upon a short figure lurking in the shadow of one of the piers. He saw it was that of an artist hastily transferring to his sketch-book the sense of some emphasised instant, there, of the immense procession of the hours; and in a moment he perceived the artist to be little Sam Singleton.

Singleton pocketed his notes with a guilty air, as if he had been caught picking a rose in a royal conservatory or lighting his cigarette at the lamp of a shrine. Rowland always enjoyed meeting him; talking with him in these days was as good as a wayside gush of clear cold water on a long hot walk. There was perhaps no drinking-vessel, and you had to apply your lips to some informal conduit; but the result was always a sense of extreme moral refreshment. On this occasion he mentally blessed his ingenuous friend and heard presently with regret that he was to leave Rome on the morrow. Singleton had come to take leave of the great basilica, where he was gathering a few last impressions. He had earned a pocketful of money and was meaning to take a summer's holiday; going to Switzerland, to Germany, to Paris. In the autumn he

was to return home; his family—composed, as Rowland knew, of a
father, who was cashier in a bank, and five unmarried sisters, one of
whom gave lyceum lectures on woman's rights, the whole resident at
Buffalo, N.Y.—had been writing him peremptory letters and appealing
to him as son, brother and fellow-citizen. He would have been grateful
for another year in Rome, but he submitted to fate the more patiently
that he had laid up treasure which at Buffalo would seem infinite. They
talked some time; Rowland hoped they might meet in Switzerland and
take a walk or two together. Singleton seemed to feel that Buffalo had
marked him for her own; he was afraid he should not see Rome again
for many a year.

"So you expect to live at Buffalo?" Rowland inquired as they looked
down the splendid avenue of the nave.

"Well, it will depend upon the views—upon the attitude—of my
family. Oh, I think I shall get on; I think it can be done," Singleton
went on. "If I find it can be done I shall really be quite proud of it;
as an artist, of course I mean, don't you know? Do you know I've
some nine hundred sketches? I shall live in my portfolio. And so long
as one's not in Rome, pray what does it matter where one is? But how
I shall envy all you Romans—you and Mr. Gloriani and Mr. Hudson
in particular."

"Don't envy Hudson; he has nothing to envy," Rowland couldn't
help risking.

Singleton wondered—but it might be a harmless jest. "Why, isn't he
going to be the great man of our time? And isn't it quite a treat to think
that it's *we* who have turned him out?"

Rowland's heart was full, and the tender touch of this personage
made it overflow a little where a harder knock might have steadied it.
"Between ourselves, since you ask, he has rather disappointed me."

Singleton stared open-mouthed. "Dear me then, what did you
expect?"

"Verily," Rowland said to himself, "what *did* I expect?"

"I confess," Singleton pursued, "I can't judge him rationally. He
fascinates me; he's the sort of man one makes one's hero of."

"Strictly speaking, he's not a positive ideal hero," Rowland
remarked.

Singleton looked intensely grave, and with almost scared eyes, "Is
there anything amiss with him, anything there shouldn't be?" he
timidly asked. Then as Rowland hesitated to reply he quickly added:
"Please, if there is, don't tell me! I want to know no evil of him, and

I think I should hardly believe it. In my memories of this Roman artist life he will be the central figure. He will stand there in extraordinary high relief, as beautiful and clear and complete as one of his own statues!"

"Amen!" said Rowland gravely. He remembered afresh that the sea is inhabited by big fishes and little, and that the latter often find their way down the throats of the former. Singleton was going to spend the afternoon in taking last looks at certain other places, and Rowland offered to join him on his sentimental circuit. But as they were preparing to leave the church he heard himself suddenly addressed from behind. Turning, he beheld a young woman whom he immediately recognised as Madame Grandoni's maid. Her mistress was on the spot, she said, and begged to confer with him before he departed.

This summons obliged Rowland to separate from Singleton, to whom he bade farewell. He followed the messenger and presently found Madame Grandoni in possession of rather more than a mere pilgrim's portion of the steps of the tribune behind the great altar, where, spreading a shawl on the polished red marble, she had spaciously seated herself. He suspected that she had been nursing a germ of truth and she lost no time in bringing forth her treasure.

"Don't shout very loud," she said; "remember that we're in church: there's a limit to the noise one may make even in Saint Peter's. Christina Light was married this morning to her Prince—or at least to her mother's."

Rowland exhaled a long breath. "Married—this morning?"

"Married this morning, at seven o'clock, *le plus tranquillement du monde*, before three or four persons. The young couple left Rome an hour afterwards."

For some moments this seemed to him really terrible; the obscure little drama of which he had caught a glimpse had played itself almost violently out. He had believed that Christina would resist; that she had succumbed was a proof that the way taken with her had had some last dire directness. His excited vision followed her, with much blinking, into the world towards which she was rolling away with her unappreciated husband and her stifled ideal; but it must be confessed that if the first impulse of his compassion was for Christina the second was now for Prince Casamassima. Madame Grandoni acknowledged an extreme curiosity as to the secret springs of these strange doings—Casamassima's sudden dismissal, his still more sudden recall, the hurried private marriage. "Listen," said Rowland presently, "and I will tell you something." And he related in detail his last visit to Mrs. Light and his talk with this lady, with Christina, and with the Cavaliere.

"Good," she said; "it's all very curious. But it's a riddle, and I only half guess it."

"Well," said Rowland, "it's all none of my business, and perhaps I see things melodramatically. But certain suppositions have taken shape in my mind which serve as answers to two or three riddles."

"It's very true," Madame Grandoni replied, "that the Cavaliere, as he stands, has always needed to be explained."

"He's explained by the hypothesis that four-and-twenty years ago, at Ancona, Mrs. Light had a lover."

"I see. Ancona was dull, Mrs. Light was lively, and—four-and-twenty years ago perhaps—the Cavaliere was dangerous. Such *are* the dangers of dull places. Poverino!"

"He has had his compensation," Rowland said. "It has been a life for him to be near Christina. What other life could he have had?"

"What indeed? But has the girl never wondered why hers should have had to have so much of *him*?"

"If she had been near guessing," Rowland replied, "her mother's high way with him would have put her off the trace. Mrs. Light's view has apparently been that she could minimise her fault by minimising her lover. She has lived it down by living *him* down, and so she has kept her secret. But what's the profit of a secret—*as* a secret!—unless you can make some use of it? The day at last came when she could turn hers to account; she could let the skeleton out of the closet and produce an effect with it."

"I don't understand."

"Neither do I, morally," said Rowland. "I only conceive that there was an odious, dangerous, desperate, a very possibly vain, but, as it *has* turned out for her, quite successful scene. The poor Cavaliere stood outside, at the door, as livid as a corpse and as dumb. The mother and daughter had it out together. Mrs. Light burned her ships. When she came out she had three lines of writing in her daughter's hand, which the Cavaliere was despatched with to the Prince. They overtook the young man in time, and when he reappeared he was delighted to dispense with further waiting. I don't know what he thought of the grand manner of his bride's amends to him; but that's how I roughly reconstruct history."

"You mean her mother told her—— ?" The old lady wondered. "I don't really see the difference that that was to make to her."

"Well," said Rowland, "it was to make the difference of her deciding that she couldn't afford not really to place herself. I've figured it out, you see. She had to knock under to a revelation—to a humiliation. She was shown that it was not for her to make conditions, but to thank her stars that there were none made for her. If she persisted she might find it coming to pass that there would be conditions, and the formal rupture—the rupture that the world would hear of and pry into—would then have proceeded from the Prince and not from her."

Madame Grandoni thought of these things. "But mustn't Christina have long ago guessed?"

"Her mother appears to have been satisfied she hadn't."

"People in this enlightened age don't mind that sort of thing," Madame Grandoni objected. "The old obloquy attaching to irregular birth is now mere stage convention and melodrama."

"Well, Christina has a taste for that—she was glad immediately to be able to see herself in a new high light. You and I don't 'mind,' but I can easily put myself in the place of the proudest girl in the world, deeply wounded in her pride and not stopping to calculate probabilities, but muffling her wound with an almost sensuous relief in a splendour that stood within her grasp and would cover everything. Is it not possible that the late Mr. Light had made an outbreak before witnesses who are still living?—that the child's coming into the world was in itself a scandal? Say Light had quarrelled with his wife and was at the time virtually separated from her. Say too," Rowland went on, "that it quite imaginably came home to her—this first of all appeals from her father *as* a father."

"Ah, she won't have liked him for that!" Madame Grandoni declared. "Her being the Cavaliere's daughter must, if she had really been ignorant, have been a stiff dose for her to swallow."

"A reason the more then for her consenting to become grand!"

The old woman got up at last, resuming her progress and her sense of the situation. "Well, she has done what she *was* to do. She was nobly to decline it—yet not to miss it. Which *would* have been a pity."

It threw Rowland, as they went, into meditation again. "Yes, she clearly wasn't made to miss!"

He called on the evening of the morrow upon Mrs. Hudson and found Roderick with the two ladies. Their companion seemed to have but lately joined them, and Rowland afterwards learned that it was his first appearance since the writing of the note which had so distressed his mother. He had dropped upon a sofa, where he lounged like a young

Pasha bored with a state seraglio; greeting Rowland with hardly more form than if he had been one of the usual guards of such *penetralia*. The manner of his advent had visibly not been happy; Mrs. Hudson had seated herself near him in mute appeal, while Mary was sunk, up to her firm chin, in one of her eternal pretexts for the fine needle and the occupied attention.

Mrs. Hudson, however, instantly broke out to Rowland. "Oh, we have such comfortable news ! Roderick's now ready to leave Rome."

"It isn't decent to be too glad," said Roderick. "There isn't a harm this place can do us, or has done us, that hasn't had something in it we shall ache for again in some better one."

She had but a wan stare for this perversity. "If you mean we shall never get over it—perhaps ! And the proof may very well be in your looking so pulled down—whatever *that* may mean ! Isn't he, Mr. Mallet, too thin to live ? It shows in all your bones that you need a change. I'm sure we'll go wherever in the world you like. Where should you like to go ?"

Roderick had let her take his hand, which she pressed tenderly in her own, but he looked at her from terribly far off. "Poor sweet old mother !" he said at last all gently, if very inconclusively.

"My own dear precious son !" Mrs. Hudson as responsively and as vaguely wailed.

"I don't care a straw where you go ! I don't care a straw for anything !"

"Oh, my dear boy," she remonstrated, "you mustn't say that before us all here—before Mary, before Mr. Mallet !"

"Mary—Mr. Mallet ?" He took up these names as after a long disuse and seemed to look at them as at objects of obscure application. Then he released himself from his mother's locked clasp and turned away, leaning his elbows on his knees and holding his head in his hands. There was a silence, Rowland's share in which was the intensity of his consciousness of the young woman at the window. "Why should I stand on ceremony with Mary and Mr. Mallet ?" Roderick presently demanded. "Mary pretends to believe I'm a great man, and if she believes it as she ought nothing I can say will alter her opinion. Mallet knows I'm a hopeless humbug ; so I needn't mince my words with *him*."

"Ah, my dear, don't use such dreadful language !" Mrs. Hudson quavered. "Aren't we all devoted to you, and proud of you, and waiting only to hear what you want, so that we may do it ?"

Roderick had got up and he began to walk about the room ; Rowland

271

felt how as never yet there was something reckless in him to count with. He observed further, with all anxiety, that Mrs. Hudson, without a sense of the delicate ground under her feet, was disposed to chide him endearingly, to show the intimacy of her tenderness. He foresaw that she would bring down the hovering thunderbolt on her head.

"Ah, in God's name," Roderick in fact broke out, "don't remind me of my obligations ! It's intolerable to me, and I don't believe it's pleasant to Mallet. I know they're tremendous—I know I shall never repay them. I'm bankrupt, bankrupt ! Do you know what that means?"

The poor lady gazed in dismay, and Rowland sharply interfered. "Oh, spare your mother your wild figures ! Don't you see you're frightening her half to death ?"

"Frightening her ? She may as well then be frightened first as last. Do I frighten you, mother ?"

"Oh, Roderick, what *do* you mean ?" she impatiently whimpered. "Mr. Mallet, what's he talking about ?"

"I'm talking about *this*," Roderick replied—"that I'm an angry, savage, disappointed, miserable man. I mean that I can't do a stroke of work nor think a profitable thought. I mean that I'm in a state of helpless rage and grief and shame. Helpless, helpless—that's what it is. You can't help me, poor mother—not with kisses nor tears nor prayers. Mary can't help me—not for all the honour she does me nor all the big books on art that she pores over. Mallet can't help me—not with all his money nor all his good example nor all his friendship, which I'm so immensely well aware of; not with all it multiplied a thousand times and repeated to all eternity. I thought you would help me, you and Mary; that's why I sent for you. But you can't—don't think it ! The sooner you give up the idea the better for you. Give up being proud of me too; there's nothing left of me to be proud of. A year or two ago I don't say, for I myself then really believed I was a swell. But do you know what has become of me now ? I've gone utterly to the devil."

There was something in the ring of his voice as he uttered these words which sent them home with convincing force. He was not talking for effect or for the mere personal pleasure of extravagant and paradoxical utterance, as had often enough been the case ere this; he was not even talking viciously or ill-humouredly. He was talking passionately, desperately, sincerely, from an irresistible need to throw off the oppressive burden of his mother's confidence. His cruel eloquence brought the poor lady to her feet, and she stood there with clasped hands, petrified and voiceless. Mary Garland quickly left her place and, coming straight to him and laying her hand on his arm, let her eyes fix him with an effort of influence of which she seemed now to wish to test for the first time the real, the sovereign power. But the power proved the mere weak fumble of a key in a lock too hard for it; he made no movement to disengage himself, but it was as if he wondered for the moment what she could want. Rowland had been living for the past month in such intolerable expectancy of disaster that, now that the ice was broken and the fatal cold splash administered, his foremost feeling on receiving his share of the spray was almost elation. But the next instant his eternal second thought, his vision of the case for others, had corrected it.

"I really don't make out," he observed, "the profit of your talking in just this way at just this time. Don't you see how you're making your mother suffer?"

"Do I enjoy it myself?" cried Roderick. "Is the suffering all on your side and theirs? Do I look as if I were happy and were stirring you up with a stick for my amusement? Here we all are in the same boat; we might as well understand each other. These women must know that I'm not to be counted on. That has a sound of the last impudence, no doubt, and I certainly don't deny your right to be disgusted with me."

"Will you keep what you've got to say till another time," said Mary, "and let me hear it alone?"

"Oh, I'll let you hear it as often as you please; but what's the use of keeping it? I'm in the humour now; it won't keep! It's a very simple matter—it isn't worth keeping. I'm a dead failure, that's all; I'm not a first-rate man. I'm second-rate, tenth-rate, anything you please. After that it's all one!"

Mary turned away and buried her face in her hands; but Roderick, affected apparently now in some unwonted fashion by her gesture, drew her towards him again and went on a little differently. "It's hardly worth while we should have any private talk about this, Mary '
—and he had one of his strange, straight drops (stranger than any flare of passion or of irony) into simple kindness. "The thing would be comfortable for neither of us. It's better, after all, that it be said once for all and dismissed. There are things I can't talk to you about. Can I, at least? You strike me sometimes as deep, you know—one never can tell."

"I can imagine nothing you shouldn't talk to me about," she returned impenetrably enough—impenetrably, that is, to Rowland.

"You're not afraid?"—Roderick pressed her with a sharpness that was, for the few seconds, almost like interest.

She turned away abruptly, with lowered eyes, intensely hesitating. "Anything you think I should hear I'll hear." And she went back to her place at the window and took up her work.

"I've had a great smashing blow," Roderick pursued. "I was the biggest ass to be seen anywhere, but it doesn't make the blow any easier to bear."

"Mr. Mallet, tell me exactly what Roderick means!" said Mrs. Hudson, who had found her voice, in a tone more peremptory than Rowland had yet heard her use.

"He ought to have told you before," Roderick interposed. "Really, Rowland, if you'll allow me to say so, you ought! You could have given a much better account of all this than I myself; better especially in that it would have been more lenient to me. You ought to have let them down gently; it would have saved them a great deal of pain. But you always want to keep things so uncannily quiet. Allow me to tell you it's very weak of you."

"Speaking too well of you's a fault that's easily mended!" said Rowland with a laugh.

"Oh, what is it, sir; what is this horror?" Mrs. Hudson insistently groaned.

"It's what Roderick says. He's a most unexpected failure!"

Mary Garland, on hearing this statement, gave the speaker a single glance and then rose, laid down her work and walked rapidly out of the room. Mrs. Hudson tossed her head and timidly bristled. "This from *you*, Mr. Mallet?" she said, with an injured air which Rowland found harrowing.

But Roderick, most characteristically, did not in the least resent his friend's assertion; he sent him, on the contrary, one of the large, clear, beautiful looks, so often at his command, which made his approval, or his patience, so unexpectedly shine, and which set his companion wondering again, as all too frequently before, at the extraordinary disparities of his nature. "My dear mother, if you had had eyes that weren't blinded by this sad maternal vanity you would have seen all this for yourself; you would have seen that I'm anything but prosperous."

"Is it anything about money?" cried Mrs. Hudson. "Oh, do write at once to Mr. Striker!"

"Money?" said Roderick. "I've not a cent of money. Where and how should I have got it?"

"Oh, Mr. Mallet, how could you let him?" Mrs. Hudson asked terribly.

"Everything I have is at his service," said Rowland, sick now of the scene.

"Of course Mr. Mallet will help you, my son!" the poor lady hastened to proclaim.

"Ah, leave Mr. Mallet alone!" said Roderick. "I've squeezed him dry; it's not my fault if he has anything left!"

"Roderick, what have you done with all your money?" his mother demanded.

"Thrown it away. It was no such great amount. I've done nothing this winter."

"You've done nothing?"

"I've done no manner of work! Why in the world didn't you guess it and spare me all this? Couldn't you see I was empty, distracted, debauched?"

"Debauched, my dear son?" Mrs. Hudson repeated.

"That's over for the present! But couldn't you see—couldn't Mary see—that I was in a damnably bad way?"

"I've no doubt Miss Garland saw," Rowland said.

"But Mary has said nothing whatever!" Mrs. Hudson protested.

"Oh, she's too wonderful," Rowland permitted himself to observe.

"Have you done anything that will hurt poor Mary?" Mrs. Hudson gasped.

"I've only been thinking night and day of another woman."

She dropped helplessly into her seat again. "Oh dear, dear, hadn't we better go home?"

"Not to get out of her way!" Roderick said. "She has started on a career of her own, and she doesn't care a rap for me. My head was filled with her; I could think of nothing else; I would have sacrificed everything to her—you, Mary, Mallet, my work, my fortune, my future, my honour. I was in a lovely state, eh? I don't pretend to be giving you good news; but I'm telling the simple, literal truth, so that you may know why I've gone to the dogs. She pretended to care greatly for all this, and to be willing to make any sacrifice in return; she had a magnificent chance, for she was being bullied and hustled, horribly against her will, into a mercenary marriage with a man she couldn't bear. She led me to believe that she would send her Prince about his business and keep herself free and sacred and pure for me. This was a great honour, and you may believe I valued it. It turned my head, and

275

I lived only to see my happiness come to pass. She did everything to encourage me to hope it would; everything her infernal coquetry and falsity could suggest."

"Oh, I say, this is too much!" Rowland bewilderedly interposed.

"So you back her up, eh?" Roderick cried with a renewal of his passion. "Do you pretend to say she gave me no hopes?" He had been speaking with growing bitterness, quite losing sight of his mother's pain and bewilderment in the passionate joy of publishing his wrongs. Since he was hurt he must cry out; since he was in pain he must scatter his pain abroad. Of his never thinking of others save as they figured in his own drama this extraordinary insensibility to the injurious effects of his eloquence was a capital example; the more so as the motive of his eloquence was never an appeal for sympathy or compassion—things to which he seemed perfectly indifferent and of which he could make no use. The great and characteristic point with him was the perfect separateness of his sensibility. He never saw himself as part of a whole; only as the clear-cut, sharp-edged, isolated individual, rejoicing or raging, as the case might be, but needing in any case absolutely to affirm himself. All this to Rowland was ancient history, but his perception of it stirred within him afresh at the sight of Roderick's sense of having been betrayed. That *he*, under the circumstances, was hardly the person to raise the cry of treason, was a point to which at his leisure Rowland was of course capable of rendering impartial justice; but his friend's present collapse was so absolute that it imposed itself on his sympathies. "Do you pretend to say," the interesting youth went on, "that she didn't lead me along to the very edge of fulfilment and stupefy me with all she suffered me to believe, all she provoked me, invited me, to count upon? It amused her to do it, and she knew perfectly well what she really meant. She never meant to be sincere; she never dreamed she *could* be. She's a ferocious flirt, and why a flirt's a flirt is more than I can tell you now. I can't understand playing with such a relation; for me it can only be a serious thing, but too deadly serious, whether to go in for or to be afraid of. I don't see what's in your head, my boy, to attempt to defend such a person—since you were the first, you'll remember, to cry out against her and to warn me. You told me she was dangerous, and I pooh-poohed you. You were intensely right; you're always so intensely right. She's as cold and false and heartless as she's beautiful—which is saying all; and she has sold her heartless beauty to the highest bidder. I hope he knows what he gets!"

"Oh, my son," Mrs. Hudson plaintively wailed, "how could you ever care for such a dreadful creature?"

"It would take long to tell you, dear mother!"

Rowland's lately quickened interest in Christina had still its fine capacity to throb, and he felt that in loyalty to it as to an at least more enlightened view he must say a word for her. "You took her, I did think, too seriously at first," he remarked, "but you take her too harshly now. She had no idea of wronging or of so terribly upsetting you."

Roderick looked at him on this with eyes almost lurid. "She's a ministering angel then after all?—that's what you want to prove!" he cried. "That's consoling for me who have lost her! You're always right, I say; but, my dear fellow, be, in mercy, just a little wrong for once!"

"Oh yes, Mr. Mallet, show a little mercy!" said Mrs. Hudson in a tone which, for all its gentleness, made Rowland stare. This demonstration on his part covered a great deal of concentrated wonder and apprehension—a presentiment of what a small, sweet, feeble, elderly lady might be capable of in the way of abrupt and perverse animosity. There was no space in Mrs. Hudson's tiny maternal mind for complications of feeling, and one emotion existed only by turning another over flat and perching on top of it. She had evidently not penetrated at all, having no imagination for it whatever, the strange cloud of her son's personal situation. Sitting without, in dismay, she only saw that all was darkness and trouble, and as his gained position, or what she had been deeming such, appeared quite to exceed her original measure and lift him beyond her jurisdiction, so that he had become a thing too precious and sacred for blame, she found it infinitely comfortable to lay the burden of their common affliction upon Rowland's broad shoulders. Had he not promised to make them all rich and happy? And this was the end of it! Rowland felt as if his trials were only beginning. "Hadn't you better forget all this, my dear?" Mrs. Hudson said to Roderick. "Hadn't you better just quietly attend to your work?"

"Work, madam?" cried Roderick. "My work's over. I can't work —I haven't worked all winter. If I were fit for anything this tremendous slap in the face would have been just the thing to cure me of my apathy. But there's a perfect vacuum here!" And he tapped his forehead. "It's bigger than ever; it grows bigger every hour!"

"I'm sure you've made a beautiful likeness of your poor dreary little mother," said Mrs. Hudson coaxingly.

"I had done nothing before, and I've done nothing since! I quarrelled with an excellent man the other day from mere exasperation of my nerves, and threw away five thousand dollars."

"Threw away—five thousand dollars!" Roderick had been wandering among formidable abstractions, complications that bristled and defied her touch; but here was a concrete fact, lucidly stated, and she looked it for a moment in the face. She repeated his words a third time with a gasping murmur, and then suddenly she burst into piteous tears. Roderick went to her, sat down beside her, put his arm round her, fixed his eyes coldly on the floor and waited for her to weep herself out. She leaned her head on his shoulder and sobbed broken-heartedly. She said not a word, she uttered no judgement, but the desolation of her tears was dire. It lasted some time—too long for Rowland's courage. He had stood silent, wishing simply to appear very respectful; but his first weary relief, that of finding their crisis really there, in definite and measurable form, to be practically dealt with, had utterly ebbed, and he found his situation intolerable. He was reduced to the vulgar expedient of leaving the room.

His servant, the next morning, brought him the card of a visitor. He read with surprise the name of Mrs. Hudson and hurried forward to meet her. He found her in his sitting-room, leaning on the arm of her son and looking very pale, her eyes red with weeping and her lips tightly compressed. Her advent puzzled him, and it was not for some time that he began to understand her. Roderick's countenance threw no light; but Roderick's explanatory power was but too subject to rich intermittences. He had not for several weeks graced the scene now open to him, and he immediately began to look at those of his own works that adorned it. He gave himself up to independent contemplation. Mrs. Hudson had evidently armed herself with dignity, and so far as she might she meant to be impressive. Rowland took comfort, however, in her small quaint majesty, which might have been that of a shorn sheep roused to discriminations and trying to correct both nature and fate; for anything was better than seeing her again break down. She told him that she had come to him for practical advice; she took leave to remind him that she was a stranger in the land. Where were they to go, please? What were they to do? His eyes, for a moment, took in Roderick—Roderick who had his back turned and, with his head on one side like a tourist in a church, was lost in the consideration of his own proved power. The proof, meeting him there in its several forms, had made him catch his breath.

"Roderick says he doesn't know, he doesn't care," Mrs. Hudson meanwhile observed. "He leaves it entirely to you."

Many another man, in Rowland's place, would have greeted this information with an irate and sarcastic laugh, telling his visitors that he thanked them infinitely for their confidence, but that really, as things stood now, they must settle these little matters between themselves; many another man might have so comported himself even had he been, deep within, equally occupied with the image of Mary Garland, and not less amply conscious that her destiny was also part of the question. But Rowland was now fairly used to his daily dose of bitterness, and after a hard look, as always, at the cup, he again swallowed the draught and entered, responsively and formally, into Mrs. Hudson's dilemma. His wits, however, were but indifferently at his command; they were dulled by his sense of the singular change that had taken place in the attitude of this bewildered woman. Her visit was evidently intended as a grave reminder of forgotten vows. She was doubtless too sincerely humble a person to suppose that if he had had the wicked levity to break faith with her any shadow she might cast would act as a lash on his shoulders. But she had convinced herself by some elaborate lonely logic that she had been weakly wanting in "style" and had suffered him to think too meanly not only of her understanding but of her social consequence. A visit in her best gown would have an admonitory effect as regards both of these attributes; it would cancel some favours received and show him that she was not incapable of grasping the theory, at least, of retribution. These were the reflexions of a very shy woman, who, determining for once in her life to hold up her head, was actually flying it like a kite.

"You know we've very little money to spend," she said while her host waited for the full expression of her idea. "Roderick tells me he has debts and has also nothing at all to pay them with. He says I must write to Mr. Striker to sell my house for what it will bring and send me out the money. When the money comes I must give it to him. I'm sure I don't know; I never heard of anything so dreadful. My house is really the principal part of my property. But that's all Roderick will say. We must be very economical."

Before this speech was finished her voice had begun to quaver softly, and her face, after all so inadequately grim, to have motions that beat the air like the wild arms of the sinking. Rowland found himself turning hereupon to their companion and speaking almost as a school-master. "Come away from those statues and sit down here and listen to me."

Roderick started, but obeyed with the most graceful docility, choosing a stiff-backed antique chair.

"What do you propose to your mother to do?" Rowland then inquired.

"Propose?" said Roderick absently. "Oh, I propose nothing."

The tone, the look, the gesture with which this was said were horribly irritating, and for an instant an imprecation rose to Rowland's lips. But he checked it, and was afterwards glad he had done so. "You must do something of *some* sort, you know," he said. "Choose, select, decide."

"My dear Rowland, how impossibly you talk!" his companion hereupon exclaimed. "The very point of the whole thing is that I can't do anything. I'll do as I'm told, of course, and be thankful, but I don't call that doing. We must leave Rome, I suppose, though I don't see why. We've no money, and you have to pay cash, you know, on the railroads."

Mrs. Hudson surreptitiously wrung her hands. "Listen to him, please! Not leave Rome, when we've stayed here later than any respectable family ever did before! It's this dreadful place that has made us so unhappy. If Roderick's so relaxed it's no more than I am too, and it's all the poison of the air."

"It's very true that I'm relaxed," said Roderick serenely. "If I hadn't come to Rome I shouldn't have risen, and if I hadn't risen I shouldn't have fallen."

"Fallen—fallen!" sighed Mrs. Hudson. "Just hear him!"

"I'll do anything you say, my dear man," Roderick continued. "I'll do anything you want. I've not been unkind to my mother—have I, mother? I was unkind yesterday, without meaning it; for, after all, you know, all that had to be said. Murder will out, and my little troubles can't be hidden. But we talked it over and made it up, didn't we? It seemed to me we did. Let Rowland decide it, mother; whatever he suggests will be the right thing." And Roderick, who had hardly removed his eyes from the exhibition of his work, got up again and went back to the great figure in which, during his divine first freshness, he had embodied his idea of the primal Adam.

Mrs. Hudson fixed her eyes upon the opposite wall. There was not a trace in Roderick's face or in his voice of the bitterness of his emotion of the day before, and not a hint of his having the lightest weight upon his conscience. He looked at his friend, all radiance and intelligence, as if there had never been a difference of opinion between them; as if each had ever been for both, unalterably, and both unalterably for each.

Rowland had received a few days before a letter from a lady of his acquaintance, a worthy Scotswoman domiciled in a villa upon one of the olive-covered hills near Florence. She held her apartments in the villa upon a long lease, and she enjoyed for a sum not worth mentioning the possession of an extraordinary number of noble, stone-floored rooms, with ceilings vaulted and frescoed, with barred windows commanding the loveliest view in the world. She was a needy and thrifty spinster who never hesitated to declare that the lovely view was all very well, but that for her own part she lived in the villa for cheapness and that with five hundred a year assured she would undertake to lead a worthier life near her sister, a knight's lady at Glasgow. She was now proposing a visit to that seat of discipline, and she desired to turn an honest penny by subletting for a few weeks her historic Italian chambers. The terms on which she occupied them enabled her to ask a rent scarce worth mention, and she had begged Rowland to do what she called a little genteel advertising for her. Would he say a good word for her rooms to his numerous friends in Rome? He said a good word for them now to Mrs. Hudson and told her in dollars and cents how cheap a summer's lodging she might secure. He dwelt upon the fact that she would strike a truce with *tables-d'hôte*, and have a servant of her own, amenable possibly to instruction in the Northampton mysteries. He had touched a tender chord, and his visitor gave out a vague hum of reassurance. Her sentiments upon the *table-d'hôte* system and upon foreign household habits generally had arrived at a high development, and if we had space for it would repay analysis; and the idea of reclaiming a lost soul to the conception of a good New England "tea" set before her a light at which she could dimly blink. While Rowland argued his case Roderick slowly walked through the rooms with his hands in his pockets. Rowland waited for him to show some interest in their discussion, but he had no attention for his friend's ingenuity. Rowland had always at his friends' service and his own his vision of the how and the how much; he possessed conspicuously the sense of detail. He entered into Mrs. Hudson's position minutely and told her exactly why it seemed good that she should remove immediately to the Florentine villa. She received his advice, but sat on her guard for it, averting her eyes much and sighing like a person suspicious of a plausibility which might be, on her entertainer's part, but an escape from penalties. Yet she had nothing better to propose, and Rowland received her permission to write to his friend that she would take the rooms.

281

Roderick assented to this decision with a large placidity. "Those Florentine villas are capable of anything! I'm perfectly at your service."

"Then I'm sure I hope you'll recover your tone up there," his mother moaned while she gathered her shawl together.

Roderick laid one hand on her arm and with the other pointed to Rowland's marbles. "This is my tone just now. Once upon a time I did those things—if it's possible to believe it."

Mrs. Hudson gazed at them vaguely, and Rowland dropped the remark that such a tone was a capital tone.

"They're too hideously beautiful!" said Roderick.

Rowland solemnly shrugged his shoulders; it seemed to him he had nothing more to say. But as the others were going a last deep throb of the sense of undischarged duty led him to address to Roderick a few words of parting advice. "You'll find the Villa Pandolfini very delightful, very comfortable. You ought to be very contented there. Whether you work or whether you do what you're doing now, it's a place for an artist to be happy in. But I hope you'll work."

"I hope to heaven I may!" It was full of expression, but he might have been speaking of some interesting alien.

"When we meet again," Rowland said, "try then to have something to show me."

"When we meet again? Where the deuce are *you* going?" Roderick demanded.

"Oh, I hardly know; over the Alps."

"Over the Alps! You're going to leave me?"

Rowland had certainly meant to leave him, but his resolution was not proof against this bare ejaculation. He glanced at Mrs. Hudson and saw that her eyebrows were lifted and her lips parted in delicate reprehension. She seemed to accuse him of a craven shirking of trouble, to demand of him to repair his cruel havoc in her life by a solemn renewal of zeal. But Roderick's expectations were the oddest! Such as they were, Rowland asked himself why he shouldn't make a bargain with them. "You want me to go with you?" he asked.

"If you don't go I won't—that's all! How in the name of goodness shall I get through the next six months without you?"

"How will you get through them *with* me? That's the question!"

"I don't pretend to say; the future's a dead blank. But without you it's not a blank—it's certain damnation!"

"Mercy, mercy, mercy!" murmured Mrs. Hudson.

Rowland made an effort to turn to account this precious sympton of a positive wish. "If I go with you, will you try to work?"

Roderick had up to this moment been looking as unperturbed as if the deep agitation of the day before were a thing of the remote past. But at these words his face changed formidably; he flushed and scowled, and all his passion returned. "Try to work!" he cried. "Try —try! Work—work! In God's name don't talk that way, or I shall think you do it on purpose. Do you suppose I'm trying *not* to work? Do you suppose I stand rotting here for the fun of it? Don't you suppose I would try to work for myself before I tried for you?"

"Mr. Mallet," cried Mrs. Hudson piteously, "will you leave me alone with *this*?"

Rowland turned to her and informed her gently that he would go with her then to Florence. After he had taken this engagement he thought not at all of the pain of his position as mediator between the mother's resentful grief and the son's incurable weakness; he drank deep, only, of the satisfaction of not cutting himself off from their other companion. If the future was a blank to Roderick it was hardly less so to himself. He had at moments a sharp foreboding of ill things yet to come. He paid it no special deference, but it seemed to warn him not to count on the future for anything he might squeeze out of the present. On his going to take leave of Madame Grandoni this lady asked when he would come back to Rome, and he answered that he would return either never or for always. When she asked him what he meant he said he really couldn't tell her; but this moved her to embrace him in a motherly manner, as if she understood. She did more, she pronounced him a paragon among men; only that afterwards made his ears burn— it was so like a consecration afresh of the overstrained use of his reason and his charity. There were moments now when these faculties in him felt limp and lifeless.

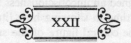

XXII

THE VILLA Pandolfini leaned largely upon a grass-grown piazzetta at the top of a hill which sloped straight from one of the gates of Florence. It offered to the outer world an ample front, though not of rare elevation, coloured a dull dark yellow and pierced with windows of various sizes, no one of which save those on the ground floor was on the same level with any other. Within was a great cool grey cortile, graced round about with high light arches and heavily-corniced doors of majestic altitude and furnished on one side with a grand old archaic well. Mrs. Hudson's rooms opened into a small garden founded on substructions of immense strength, rising from the part of the hill that sloped steeply away. This garden was a charming place. Its southern wall was curtained with a screen of orange-blossoms, a dozen fig-trees here and there offered you their large-leaved shade, and over the low parapet the soft grave Tuscan landscape kept you company. The rooms themselves were as high as chapels and as cool as royal sepulchres. Silence, peace and security seemed to abide in the ancient house, to make of it a square fortress against further assault of fortune. Mrs. Hudson took into her service a stunted brown-faced Maddalena, who wore a crimson handkerchief passed over her coarse black locks and tied under her sharp pertinacious chin, and played over the domestic question in general a smile as vivid, though perhaps as treacherous, as some flaring mediæval torch, the signal to confederates without. A glance, a word, a motion, made her show her teeth like a friendly she-wolf. This formidable flicker formed her sole substitute for speech with her melancholy mistress, to whom she had been bequeathed by the late occupant of the apartment and who, to Rowland's satisfaction, promised to be diverted from the study of his predicament by the still deeper perversity of Maddalena's theory of roasting, sweeping and bed-making.

Rowland took rooms at a villa a trifle nearer Florence, whence in the summer mornings he had five minutes' walk in the sharp black shadow-strip projected by winding flower-topped walls to join his friends. The life at Villa Pandolfini, when it had begun to fill out its measure, took the rhythm of the slow summer days, during which nothing would have been more open to it than to confess itself charmed to patience. If it was under a sensible shadow this was because it had an inherent vice; it feigned an unconsciousness that it too scantily felt. Roderick had lost no time in showing how little he was still able to save, and as he was the central figure of the small group, as he held its heart-strings all in his hand, it reflected faithfully the eclipse of his genius. No one had ventured upon the cheerful commonplace of saying that the change of air and of scene would restore his spirits; this would have had, in the conditions, altogether too silly a sound. The change had clearly done nothing of the sort, and his companions had at least the comfort of their mute recognition. An essential spring had dried up within him, and there was no household magic, no waving of any blest wand, to make it flow again. He was rarely violent, he expressed little of the irritation and ennui he must have constantly felt; it was as if he believed that an inward miracle—but only a miracle—might yet take place for him and was perhaps worth waiting for. The most that one could do, however, was to wait grimly and doggedly, suppressing an imprecation as from time to time one looked at one's watch. An attitude of positive urbanity towards life was not to be expected; it was doing one's duty to hold one's tongue and keep one's hands off one's own windpipe and other people's. He had long sad silences, fits of a deeper detachment than any before, during which he sat in the garden by the hour, with his head thrown back, his legs outstretched, his hands in his pockets and his eyes attached to the blinding summer sky. He would gather a dozen books about him, tumble them out on the ground, take one into his lap and leave it with the pages unturned. These moods would alternate with attacks of high restlessness, when, at unnatural hours, he made unexplained absences. He bore the heat of the Italian summer like a salamander and used to start off in the glare of noon for long walks over the hills. He often went down into Florence, rambled through the close dim streets and lounged away mornings in the churches and galleries. On several of these occasions Rowland bore him company, for they were the times when his contact had most of its early charm. Before Michael Angelo's statues and the pictures of the early Tuscans he quite forgot his disaster and picked up the thread of his old love of ideas. He found again in Florence certain of his Roman friends and made with them appointments more or less genial. More than once he asked Mary Garland to accompany him to the city, where he showed her the things he most cared for. He had a mass of sculptor's clay brought up to the villa and deposited in a room suitable for his work, but when this had been done he turned the key in the door and the clay was never touched. His eye was heavy and his hand cold, and his mother was more than once caught in the act of praying that he might be induced to see a doctor. On one of these occasions he had a great outburst of anger, begging her to know once for all that his health in these days fairly mocked him with its excellence. On the whole, and most of the time, he irresistibly appealed, the air being charged with him as with some rich wasted essence, some spirit scattered by the breaking of its phial and yet unable, for its very quality, to lose itself. If he was not querulous and bitter it was because he had taken an extraordinary vow not to be; a vow heroic for him and which those who knew him well had the tenderness to appreciate. Talking with him was like skating on thin ice, and his companions had a constant mental vision of spots marked dangerous.

This was an arduous time for Rowland; he said to himself that he would see it through but must never court again such perils. Mrs. Hudson divided it between looking askance at her son, with her hands tightly clasped about her pocket-handkerchief, as if she were wringing it dry of the last hour's tears, and turning her eyes much more directly to his perfidious patron, on whom they rested in the mutest, the feeblest, the most unbearable reprehension. She never phrased her accusations, but he felt them gather in the poor lady's inward gloom like monsters and spectral shapes. These things were a felt weight, of the heaviest, to him, and if at the outset of his experiment he had seen the possibility of them, how dimly soever, in the opposite scale, the brilliancy of Roderick's promises would have counted for little. It would have been better perhaps had she appeared voluble and vulgar, for neat and noiseless and dismally ladylike as she sat there, keeping her grievance green with her soft-dropping tears, her forbearance had somehow an edge and her propriety a chill. He did his best to be thoroughly civil to her and to treat her with distinguished deference, but perhaps his exasperated nerves made him overshoot the mark and rendered his attentions too grimly formal. She met them at moments almost as if they had represented a longer stretch of duplicity. She seemed capable of believing that he was trying to make a fool of her; she would have thought him cruelly recreant if he had suddenly turned his back, and yet she gave him no visible credit for consistency. It often struck him that he had too abjectly forfeited his freedom. Wasn't it grotesque, at his age, to be put into a corner for punishment?

But Mary Garland had helped him before and she helped him now— helped him not less than he had assured himself she would when he found himself drifting to Florence. Yet her help was rendered as unconsciously, he believed, and certainly as indirectly as before: he had made no apologies, and she had offered to remit no penalties. After that dreadful scene in Rome which had hurried their departure it was of course impossible that there should not be on the girl's part some frankness of allusion to Roderick's so pronounced and so public perversity. She had been present, the reader will remember, during only half this supreme demonstration of it, and Rowland had not seen her confronted with any absolute proof of the dependence of their friend's equilibrium on a crookedness the more or less in the tortuous progress of Christina Light. But he knew that she knew too much for her trust or her peace—even for the most indulgent view of her dignity: Roderick had told him, shortly after their settlement at the Villa Pandolfini, that he had had a "tremendous talk" with his cousin. Rowland asked no questions about it; he preferred not to have to take this knowledge into account. If the interview had but stirred the waters of bitterness he wished to ignore it for Mary's sake; and if it had sown the seeds of reconciliation he wished to close his eyes to it for his own —for the sake of that shy contingency, for ever dismissed and yet for ever present, which hovered in the background of his consciousness with a hanging head and yet an unshamed glance, and which had only, like a sentry in a narrow niche, to shift from one foot to the other, in order to become a fresh bribe to patience. Was the old understanding "off," or was Mary, in spite of humiliation, keeping it on?—was she in short consenting to *that*, to humiliation? Rowland looked at the question rather than asked it, since everything hung for him on her possible appetite for sacrifice, on his measure, so to call it, of what she would abjectly "take." Was she one of those who would *be* abject for some last scrap of the feast of their dream? It wronged her, as he liked to think of her, to believe either that she was or that she wasn't, and, as if the matter were none of his business, he tried to turn away his head. There are women whose love is care-taking and patronising and who attach themselves to those persons of the other sex in whom the manly grain is soft and submissive. It did not in the least please him to hold her one of these, for he regarded such women as mere males in petticoats, and he was convinced that this young lady was intensely of her sex. That she was a very different person from Christina Light didn't at all prove that she was a less considerable one, and if the Princess Casamassima had gone up into a high place to publish her dismissal of a man who couldn't strike out like a man, it had been hitherto presumable that she was not of a complexion to put up at any point with what might be called the Princess's leavings. It was Christina's constant practice to remind you of the complexity of her character, of the subtlety of her mind, of her troublous faculty of seeing everything in a dozen different lights. Mary had never pretended not to be simple; but Rowland had a theory that she had really a finer sense of human things and had made more, for observation and for temper, of her scant material of experience, than Christina had ever made of the stuff of *her* wild weaving. She did you the honours of her intelligence with a less accomplished grace, but was not that retreat as fragrant a maiden's bower ? If in poor Christina's strangely mixed nature there was a circle within circle and depth beneath depth, it was to be believed that the object of Rowland's preference, though she did not amuse herself with dropping stones into her soul and waiting to hear them fall, could none the less draw from the reservoir in question as brimming a bucket of energy. She had believed Roderick was "splendid" when she bade him farewell beneath their New England elms, and this synthetic term, to her young, strenuous, concentrated imagination, had meant many things. If it was to know itself chilled to the core, that would be because disenchantment had won the battle at each successive point and was now encamped on the field.

She showed even in her face and step, meanwhile, the tension of the watcher and the time-keeper: poor Roderick's muddled sum was a mystifying page to a girl who had supposed genius to be to one's spiritual economy what a large balance at the bank is to one's domestic. And yet our friend never tasted with her, as with Mrs. Hudson, of that acrid undercurrent—the impertinent implication that he had defrauded her of a promised security. Did this spring in her from a vague imagination of his own feeling, or even from a vague pity for it ? The answer might have been hopeful, inasmuch as she had almost let him think before leaving Rome that she liked him well enough to forgive him an injury. It was partly, he fancied, that there were occasional lapses, deep and sweet, in her sense of what had happened. When on arriving at Florence she saw the place he had brought them to in their trouble, she had given him a look, and said a few words, that had seemed almost more than a remission of penalties. This happened in the court of the villa—the large grey quadrangle, overstretched, from edge to edge of the red-tiled roof, by the deep Italian sky. Mary had felt on the spot the sovereign charm of the place; it was reflected in her sincere eyes, and, immediately promising himself to work it, as the phrase was, for all it was worth, Rowland as promptly accepted the odium of not having done the villa justice. She fell in love on the spot with Florence, and used to look down wistfully at the towered city from their terraced garden. Roderick having now no pretext for not being her cicerone, Rowland was no longer at liberty, as he had been in Rome, to propose frequent excursions to her. Roderick's own invitations, however, were much interspaced, and their companion more than once ventured to introduce her to a gallery or a church. These expeditions were not so blissful, to Rowland's sense, as the rambles they had taken together in Rome, for the excellent reason that they made, unmistakably, a more embarrassed appeal to hers. She was trying what they could do for her—little indeed as she might betray it if they failed. She had at her command but half her attention, and often, when she had begun with looking closely at a picture, her silence, after an interval, made him turn and see that if her eyes were fixed, her thoughts were wandering and an image more vivid than any Raphael or Titian had superposed itself upon the canvas. She asked fewer questions than before and seemed to have lost heart for consulting guide-books and encyclopædias. From time to time, however, she uttered a deep full murmur of gratification. Florence in midsummer was perfectly void of travellers, and the dense little city gave forth its historic soul with that larger passion with which the nightingale sings when listeners have ceased to be visible. The churches were deliciously cool, but the grey streets stifling and the great dovetailed polygons of pavement hot to the lingering tread. Rowland, who suffered from deadness of air, would have found all this uncomfortable in solitude; but Florence had never charmed him so completely as during these midsummer strolls with his preoccupied companion. One evening they had arranged to go on the morrow to the Academy. Mary kept her appointment, but as soon as she appeared he saw that, though she was doing her best to look at her ease, she had had some evil hour. When he hinted that he feared she was ill and that if she preferred to give up their adventure he would submit with what grace he might, she replied, after hesitation, that she would adhere to their plan. "I'm certainly not 'well,'" she presently added, "but it's a moral malady, and in such cases I regard your company as a tonic."

"But if I'm to administer your remedies," he said, "you must tell me how your indisposition came on."

"I can tell you very little. It came on with Mrs. Hudson's doing me an injustice—for the first time in her life. And now I'm already better."

This scant passage confirmed for Rowland an impression he had tried positively to cultivate. He was but too aware of the shocked, scared element in Mrs. Hudson's view of her son's "sentimental" infidelity, but he was surer than ever now that the young man himself, much more than his wronged bride-that-was-to-be, had been marked by it for her indulgence. She was fond enough, obviously, of her serviceable little cousin, but she had valued her primarily, during the last two years, as an assistant priestess at Roderick's shrine. Roderick had paid her the compliment of asking her to become, at his later convenience, his wife, but that poor Mary's own, and her present, convenience was sharply involved appeared not to have occurred to his mother. Her understanding of the matter was of course not rigidly formulated, but it was as if she felt that Roderick and she together sufficed as victims, without their counting in their kinswoman. It would be Rowland and Rome and the artistic temperament that had victimised them, but it would be the people naturally enamoured of Roderick most of all. He had been wretchedly upset—that was enough; and Mary's duty was to join her patience and her prayers to those of a disinterested parent. He might feel the force of charms greater than Mary's; no doubt women trained in the subtle Roman arts were only too proud and too happy to make it easy for him; and it was very presuming in a plain second cousin to make a wonder of the inevitable. Mrs. Hudson kept clear of the reflexion that a mother may forgive where a mistress may not, and she seemed to feel it a further drain on her own depletion that Mary shouldn't be glad to act as a handmaid without wages. She was ready to hold her breath so that Roderick might howl, if need be, at his ease, and she was capable of seeing any one else gasp for air without a tremor of compassion. The girl had now perhaps given some intimation of her belief that if constancy is the flower of devotion reciprocity is the guarantee of constancy, and Mrs. Hudson had denounced this as arrogant doctrine. That she had found it hard to reason with her protectress, that something was expected of her which she couldn't give, and that in short he had companionship in misfortune—these things relieved a little the pressure of which Rowland was conscious.

The party at Villa Pandolfini used to sit in the garden in the evenings, which Rowland almost always spent with them. Their entertainment was in the heavy scent of the air, in the dim, far starlight, in the crenellated tower of a neighbouring villa, which loomed vaguely above them through the warm darkness, and in such conversation as depressing reflexions permitted. Roderick, habited always in white, stalked about like a restless ghost, silent for the most part, but making from time to time an observation in which, as it seemed to the elder man, the spirit of vain paradox and of loose pessimism too freely overflowed. With Rowland alone he talked more, and as well as ever, and even about the things that had formerly interested him; but, taking a vicious twist always, it ended for the most part in some abrupt profession of despair and disgust. When this current set in our friend straightway turned his back and stopped his ears, and Roderick now witnessed these movements with perfect indifference. When the latter was absent from the starlit circle in the garden, as often happened, they knew nothing of his whereabouts: Rowland supposed him to be in Florence, but never learned what he did there. All this was not enlivening; yet with an even, muffled tread the days followed each other and brought the month of August to a close. One particular evening at this time was admirable; there was a perfect moon, looking so extraordinarily large that it made everything its light fell on turn pale and shrink; the heat was tempered by a soft west wind and the air laden with the breath of the early harvest. The hills, the vale of the Arno, the yellow river, the domes of Florence, were not so much lighted as obscured by the white glow. Rowland had found the two ladies alone at the villa, and he had dropped into a seat as discreetly as if they had been, as he said, at a "show." He felt hushed by the solemn splendour of the scene, but he risked the remark that, whatever life might yet have in store for either of them, this was a night they would never forget.

"It's a night that makes a success," Mary Garland replied, "of one's having lived at all."

"'At all,' dear?" Mrs. Hudson echoed. "You surely haven't waited till this evening to feel that you've lived very comfortably!" And she surveyed the scene as in vague reprehension and as finding in the accumulated loveliness of the hour something shameless and unholy.

They were silent after this for some time, but at last Rowland addressed to the girl some tentative idle word. She made no reply, and he turned to look at her. She was sitting motionless, with her head pressed to Mrs. Hudson's shoulder, and the latter lady was gazing at him through the silvered dusk with an air that gave a sort of spectral solemnity to the sad weak meaning of her eyes. She might have been for the moment a little old malevolent fairy. Mary, Rowland perceived in an instant, was not absolutely motionless; some strange agitation had shaken her. She was softly crying, or about so to cry, and unable to trust herself to speak. Rowland left his place and wandered to another part of the garden, affected by this sudden access and asking himself what had determined it. Of women's weeping in general he had a developed dread, but this particular appearance moved him to odd rejoicing. When he returned to his place Mary had raised her head and composed her aspect. She came away from Mrs. Hudson, and they stood for a short time together, leaning against the parapet.

"It seems to you very strange, I suppose," Rowland presently said, "that there should have to be anxiety and pain in such a world as this."

"I used to think," she answered, "that if any trouble came to me I should bear it like a stoic. But that was at home, where things don't speak to us of enjoyment as they do here. Here it's such a mixture; one doesn't know what to choose, what to believe. Beauty stands there—beauty such as this night and this place and all this sad strange summer have been so full of—and it penetrates to one's soul and lodges there and keeps saying that man wasn't made, as we think at home, to struggle so much and miss so much, but to ask of life as a matter of course some beauty and some charm. This place has destroyed any scrap of consistency that I ever possessed, but even if I must myself say something sinful I love it !"

"If it's sinful, I absolve you—in so far as I have power. We shouldn't be able to enjoy, I suppose, unless we could suffer, and in anything that's worthy of the name of experience—that experience which is the real *taste* of life, isn't it ?—the mixture is of the finest and subtlest. Just now and here it's certainly wonderful enough. Yet we must take things as much as possible in turn."

His words had a singular aptness, for he had hardly uttered them when Roderick came out from the house, not, as appeared, on pleasure bent. He stood for a moment taking in the effulgence.

"It's a very beautiful night, my son," said his mother, going to him timidly and touching his arm.

He passed his hand through his hair and let it stay there, clasping his thick locks. "Beautiful ?" he cried. "Of course it's beautiful ! Everything's beautiful; everything's insolent, defiant, atrocious with beauty. Nothing's ugly but me—me and my poor dead brain !"

"Oh, my dearest son," pleaded the poor lady; "don't you feel any better ?"

Roderick made no immediate answer, but at last he spoke in a different voice. "I came expressly to tell you that you needn't trouble yourselves any longer to wait for something to turn up. Nothing *will* turn up. It's all over. I said when I came here I would give it a chance. I've given it a chance. Haven't I, eh ? Haven't I, Rowland ? It's no use; our little experiment's a failure. Do with me now what you please. I recommend you to set me up there at the end of the garden and shoot me dead."

"I feel strongly inclined," said Rowland gravely, "to go and get my revolver."

"Oh, mercy on us, what language !" cried Mrs. Hudson.

"Why not ?" Roderick went on. "This would be a lovely night for it, and I should be a lucky fellow to be buried in this garden. But bury me alive if you prefer. Take me back to Northampton."

"Roderick, will you really come?" his mother quavered.

"Why shouldn't I go? I might as well be there as anywhere—reverting to idiocy and living on alms. I can do nothing with all this; perhaps I should really like again the opposite pole. If I'm to vegetate for the rest of my days I can do it there better than here."

"Oh, come home, come home," Mrs. Hudson pleaded, "and we shall all be safe and quiet and happy. My dearest son, come home with your poor little mother!"

"Let us go then—quickly!"

She flung herself on his neck for gratitude. "We'll go to-morrow! The Lord's very good to me!"

Mary Garland said nothing to this; but she looked at Rowland, and her eyes struck him as containing a deep, an alarmed appeal. He observed it with exultation, but even without it he would have broken into an eager protest.

"Are you serious, Roderick?" he demanded.

"Serious? Of course not! How can a man with a crack in his brain be serious, how can a damned fool reason? But I'm not jesting either; I can no more crack jokes than utter oracles!"

"Are you willing to go home?"

"Willing? God forbid! I'm simply amenable to force; if my mother chooses to take me I won't resist. I can't! I've come to that!"

"Let *me* resist then," said Rowland. "Go home as you're now acting and talking? I can't stand by and see it."

It may have been true that Roderick had lost his sense of humour, but he scratched his head with a gesture of comic effect. "You *are* a funny man. I should think I would disgust you horribly."

"Stay another year," Rowland simply said.

"Doing nothing?"

"You shall do more than you've bargained for yet. I'm responsible for your doing it."

"To whom are you responsible?"

Rowland, before replying, glanced at Mary Garland, and his glance made her speak quickly. "Not to me!"

"I'm responsible to myself," he substituted.

"Ah, but my poor dear fellow!" his friend inconclusively demurred.

"Oh, Mr. Mallet, aren't you satisfied?" asked Mrs. Hudson in the tone in which Niobe may have addressed the avenging archers after she had seen her eldest-born fall. "It's out of all nature keeping him here. When our poor hearts are broken, surely our own dear native land is the place for us. Do leave us to ourselves, sir !"

This just failed of being a dismissal in form, and Rowland made a note of it. Roderick was silent for some moments; then suddenly he covered his face with his two hands. "Take me, at least, out of this terrible Italy," he cried, "where everything mocks and reproaches and torments and eludes me ! Take me out of this land of impossible beauty and put me in the midst of ugliness. Set me down where nature is coarse and flat and men and manners are vulgar. There must be something ugly enough in Germany. Pack me off, for goodness' sake, there !"

Rowland answered that if he wished to leave Italy the thing might be arranged; he would think it over and submit a proposal on the morrow. He suggested to Mrs. Hudson in consequence that she should spend the autumn in Switzerland, where she would find a fine tonic climate, plenty of fresh milk and several very inexpensive *pensions*. Switzerland of course was not reputed ugly, but one couldn't have everything !

Mrs. Hudson neither thanked him nor assented, but she wept and packed her trunks. Rowland had a theory, after the scene which led to these preparations, that Mary was weary of waiting for Roderick to come to his senses, that the faith which had borne him company on the tortuous march he was leading it had begun to falter and droop. This theory was not vitiated by a word falling from her on the day before that on which Mrs. Hudson had settled to leave Florence.

"Cousin Sarah, the other evening," she said, "asked you to leave us to ourselves. I think she hardly knew what she was saying, and I hope you've not taken offence."

"By no means; but I honestly believe that my leaving you would contribute greatly to Mrs. Hudson's comfort. I can be your hidden providence, you know; I can watch you at a distance and come upon the scene at critical moments."

The girl looked at everything but himself, then spoke with sudden earnestness, "I particularly want you to come with us !"

It need hardly be added that after this Rowland went with them.

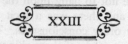

XXIII

HE HAD a very friendly memory of a little mountain inn, accessible with moderate trouble from Lucerne, where he had once spent ten idle unadventurous days. He had at that time been trudging, knapsack on back, over half Switzerland, and, having had a sturdy conscience about covering ground, it was no shame to him to confess that he was mortally tired. The inn of which I speak appeared to have but recently exchanged the care of the stalled ox for that of the hungry tourist; but Rowland at least had felt himself only a feebler ruminant. It stood in a high shallow valley, with flower-strewn Alpine meadows sloping down to it from the base of certain rugged rocks whose outlines were grim against the late sky. Our friend had seen grander places that pleased him less, and whenever afterwards he wished to think of Alpine opportunities at their best he recalled this grassy concave among the steeper ridges and the August days passed in resting at his length in the lee of a sun-warmed boulder, with the light cool air astir about his temples, the wafted odours of the pines in his nostrils, the tinkle of the cattle-bells in his ears, the vast procession of the mountain-hours before his eyes and a volume of Wordsworth in his pocket. His face, on the Swiss hillsides, had been scorched to a brilliant hue, and his bed was a pallet in a loft, which he shared with a German botanist of colossal stature—every inch of whom quaked at an open window. These had been drawbacks to selfish ease, but Rowland hardly cared whether or how he was lodged, for his place of preference and of main abode was under the sky, on the crest of a slope that looked at the Jungfrau. He remembered all this on leaving Florence with his friends, and he reflected that, as the midseason was over, accommodations would be more ample and charges more modest. He communicated with his old friend the landlord, and while September was yet young his companions established themselves under his guidance in this hollow of the hills.

He had crossed the Saint-Gotthard Pass with them in the same vehicle. During the journey from Florence, and especially during this portion of it, the cloud that hung over the little party had almost cleared, and they had looked at each other, in the close intimacy of train and vettura, without either the retributive or the argumentative glare. It was impossible not to hang upon the perpetual rich picture of Apennine and Alp, and there was a tacit agreement among the travellers to sink every other consciousness. The effect of this discretion was of the best; it made of them shipwrecked swimmers who had clambered upon a raft. Roderick sat with a fascinated far-reaching stare and a perfect docility of attitude. He concerned himself not a particle about the intinerary or the wayside arrangements; but if he took no trouble he also gave quite touchingly little. His friend tacitly compared him to some noble young *émigré* of the French Terror, seized before reaching the frontier and showing, while brought back, a white face, indescribable, that anticipated the guillotine. He assented to everything that was proposed, and was perched apparently on heights of contemplation inaccessible to the others. His mother rarely removed her eyes from him; and, if a while before this would greatly have irritated him, he now seemed wholly unconscious of her observation and deeply indifferent to anything that might befall him. They spent a couple of days on the Lake of Como, at an hotel with white porticoes smothered in oleander and myrtle and terrace-steps leading down to little boats under striped awnings. They agreed it was the earthly paradise, and they passed the mornings in strolls through the cedar alleys of classic villas and the evenings afloat beneath the stars, in a circle of outlined mountains, to the music of silver-trickling oars. One afternoon the two young men wandered away together as they had wandered of old. They followed the winding footpath that led towards Como, close to the lakeside, past the gates of villas and the walls of vineyards, through little hamlets propped on a dozen arches and bathing their feet and their pendent tatters in the grey-green ripple; past frescoed walls and crumbling campanili and grassy village piazzettas and the mouth of soft ravines that wound upward, through belts of swinging vine and vaporous olive and wide-armed chequering chestnut, to high ledges where white chapels gleamed amid the paler boskage and bare cliff-surfaces, with their blistered lips, drank in the liquid light. It was all consummately romantic; it was the Italy we know from the steel-engravings in old keepsakes and annuals, from the vignettes on music-sheets and the drop-curtains at theatres; an Italy we can never confess ourselves—in spite of our own changes and of all the local perversions and the lost causes, as well the gained—to have ceased to need and to believe in. The companions turned aside from the little paved footway that clambered and dipped and wound and doubled beside the lake, and stretched themselves idly beneath a fig-tree on a grassy headland. Rowland had never known anything so divinely soothing as the dreamy softness of these early autumn hours. The iridescent mountains shut him in; the small waves beneath him fretted the white pebbles at the laziest intervals; the festooned vines above him swayed just visibly in the all but motionless air.

Roderick lay observing it all with his arms thrown back and his hands under his head. "This suits me," he said at last; "I could be happy here and forget everything. Why not stay here for ever?" He kept his position a long time and seemed lost in his thoughts. Rowland spoke to him, but he made vague answers; finally he closed his eyes. It seemed to Rowland also a place of irresistible persuasion, with the very taste of the lotus in the air. Suddenly Roderick turned over on his face and buried it in his arms. The movement had been a nervous spasm, but our friend nevertheless winced, on his jerking himself round again and sitting up, at the sight of his suffused eyes. Roderick turned to him, stretching out both hands to the lake and mountains and shaking them as from a heart too full for utterance.

"Pity me, my friend; pity me !" he presently cried. "Look at this lovely world and think what it must be to be dead to it !"

"Dead?" poor Rowland temporised.

"Dead, dead; dead and buried ! Buried in an open grave where you lie staring up at the sailing clouds, smelling the waving flowers and hearing all nature live and grow above you. That's the way I feel."

"I'm very glad to hear it. Death of that sort's very near to re-surrection."

"It's too horrible," Roderick went on; "it has all come over me here. If I were not ashamed I could shed a bushel of tears. For one hour of what I *have* been I'd give up—everything I'm not."

"Never mind what you 'have' been; be something better !"

"I shall never be anything again; it's no use talking ! But I don't know what secret spring has been touched since I've lain here. Some-thing in my heart seems suddenly to open and let in a flood of beauty and desire. I know what I've lost and I think it horrible. Mind you, I know it, I feel it. Remember that hereafter. Don't say that he was stupefied and senseless, that his perception was dulled or his aspiration dead. Say he trembled in every nerve with a sense of the beauty and sweetness of life; say he rebelled and protested and struggled; say he was buried alive, with his eyes open and his heart beating to madness; say he clung to every blade of grass and every wayside thorn as he passed; say it was the most pathetic thing you ever beheld. "Say," he wound up, "that it was a sacrifice and a scandal."

Rowland fairly turned pale as their eyes met. "I think that if you're not mad you'll at least soon make *me* so."

"Oh, I can trust you, old chap, and I assure you I can be trusted. I've never been saner. I don't want to be bad company, and in this beautiful spot, at this delightful hour, it seems an outrage to break the charm. But I'm bidding farewell to Italy, to beauty, to honour, to life. I only want to assure you that I know what I lose. I know it in every pulse, in every inch of me. Here where these things are all loveliest I take leave of them. Good-bye, adorable world !"

During their slow ascent into Switzerland he absented himself much of the time from the carriage and rambled, far in advance, along the zigzags of the road and in constant deviation from them. He showed a tireless activity; his light weight and long legs carried him every-where, and his friends saw him skirt the edge of plunging chasms, loosen the stones on vast steep slopes and lift himself against the sky from the top of rocky pinnacles. Mary Garland took scarcely less to her feet, but she remained near the carriage to be with Mrs. Hudson, while Rowland remained near it to be with Mrs. Hudson's companion. He measured the great road by her side and found himself sorry the Alps were so low and that their walk was not to last a week. She was exhilarated; she rejoiced in their adventure; in the way of mountains, until within the last few weeks, she had seen, for a near view, nothing greater than Mounts Holyoke and Tom and the mild Alban hills, so that she recognised in the Alps the just ground of their glory. Rowland had noted her own vision of natural objects, but he was struck afresh with her quick eye for them and with her knowledge of plants and rocks and "formations." At that season many of the wild flowers had gone, but others lingered, and Mary never failed to "spot" them in their outlying corners. She gave herself up to them, interested when they were old friends and charmed when they were new. Her foot was light in quest of them and she had soon covered the front seat of the carriage with a tangle of strange vegetation. Rowland had always supposed himself to dislike the race of weed-gathering, vase-dressing women, disposers, over the domestic scene, of bristling, tickling greenery; but he was none the less alert in her service and gathered for her several fine specimens which had at first seemed inaccessible. One of these indeed had appeared an easier prize than it was likely to prove, and he had paused a moment at the base of the little peak on which it grew, measuring the risk of further pursuit. Suddenly, as he stood there, he remembered Roderick's defiance of danger and of Christina Light during that sharp moment at the Coliseum, and he was seized with a strong desire to test the quality of his own companion. She had just scrambled up a grassy slope near him and had seen that the flower was out of reach. As he prepared to approach it she called to him eagerly to stop and yield to the impossibility. Poor Rowland, whose interest in her had so much more nourished itself on plain fare than snatched at any golden apple of reward, enjoyed immensely the sense of her caring for three minutes what should become of him. He was the least brutal of men, but for a moment he was perfectly indifferent to her nerves.

"I can get the flower," he called to her. "Will you trust me ?"

"I don't want it; I'd rather not have it !" she cried.

"Will you trust me ?" he repeated, looking at her hard.

She looked at him in return and then at the flower; he wondered whether she would shriek and swoon as Christina had done. "I wish it were something better !" she said simply; and she stood watching him while he began to clamber. Rowland was not a trained acrobat, and his enterprise was difficult; but he kept his wits about him, made the most of narrow footholds and coigns of vantage and at last secured his prize. He managed to stick it into his button-hole, after which he worked his way down again. There was more than one chance for an ugly fall, but he had not lost his head or his hold. It was doubtless not gracefully done, but it was done, and that was all he had proposed to himself. He was red in the face when he offered Mary the flower, and she was visibly pale. She had kept her eyes on him without moving. All this had passed without the knowledge of Mrs. Hudson, who was dozing beneath the hood of the carriage. Mary's eyes did not perhaps quite display the ardent admiration anciently offered to the victor by the queen of beauty at a tournament; but they told him that his existence had for the time mattered to her. He liked having proof of this to put in his pocket, very much as a "handsome" subscriber to an important cause likes an acknowledgement of his cheque. "Why did you do that ?" she asked gravely.

He hesitated, conscious of the deep desire to answer "Because I love you !" But he had not kept his head before to lose it now. He lowered his pitch and replied simply: "Because I wanted to do something for you."

"Suppose you had broken your neck."

299

"I believed I shouldn't. And you believed it, I think."

"I believed nothing. I simply trusted you, as you asked me."

"*Quod erat demonstrandum !*" cried Rowland. "I think you know Latin."

When our four friends were established in what I have called their hollow in the hills there was much scrambling over slopes both grassy and stony, a good deal of flower-plucking on narrow ledges, a great many long walks and, thanks to the tonic mountain air, not a little relief and oblivion. Mrs. Hudson was reduced to forgetting, above all, that the poison of Europe—as she knew Europe—might lurk in the breeze, and even to admitting that the eggs of Engelthal were almost as fresh and the cream almost as thick as those of the Connecticut Valley. She was certainly more in her element that she had been in Italy; having always lived in the country she had missed in Rome and Florence that social solitude mitigated by bushes and rocks, primarily dear to the true England temperament. The little unpainted Oberland inn, with its plank partitions, its milk-pans standing in the sun, its "help," in the form of angular young women of the countryside, reminded her of places of summer sojourn in her native land; and the beautiful historic chambers of Villa Pandolfini passed from her conscience without a regret and without having in the least modified her conception of the house submissive to "keeping." If Roderick, on the other hand, had changed his sky, he had still not changed his mind; he was not sensibly nearer to having got back into the traces than he had shown himself during his declaration of despair by the Italian lakeside. He now kept this despair to himself and went decently enough about the ordinary business of life; but it was easy to see that he wasn't, in the new phrase, "there"—his meekness was so mechanical and his present motives somehow so inscrutable. In that sad half-hour on the Como promontory there had been a fierce truth under the impression of which Rowland found himself at last forswearing criticism and censure. He began to feel it quite idle to appeal to his comrade's will; there was no will left —its place was a mocking void. This view of the case indeed was occasionally contravened by certain indications on Roderick's part of the surviving faculty of resistance to disagreeable obligation: one might still have said, if one had been disposed to improve the occasion at any hazard, that there was a method in his madness, that his moral energy had its sleeping and its waking hours, and that in an attractive cause it would yet again be capable of rising with the dawn. This name, however, for a possible knock at his door, what was it, truly, but another word for an inspiration? Oh, for such a visitor, the appealing plastic idea, he would spring up and open wide his eyes and look out at the dawn; but where was the precious pebble to come from that might be cast with the right sharp tap at his window-pane? It was now impossible, at all events, not to be indulgent to a consciousness that had so ceased to be aggressive—not to forgive much apathy to a temper that had turned its rough side inward. Roderick said frankly that Switzerland made him less miserable than Italy, and that the Alps were less of a reproach to idle skilled hands than the Apennines. He went in for long rambles, generally alone, and was very fond of climbing into dizzy places where no sound could overtake him and there, stretched at his length on the never-trodden moss, of pulling his hat over his eyes and lounging away the hours in perfect immobility. Rowland was sometimes the associate of these walks, for if his friend never directly proposed it he yet as little visibly resented it; and the only way at present to treat him was as a graceful, an almost genial, a certainly harmless eccentric, with whom one assumed that all things were well and held one's tongue about the prosperity he had forfeited, or maintained to any questioner—much rejoicing, for the time, there were none—that such were the interlunar swoons of the true as distinguished from the false artist, and that the style of genius was as much in them as in the famous Homeric nod. His interest in Mary's relations with her cousin had lost meanwhile none of its point, though mystified as he was on all sides he found nothing penetrable here. After their arrival at Engelthal Roderick appeared to care more for her society than he had done hitherto, and this revival of appetite couldn't fail to come home to their friend. They sat together and strolled together, and she often read aloud to him. One day, on their arrival at luncheon, after he had been lying half the morning at her feet in the shadow of a rock, Rowland asked him what she had been reading.

"I don't know," Roderick said, "I don't heed the sense." Mary heard this and Rowland looked at her, but it only made her look hard at Roderick. "I listen to Mary," he continued, "for the sake of her voice. It's soothing and stupefying—it's really demoralising." At this the girl coloured and turned away.

Rowland, as we know, had speculated much, in the interest of his ultimate chance, had asked himself if her constancy had been proof; and that demand, on her lips, which had brought about his own

301

departure for Switzerland had seemed almost equivalent to a confession that she needed his help to keep her faith. He had, in his high modesty, not risked the supposition that Mary could contrast him with Roderick to the advantage of his personal charm; but his consciousness of duty done had a hand to hold out for any such stray grain of enthusiasm as might have crumbled away from her estimate of his companion. If some day she had declared in a sudden burst of bitterness that she was completely disillusioned and that she gave up her recreant lover our friend's expectation would have gone half-way to meet her. And certainly, if her troubled spirit had taken this course, no generous critic, he reasoned, would have pronounced her vain. She had been offered an extent of cold shoulder on which few girls could have schooled themselves to rest their eyes so long. There were girls indeed the beauty of whose nature, like that of Burd Helen in the ballad, lay in clinging to the man of their love through bush and brier and in bowing their head to all hard usage. That behaviour had of course a grace of its own, but Rowland was far from seeing it as proper to Mary Garland. She asked something for what she gave, and he was yet to make out what had been given her. She believed in the conquests of ambition, and would surely never long persuade herself that it was as interesting to see them missed—even helplessly and pathetically— as to see them strenuously reached. Rowland passed, before he had done, an angry day; for he had not been able to stifle a sense that she had in a manner—how did he like to put it?—"transferred her esteem" to him. And yet here she was throwing herself back into Roderick's arms at his slightest overture—so that a fatuous man (which, thank goodness, *he* wasn't) might almost have called her a coquette, or at least have asked her what she "meant." He stated to himself that his position was abject and that all the philosophy he could bring to bear upon it would make it neither honourable nor comfortable. He would go away and cut it short. He didn't go away; he simply took a long walk, made an absence of hours, and on his return found Mary sitting out in the moonlight with their friend.

Communing with himself during the restless ramble in question, he had determined that he would at last cease to observe, to heed or to care for what these two young persons might do or might not do to-gether. Nevertheless some three days afterwards, the opportunity presenting itself, he deliberately broached the subject with Roderick. He felt it inconsistent and faint-hearted; it was an allowance to fingers that itched to handle forbidden fruit. But he said to himself that it was really more logical to return to the question than to drop it, for they had formerly discussed these mysteries sharply enough. Wasn't it perfectly reasonable that he should wish to know the sequel to the situation Roderick had then delineated? Roderick had made him promises, and it was to be expected that he should wish to ascertain how the promises had been kept. So he took occasion to break ground on the morrow of the day just mentioned. "I imagine you're not sorry at present to have allowed yourself to be dissuaded from putting an end to your affair with your cousin." He liked somehow calling their engagement an affair.

Roderick eyed him with the vague and absent look lately habitual to his face. "Dissuaded?"

"Don't you remember that in Rome you wished to break off, and that I urged you to hold fast, on the contrary—thin as your link appeared to have become? I wanted you to see what would come, for you, of your taking no first step. If I'm not mistaken you're now reconciled to your having let things alone."

"Oh yes," said Roderick, "I remember what you said; you made it a kind of personal favour to yourself that I should *not* clear anything up. I consented, but afterwards, when I thought of it, your attitude struck me as having its oddity. Had it ever been seen before?—a man asking another man to gratify him, in such a case—I mean the case of such an attractive girl—by still blocking the way."

"Well, my view was about as selfish as another," said Rowland. "One man puts his selfishness into this thing, and one into that. It wouldn't at all have suited me to see your cousin in low spirits."

"But you liked her—you admired her, eh? So you intimated."

"I admire her extremely."

"It was your originality then—to do you justice you've a great deal of a certain sort—to wish her happiness secured in just that fashion. Many a man would have liked better himself to make the woman he admired happy, and would have welcomed her low spirits as an opening for sympathy. You were very quaint and unexpected—though I'm bound to say very reasonable and even very charming—about it."

"So be it!" said Rowland. "The question is, Aren't you glad I was all those interesting things? Aren't you finding much of your old feeling for your cousin now come back to you?"

"I don't pretend to say. When she arrived in Rome I discovered I had ceased to care for her, and I honestly proposed that we should

303

have no humbug about it. If you, on the contrary, thought there was something to be gained by having a little humbug I was willing to try it ! I don't see that the situation is really changed. Mary is all she ever was—all the cardinal virtues, and if possible more than all. But she doesn't, poor dear, in the least *interest* me—so what's a fellow to do ? Nothing does interest me—not really—of course, and how can I pretend she's a brilliant exception ? The only difference is that I don't care now whether she interests me or not. Of course marrying such a useless lout as I am is out of the question for any woman, and I should pay Mary a poor compliment to assume that she's in a hurry to celebrate our nuptials."

"Oh, you'll do—you're in love !" Rowland not very logically answered. It must be confessed that this assertion was made for the sole purpose of hearing his companion deny it.

But it quite failed of its aim. Roderick gave a liberal shrug of his shoulders and an irresponsible toss of his head. "Call it what you please ! I'm past caring for the names of things."

Rowland had not only failed of logic, he had also failed of candour. He believed not the least little mite that Roderick was in love; he had only argued the false to learn the true. The "true" was then that this troubled youth was again, despite everything, in some degree under a charm, and that one couldn't be so ministered to without either liking it or hating it. Roderick might say what he would, he didn't hate it. So it came round to her having, behind everything, an insidious art. Rowland liked, for his part, to think of her insidious art. Since she had asked him as a favour to herself, at any rate, to come with them to Switzerland, he thought she might by this time have let him know if he seemed to have done her a service. The days passed without her doing so, and at last he walked away to an isolated eminence some five miles from the inn and murmured to the silent rocks that she was ungrateful. Listening nature appeared not to contradict him, so that on the morrow he asked the girl with a touch of melancholy malice whether it struck her that his deflexion from his other plan had been attended with brilliant results.

"Why, we're delighted you're with us !" she simply answered.

He was anything but satisfied with this; it seemed to imply that she had forgotten how she had put it to him that he would particularly oblige her. He reminded her of her request and recalled the place and time. "That evening on the terrace, late, after Mrs. Hudson had gone to bed, and Roderick being absent."

She perfectly remembered, but the memory seemed to trouble her. "I'm afraid your kindness has been a great charge upon you then. You wanted very much to do something else."

"I wanted above all things to do what you would like, and I made no sacrifice. But if I had made an immense one it would be more than made up to me by any assurance that I've helped Roderick to better conditions."

She was silent a while, and then, "Why do you ask me?" she said. "You're able to judge quite as well as I."

Rowland cast about him; he desired to justify himself in the most veracious manner. "The truth is I'm afraid I care only in the second place for Roderick's holding up his head. What I care for in the first place is your tranquillity and security."

"I don't know why that should be," she returned. "I've certainly done nothing to make you so much my friend. If you were to tell me you intend to leave us to-morrow I'm afraid that I shouldn't venture to ask you to stay. But whether you go or stay, let us not talk of Roderick."

"Then that," said Rowland, "doesn't answer my question. *Is* he better?"

"No !" she brought out, and turned away.

He was careful not to tell her he intended to leave them.

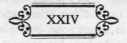

XXIV

ONE DAY shortly after this, as the two young men sat at the inn door watching the sunset, which on that evening was very rich and clear, Rowland made an attempt to sound his companion's actual sentiment touching Christina Light. "I wonder where she is," he permitted himself to begin, "and what sort of a life she's leading her Prince."

Roderick at first made no response. He was watching a figure on the summit of some distant rocks opposite. The figure was apparently descending into the valley, and in relief against the crimson screen of the western sky it looked gigantic. "Christina Light?" he at last repeated, as if rousing himself from a reverie. "Where she is? It's 'rum' how little I care !"

"Have you completely got over caring?"

To this he made no direct reply; he sat brooding a while. "She's a fearful fraud!" he presently exclaimed.

"She's certainly not a mere child of nature. But she had elements of interest."

"She didn't at all come up to my original idea of her," Roderick pursued.

"In what manner then did she fall away from it?"

"Oh, don't ask me or remind me!" Roderick cried. "What's the use of going into it now? It was only three months ago, but it seems like ten years." His friend said nothing more, and after a while he went on of his own accord. "I believed there was a future in it all! She gave me pleasure—extraordinary pleasure; and when an artist, such a one as I was, receives extraordinary pleasure, you know——!" And he paused again. "You never saw her as I did, you never heard her in her great moments. But there's no help in talking about that! At first she wouldn't regard me seriously; she only chaffed me and made light of me and kept me off. Then at last I forced her to admit I was a great man. She told me she believed that, and it gave me more extraordinary pleasure than anything else. A great man was what she was looking for, and we agreed to find our happiness for life in each other. To please me she promised not to marry till I should say I was prepared—so far as I *could* be prepared—to see her. I was of course not in a marrying way myself, but it was a stiff dose—which I kept begging off from—to have to think of another man's possessing her. To spare my sensibilities she promised to turn off her Prince, and the idea of her doing so made me as happy as to see some blest idea shaping itself in the block. You've seen how she kept her promise. When I learned it, it was as if my block had suddenly split and turned rotten. She died for me, like that!" And he snapped his fingers. "Was it wounded vanity, disappointed desire, betrayed confidence? I'm sure I don't know. I make the beastly mistakes, and you find the proper names for them."

Rowland, after an instant, could but temporise. "The poor girl did the best she could."

"That that was her best then was exactly the grand sell! I've hardly thought of her these two months, but you see, and I'm in fact myself surprised to find, how little I've forgiven her."

"Well, you may probably take it that you're avenged. I can't think of her as very happy."

306

"Ah, I can't pity her!" said Roderick. After which he relapsed into silence, and the two sat watching the colossal figure as it made its way downward along the jagged silhouette of the rocks. "Who's this mighty man," he finally demanded, "and what's he coming down on us for? We're small people here, and we can't keep company with giants."

"Wait till we meet him on our own level," said Rowland, "and perhaps he'll not overtop us."

"He's like me," Roderick rejoined; "he'll have passed for ten minutes for bigger than he is." At this moment the figure sank beneath the horizon and became invisible in the uncertain light. Suddenly he went on: "I should like to see her once more—simply to look at her."

"I wouldn't advise it," his companion observed.

"It was the wonderful nature of her beauty that did it!" Roderick kept on. "It was all her beauty—so fitful, so alive, so *subject to life*, yet so always there and so interesting and so splendid. In comparison the rest was nothing. What befooled me was to think of it as my own property and possession—somehow bought and paid for. I had mastered it and made it mine; no one else had studied it as I had, no one else so understood it. What does that stick of a Casamassima know about it at this hour? There were things I could say of her, things I could say *to* her—because I know, or at least did know—that made her *more* beautiful, put her into possession of more of her value. Therefore I should like to see it just once more; it's the only thing in the world of which I can say so."

"I wouldn't advise it," Rowland felt himself too meagrely repeat.

"That's right, my dear fellow," his friend returned. "Don't advise! That's no use now."

The dusk meanwhile had thickened, and they had not perceived a figure approaching them across the open space in front of the house. Suddenly it stepped into the circle of light projected from the door and windows and they beheld little Sam Singleton stopping to stare at them. He was the giant they had seen so strikingly presented. When this was made apparent Roderick was seized with high amusement; it was the first time he had laughed for ever so many weeks. Singleton, who carried a knapsack and walking-staff, received from Rowland the friendliest welcome. He was still the same almost irritating little image of happy diligence, and if in the way of luggage his knapsack contained nothing but a comb and a second shirt, he extracted from it a dozen admirable sketches. He had been trudging over half Switzerland and making

307

everywhere the most vivid pictorial notes. They were mostly in a box at Interlaken, and in gratitude for Rowland's appreciation he presently telegraphed for his box, which, according to the excellent Swiss method, was punctually delivered by post. The nights were cold, and our friends, with three or four other chance sojourners, sat indoors, over a fire of great logs. Even with Roderick hovering moodily apart they made a sympathetic little circle, and they turned over Singleton's drawings while he perched in the chimney-corner, blushing and explaining, with his feet on the rounds of his chair. He had been pedestrianising for six weeks, and he was glad to rest a while at Engelthal. It was no empty interval, however, for he sallied forth every morning, his utensils on his back, in search of material for new studies. Roderick's ironic sense of him, after the first evening, had spent itself, and he might have been listening, as under a sombre spell, to the hum of some prosperous workshop from which he had been discharged for incompetence. Singleton, who was not in the secret of his personal misfortunes, still treated him, with romantic reverence, as the rising star of American art. Roderick had said to Rowland at first that their friend reminded him of some curious insect with a remarkable mechanical instinct in its antennæ; but as the days went by it was apparent that the modest landscapist's successful method grew to have an oppressive meaning for him. It pointed a moral, and Roderick used to sit and con the moral as he saw it figured in the little painter's bent back, on the hot hillsides, protruding from beneath a white umbrella. One day he wandered up a long slope and overtook him as he sat at work; Singleton related the incident afterwards to Rowland, who, since giving him in Rome a hint of the other's aberrations, had strictly kept his own counsel.

"Are you *always* just like this?" Roderick had asked in almost sepulchral accents.

"Like this?" Singleton, startled, had repeated with a guilty blink.

"You remind me of a watch that never runs down. If one listens hard one hears you always at it. Tic-tic-tic, tic-tic-tic."

"Oh, I see," Singleton had returned while he beamed ingenuously. "I'm very regular."

"You're very regular, yes. And I suppose you find it very pleasant to be very regular?"

Singleton had hereupon turned and smiled more brightly, sucking the water from his camel's-hair brush. Then with a quickened sense of his indebtedness to a Providence that had endowed him with intrinsic facilities: "Oh, most delightful!" he had exclaimed.

Roderick had stood looking at him a moment. "Damnation!" was the single word that then had fallen from him; with which he had turned his back.

Later in the week our two friends took together one of their longest rambles. They had walked before in a dozen different directions, but had not yet crossed a charming little wooded pass which shut in their valley on one side and descended into the vale of Engelberg. In coming from Lucerne they had approached their inn by this path, and then, feeling that they knew it, had neglected it for more untrodden ways. But at last the list of these was exhausted, and Rowland proposed the walk to Engelberg as a novelty. The place is half bleak and half pastoral; a huge white monastery rises abruptly from the green floor of the valley and contributes to the somewhat spare concert of blue-green and blue-grey the diversion of a sharp discord. Hard by is a group of châlets and inns, with the usual appurtenances of a prosperous Swiss resort —lean brown guides in baggy homespun loafing under carved wooden galleries, stacks of alpenstocks in every doorway, sun-scorched Englishmen without shirt-collars. The companions sat a while at the door of an inn and discussed a pint of wine, and then Roderick, whose light, elegant legs never gave way, whatever else in him did, announced his intention of climbing to a certain rocky pinnacle which overhung the valley and, according to the testimony of one of the guides, commanded a view of the Lake of Lucerne. To go and come back was only an hour, but Rowland, with the prospect of his homeward march before him, confessed to a preference for lounging on his bench or, at most, strolling a trifle farther and paying a visit to the monastery. Roderick went off alone, and the elder man took after a little the direction of the monasterial church. It was remarkable, like most of the churches of Catholic Switzerland, for a coarse floridity, but one was free to view this, if one would, as brave romantic character. Rowland lingered a quarter of an hour under the influence of that suggestion. While he was near the high altar another visitor or two appeared to have come in at the west door, but he gave no heed and was presently engaged in deciphering a curious old German epitaph on one of the mural tablets. At last he turned away, wondering if its syntax or its theology were the more uncomfortable, and, to his infinite surprise, found himself confronted with Prince and Princess Casamassima.

The surprise on Christina's part, for an instant, was equal, and its first effect might have been to make her seek, for the time, the refuge of assumed unconsciousness. The Prince, however, saluted gravely, and then Christina, in silence, put out her hand. Rowland immediately asked if they were staying at Engelberg, but Christina only looked at him hard, and still without speaking. The Prince answered his questions and related that they had been making a month's tour in Switzerland, that at Lucerne his wife had been somewhat obstinately indisposed, and that the physician had recommended a week's trial of the tonic air and goat's milk of Engelberg. The scenery, said the Prince, was stupendous, but the life was terribly sad—and they had three days more ! It was a blessing, he urbanely added, to see a good Roman face.

Christina's odd attitude, her voluntary silence and her inscrutable gaze, seemed to Rowland at first to promise, a little alarmingly, or even boringly, some new "line"; but he then perceived that she was really moved by the sight of him and was afraid of betraying herself. "Do let us leave this Swiss hideousness," she said; "the whole place seems horribly to 'jodel' at us!" They passed slowly to the door, and when they stood outside, in the sunny coolness of the valley, she turned more frankly to her old acquaintance. "It *is* a blessing, you know—such a meeting. I'm too delighted to see you." She glanced about her and observed against the wall of the church a large stone seat. She looked at her companion a moment, and he smiled more intensely, Rowland thought, than the occasion demanded. "I should like to sit here a little and speak to this good friend—alone."

"At your pleasure, *cara mia*," said the Prince.

The tone of each was measured, to Rowland's ear; but that of Christina was not imperceptibly dry and that of her husband irreproachably urbane. Rowland remembered how the Cavaliere had told him that Mrs. Light's candidate had, in his way, the inner as well as the outer marks of the *grand seigneur*, and our friend wondered how he relished a certain curtness. He was, comparatively speaking, an Italian of the undemonstrative type, but Rowland nevertheless divined that, like other potentates, great and small, before him, he had had to look concessions in the face. "Shall I come back ?" he imperturbably asked.

"In half an hour," said Christina.

In the clear outer light Rowland's first impression of her was that her beauty had received some strange accession, affecting him after the manner of a musical composition better "given," to his sense, than ever before. And yet in three months she could hardly have changed; the change was in Rowland's own vision of her, in which that last interview on the eve of her marriage had sown the seeds of a new appreciation.

"How came you to be in this queer place?" she asked. "Are you making a stay?"

"I'm staying at Engelthal, some ten miles away. I walked over."

"Then you're alone?"

"I'm with Roderick Hudson."

"Is he here with you now?"

"He went half an hour ago to climb a rock for a view."

"And his mother and—and the *promessa*—where are they?"

"They also are at Engelthal."

She had a pause. "What then are you all doing there?"

"What are you doing here?" Rowland returned.

"Counting the minutes till my week's over. I hate mountains; they always strike me as great rough lumps and chunks of Nature— hopeless confessions of her stupidity. I'm sure Miss Garland likes them."

"She's very fond of them I believe."

"You believe—don't you know? But I think I've given up trying to imitate Miss Garland," said Christina.

"You surely need imitate no one."

"Don't say that," she said gravely. "So you've walked ten miles this morning? And you're to walk back again?"

"Back again to dinner."

"And Mr. Hudson too?"

"Mr. Hudson especially. He's a great walker."

"You men are happy!" Christina cried. "I believe I should enjoy the mountains if I could do such things. It's sitting still and having them scowl down at you. The Prince never walks. He only goes on a mule. He was carried up the Faulhorn in a palanquin."

"In a palanquin?"

"In one of those machines—a *chaise-à-porteurs*—like a woman." And then when Rowland had received this information in silence, since it was equally unbecoming to be either amused or shocked: "Is Mr. Hudson to join you again? Will he come to this spot?"

"I shall soon begin to expect him."

"What shall you do when you leave Switzerland?" she continued. "Shall you go back to Rome?"

"I rather doubt it. My plans are very uncertain."

"They depend upon Mr. Hudson, eh?"

"In a great measure."

"I want you to tell me about him. Is he still in that perverse state of mind that distressed you so much?"

Rowland looked at her mistrustfully, making no answer. He was indisposed, instinctively, to tell her Roderick was out of sorts; it was so possible she might offer to try to bring him round. She immediately perceived his hesitation.

"I see no reason why we shouldn't be frank," she said. "I should think we were excellently placed for that sort of thing. You remember that formerly I cared very little what I said, don't you? Well, I care absolutely not at all now. I say what I please, I do what I please! How did Mr. Hudson receive the news of my marriage?"

"Very badly," said Rowland.

"With rage and reproaches?" And as he hesitated again: "With silent contempt?"

"I can tell you but little. He spoke to me on the subject, but I stopped him. I told him it was none of his business nor of mine."

"That was an excellent answer," Christina observed. "Yet it *was* a little your business, after those sublime protestations I treated you to. I was really very fine that morning, eh?"

"You do yourself injustice," said Rowland. "I should be at liberty now to believe you were insincere."

"What does it matter now whether I was insincere or not? I can't conceive of anything mattering less. I *was* very fine—isn't it true?"

"You know what I think of you," he replied. And for fear of being forced to betray his suspicion of the influence brought to bear upon her crisis he took refuge in a commonplace. "I hope your mother's well."

"My mother's in the enjoyment of superb health, and may be seen every evening in the Casino at the Baths of Lucca confiding to every new-comer that she has married her daughter—tremendously."

Rowland was anxious for news of Mrs. Light's companion, and the natural course was frankly to inquire about him. "And the dear Cavaliere's well?"

Christina hesitated, but she betrayed no other embarrassment. "The dear Cavaliere has retired to his native city of Ancona, upon a pension, for the rest of his natural life. Poverino!"

"I've a great regard for him," said Rowland gravely, at the same time that he privately wondered if Poverino's pension were paid by Prince Casamassima for services rendered in connexion with his marriage. "And what do you do," he continued, "on leaving this place?"

"We go to Italy—we go to Naples." She rose and stood silent some minutes, looking down the valley. The figure of Prince Casamassima appeared in the distance, balancing his white umbrella. As her eyes took it in Rowland could feel he saw something deeper in the strange expression that had lurked in her face while he talked to her. Was it pure imagination, or did they grow harder with this view, and was the bitterness so suggested the outward mark of her sacrificed ideal? When she presently afterwards turned them on himself they showed to Rowland as almost tragic. There was a new dread in his sympathy; he wished to give her a proof of friendship, and yet it seemed to him that she had now fixed her face in a direction where friendship was powerless to interpose. She half read his feelings apparently, and she had a beautiful sad smile. "I hope we may never meet again!" she said. And as Rowland appeared to protest: "You've seen me at my best. I wish to tell you solemnly, I *was* sincere. I know the whole look of it's against me," she went on quickly. "There's a great deal I can't tell you. Perhaps you've guessed it; I care very little. You know at any rate I did my best. It wouldn't serve; I was beaten and broken; they were stronger than I. Now it's another affair!"

"It seems to me you've a large opportunity for happiness yet," he vaguely remarked, seeming foolish even to himself.

"Happiness? I mean to cultivate delight; I mean to go in for passing my time. You remember I told you that I was in part the world's and the devil's. Now they've taken me all. It was their choice; may they never repent!"

"I shall hear of you," said Rowland.

"You'll hear of me. And whatever you do hear, remember this: I *was* sincere!"

Prince Casamassima had approached, and Rowland looked at him with a good deal of simple compassion as a part of that "world" against which Christina had launched her mysterious menace. It was obvious that he was what is called a well-meaning person, and that he could not in the nature of things be a positively bad husband; but his distinguished inoffensiveness only deepened the infelicity of Christina's situation by depriving her defiant attitude of the sanction of relative justice. So long as she had been free to choose she had esteemed him; but from the moment she was forced to marry him she had detested him. Rowland read in the young man's elastic Italian mask a profound consciousness of all this; and as he found there also a record of other curious things—of pride, of temper, of bigotry, of an immense heritage of more or less aggressive traditions—he reflected that the matrimonial conjunction of his two companions might be sufficiently prolific in incident.

"You're going to Naples?" he inquired by way of conversation.

"We're going to Paris," Christina interposed slowly and softly. "We're going to London. We're going to Vienna. We're going to St. Petersburg. We may even go to China."

The Prince dropped his eyes and fretted the earth with the point of his umbrella. While he engaged Rowland's attention Christina turned away, and when our friend observed her again a fresh impression was reflected in her face. She had noticed something concealed from his own sight by the angle of the church wall. In a moment Roderick stepped upon the scene.

He stopped short, astonished; his face and figure were jaded, his garments dusty. He looked at Christina from head to foot, and then, slowly, his cheek flushed and his eyes darkened. Christina returned this unadorned recognition, and for some moments there was a singular silence. "You don't look well!" she said at last.

Roderick answered nothing; he only kept his attention on her as if she had been some striking object in the picture. "I don't see that you're less wonderful, you know," he presently remarked.

She turned away with a smile and stood a while gazing down the valley; Roderick then simply stared at her husband. Christina put out her hand to Rowland. "Farewell," she said. "If you're near me in future don't try to see me." And after a pause, in a lower tone: "I *was* sincere!" She addressed herself again to Roderick and asked him some commonplace about his walk; but his answer, barely articulate, was all in his eyes. Rowland at first had expected an outbreak of reproach, but it was evident that the danger was every moment diminishing. He was forgetting everything but her beauty, and as she stood there and let him feast upon it Rowland was sure she acted with intention. "I won't say good-bye to *you*," she rang out clear; "we shall meet again!" And she moved gravely away. The Prince took courteous leave of Rowland; upon Roderick he bestowed a bow of exaggerated civility. The latter appeared not to notice; he was watching Christina as she passed over the grass. His eyes followed her until she reached the door of her inn. Here she stopped and looked back at him.

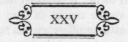

XXV

ON THE homeward walk that evening he preserved an ominous silence, and early on the morrow, saying nothing of his intentions, he started off alone : Rowland saw him measure with light elastic steps the rugged path to Engelberg. He was absent all day and gave no account of himself on his return, simply saying he was impossibly tired and going to bed early. When he had left the room Mary Garland drew near to their friend.

"I wish to ask you a question," she said. "What happened to Roderick yesterday at Engelberg ?"

"You've discovered that something did happen ?"

"I'm sure of it. Was it anything disagreeable ?"

"I don't know how at the present moment he judges it. He met Princess Casamassima."

"Thank you !" said Mary; and she turned away.

The conversation had been brief, but it had not been the first exchange of words important far beyond its duration. Mary's question had at any rate for Rowland a great and particular sign—being the first she had ever asked him which Roderick himself could have answered better. Therefore she had betrayed as not before how little she "got out" of the latter. Rowland ventured to think this fact marked an era.

The next morning was sultry, and the air, usually so fresh at those altitudes, was oppressively heavy. Rowland lounged on the grass a while, near Singleton, who was at work under his white umbrella within view of the house; and then in quest of coolness he wandered away to the rocky ridge whence the view was across to the Jungfrau. To-day, however, the white summits were invisible; their heads were muffled in sullen clouds and the valleys beneath them curtained in dun-coloured mist. Rowland had a book in his pocket, which he took out and opened. But his page remained unturned; his own thoughts were more absorbing. His interview with Christina had left him all vibrating, and he was haunted with the memory of her almost blame-less bitterness and of something sinister in this fresh physiognomy she had chosen to present. These things were immensely appealing, and he thought with richly renewed impatience of Roderick's having again become acquainted with them. It required little ingenuity to make it probable that certain visible marks in him had also appealed to Christina. His consummate indifference, his supreme defiance, would make him a magnificent trophy, and she had announced with sufficient distinctness that she had said good-bye to scruples. It was her fancy at present to treat the world as a garden of pleasure, and if hitherto she had played with Roderick's passion on its stem there was little doubt that she would now pluck it with a more merciless hand and drain it of its acrid sweetness. And why in the name of common consistency— though indeed it was the only consistency to have looked for—need Roderick have gone marching back to destruction? Rowland's meditations, even when they began in rancour, often brought him comfort; but on this occasion they hurt him as if they had been sharp-cornered objects bumped against in darkness. He recognised a sudden collapse of his moral energy; a current that had been flowing for two years with a breadth of its own seemed at last to submit to shrinkage and thinness. He looked away at the sallow vapours on the mountains; their dreariness had an analogy with the stale residuum of his own generosity. At last he had arrived at the very limit of the deference a sane man might pay to other people's folly; nay, rather, he had transgressed it, he had been befooled on a gigantic scale. He turned to his book and tried to woo back patience, but it gave him cold comfort and he tossed it angrily away. He pulled his hat over his eyes and tried to wonder dispassionately if atmospheric conditions mightn't have to do with his gloom. He remained some time in this attitude, but was finally roused from it by an odd sense that although he had heard nothing some one had approached him. He looked up and saw Roderick standing before him on the turf. His mood made the spectacle unwelcome, and for a moment he felt himself ungraciously glare. Roderick's face, on the other hand, took up, even before he spoke, something that evidently figured to him as their old relation. It was as if he had come back to him—and that, after a moment, made our friend sit up.

"I should like you to do me a favour," the young man presently said. "I should like you to lend me some money."

"How much do you wish?" Rowland asked.

"Well, say a thousand francs."

Rowland considered. "I don't wish to be indiscreet, but may I ask you what you propose to do with a thousand francs?"

"To go to Interlaken."

"And why should you go to Interlaken?"

The answer came at once. "Because that woman's to be there."

Rowland broke into laughter, but his friend remained serenely grave. "You've forgiven her then?" said Rowland.

Roderick, before answering, dropped upon the grass. But then, beside his companion, he spoke with emphasis. "Not a bit!"

"I don't understand."

"Neither do I. I only know that her beauty has the same extraordinary value as ever and that it has waked me up amazingly. Besides, she has asked me to come."

"She has asked you?"

"Yesterday, in so many words."

"Ah, the cruel creature!" cried Rowland, who was thinking of Mary Garland.

"Well," said Roderick, "I'm perfectly willing to take her for that."

"But why need you take her for anything? Why, in the name of common sense, did you go back to her?"

"Why did I find her standing there like a goddess who had just stepped out of her cloud? Why did I look at her at all? Before I knew where I was the spell was cast."

Rowland, who had been sitting erect, threw himself back on the grass and lay for some time staring up at the sky. At last, raising himself again, "Are you perfectly serious?" he demanded.

"Deadly serious."

"Your idea's to remain at Interlaken some time?"

"Indefinitely!" said Roderick; and it seemed to his companion that the tone in which he spoke this made it immensely well worth hearing.

"And your mother and cousin meanwhile are to remain here? It will soon be getting very cold, you know."

"It doesn't seem much like it to-day."

"Very true; but to-day's a day by itself."

"There's nothing to prevent their going back to Lucerne. I quite depend upon your taking charge of them."

At this Rowland threw himself at his length again, and then again, after reflection, faced his interlocutor. "How would you express," he asked, "the nature of the profit that you expect to derive from your excursion?"

"I see no need of expressing it. I shall express it by going. The case is simply that that appeals to me as an interest, and I find myself so delighted to recognise an interest that I haven't it in my heart to dash it away. As I say, she has waked me up, and it's possible that something may come of that. She makes me live again—though I admit there's a strange pain in the act of *coming* to life. But at least it's movement, and what else, or who else, for so many weeks, has moved me?"

Of this again Rowland considered. "You really feel then on the way—— ?"

"Don't ask too much. I only know that she makes my heart beat, makes me see visions."

"You feel at least encouraged?"

"I feel excited."

"You're really looking better," Rowland went on after a moment.

"I'm glad to hear it. Now that I've answered your questions, therefore, please give me the money."

Rowland shook his head. "For that dire purpose I can't!"

"You can't?"

"It's impossible. Your idea's too great a folly. I can't help you to it."

Roderick flushed a little, and his eyes lighted. "I'll borrow what money I can then from Mary!" This was not viciously said; it had simply the ring of passionate resolution.

Instantly it brought Rowland to terms. He took a bunch of keys from his pocket and tossed it upon the grass. "The little brass one opens my dressing-case. You'll find money in it."

Roderick let the keys lie; something seemed to have struck him; he looked askance at his friend. "You're awfully considerate of Mary!"

"You certainly are not. Your proposal's an outrage."

"Very likely. It's proof the more of my desire."

"If you've so much steam on, then, use it for something else! You say you're awake again. I'm delighted to believe it; only be so in the best sense. Isn't it very plain? If you've the energy to desire you've also the energy to reason and to judge. If you can care to go you can also care to stay, and, staying being the more profitable course, the inspiration, on that side, for a man who has his self-confidence to win back again, should be greater."

Roderick plainly failed to relish this lesson, and his face darkened as he listened to its echo. "I think, my dear man, you're making a mistake."

Well, Rowland would at least drive his mistake home. "Do you

318

believe that hanging about the Princess, on such terms, will do you any good ? Do you believe it won't ? In either case you should keep away from her. If it won't, it's your duty; and if it will, you can get on without it."

"Do me good ?" cried Roderick. "What do I want of 'good'— what should I do with 'good' ? I want what she gives me, call it by what name you will. I want to ask no questions, but to take what comes and let it fill the impossible hours ! But I didn't come to you to discuss the matter."

"I've not the least desire to discuss it," said Rowland. "I simply protest."

Roderick meditated a moment. "I've never yet thought twice about accepting any favour of you, but this one sticks in my throat."

"It's not a favour. I lend you the money only under compulsion."

"Well, then, I'll take it only under compulsion !" And, springing to his feet, Roderick marched away.

His words were ambiguous; Rowland lay on the grass wondering what they meant. Half an hour had not elapsed before he reappeared, heated with rapid walking and wiping his forehead. He flung himself down, and the difference between his perversity and his sincerity was somehow vivid in his eyes.

"I've done my best !" he said. "My mother's out of money; she's expecting next week some circular notes from London. She had only ten francs in her pocket. Mary Garland gave me every sou she possessed in the world. It makes exactly thirty-four francs. That's not enough."

"You asked Mary Garland ?" Rowland cried.

"Yes, I asked her."

"And told her your purpose ?"

"I named no names. But she knew."

"What then did she say ?"

"Not a syllable. She simply emptied her purse."

Rowland turned over and buried his face in his arms. He felt a movement of irrepressible elation and barely stifled a cry of joy. Now, surely, Roderick had shattered the last link in the chain that bound Mary to him, and after this she would be free―― ! When he recovered his posture Roderick was still sitting there and had not touched the keys that lay on the grass.

"I don't know what's the matter with me," said this young man, "but I've an insurmountable aversion to taking your money."

"The matter, I suppose, is that you've a grain of reason left."

"No, it's not that. It's a kind of brute instinct. I find it extremely provoking!" He sat there for some time with his head in his hands and his eyes on the ground. His expression had turned hard—his difficulty was clearly greater than he had expected. "You've succeeded in making this thing uncommonly unpleasant!" he at last exclaimed.

"I'm sorry," said Rowland, "but I can't see it in any other way."

"That I believe, but what I resent is that the range of your vision should pretend to be the limit of my action. You can't feel for me nor judge for me, and there are certain things you know nothing about. I have suffered, sir!" Roderick went on with increasing emphasis and with the reawakened ring of his fine old Virginian pomposity. "I've suffered damnable torments. Have I been such a placid, contented, comfortable creature these last six months that when I find a chance to forget my misery I should take such pains not to profit by it? You ask too much, it seems to me—for a man who himself has no occasion to play the hero. I don't say that invidiously; it's your disposition, and you can't help it. But decidedly there are certain things you know nothing about."

Rowland listened to this outbreak with open eyes, and Roderick, if he had been less intent upon his own unhappy cause, would probably have perceived that he turned pale. "These things—what are they?" Rowland asked.

"Why, they're women, principally, and what relates to women. Women for you, by what I can make out, scarce have an existence. You've no imagination of them, no sense of them, nothing in you to be touched by them."

"That's a funny charge," said Rowland gravely.

"I don't make it without evidence."

"Then with what evidence?"

Roderick hesitated. "The way you treated Christina Light. I call that grossly obtuse."

"Obtuse?" Rowland repeated, frowning.

"Thick-skinned, beneath your good fortune."

"My good fortune?"

"There it is—it's all news to you! You had pleased her, interested her. I don't say she was dying of love for you, but she liked you so much that she would have been glad if you could have become a little aware of it."

"We'll let this pass!" Rowland said after a silence.

320

"Oh, I don't insist. I've only her own word for it."

"Her own word ?"

"You've noticed, at least, I suppose, that she's not in general afraid to speak. I never repeated it, not because I was jealous, but because I was curious to see how long your ignorance would last if left to itself."

"I frankly confess it would have lasted for ever. And yet I don't at all hold my insensibility proved."

"Oh, don't say that," cried Roderick, "or I shall begin to suspect—what I must do you the justice to say I never *have* suspected—that you take yourself even more seriously than we, your good friends, take you. Upon my word, when I think of all this, your protest, as you call it, against the vivacity of my attention to that young lady strikes me as having its absurd side. There's something monstrous in a man's pretending to lay down the law to a state of sensibility with which he's unacquainted—in his expecting of a fellow a kind of sacrifice that it has been so easy for *him* not to have the occasion to make, and of which he doesn't understand the very terms."

"Oh, oh !" cried Rowland.

"It's very easy to exclaim," Roderick went on; "but you must remember that there are such things as nerves and needs and senses and desires and a restless demon within, a demon that may sleep sometimes for a day, or for six months, but that sooner or later starts up and thumps at your ribs till you listen to him. If you can't conceive it, take it on trust and let a poor visionary devil live his life as he can !"

These words affected his sad auditor as something heard in a dream; it was impossible they had been actually spoken—so supreme an expression were they of the high insolence of egotism. Reality was somehow never so consistent and complete. But Roderick sat there balancing his beautiful head, and the echoes of his ugly mistake still lingered along the half-muffled mountain-side. Rowland suddenly felt the cup of his own ordeal full to overflowing, and his long-gathered bitterness surged into the simple clear passion of pain at wasted kind' ness. But he spoke without violence, and Roderick was probably a first far from measuring the depths beneath his tone.

"You're incredibly ungrateful, I think, and you're talking arrogant nonsense. What do you know about my needs and senses and my imagination ? How do you know whether I've loved or suffered ? If I've held my tongue and not troubled you with my complaints, you find it the most natural thing in the world to put a belittling construction on my silence ! I've loved quite as well as you; indeed I think I may

321

say rather better, since I've been constant. I've been willing to give more than I received. I've not forsaken one mistress because I thought another more beautiful, nor given up the other and believed all manner of evil about her because I hadn't my way with her. I've been a good friend to Christina Light, and it seems to me my friendship does her quite as much honour as your love!"

"Your love—your suffering—your silence—your friendship!" cried Roderick. "I declare I don't understand!"

"I daresay not. You're not used to having to, in the least, where I'm concerned; you're not used to hearing me talk of my feelings or even to remembering that such things are possible, such luxuries thinkable to me. You're altogether too much taken up with your interests. Be as much so as you like or as you must; I've always respected your right. Only when I have kept myself in durance on purpose to leave you an open field, don't, by way of thanking me, come and call me an idiot."

"Oh, you claim then that you've *made* sacrifices?"

"Several! You've never suspected it?"

"If I had, do you suppose I would have allowed them?" Roderick magnificently demanded.

"They were sacrifices to friendship, and they were easily, eagerly, rejoicingly made. Only I don't enjoy having them thrown back in my teeth."

This was in all the conditions a sufficiently generous speech; but Roderick scanned it as he might have scanned the total of an account not presented in items. "Come, be more definite," he said. "Let me know where it is the shoe has pinched."

Rowland frowned; if he wouldn't take generosity he should have full justice. "It's a perpetual sacrifice then to live with a remorseless egotist!"

"I'm a remorseless egotist?" Roderick returned.

"Did it never occur to you?"

"An egotist to whom you have made perpetual sacrifices?" He repeated the words in a singular tone; a tone that denoted neither exactly indignation nor incredulity, but (strange as it might seem) a sudden violent curiosity for news about himself.

"You're selfish," said Rowland; "you think only of yourself and believe only in your own history. You regard other people only as they play into your own hands. You've always been very frank about it, and the thing seemed so mixed up with the nature of your genius and the very breath of your life that often one was willing to take the evil with the good and to be thankful that, considering your great talent, you were no worse. But if one was to believe in you as I've done one was to pay a tax on one's faith!"

Roderick leaned his elbows on his knees, clasped his hands together and crossed them shadewise over his eyes. In this attitude for a moment he sat looking coldly at his friend. "So I've made you very uncomfortable?" he went on.

"Extremely so."

"I've been eager, grasping, obstinate, vain, ungrateful, indifferent, cruel?"

"I've accused you mentally of all these things—with the particular exception of vanity."

"You've therefore often hated me?"

"Never. I should have parted company with you before coming to that."

"But you've wanted to part company, to bid me go on my way and be hanged?"

"Repeatedly. Then I've had patience and forgiven you."

"Forgiven me, eh? Suffering all the while?"

"Yes, you may call it suffering."

Roderick thought a moment. "Why did you never tell me all this before?"

"Because my affection was always stronger than my resentment; because I preferred to err on the side of kindness; because I had myself in a measure launched you in the world and thrown you among temptations; and because nothing short of your unwarrantable aggression just now could have made me, with this effect of harshness, break my silence."

Roderick picked up a blade of long grass and began to bite it; Rowland was puzzled by his expression and manner. They were strangely detached and as if unnaturally quiet. "I must have been horrible," he presently resumed.

"I'm not talking for your entertainment," his companion declared.

"Of course not. For my edification!" And as he spoke the air seemed colder for his breath.

"I've spoken for my own relief," Rowland went on, "and so that you need never again go so utterly astray as you've done this morning."

"It has been a terrible mistake then?" What his tone represented was doubtless no direct purpose of irony, but irresponsible, void of positive compunction, it jarred at moments almost like an insult.

Rowland answered nothing. "And all this time," Roderick continued, "you've been in love? Tell me then, please—if you don't mind—with whom."

Rowland felt the temptation to give him a palpable pang. "With whom but with the nearest——?"

"The nearest——?" Roderick maintained his cold, large stare, which seemed so to neglect and overshoot the near. But then he brought it down. "You mean with poor Mary?"

"I mean with Miss Garland."

At the tone, suddenly, he coloured; something had touched him somewhere. He gave, however, at first, under control, the least possible sign. "How extraordinary! But I see. Heaven forgive us!"

Rowland took notice of the "us," while his companion, for further comment, simply fell back on the turf and lay for some time staring at the sky. At last he sprang to his feet, and Rowland rose also, conscious for the first time, with any sharpness, in all their intercourse, of having made an impression on him. He had driven in, as it were, a nail, and found in the tap of his hammer, for once in a way, a sensation.

"For how long has this been?" the young man went on.

"Since I first knew her."

"Two years! And you've never told her?"

"Never."

"You've told no one?"

"You're the first person."

"Why then have you been silent?"

"Because of your engagement."

"But you've done your best to keep that up."

"That's another matter!"

"It's very wonderful," Roderick presently continued. "It's like something in a bad novel."

"We needn't expatiate on it," said Rowland. "All I wished to do was to rebut your charge that I've enjoyed any special immunity."

But still his friend pondered. "All these months, while I was going my way! I wish you had some time mentioned it."

"I acted as was necessary, and that's the end of the matter."

"You've a very high opinion of her?"

"The highest."

"I remember now your occasionally expressing it and my being struck with it. But I never dreamed you were in love with her. It's a pity," Roderick added, "that she doesn't care for you."

Rowland had made his point and had no wish to prolong the conversation; but he would have liked to hear more of this, and he remained silent.

"You hope, I suppose, that she may some day be moved?" Roderick inquired.

"I shouldn't have offered to say so; but since you ask me, I do."

"Well, I don't believe it, you know. She idolises me, and if she never were to see me again she would idolise my memory."

This might be vivid insight and it might be deep fatuity. Rowland turned away; he couldn't trust himself to speak.

"My indifference, my neglect of her, must have seemed to you too base," his companion pursued. "Altogether I must have appeared simply hideous."

"Do you really care," Rowland was prompted to ask, "for what you may have appeared?"

"Certainly. I've been damnably stupid. Isn't an artist supposed to be a man of fine perceptions? I haven't, as it turns out, had *one*."

"Well, you've a beautiful one now, and we can start afresh."

"And yet," said Roderick, "though you've suffered, in a degree, I don't believe you've suffered so much as some other men would have done."

"Very likely not. In such matters quantitative analysis is difficult."

Roderick picked up his stick and stood looking at the ground. "I must nevertheless have seemed hideous," he repeated—"hideous." He turned away frowning, and Rowland offered no contradiction.

They were both silent a while, and at last Roderick gave a long, subdued exhalation, the discharge of a consciousness too suddenly overloaded, and began to move off.

"Where are you going?" Rowland then demanded.

"Oh, I don't care! To walk, to look about, to 'commune with nature.' You've given me an idea, and I nowadays have so few that I'm taking this one with me. I don't quite know what I can do with it, but perhaps I shall find out. Leave me to try—though I've already been so stupid." This seemed a salutary impulse, yet Rowland felt a nameless doubt. "*That*, you know, damns me more than anything," Roderick went on. "Certainly I can shut up shop now."

Rowland's immediate, his personal relief had dropped after speaking; yet at sight of the way such a character could hang together he still felt justified. It was egotism always—the shock of taste, the humiliation of a proved blunder, the sense, above all, of a flagrant want of grace;

but never a hint of simple sorrow for pain inflicted. He let the poor boy go and for some moments stood watching him; then of a sudden he yielded to an impulse all inconsequent, a desire to stop him, to have another word with him, not to lose sight of him. He called out, and Roderick turned. "I should like to go with you," said our friend.

"Oh, I'm fit only to be alone. It's awful!"

"You had better not think of it at all," Rowland cried, "than think in that way."

"There's only one way. I've been grotesque!" And he broke off and marched away, taking long steps and swinging his stick. Rowland still watched him and in another instant called to him again. Roderick stopped and looked back in silence; after which, abruptly turning, he disappeared below the crest of a hill.

XXVI

ROWLAND PASSED the remainder of the day as best he could. He could scarce have said whether he were exalted or depressed; he felt, uneasily, placed in the wrong in spite of his excellent cause. Roderick made no appearance at luncheon; but of this, with his passion for mooning away the hours on far-off mountain-sides, he had almost made a habit. Mrs. Hudson's face, at the noonday repast, showed how his sharp demand for money had unsealed the fountains of her distress. Little Singleton consumed an enormous and well-earned meal. Mary Garland, Rowland observed, had not contributed her scanty assistance to her kinsman's pursuit of the Princess Casamassima without an effort that had ploughed deep. She had clearly, in fact, been ravaged by it, and she looked so ill and remained so silent that, the repast over, Rowland expressed to her the fear that she was seriously unwell. They had come out upon the grass in front of the inn.

"I've a bad headache—that's all." And then suddenly, looking about at the menacing sky and motionless air, "It's this horrible day!" she said.

He that afternoon tried to write a letter to his cousin Cecilia, but his head and his heart were alike heavy, and he traced upon the paper but a single line. "I believe there's such a thing as being too reasonable.

Yet when once the habit's formed what is one to do ?" He had occasion to use his keys, and he felt for them in his pockets; they were missing, and he remembered that he had left them lying on the hill-top where he had had his talk with Roderick. He went forth in search of them and found them where he had thrown them. He flung himself down in the same place again; he felt it impossible to walk. He was conscious that his mood had greatly changed since the morning; his extra-ordinary acute sense of his rights had been replaced by the familiar chronic sense of his duties. His duties, however, now seemed only to defy him; he turned over and buried his face in his arms. He lay so a long time, thinking of many things; the sum of them all was that Roderick had beaten him. At last he was startled by an extraordinary sound, which defined itself the next instant as a portentous growl of thunder. He got up and saw that the whole face of the sky had altered. The clouds that had hung motionless all day were moving from their stations and getting into position for a battle. The wind was rising, the turbid vapours growing dark and thick. It was a striking spectacle, but Rowland judged best to observe it briefly, as a storm was evidently imminent. He took the path to the inn and found Singleton still at his post, profiting by the last of the rapidly-failing light to finish his study and yet at the same time making rapid notes of the actual condition of the clouds.

"We're going to have the biggest show the Alps can give," the little painter gleefully cried. "I should like awfully to *do* it."

Rowland adjured him to pack up his tools and decamp, and then repaired to the house. The air by this time had become densely dark, and the thunder was incessant and deafening; in the midst of it the lightning flashed and vanished as the treble shrills upon the bass. The innkeeper and his servants, wondering and blinking, pale in the frequent flare, had pressed to the doorway, and, as Rowland approached, the group divided to let some one pass from within. Mrs. Hudson, her face white and convulsed, waving her arms, came out as if, on some alarm of a flood, she were walking in the water breast-high.

"My boy, my boy, where's my boy?" she cried. "Mr. Mallett, why are you here without him? Bring him straight home to me!"

"Has no one seen Mr. Hudson?" Rowland asked of the others. "Has he not returned?"

Each one shook his head and looked grave, and Rowland represented to the poor lady, and by the same urgency to himself, that Roderick would of course have sought asylum in some secure châlet.

"Go and find him, go and find him!" she none the less imperiously quavered. "Don't stand there and talk, or my reason will give way!" It was now as dark as evening, and Rowland could just distinguish the figure of Singleton scampering home with his box and easel. "And where's Mary?" Mrs. Hudson went on; "what in mercy's name has become of *her*? Mr. Mallett, why did you ever bring us here?"

There came a huge white glare, under which, for thirty seconds, all nature stood still and Rowland, making out a slight figure on the top of an eminence near the house, recognised the younger woman, urged forth by her anxiety and almost insanely exposed. He sprang out to join her, but in a moment he met her coming back. He seized her hand and hurried her to the house, where, as soon as she stepped into the covered gallery, Mrs. Hudson fell upon her with frantic lamentations.

"Did you see anything—nothing? Tell Mr. Mallett he must go and find him, with some men, some lights, some wraps, some wine. Go, go, go, sir! In mercy, go!"

Rowland, thus assaulted by the terrors of others, threw himself back with force on his own argument. He had offered it in all sincerity; nothing was more probable than that Roderick had found shelter in a herdsman's cabin. These were numerous on the neighbouring mountains, and the storm had given fair warning of its approach. Mary stood there at first without a word, only looking hard at him. He expected she would try to soothe her cousin. "*Could* you find him?" she suddenly asked. "Would it be of use?"

The question struck him as a flash intenser than when the jaws of the night opened to the whiteness of a thousand teeth. It shattered his dream that he weighed in the scale. But before he could answer the tempest was in possession and the rain, about them, like the sound of the deeps about a ship's sides. Every one fell back into the house. There had been no time to light lamps, and in the little uncarpeted parlour, in the unnatural darkness, Rowland felt Mary's hand on his arm. He imputed for a moment a meaning to it, some attenuation of her vain challenge, an assurance that she accepted, for Roderick, whatever he thought probable. But, nevertheless, thought Rowland, the cry had come, her passion had spoken; her first impulse had been to sacrifice him. He had been uncertain before; here at least was the comfort of certainty.

It must be confessed, however, that the certainty did little to enliven the gloom of that formidable evening. There was a noisy crowd everywhere—noisy even beyond the uproar without; lodgers and servants, chattering, shuffling, bustling, vociferating; breaking in, as he felt, upon the dignity of the storm. It was some time, in the confusion, before a lamp was lighted, and the first thing it showed him when swung from the ceiling was the closed eyes of Mrs. Hudson, carried away in a faint by two stout maid-servants and with Mary Garland forcing a passage. He rendered what help he could, but when they had laid their companion on her bed Mary motioned him away.

"I think you make her worse," was all the girl's comment.

He could but betake himself then to his own room. The partitions in Swiss mountain-inns are thin, and he heard Mrs. Hudson's wail three doors away. The rage of the weather, for all its violence, was slow to abate; it held its own for two long hours. With the drop of the thunder the rush of water continued, and night had come on impenetrably black. Rowland thought of Mary Garland's question in the porch, but he thought still more that, although the fetid interior of a high-nestling châlet may offer a convenient refuge from an Alpine tempest, there was no possible music in the universe so sweet as the sound of Roderick's voice. At midnight, from his window, through the ebb of the tide, he made out a star and immediately went below and out into the gallery. The rain had ceased, the cloud-masses showed gaps and the gaps cold points of light. In a few minutes he heard a step behind him and, turning, saw Mary Garland. He asked about Mrs. Hudson and learned that she was sleeping, exhausted by her long tension. Mary's eyes kept sounding the night, but she said nothing to cast doubt on the idea of Roderick's having found a refuge. Rowland noticed it and knew this assurance then for a matter as to which he would be held responsible. There was something she further wished to learn, and a question presently revealed it. "What made him start on a long walk so suddenly?" she asked. "I saw him at eleven o'clock, and then he meant to go to Engelberg and sleep."

"On his way to Interlaken!" Rowland said.

"Yes," she answered under cover of the darkness.

"We had some talk," said Rowland, "and he seemed, for the day, to have given up Interlaken."

"Did you dissuade him?"

"Not exactly. We discussed another question, which for the time appeared to have superseded his plan."

Mary was silent; after which, "May I ask whether your discussion was violent?" she went on.

"I'm afraid it was easy for neither of us."

329

"And Roderick left you in—in irritation?"

"I offered him my company on his walk, but he wouldn't have me."

Mary paced to the end of the gallery and came back. "If he had gone to Engelberg he would have reached the hotel before the storm began."

Rowland felt himself suddenly break out. "Oh, if you like, he can start for Interlaken as soon as he comes back!"

But it was as if she were unconscious of his remark. "Will he come back early?" she pursued.

"We may suppose so."

"He'll know how anxious we are, and he'll start with the first light."

He was on the point of declaring that Roderick's readiness to throw himself into the feelings of others made this extremely probable; but he checked himself and said simply: "I expect him at sunrise."

She gave again, into the darkness round her, a long, strained stare and then went into the house. Rowland, it must be averred, in spite of his determination not to worry, found no sleep that night. When the early dawn began to tremble in the east he came forth again into the open air. The storm had completely cleared it, and the day gave promise of cloudless splendour. He watched the first sunshafts slowly reach higher and remembered that if Roderick should not be back to breakfast there were two points to be made. One was the heaviness of the soil on the mountain-sides, saturated with the rain, which would make him walk slowly; the other was the fact that, speaking without irony, he was not remarkable for his divination of the convenience of others. Breakfast at the inn was early, and Roderick had not then reappeared. Rowland admitted with this that he was worrying. Neither Mrs. Hudson nor her companion had left their apartment; Rowland had a mental vision of the two women sitting there face to face and listening; he had no desire to see them in fact. There were a couple of men who hung about the inn as guides for going up the Titlis; Rowland sent each of them forth in a different direction to ask for news wherever news might be gathered. Then he called Sam Singleton, whose peregrinations had made him a prime rambler and whose zeal and sympathy were now unbounded, and the two started together to ascertain what they might. By the time they had lost sight of the inn they were obliged to confess that decidedly their friend had had time to come back.

Ours, poor man, wandered about for several hours, but found only the sunny stillness of the mountain-sides. Before long he had parted company with Singleton, who, to his suggestion that separation would extend their search, assented with fixed eyes that reflected his own dire obsession. The day was magnificent, the sun everywhere; the storm had lashed the lower slopes into a deeper flush of autumnal colour and the snow-peaks reared themselves above the near horizon in shining blocks and sharp incisions. He made his way to several far-perched huts, but most of them were empty and some of them closed. He thumped at their low foul doors with nervous savage anger; he challenged the stupid silence to speak to him of his friend. Some of these places had evidently not been open for months. The silence everywhere was horrible; it mocked at his impatience, it was charged with cruelty and danger. In the midst of it, at the door of one of the cabins, quite alone, sat a hideous *crétin* who grinned at him over a vast goitre when, hardly knowing what he did, he put vain questions. This creature's family was scattered on the mountain; he could give no help towards finding them. Rowland climbed into the awkward places Roderick loved; he looked down into ugly chasms from narrow steep-dropping ledges; and he was to consider afterwards, uneasily, how little he had heeded his foothold. But the sun, as I have said, was everywhere; it illumined the depths and heights in presence of which, not knowing where to turn next, he halted and lingered, and showed him nothing but the stony Alpine void—nothing so human even as a catastrophe or a trace. At noon he paused in his quest and sat down on a stone; the conviction pressed him hard that the worst now conceivable was true. He stopped looking; he was afraid to go on. He sat there for an hour, sick to his innermost soul. Without his knowing why, several things, chiefly trivial, that had happened during the last two years and that he had quite forgotten, lived again before him and breathed their mortal chill into his face. He was roused at last by the sound of a stone dislodged near by, which rattled down the mountain. In a moment, on a rough slope opposite, he beheld a figure cautiously descending—a figure which was not Roderick's. It was Singleton's, who had seen him and begun to beckon.

"Come down—come down!" cried this companion, steadily making his own way down. Rowland saw that as he moved, and even as he selected his foothold and watched his steps, he was looking at something at the bottom of the cliff. This was a great rugged wall that sloped backward from the perpendicular, and the descent, though difficult, was with care sufficiently practicable.

"What do you see?" Rowland managed to call.

Singleton stopped, looked across at him and seemed to hesitate; then, "Come down—come down!" he simply repeated.

Rowland's course was also precipitous, and he attacked it so dizzily that he marvelled, later on, he had not broken his neck. It was a ten minutes' headlong scramble. Half-way down he saw something that for a minute did make him reel; he saw what Singleton had seen. In the gorge below a vague white mass lay tumbled upon the stones. He let himself go, blindly, fiercely, to where Singleton, reaching the rocky bottom of the ravine first, had bounded forward and fallen upon his knees. Rowland overtook him, and his own legs gave way for horror. The thing that yesterday was his friend lay before him as the chance of the last breath had left it, and out of it Roderick's face stared open-eyed at the sky.

He had fallen from a great height, but he was singularly little disfigured. The rain had spent its torrents upon him, and his clothes and hair were as wet as if the billows of the ocean had flung him upon the strand. An attempt to move him would attest some fatal fracture, some horrible physical dishonour, but what Rowland saw on first looking at him was only a noble expression of life. The eyes were the eyes of death, but in a short time, when he had closed them, the whole face seemed to revive. The rain had washed away all blood; it was as if violence, having wrought her ravage, had stolen away in shame. Roderick's face might have shamed her; it was indescribably, and all so innocently, fair.

Then Singleton spoke as for the time of his life. "He was the most beautiful of men!"

They looked up through their dismay at the cliff from which he had unmistakably fallen and which lifted its blank and stony face above him, with no care now but to drink the sunshine on which his eyes were closed; and Rowland had thus a wild outbreak of pity and anguish. His friend put round him a supporting arm, and the pair gasped together, for a long minute, in their pain, like guilty creatures discovered. At last they spoke of carrying their comrade home. "There must be three or four men," Rowland said, "and they must be brought fast. I haven't the least idea where we are."

"We're at about three hours' walk from the inn. It's I who must go for help," Singleton insisted; "I can easily find my way."

"Remember then whom you'll have to face!" said Rowland.

"I remember," the little artist answered. "There was nothing I could ever do for him before; I'll do what I can now."

He went off and Rowland remained alone. He watched in the flesh for seven long hours, but the vigil of his spirit was a thing that would never cease. The most rational of men wandered and lost himself in the dark places of passion, lashed his "conduct" with a scourge of steel, accusing it of cruelty and injustice: he would have lain down there in Roderick's place to unsay the words that had yesterday driven him forth on his ramble of despair. Roderick had been fond of saying that there are such things as necessary follies, and he, of all men, was now proving it. The great gaunt wicked cliff above them became almost company to him, as the chance-saved photograph of a murderer might become for a shipwrecked castaway a link with civilisation: it had but done *its* part too, and what were they both, in their stupidity, he and it, but dumb agents of fate ? He tried at any rate to understand what had hideously happened. Not that it offered one healing touch; before the absoluteness, the grim majesty, of the fact explanations and suppositions had only an effect of contributive meanness. Roderick's stricken state had driven him, in the mere motion of flight, higher and further than he knew; he had outstayed supposably the first menace of the storm and perhaps even found a dark distraction in watching it. Perhaps he had simply lost himself. The tempest had overtaken him, and when he tried to return it had been too late. He had attempted to descend the cliff in the treacherous gloom, he had made the inevitable slip, and whether he had fallen fifty feet or three hundred little mattered now. Even if it had not been far, it had been far enough. Now that all was over Rowland understood how up to the brim, for two years, his personal world had been filled. It looked to him at present as void and blank and sinister as a theatre bankrupt and closed.

Singleton came back with four men—one of them the landlord of the inn. They had formed a rude bier of the frame of a *chaise-à-porteurs* and by taking a very roundabout course homeward were able to follow a tolerably level path and carry their burden with due decency. To Rowland it seemed as if the little procession would never reach the inn, yet as they drew near it he would have given his right hand for a longer holding-off. The few lingerers came forward to do them silent solemn homage, and in the doorway, clinging together, appeared the two bereaved women. Mrs. Hudson tottered forward with outstretched hands divided between yearning and terror; but before she reached her son Mary Garland had rushed past her and, in the face of the staring, pitying, awe-stricken crowd, had flung herself, with the magnificent movement of one whose rights were supreme and with a loud tremendous cry, upon the senseless vestige of all she had cherished.

That cry still lives in Rowland's ears. It interposes persistently against the consciousness that when he sometimes—very rarely—sees her, she is inscrutably civil to him; against the reflexion that during the awful journey back to America, made of course with his assistance, she had used him, with the last rigour of consistency, as a character definitely appointed to her use. She lives with Mrs. Hudson under the New England elms, where he also visits his cousin Cecilia more frequently than of old. When he calls on Mary he never sees the elder lady. Cecilia, who, having her shrewd impression that he comes for the young person, the still young person, of interest at the other house as much as for any one else, fails to show as unduly flattered, and in fact pronounces him, at each reappearance, the most restless of mortals. But he always says to her in answer: "No, I assure you I'm the most patient!" And then he talks to her of Roderick, of whose history she never wearies and whom he never elsewhere names.